Pride and Prejudice's Vampires

By Jane Austen
Adapted by Ann Hassell

Netherfield House Press

Printed in the United States of America

Published by Netherfield House Press
www.NetherfieldHousePress.com

ISBN 978-1-935649-02-1

Library of Congress Control Number: 2010926477
Library of Congress subject headings:
Austen, Jane, -- 1775-1817. -- Pride and prejudice -- Parodies, imitations, etc.
Bennet, Elizabeth (Fictitious character) -- Fiction.
Darcy, Fitzwilliam (Fictitious character) -- Fiction.
England -- Social life and customs -- 19th century -- Fiction.
Parodies.
Sisters -- Fiction.
Social classes -- England -- Fiction.
Vampires -- Fiction.
Young women -- England -- Fiction.

Book editing and design: Melissa Darnell
Cover design and illustrations: SavannahAnn McMillan
Cover credits:
Background Copyright © Wyldraven.
Female model Copyright © TaraFly.

Dear Readers,

I am an ardent fan of all of Jane Austen's works. So naturally when I was considering which classics would make great fantasy and monster adaptations, the first that immediately came to my mind was Ms. Austen's Pride and Prejudice. The original was already close to perfect as a vampire story and needed only a few additions to add this fantasy element to it.

I debated at length as to whether I should rewrite the story entirely in my own words, or simply build upon Ms. Austen's original. I chose the latter option for two reasons…one, because as previously stated, the original story was already so perfectly suited for a vampire adaptation. And two, because I am such an admirer of Jane Austen's writing, I wanted to encourage readers who might never have read her books before to experience exactly why her stories are so beloved, as well as give her already existing fans a new version of her work to experience in a new way. Therefore, you will find upon reading this adaptation that a majority of the text is from the original version.

However, I also understand that many readers of Ms. Austen's classics have found her style of writing with its long sentences of highly complex syntax to be a bit challenging to follow. So in this adaptation, I have added grammatical changes throughout to make her style of writing easier to follow and appreciate. I hope that my fellow fans of Ms. Austen will understand that such changes were performed with the sole aim to make her writing easier and more enjoyable to read without lessening the author's original intentions or authorial voice.

I hope that you enjoy this vampire adaptation of Pride and Prejudice, and welcome readers to visit my blog at http://annhassell.blogspot.com.

Yours, etc.,
Ann Hassell

Dedicated to my family for all their continued support over the years, especially my own "Mr. Darcy", the most supportive husband in the entire world past or present.

Chapter One

It is a truth universally acknowledged that a single man in possession of a good fortune must be in want of a wife.

However little known the feelings or views of such a man may be on his first entering a neighborhood, this truth is so well fixed in the minds of the surrounding families that he is considered the rightful property of some one or other of their daughters.

And if he should be something quite other than a human, even that might not matter at all.

"My dear Mr. Bennet," said his lady to him one day, "have you heard that Netherfield Park is let at last?"

Mr. Bennet replied that he had not.

"But it is," returned she. "For Mrs. Long has just been here, and she told me all about it."

Mr. Bennet made no answer.

"Do you not want to know who has taken it?" cried his wife.

"*You* want to tell me, and I have no objection to hearing it."

This was invitation enough.

"Why, my dear, you must know, Mrs. Long says that Netherfield is taken by a young man of large fortune from the north of England; that he came down on Monday in a chaise and four to see the place and was so much delighted with it that he agreed with Mr. Morris immediately; that he is to take possession before Michaelmas, and some of his servants are to be in the house by the end of next week."

"What is his name?"

"Bingley."

"Is he married or single?"

"Oh! Single, my dear, to be sure! A single man of large fortune, four or five thousand a year. What a fine thing for our girls!"

"How so? How can it affect them?"

"My dear Mr. Bennet, how can you be so tiresome! You must know that I am thinking of his marrying one of them."

"Is that his design in settling here?"

"Design! Nonsense, how can you talk so! But it is very likely that he *may* fall in love with one of them, and therefore you must visit him as soon as he comes."

"I see no occasion for that. You and the girls may go."

"But, my dear, you must indeed go and see Mr. Bingley when he comes into the neighborhood."

"It is more than I engage for, I assure you."

"But consider your daughters. Only think what an establishment it would be for one of them. You must go, for it will be impossible for *us* to visit him if you do not."

"You are over-scrupulous, surely. I dare say Mr. Bingley will be very glad to see you, and I will send a few lines by you to assure him of my hearty consent to his marrying whichever he chooses of the girls. Though I must throw in a good word for my little Lizzy."

"I desire you will do no such thing. Lizzy is not a bit better than the others, and I am sure she is not half so handsome as Jane, nor half so good-humored as Lydia. But you are always giving *her* the preference."

"They have none of them much to recommend them," replied he. "They are all silly and ignorant like other girls. But Lizzy has something more of quickness than her sisters."

"Mr. Bennet, how *can* you abuse your own children in such a way? You take delight in vexing me. You have no compassion for my poor nerves."

"You mistake me, my dear. I have a high respect for your nerves. They are my old friends. I have heard you mention them with consideration these last twenty years at least."

Mr. Bennet was so odd a mixture of quick parts, sarcastic humor, reserve, and caprice, that the experience of three-and-twenty years had been insufficient to make his wife understand his character. *Her* mind was less difficult to develop. She was a woman of mean understanding, little information, and uncertain temper. When she was discontented, she fancied herself nervous. The business of her life was to get her daughters married; its solace was visiting and news.

Mr. Bennet was among the earliest of those who waited on Mr. Bingley. He had always intended to visit him, though to the last always assuring his wife that he should not go, and till the evening after the visit was paid she had no knowledge of it. It was then disclosed in the following manner.

Observing his second daughter employed in trimming a hat, he suddenly addressed her with, "I hope Mr. Bingley will like it, Lizzy."

"We are not in a way to know *what* Mr. Bingley likes since we are not to visit," said her mother.

"But you forget, Mamma, that we shall meet him at the assemblies," said Elizabeth.

Mrs. Bennet deigned not to make any reply, but, unable to contain herself, began scolding one of her daughters. "Don't keep coughing so, Kitty, for Heaven's sake! Have a little compassion on my nerves. You tear them to pieces."

"Kitty has no discretion in her coughs," said her father. "She times them ill."

"I do not cough for my own amusement," whined Kitty. "When is your next ball to be, Lizzy?"

"Tomorrow fortnight."

"Aye, so it is," cried her mother. "And it will be impossible to introduce Mr. Bingley to our girls when I do not know him myself. Oh, how sick I am of Mr. Bingley!"

"I am sorry to hear *that*," said Mr. Bennet. "But why did not you tell me that before? If I had known as much this morning I certainly would not have called on him. It is very unlucky; but as I have actually paid the visit, we cannot escape the acquaintance now."

The astonishment of the ladies was just what he wished, that of Mrs. Bennet perhaps surpassing the rest. Though when the first tumult of joy was over, she began to declare that it was what she had expected all the while.

"How good it was of you, my dear Mr. Bennet! But I knew I should persuade you at last. I was sure you loved your girls too well to neglect such an acquaintance. Well, how pleased I am! And it is such a good joke, too, that you should have gone this morning and never said a word about it till now."

"Now, Kitty, you may cough as much as you choose," said Mr. Bennet, and as he spoke, he left the room, fatigued with the raptures of his wife.

"What an excellent father you have, girls!" said she when the door was shut. "I do not know how you will ever make him amends for his kindness; or me, either, for that matter. At our time of life it is not so pleasant, I can tell you, to be making new acquaintances every day; but for your sakes, we would do anything. Lydia, my love, though you *are* the youngest, I dare say Mr. Bingley will dance with you at the next ball."

"Oh!" said Lydia. "I am not afraid; for though I *am* the youngest, I'm the tallest."

The rest of the evening was spent in conjecturing how soon he would return Mr. Bennet's visit, and determining when they should ask him to dinner.

An invitation to dinner was soon afterwards dispatched, and already had Mrs. Bennet planned the courses that were to do credit to her housekeeping, when an answer arrived which deferred it all. Mr. Bingley was obliged to be in town the following day, and, consequently, unable to accept the honor of their invitation, etc. Mrs. Bennet was quite disconcerted. She could not imagine what business he could have in town so soon after his arrival in Hertfordshire, and she began to fear that he might be always flying about from one place to another and never settled at Netherfield as he ought to be. Lady Lucas quieted her fears a little by starting the idea of his being gone to London only to get a large party for the ball. A report soon followed that Mr. Bingley was to bring twelve ladies and seven gentlemen with him to the assembly. The girls grieved over such a number of ladies, but were comforted the day before the ball by hearing that instead of twelve he brought only six with him from London—his five sisters and a cousin. And when the party entered the assembly room it consisted of only five altogether—Mr. Bingley, his two sisters, the husband of the eldest, and another young man.

Upon their first arrival in the ballroom, the party bore several striking resemblances to one another that Elizabeth found difficult to sort out. Everyone within Elizabeth's hearing began to whisper such things as "Good Heavens! Have they come bearing an illness from town?". And indeed, one had to wonder if perhaps the entire party had come in ill health, for Mr. Bingley, Miss Bingley, and Mr. Darcy all bore the same purple smudges beneath their eyes, while Mr. and Mrs. Hurst's countenances were quite pale and of a sickly nature, which was most alarming upon first glance. Yet this appearance of ill health proved to be a mere illusion, for once the party fully entered the room's light, all pale coloring and shadows were replaced by healthier, more universally pleasing aspects. Though even in the light, there was a certain something about the way those three walked, as if their feet did not quite touch the floor beneath them, that drew the eye and held it.

Mr. Bingley was good looking and gentlemanlike; he had a pleasant countenance and easy, unaffected manners. Unfortunately, he was the only one of his circle who was so charming. Undoubtedly his sisters were fine women with an air of decided fashion, and his brother-in-law, Mr. Hurst, looked the gentleman. But excepting Mr. Bingley, they all seemed quite miserable to be there, their expressions cold and filled with disdain. In spite of this, Mr. Bingley's friend Mr. Darcy soon drew the attention of the room by his fine, tall person, handsome features, and the report which was in general circulation within five minutes after his entrance of his having ten thousand a year. The gentlemen pronounced him to be a fine figure of a man, the ladies declared he was much handsomer than Mr. Bingley, and he was looked at with great admiration for about half the evening. But then his manners gave a disgust which turned the tide of his popularity; for he was discovered to be proud, to be above his company, and above being pleased. Then not even his large estate in Derbyshire could save him from having a most forbidding, disagreeable countenance and being unworthy to be compared with his friend. Elizabeth's gaze unerringly found that unhappy countenance often throughout the first half of the evening, only to see that his frown did not once lift into even a semblance of a smile.

Mr. Bingley had soon made himself acquainted with all the principal people in the room. He was lively and unreserved, danced every dance, was angry that the ball closed so early, and talked of giving one himself at Netherfield. Such amiable qualities must speak for themselves. Though he should have half as much fortune, he would have been sure to draw every single female present to him. What a contrast between him and his friend! Mr. Darcy danced only once with Mrs. Hurst and once with Miss Bingley, declined being introduced to any other lady, and spent the rest of the evening in walking about the room, speaking occasionally to one of his own party. His character was decided. He was the proudest, most disagreeable man in the world, and everybody hoped that he would never come there again. Amongst the most violent against him was Mrs. Bennet, whose dislike of his general behavior was sharpened into particular resentment by his having slighted one of her daughters.

Elizabeth Bennet had been obliged, by the scarcity of gentlemen, to sit down for two dances. During that time, her gaze was especially drawn toward Mr. Darcy as he walked about the room, at last coming to stand near enough for her to hear a conversation between him and Mr. Bingley, who came from the dance for a few minutes to press his friend to join it.

"Come, Darcy," said he. "I must have you dance. I hate to see you standing about by yourself in this stupid manner. You had much better dance."

"I certainly shall not. You know how I detest it unless I am particularly acquainted with my partner. At such an assembly as this it would be insupportable. Your sisters are engaged, and there is not another woman in the room whom it would not be a punishment to me to stand up with."

"I would not be so fastidious as you are for a kingdom!" cried Mr. Bingley. "Upon my honor, I never met with so many pleasant girls in my life as I have this evening, and there are several of them you see uncommonly pretty."

"Of course you would find every girl here handsome." Mr. Darcy almost smiled at last. "However, y*ou* are dancing with the only truly handsome girl in the room." He nodded towards the eldest Miss Bennet.

"Oh! She is the most beautiful creature I ever beheld! But there is one of her sisters sitting down just behind you who is very pretty, and I dare say very agreeable. Do let me ask my partner to introduce you."

"Which do you mean?" And turning round, he looked for a moment at Elizabeth, till catching her eye, he withdrew his own. "She is tolerable, but not handsome enough to tempt *me*. You had better return to your partner and enjoy her smiles, for you are wasting your time with me."

Elizabeth bit the inside of her cheek so that she might refrain from giving an indignant gasp.

Mr. Bingley followed his friend's advice. Mr. Darcy walked off, and Elizabeth remained with no very cordial feelings toward him. However, she told the story with great spirit among her friends, for she found delight in anything ridiculous and could at least soothe her wounded feelings with laughter.

The evening altogether passed off pleasantly to the whole family. Mrs. Bennet had seen her eldest daughter much admired by the Netherfield party. Mr. Bingley had danced with her twice, and she had been distinguished by his sisters. Jane was as much gratified by this as her mother could be, though in a quieter way. Elizabeth felt Jane's pleasure. Mary had heard herself mentioned to Miss Bingley as the most accomplished girl in the neighborhood. And Catherine and Lydia had been fortunate enough never to be without partners, which was all that they had yet learned to care for at a ball. They returned, therefore, in good spirits to Longbourn, the village where they lived and of which they were the principal inhabitants.

Chapter Two

When Jane and Elizabeth were alone in their shared bedroom after the ball, the former, who had been cautious in her praise of Mr. Bingley before, expressed to her sister just how very much she admired him.

"He is just what a young man ought to be," said she. "Sensible, good-humored, lively, and I never saw such happy manners! So much ease, with such perfect good breeding!"

"He is also handsome, which a young man ought likewise to be, if he possibly can," replied Elizabeth. "His character is thereby complete."

"I was very much flattered by his asking me to dance a second time. I did not expect such a compliment."

"Did not you? I did. But that is one great difference between us. Compliments towards your goodness always take *you* by surprise, and *me* never. What could be more natural than his asking you again? He could not help seeing that you were about five times as pretty as every other woman in the room. No thanks to his gallantry for that. Well, he certainly is very agreeable somehow, though why I can not exactly say, for it is certainly not for the sake of any great intelligence on his part. Still, there is something that draws one to him, and I give you leave to like him. You have liked many a stupider person."

"Dear Lizzy!"

"Oh! You are a great deal too apt to like people in general, you know. You never see a fault in anybody. All the world is good and agreeable in your eyes. I never heard you speak ill of a human being in your life."

"I would not wish to be hasty in censuring anyone, but I always speak what I think."

"I know you do, and it is *that* which makes the wonder. With *your* good sense, to be so honestly blind to the follies and nonsense of others! Affectation of candor is common enough—one meets with it everywhere. But to be candid without ostentation or design—to take the good of everybody's character and make it still better, and say nothing of the bad—belongs to you alone. And so you like this man's sisters, too, do you? Their manners are not equal to his, though they still managed to draw quite the crowd."

"Certainly not—at first. But they are very pleasing women when you converse with them. Miss Bingley is to live with her brother and keep his house, and I am much mistaken if we shall not find a very charming neighbor in her."

Elizabeth listened in silence but was not at all convinced. Their behavior at the assembly had not been calculated to please in general, however much their finely cultivated manner of speaking might attract others to them. And with more quickness of observation and less pliancy of temper than her sister, and with a judgement too unassailed by any attention to herself, she was very little disposed to approve them. They were in fact very fine ladies, not deficient in good humor when they were pleased, nor in the power of making themselves agreeable when they chose it, but proud and conceited. One merely had to stand beyond the reach of their charming voices to understand them more clearly.

* * * * *

Of their circle, it was only Bingley who succeeded in being roundly liked by all. And yet, had Darcy heard such a report, he would have been satisfied. Between him and Darcy there was a very steady friendship, in spite of great opposition of character. Bingley was endeared to Darcy by the easiness, openness, and ductility of his temper, though no disposition could offer a greater contrast to his own, and though with his own he never appeared dissatisfied. On the strength of Darcy's regard, Bingley had the firmest reliance, and of his judgement the highest opinion. And thank the Heavens, for in understanding of their circle's true dire situation, Darcy was the reluctant superior. Bingley was by no means deficient in general, but Darcy was by dark necessity clever. He was also self-aware, and knew that he appeared haughty, reserved, and fastidious. His manners, though well-bred, repulsed any who might otherwise fall prey to his unnatural charms.

In that lack of full knowledge his friend had greatly the advantage, which only served to make their situation still more dire. Bingley, unaware that he had become a vampire of late along with Darcy and Miss Bingley, was able to put his most pleasing foot forward and was thus sure of being liked wherever he went. Darcy was continually giving offense, weighed down by the responsibility of ensuring that none liked his friend too much for their own safety.

Though Miss Bingley shared this dark nature and the knowledge of it with Darcy, the weight of keeping such secrets from Bingley and the world in general rested heavier upon Darcy's shoulders than it did Miss Bingley's, who did not seem to mind the changes. In fact, Darcy believed her vanity even welcomed what they had become. In her mind, it seemed the weekly need for blood, so willingly provided by her eldest sister and brother-in-law in return for a comfortable life of leisure, was a small price to pay for immortality. She found joy in being a vampire, and wanted only Darcy's affection to make her eternal future complete. Yet it was her very willingness to embrace their newly evil natures that made her entirely unsuitable for him. If not for his continual restraint upon her will, she would have them dining upon the entire neighborhood, heedless of the mob of villagers with pitchforks and torches that would be sure to result.

Therefore it was entirely upon Darcy's inexperienced abilities that all the responsibility lie of keeping this knowledge within their own trusted circle, and ensuring that their trio's actions and appearances did not arouse suspicions within their new neighborhood. Unfortunately, never was such a secret heavier for Mr. Darcy to bear than when they were surrounded by the temptation of humans. In such dire moments as at the assemblies, when all was at stake—the safety of those who unknowingly gathered their pulsing heartbeats round them, the protection of their own reputations, and the very sanity of Bingley himself should the truth be revealed—it took the entirety of Darcy's focus to create and control the vampire's illusion that all was well and normal with them.

Such a strain on such inexperienced shoulders as his left little energy or attention available for enamoring himself toward others beyond the glamour of making himself seem human again. Oh, but if only such a horrid social contraption as a dance had never been designed! Yet they had, they were given continuously in the neighborhood, and as the newest additions his circle must be called upon to attend again and again and again.

And so continually must he also be thrust into the presence of the only human who had thus far tempted his darker desires. For apparently the Bennets were equally relied upon to be part of every assembly.

Though perhaps this torture was the rightful justice due to one who could have prevented such darkness from falling upon his friends with but a little more care on his part. In such a view of penance, Darcy was resolved that all his efforts were to be forever spent upon the protection and welfare of his friend and Bingley's family, and if he should give the appearance to himself of being haughty and cold in the process and lose all chance of winning the affections of a certain Bennet daughter, so be it.

* * * * *

Within a short walk of Longbourn lived a family with whom the Bennets were particularly intimate. Sir William Lucas had been formerly in trade in Meryton, where he had made a tolerable fortune and risen to the honor of knighthood by an address to the king during his mayoralty. The distinction had perhaps been felt too strongly. It had given him a disgust to his business and his residence in a small market town. In quitting them both, he had removed with his family to a house about a mile from Meryton, denominated from that period Lucas Lodge, where he could think with pleasure of his own importance, and unshackled by business, occupy himself solely in being civil to all the world. For, though elated by his rank, it did not render him supercilious; on the contrary, he was all attention to everybody. By nature inoffensive, friendly, and obliging, his presentation at St. James's had made him courteous.

Lady Lucas was a very good kind of woman, not too clever to be a valuable neighbor to Mrs. Bennet. They had several children. The eldest of them, Charlotte, a sensible, intelligent young woman, about twenty-seven, was Elizabeth's intimate friend.

That the Miss Lucases and the Miss Bennets should meet to talk over a ball was absolutely necessary, and the morning after the assembly brought the former to Longbourn to hear and to communicate.

"*You* began the evening well, Charlotte," said Mrs. Bennet with civil self-command. "*You* were Mr. Bingley's first choice."

11

"Yes, but he seemed to like his second better." She smiled at Jane.

"Oh! You mean Jane, I suppose, because he danced with her twice." Mrs. Bennet set her embroidery work down in her lap. "To be sure that *did* seem as if he admired her—indeed I rather believe he *did*—I heard something about it—but I hardly know what—something about Mr. Robinson."

"Perhaps you mean what I overheard between him and Mr. Robinson; did not I mention it to you?" Charlotte leaned forward upon the edge of the settee. "Mr. Robinson's asking him how he liked our Meryton assemblies, and whether he did not think there were a great many pretty women in the room, and *which* he thought the prettiest? And his answering immediately to the last question, 'Oh! The eldest Miss Bennet, beyond a doubt; there cannot be two opinions on that point.'"

"Upon my word! Well, that is very decided indeed—that does seem as if—but, however, it may all come to nothing, you know." Mrs. Bennet's confident smile seemed to say otherwise.

"*My* overhearings were more to the purpose than *yours*, Eliza," said Charlotte, turning toward her friend who sat beside her. "Mr. Darcy is not so well worth listening to as his friend, is he? Poor Eliza! To be only just *tolerable*."

Elizabeth pressed her lips together in an effort to withhold all that she could say on *that* subject, for to do so would be not at all ladylike, even within such understanding company. In the end, however, such effort at self-discipline proved unnecessary; her mother said more than even she might have wished for.

"I beg you would not put it into Lizzy's head to be vexed by his ill-treatment, for he is such a disagreeable man that it would be quite a misfortune to be liked by him. Mrs. Long told me last night that he sat close to her for half an hour without once opening his lips."

Jane frowned. "Are you quite sure, ma'am? Is not there a little mistake? I certainly saw Mr. Darcy speaking to her."

"Aye—because she asked him at last how he liked Netherfield, and he could not help answering her," said Mrs. Bennet. "But she said he seemed quite angry at being spoke to."

"Miss Bingley told me that he never speaks much unless among his intimate acquaintances," said Jane. "With *them* he is remarkably agreeable."

"I do not believe a word of it, my dear. If he had been so very agreeable, he would have talked to Mrs. Long. But I can guess how it was. Everybody says that he is eaten up with pride, and I dare say he had heard somehow that Mrs. Long does not keep a carriage and had come to the ball in a hack chaise."

"I do not mind his not talking to Mrs. Long," said Charlotte. "But I wish he had danced with Eliza."

"Another time, Lizzy," said her mother, "I would not dance with *him*, if I were you."

"I believe, ma'am, I may safely promise you *never* to dance with him."

"His pride does not offend *me* so much as pride often does, because there is an excuse for it," said Charlotte. "One cannot wonder that so very fine a young man, with family, fortune, everything in his favor, should think highly of himself. If I may so express it, he has a *right* to be proud."

"That is very true," replied Elizabeth. "And I could easily forgive *his* pride, if he had not mortified *mine*."

"Pride is a very common failing, I believe," observed Mary, who piqued herself upon the solidity of her reflections. "By all that I have ever read, I am convinced that it is very common indeed, that human nature is particularly prone to it, and that there are very few of us who do not cherish a feeling of self-complacency on the score of some quality or other, real or imaginary. Vanity and pride are different things, though the words are often used synonymously. A person may be proud without being vain. Pride relates more to our opinion of ourselves, vanity to what we would have others think of us."

Mary's sermon soon ended the visit with a round of suppressed smiles and yawns.

Chapter Three

The ladies of Longbourn soon waited on those of Netherfield. Miss Bennet's pleasing manners grew on the goodwill of Mrs. Hurst and Miss Bingley; and though the mother was found to be intolerable and the younger sisters not worth speaking to, a wish of being better acquainted with *them* was expressed towards the two eldest. By Jane, this attention was received with the greatest pleasure, but Elizabeth still saw superciliousness in their treatment of everybody, hardly excepting even her sister, and could not like them. Their kindness to Jane, such as it was, had a value as arising in all probability from the influence of their brother's admiration. It was generally evident whenever they met that he *did* admire Jane, and to Elizabeth it was equally evident that Jane was yielding to the preference which she had begun to entertain for him from the first and was in a way to be very much in love. Yet Elizabeth considered with pleasure that it was not likely to be discovered by the world in general, since Jane united with great strength of feeling a composure of temper and a uniform cheerfulness of manner which would guard her from the suspicions of the impertinent. She mentioned this to her friend Miss Lucas.

Charlotte shook her head. "It may perhaps be pleasant to be able to impose on the public in such a case, but it is sometimes a disadvantage to be so very guarded. If a woman conceals her affection with the same skill from the object of it, she may lose the opportunity of fixing him, and it will then be but poor consolation to believe the world equally in the dark. There is so much of gratitude or vanity in almost every attachment that it is not safe to leave any to itself. We can all *begin* freely—a slight preference is natural enough, but there are very few of us who have heart enough to be really in love without encouragement. In nine cases out of ten a woman had better show *more* affection than she feels. Bingley likes your sister undoubtedly, but he may never do more than like her if she does not help him on."

"But she does help him on, as much as her nature will allow. If I can perceive her regard for him, he must be a simpleton indeed not to discover it too."

"Remember, Eliza, that he does not know Jane's disposition as you do."

"But if a woman is partial to a man and does not endeavor to conceal it, he must find it out."

"Perhaps he must, if he sees enough of her. But though Bingley and Jane meet tolerably often, it is never for many hours together; and as they always see each other in large mixed parties, it is impossible that every moment should be employed in conversing together. Jane should therefore make the most of every half hour in which she can command his attention. When she is secure of him, there will be more leisure for falling in love as much as she chooses."

"Your plan is a good one where nothing is in question but the desire of being well married," replied Elizabeth. "And if I were determined to get a rich husband, or any husband, I dare say I should adopt it. But these are not Jane's feelings; she is not acting by design. As yet, she cannot even be certain of the degree of her own regard nor of its reasonableness. She has known him only a fortnight. She danced four dances with him at Meryton; she saw him one morning at his own house, and has since dined with him in company four times. This is not quite enough to make her understand his character."

"Not as you represent it. Had she merely *dined* with him, she might only have discovered whether he had a good appetite. But you must remember that four evenings have also been spent together—and four evenings may do a great deal."

"Yes. These four evenings have enabled them to ascertain that they both like Vingtun better than Commerce. But with respect to any other leading characteristic, I do not imagine that much has been unfolded."

"Well, I wish Jane success with all my heart," said Charlotte. "And if she were married to him tomorrow, I should think she had as good a chance of happiness as if she were to be studying his character for a twelvemonth. Happiness in marriage is entirely a matter of chance. If the dispositions of the parties are ever so well known to each other or ever so similar beforehand, it does not advance their felicity in the least.

They always continue to grow sufficiently unlike afterwards to have their share of vexation, and it is better to know as little as possible of the defects of the person with whom you are to pass your life."

"You make me laugh, Charlotte, but it is not sound. You know it is not sound, and that you would never act in this way yourself."

* * * * *

Occupied in observing Bingley's attentions to her sister, Elizabeth was far from suspecting that she was herself becoming an object of some interest in the eyes of his friend. Darcy had at first scarcely allowed her to be pretty. He had looked at her without admiration at the ball, and when they next met, he looked at her only to criticize. But no sooner had he made it clear to himself and his friends that she hardly had a good feature in her face, than he began to find it was rendered uncommonly intelligent by the beautiful expression of her dark eyes. To this discovery succeeded some others equally mortifying. Though he had detected with a critical eye more than one failure of perfect symmetry in her features as was so common among humans, he was forced to acknowledge her figure to be light and pleasing. And in spite of his asserting that her manners were not those of the fashionable world, he was caught by their easy playfulness and her obvious joy for life.

Unfortunately, of all this she seemed perfectly unaware; to her he was most probably only the man who made himself agreeable nowhere and who had not thought her handsome enough to dance with.

He began to wish to know more of her, and as a step towards conversing with her himself, attended to her conversation with others.

* * * * *

His doing so drew her notice. It was at Sir William Lucas's where a large party was assembled.

"What does Mr. Darcy mean by listening to my conversation with Colonel Forster?" said she to Charlotte.

"That is a question which Mr. Darcy only can answer."

"But if he does it any more I shall certainly let him know that I see what he is about. He has a very satirical eye, and if I do not begin by being impertinent myself, I shall soon grow afraid of him." These were not idle words, for already the nearness of his presence threatened to make her tremble as it always did. Such an effect upon her was most distressing and not one she could think upon with any comfort or anything other than confusion. The only cure for such an ill was to confront the source of distress in order to lessen his affect.

On his approaching them soon afterwards, though without seeming to have any intention of speaking, Miss Lucas defied her friend to speak to him.

This immediately provoked Elizabeth to do it; she turned to him. "Did you not think, Mr. Darcy, that I expressed myself uncommonly well just now when I was teasing Colonel Forster to give us a ball at Meryton?"

"With great energy," he readily agreed. "But it is always a subject which makes a lady energetic."

"You are severe on us."

"It will be *her* turn soon to be teased," said Miss Lucas. "I am going to open the instrument, Eliza, and you know what follows."

"You are a very strange creature by way of a friend! Always wanting me to play and sing before anybody and everybody! If my vanity had taken a musical turn, you would have been invaluable. But as it is, I would really rather not sit down before those who must be in the habit of hearing the very best performers." On Miss Lucas's persevering, however, she added, "Very well, if it must be so, it must." And gravely glancing at Mr. Darcy, "There is a fine old saying, which everybody here is of course familiar with: 'Keep your breath to cool your porridge'; and I shall keep mine to swell my song."

Her performance was pleasing, though by no means capital as she well knew and had expected. After a song or two, and before she could reply to the entreaties of several that she would sing again, she was eagerly succeeded at the instrument by her sister Mary.

As the only plain one in the family, Mary had worked hard for knowledge and accomplishments and was always impatient for display. Unfortunately, she had neither genius nor taste, and though vanity had given her application, it had given her likewise a pedantic air and conceited manner, which would have injured a higher degree of excellence than she had reached. Elizabeth, easy and unaffected, had been listened to with much more pleasure, though not playing half so well.

Mary, at the end of a long concerto, was glad to purchase praise and gratitude by Scotch and Irish airs at the request of her younger

17

sisters who, with some of the Lucases and two or three officers, joined eagerly in dancing at one end of the room.

* * * * *

Mr. Darcy stood near them in silent indignation at such a mode of passing the evening to the exclusion of all conversation. Oh, why must these humans always be dancing about? Such activity only made his responsibility more difficult, as soon Bingley and Miss Bingley would most likely join in with the other dancers. A second's loss of focus on his part, one slip of his glamour over them, and their human dance partners would be sure to notice their pale skin, the shadows beneath their eyes that caught the light with an animal-like shine, the cold hardness of their skin. So too did the act of dancing draw more attention to oneself than usual, thus ensuring that most every eye present would be turned upon the dancers. And then there was the small matter of how dancing quickened all those human heartbeats until they pounded at his ears and will with their distracting pulse.

Dancing was an evil temptation. Now more than ever, he must remain focused.

He became too engrossed to perceive that Sir William Lucas was his neighbor till Sir William spoke.

"What a charming amusement for young people this is, Mr. Darcy! There is nothing like dancing after all. I consider it as one of the first refinements of polished society."

"Certainly, sir, and it has the advantage also of being in vogue amongst the less polished societies of the world. Every savage can dance."

Sir William only smiled. After seeing Bingley join the dancers, he said, "Your friend performs delightfully. And I doubt not that you are an adept in the science yourself, Mr. Darcy."

"You saw me dance at Meryton, I believe, sir."

"Yes, indeed, and received no inconsiderable pleasure from the sight. Do you often dance at St. James's?"

"Never, sir."

"Do you not think it would be a proper compliment to the place?"

"It is a compliment which I never pay to any place if I can avoid it."

"You have a house in town, I conclude?"

Darcy bowed, wishing yet again to be left in peace so he could focus on maintaining his glamour over Bingley and Miss Bingley. Mrs. Long squinted her eyes as she stared at Miss Bingley to her left. Darcy redoubled his efforts with the illusion, and after a few seconds, Mrs. Long smiled and relaxed once more.

"I had once had some thought of fixing in town myself—for I am fond of superior society," Sir Lucas continued. "But I did not feel quite certain that the air of London would agree with Lady Lucas."

He paused in obvious hopes of an answer. But Darcy was not disposed to make any, and Elizabeth at that instant moving towards them, Sir William seemed struck with the action of doing a gallant thing and called out to her.

"My dear Miss Eliza, why are you not dancing? Mr. Darcy, you must allow me to present this young lady to you as a very desirable partner. You cannot refuse to dance, I am sure, when so much beauty is before you." And taking her hand, he would have given it to Darcy who, though extremely surprised, was not unwilling to receive it.

She instantly drew back and said with some discomposure to Sir William, "Indeed, sir, I have not the least intention of dancing. I entreat you not to suppose that I moved this way in order to beg for a partner."

Darcy, with grave propriety, requested to be allowed the honor of her hand, but in vain. Elizabeth was determined; nor did Sir William at all shake her purpose by his attempt at persuasion.

"You excel so much in the dance, Miss Eliza, that it is cruel to deny me the happiness of seeing you; and though this gentleman dislikes the amusement in general, he can have no objection, I am sure, to oblige us for one half hour."

"Mr. Darcy is all politeness," said Elizabeth, smiling.

"He is, indeed; but considering the inducement, my dear Miss Eliza, we cannot wonder at his complaisance—for who would object to such a partner?"

With one eyebrow raised, Elizabeth moved away, taking with her the pleasing scent of rain and wildflowers that clung to her from her long walks outdoors, as he had once overheard her mention was her habit. Yet her resistance to dancing with him tonight had not injured her with the gentleman, and after Sir Lucas left him in welcome silence, he was thinking of her with some complacency when thus accosted by Miss Bingley.

"I can guess the subject of your reverie."

"I should imagine not."

"You are considering how insupportable it would be to pass many evenings in this manner—in such weak, mortal society; and indeed I am quite of your opinion. I was never more annoyed! The insipidity, and yet the noise—the nothingness, and yet the self-importance of all these humans! What would I give to hear your strictures on them!"

"Your conjecture is totally wrong, I assure you. My mind was more agreeably engaged. I have been meditating on the very great pleasure which a pair of fine eyes in the face of a pretty woman can bestow." He spoke without consideration, his mind torn between maintaining the ever necessary glamour upon his circle, and the profile of one across the room who had since joined in laughter and conversation with her sister Jane.

Miss Bingley immediately fixed her gaze on his face and desired he would tell her what lady had the credit of inspiring such reflections.

"Miss Elizabeth Bennet."

"Miss Elizabeth Bennet!" repeated Miss Bingley. "I am all astonishment. How long has she been such a favorite? And pray, when am I to wish you joy? Unless you were reserving your preferences toward her for food alone?" She laughed.

He disregarded her allusions to their altered state's dietary preferences. "Those are exactly the questions which I expected you to ask. A lady's imagination is very rapid; it jumps from admiration to love, from love to matrimony, in a moment. I knew you would be wishing me joy."

"Ah, so she is not for food then? Well, if you are serious in persisting on becoming attached to the chattle, I shall consider the matter as absolutely settled. You will be having a charming mother-in-law, indeed; and of course she will always be at Pemberley with you. Especially if you should decide to turn her into one of us; then she may reside with you at Pemberley for all eternity!"

He listened to her with perfect indifference while she chose to entertain herself in this manner, and as his composure convinced her that all was safe, and no humans drew within hearing distance, her wit flowed long.

Chapter Four

Mr. Bennet's property consisted almost entirely in an estate of two thousand a year, which, unfortunately for his daughters, was entailed in default of heirs male on a distant relation. Their mother's fortune, though ample for her situation in life, could but ill supply the deficiency of his. Her father had been an attorney in Meryton and had left her four thousand pounds. She had come to their marriage with naught else but a sister married to a Mr. Phillips, who had been a clerk to their father and succeeded him in the business, and a brother settled in London in a respectable line of trade.

The village of Longbourn was only one mile from Meryton, a most convenient distance for the young ladies, who were usually tempted thither three or four times a week to pay their duty to their aunt and to a milliner's shop just over the way. The two youngest of the family, Catherine and Lydia, were particularly frequent in these attentions. Their minds were more vacant than their sisters', and when nothing better offered, a walk to Meryton was necessary to amuse their morning hours and furnish conversation for the evening. And however bare of news the country in general might be, they always contrived to learn some from their aunt. At present, indeed, they were well supplied both with news and happiness by the recent arrival of a militia regiment in the neighborhood. It was to remain the whole winter, and Meryton was the headquarters.

Their visits to Mrs. Phillips were now productive of the most interesting intelligence. Every day added something to their knowledge of the officers' names and connections. Their lodgings were not long a secret, and at length they began to know the officers themselves. Mr.

Phillips visited them all, and this opened to his nieces a store of felicity unknown before. They could talk of nothing but officers, and Mr. Bingley's large fortune, the mention of which gave animation to their mother, was worthless in their eyes when opposed to the regimentals of an ensign.

After listening one morning to their effusions on this subject, Mr. Bennet coolly observed, "From all that I can collect by your manner of talking, you must be two of the silliest girls in the country. I have suspected it some time, but I am now convinced."

Catherine was disconcerted and made no answer. But Lydia, with perfect indifference, continued to express her admiration of Captain Carter and her hope of seeing him in the course of the day, as he was going the next morning to London.

"I am astonished, my dear, that you should be so ready to think your own children silly," said Mrs. Bennet. "If I wished to think slightingly of anybody's children, it should not be of my own, however."

"If my children are silly, I must hope to be always sensible of it."

"Yes—but as it happens, they are all of them very clever."

"This is the only point, I flatter myself, on which we do not agree. I had hoped that our sentiments coincided in every particular, but I must so far differ from you as to think our two youngest daughters uncommonly foolish."

Mrs. Bennet was prevented replying by the entrance of the footman with a note for Miss Bennet; it came from Netherfield, and the servant waited for an answer.

Mrs. Bennet's eyes sparkled with pleasure, and she was eagerly calling out, while her daughter read, "Well, Jane, who is it from? What is it about? What does he say? Well, Jane, make haste and tell us. Make haste, my love."

"It is from Miss Bingley," said Jane and then read it aloud.

"MY DEAR FRIEND,

"If you are not so compassionate as to dine today with Louisa and me, we shall be in danger of hating each other for the rest of our lives, for a whole day's tete-a-tete between two women can never end without a quarrel. Come as soon as you can on receipt of this. My brother and the gentlemen are to dine with the officers.

Yours ever,

"With the officers!" cried Lydia. "I wonder my aunt did not tell us of *that*."

"Dining out." Mrs. Bennet shook her head with a frown. "That is very unlucky."

"Can I have the carriage?" said Jane.

"No, my dear, you had better go on horseback, because it seems likely to rain, and then you must stay all night." Mrs. Bennet gave a happy glance at the stormy view beyond the room's windows.

Jane was therefore obliged to go on horseback, and her mother attended her to the door with many cheerful prognostics of a bad day. Her hopes were answered; Jane had not been gone long before it rained hard. Her sisters were uneasy for her, but her mother was delighted. The rain continued the whole evening without intermission; Jane certainly could not come back.

"This was a lucky idea of mine, indeed!" said Mrs. Bennet more than once, as if the credit of making it rain were all her own. Till the next morning, however, she was not aware of all the felicity of her contrivance. Breakfast was scarcely over when a servant from Netherfield brought the following note for Elizabeth:

"MY DEAREST LIZZY,

"I find myself very unwell this morning, which I suppose is to be imputed to my getting wet through yesterday. My kind friends will not hear of my returning till I am better. They insist also on my seeing Mr. Jones—therefore do not be alarmed if you should hear of his having been to me—and, excepting a sore throat and headache, there is not much the matter with me. Yours, etc."

Mr. Bennet looked at his wife with raised eyebrows. "Well, my dear, if your daughter should have a dangerous fit of illness—if she should die, it would be a comfort to know that it was all in pursuit of Mr. Bingley and under your orders."

"Oh! I am not afraid of her dying. People do not die of little trifling colds. She will be taken good care of. As long as she stays there, it is all very well. I would go and see her if I could have the carriage."

23

Elizabeth, feeling really anxious, was determined to go to her, though the carriage was not to be had and, as she was no horsewoman, walking was her only alternative. She declared her resolution.

"How can you be so silly as to think of such a thing in all this dirt!" cried her mother. "You will not be fit to be seen when you get there."

"I shall be very fit to see Jane—which is all I want."

"Is this a hint to me, Lizzy, to send for the horses?" said her father.

"No, indeed, I do not wish to avoid the walk. The distance is nothing when one has a motive; only three miles. I shall be back by dinner."

"We will go as far as Meryton with you," said Catherine and Lydia.

Elizabeth accepted their company, and the three young ladies set off together in the gloom.

As they walked along the soggy ground, Lydia said, "If we make haste, perhaps we may see something of Captain Carter before he goes."

In Meryton they parted. The two youngest repaired to the lodgings of one of the officers' wives, and Elizabeth continued her walk through the shadows alone, crossing field after muddy field at a quick pace, jumping over stiles and springing over puddles with impatient activity, and finding herself at last within view of the house, with weary ankles, dirty stockings, and a face glowing with the warmth of exercise.

She was shown into the breakfast parlor, where all but Jane were assembled amongst the flickering of many candelabras lit to relegate the stormy day's darkness to the corners. Her appearance created a great deal of surprise, causing Mr. Darcy to jump to his feet while the others remained seated in shock. That she should have walked three miles so early in the day, in such dark, dirty weather, and by herself, was almost incredible to Mrs. Hurst and Miss Bingley. Elizabeth was convinced that they held her in contempt for it. She was received, however, very politely by them, though Mr. Darcy remained standing quite formally. In their brother's manners there was something better than politeness; there was good humor and kindness. Mr. Darcy said very little but only looked pale and mildly alarmed in the dancing shadows, and Mr. Hurst said nothing at all. The former was divided between admiration of the brilliancy which exercise had given to her complexion, and doubt as to whether her tempting presence there without the protection of a familial chaperone was entirely safe. The latter was thinking only of his breakfast and a morning nap if the lingering rumbles of thunder would allow it.

Her inquiries after her sister were not very favorably answered. Miss Bennet had slept ill, and though up, was very feverish and not well enough to leave her room. Elizabeth was glad to be taken to her immediately. Jane, who had only been withheld by the fear of giving alarm or inconvenience from expressing in her note how much she longed for such a visit, was delighted at her entrance. She was not equal, however, to much conversation and could attempt little besides expressions of gratitude for the extraordinary kindness she was treated with. Elizabeth silently attended her.

When breakfast was over, the apothecary came, and having examined his patient, said as might be supposed…that she had caught a violent cold and that they must endeavor to get the better of it, advised her to return to bed, and promised her some draughts. To relieve the aching pressure in Jane's head, he drew off some of her blood into a bowl, during which Miss Bingley and Mrs. Hurst started to enter the room for a visit. Mrs. Hurst led the way, so Elizabeth could not be sure, but there was a sound at her back, as if Miss Bingley had looked into the room and gasped at the sight of the blood. Elizabeth smiled to herself at such a weakness of character, the only possible explanation for why Miss Bingley would then immediately draw back from the room's entrance. With an apologetic smile, Mrs. Hurst followed her sister in haste from the room with promises to return in a moment.

The apothecary's advice was readily followed, for the feverish symptoms increased. Elizabeth did not quit Jane's room for a moment. Once Miss Bingley's maid had come to remove the bowl of Jane's blood, the other ladies returned and were then not often absent; the gentlemen being out, they had in fact nothing to do elsewhere and so chose to attend to Jane instead. Miss Bingley did not seem quite recovered from her shock during her visit, or perhaps the proximity to illness caused her to be pale with dark shadows about her eyes. Still, Elizabeth began to like the sisters when she saw how much affection and solicitude they showed for Jane. There was something truly charming about them when they attempted to endear themselves to others, which overcame Elizabeth's more logical feelings towards them when not close within their presence.

When the clock struck three, Elizabeth felt that she must go and very unwillingly said so. Miss Bingley offered her the carriage, and she only wanted a little pressing to accept it, when Jane testified such concern in parting with her that Miss Bingley was obliged to convert the offer of the chaise to an invitation to remain at Netherfield for the present. Elizabeth most thankfully consented, and a servant was dispatched to Longbourn to acquaint the family with her stay and bring back a supply of clothes.

Chapter Five

At five o'clock Mrs. Hurst and Miss Bingley retired to dress, and at half past six Elizabeth was summoned to dinner. To the civil inquiries which then poured in, and amongst which she had the pleasure of distinguishing the much superior solicitude of Mr. Bingley's, she could not make a very favorable answer. Jane was by no means better. The sisters, on hearing this, repeated three or four times how much they were grieved, how shocking it was to have a bad cold, and how excessively they disliked being ill themselves. They then thought no more of the matter, and their indifference towards Jane when not immediately before them restored Elizabeth to the enjoyment of all her former dislike, in spite of their charming voices and countenances.

Their brother, indeed, was the only one of the party whom she could regard with any complacency. His anxiety for Jane was evident, and his attentions to herself most pleasing, and they prevented her feeling herself so much an intruder as she believed she was considered by the others. She had very little notice from any but him. Miss Bingley was engrossed with Mr. Darcy, and her sister scarcely less so while struggling in vain to hide many yawns. As for Mr. Hurst, by whom Elizabeth sat, he was an indolent man who lived only to eat, drink, play at cards, and nap, and when he found her to prefer a plain dish to a ragout, had nothing to say to her.

* * * * *

When dinner was over, she returned directly to Jane. Darcy watched her leave with a mixture of relief and regret that soon turned

27

to annoyance, as Miss Bingley began abusing her as soon as she was out of the room. Her manners were pronounced to be very bad indeed, a mixture of pride and impertinence; she had no conversation, no style, no beauty.

Mrs. Hurst thought the same, and after yet another yawn, added, "She has nothing, in short, to recommend her other than being an excellent walker. I shall never forget her appearance this morning. She really looked almost wild."

"She did, indeed, Louisa. I could hardly keep my countenance," agreed Miss Bingley. "Very nonsensical to come at all! Why must *she* be scampering about the country because her sister had a cold? Her hair, so untidy, so blowsy!"

"Yes, and her petticoat; I hope you saw her petticoat, six inches deep in mud, I am absolutely certain, and the gown which had been let down to hide it not doing its office."

"Your picture may be very exact, Louisa," said Bingley. "But this was all lost upon me. I thought Miss Elizabeth Bennet looked remarkably well when she came into the room this morning. Her dirty petticoat quite escaped my notice."

Miss Bingley and Mrs. Hurst shared knowing smiles.

"But of course you would think anyone not in this circle was attractive," teased Miss Bingley before turning to his friend. "*You* observed it, Mr. Darcy, I am sure, and I am inclined to think that you would not wish to see *your* sister make such an exhibition."

"Certainly not."

"To walk three miles, or four miles, or five miles, or whatever it is, above her ankles in dirt, and alone, quite alone! What could she mean by it? It seems to me to show an abominable sort of conceited independence, a most country-town indifference to decorum."

"It shows an affection for her sister that is very pleasing," said Bingley.

Miss Bingley leaned over and half whispered, "I am afraid, Mr. Darcy, that this adventure has rather affected your admiration of her fine eyes."

"Not at all," he replied. "They were brightened by the exercise."

A short pause followed this speech, and Mrs. Hurst began again, "I have an excessive regard for Miss Jane Bennet, she is really a very sweet girl, and I wish with all my heart she were well settled. But with such a father and mother, and such low connections, I am afraid there is no chance of it."

"I think I have heard you say that their uncle is an attorney in Meryton," said Miss Bingley.

"Yes, and they have another who lives somewhere near Cheapside."

"That is capital," added her sister, and they both laughed heartily.

"If they had uncles enough to fill *all* Cheapside, it would not make them one jot less agreeable," cried Bingley.

"But it must very materially lessen their chance of marrying men of any consideration in the world," replied Darcy, ignoring the discomfort that spread through him at his own words.

To this speech Bingley made no answer; but his sisters gave it their hearty assent and indulged their mirth for some time at the expense of their dear friend's vulgar relations.

* * * * *

With a renewal of tenderness, however, they returned to Jane's room on leaving the dining parlor and sat with her till summoned to coffee. She was still very poorly, and Elizabeth would not quit her at all till late in the evening, when she had the comfort of seeing her sleep, and when it seemed to her rather right than pleasant that she should go downstairs herself. On entering the drawing room, dimly lit mainly by a small fire, she found the whole party playing cards and was immediately invited to join them. Suspecting them to be playing high, she declined it, and making her sister the excuse, said she would amuse herself for the short time she could stay below with a book.

Mr. Hurst looked at her with astonishment. "Do you prefer reading to cards? That is rather singular."

"Miss Eliza Bennet despises cards," said Miss Bingley. "She is a great reader and has no pleasure in anything else."

"I deserve neither such praise nor such censure," cried Elizabeth. "I am *not* a great reader, and I have pleasure in many things."

"In nursing your sister I am sure you have pleasure," said Mr. Bingley. "And I hope it will be soon increased by seeing her quite well."

Elizabeth thanked him from her heart and then walked towards the table where a few books were lying.

He immediately offered to fetch her others—all that his library afforded. "And I wish my collection were larger for your benefit and my own credit. But I am an idle fellow, and though I have not many, I have more than I ever looked into."

29

Elizabeth assured him that she could suit herself perfectly with those in the room.

"I am astonished that my father should have left so small a collection of books," said Miss Bingley. "What a delightful library you have at Pemberley, Mr. Darcy!"

"It ought to be good," he replied. "It has been the work of many generations."

"And then you have added so much to it yourself; you are always buying books."

"I cannot comprehend the neglect of a family library in such days as these."

"Neglect! I am sure you neglect nothing that can add to the beauties of that noble place. Charles, when you build *your* house, I wish it may be half as delightful as Pemberley."

"I wish it may," agreed Mr. Bingley.

"But I would really advise you to make your purchase in that neighborhood and take Pemberley for a kind of model. There is not a finer county in England than Derbyshire."

"With all my heart; I will buy Pemberley itself if Darcy will sell it."

Miss Bingley waved a hand in dismissal of such an idea. "I am talking of possibilities, Charles."

"Upon my word, Caroline, I should think it more possible to get Pemberley by purchase than by imitation."

Elizabeth was so much caught with what passed as to leave her very little attention for her book, and soon closing it, she drew near the card table and stationed herself between Mr. Bingley and his eldest sister to observe the game.

"Is Miss Darcy much grown since the spring?" said Miss Bingley, turning toward Mr. Darcy. "Will she be as tall as I am?"

"I think she will. She is now about Miss Elizabeth Bennet's height, or rather taller."

Elizabeth started and stared at him across the table. Mr. Darcy had noticed and remembered her height? He ignored her attention.

Miss Bingley's eyes flashed wide then narrowed. "How I long to see her again! I never met with anybody who delighted me so much. Such a countenance, such manners! And so extremely accomplished for her age! Her performance on the pianoforte is exquisite."

Mr. Bingley smiled. "It is amazing to me how young ladies can have patience to be so very accomplished as they all are."

"All young ladies accomplished!" cried Miss Bingley. "My dear Charles, what do you mean?"

"Yes, all of them, I think. They all paint tables, cover screens, and net purses. I scarcely know anyone who cannot do all this, and I am sure I never heard a young lady spoken of for the first time without being informed that she was very accomplished."

"Your list of the common extent of accomplishments has too much truth," said Mr. Darcy. "The word is applied to many a woman who deserves it no otherwise than by netting a purse or covering a screen. But I am very far from agreeing with you in your estimation of ladies in general. I cannot boast of knowing more than half a dozen, in the whole range of my acquaintance, that are really accomplished."

"Nor I, I am sure," said Miss Bingley.

"Then you must comprehend a great deal in your idea of an accomplished woman," observed Elizabeth.

"Yes, I do comprehend a great deal in it."

"Oh! Certainly," cried his faithful assistant. "A woman must have a thorough knowledge of music, singing, drawing, dancing, and the modern languages to deserve the word. And besides all this, she must possess a certain something in her air and manner of walking, the tone of her voice, her address and expressions, or the word will be but half deserved." At that moment as she stared at Elizabeth with one eyebrow arched, the firelight played most strangely over Miss Bingley's countenance, seeming to reflect with an unnatural, animal-like shine upon her eyes. The frightening effect lasted only until Elizabeth blinked, yet left her heart stuttering.

"All this she must possess," added Mr. Darcy. "And to all this she must yet add something more substantial in the improvement of her mind by extensive reading." He nodded at the book still clutched in Elizabeth's lap.

This repeat of such unexpected attention from him served to help Elizabeth recollect herself and take heed of his words. "I am no longer surprised at your knowing *only* six accomplished women. I rather wonder now at your knowing *any*."

Mr. Bingley laughed.

Mr. Darcy turned his gaze fully upon her face for the first time all evening, his expression perturbed. "Are you so severe upon your own sex as to doubt the possibility of all this?"

"I never saw such a woman." Her chin lifted in defiance of the strange effect his stare had upon her pulse.

31

Mrs. Hurst and Miss Bingley both cried out against the injustice of her implied doubt, and were both protesting that they knew many women who answered this description, when Mr. Hurst called them to order with bitter complaints of their inattention to what was going forward in the mostly forgotten card game. As all conversation was thereby at an end, Elizabeth soon afterwards left the room, her heartbeat still insistent upon a rhythm slightly faster than its usual.

* * * * *

When the door was closed behind Elizabeth, Miss Bingley said, "Elizabeth Bennet is one of those young ladies who seek to recommend themselves to the other sex by undervaluing their own; and with many men, I dare say, it succeeds. But in my opinion it is a paltry device, a very mean art."

"Undoubtedly," replied Darcy, to whom this remark was chiefly addressed. "There is a meanness in *all* the arts which ladies sometimes condescend to employ for captivation. Whatever bears affinity to cunning is despicable."

Miss Bingley was apparently not so entirely satisfied with this reply as to continue the subject.

Elizabeth joined them again only to say that her sister was worse and that she could not leave her. Bingley urged Mr. Jones being sent for immediately, while his sisters, convinced that no country advice could be of any service, recommended an express to town for one of the most eminent physicians. This she would not hear of. But she was not so unwilling to comply with their brother's proposal, and it was settled that Mr. Jones should be sent for early in the morning if Miss Bennet were not decidedly better. Bingley was quite uncomfortable; his sisters declared that they were miserable. They solaced their wretchedness, however, by duets after supper, while he could find no better relief to his feelings than by giving his housekeeper directions that every attention might be paid to the sick lady and her sister.

Chapter Six

Elizabeth passed the chief of the night in her sister's room, and in the morning had the pleasure of being able to send a tolerable answer to the inquiries which she very early received from Mr. Bingley by a housemaid, and some time afterwards from the two elegant ladies who waited on his sisters. In spite of this amendment, however, she requested to have a note sent to Longbourn desiring her mother to visit Jane and form her own judgement of her situation. The note was immediately dispatched and its contents as quickly complied with. Mrs. Bennet, accompanied by her two youngest girls, reached Netherfield soon after the family breakfast.

Had she found Jane in any apparent danger, Mrs. Bennet would have been very miserable. But being satisfied on seeing her that her illness was not alarming, she had no wish of her recovering immediately, as her restoration to health would probably remove her from Netherfield. She would not listen, therefore, to Elizabeth's proposal of being carried home; neither did the apothecary, who arrived about the same time, think it at all advisable. After sitting a little while with Jane, on Miss Bingley's appearance and invitation, the mother and three daughters all attended her into the breakfast parlor. Mr. Bingley met them with hopes that Mrs. Bennet had not found Miss Bennet worse than she expected.

"Indeed I have, sir," was her answer. "She is a great deal too ill to be moved. Mr. Jones says we must not think of moving her. We must trespass a little longer on your kindness."

"Removed!" cried Mr. Bingley. "It must not be thought of. My sisters, I am sure, will not hear of her removal."

"You may depend upon it, Madam, that Miss Bennet will receive every possible attention while she remains with us," said Miss Bingley with cold civility.

Her words gave Elizabeth an unaccountable chill and the desire to remain as close to Jane as possible throughout the remainder of their stay.

However, Mrs. Bennet was profuse in her acknowledgments.

She added, "I am sure if it was not for such good friends I do not know what would become of her, for she is very ill indeed and suffers a vast deal, though with the greatest patience in the world, which is always the way with her, for she has without exception the sweetest temper I have ever met with. I often tell my other girls they are nothing to *her.* You have a sweet room here, Mr. Bingley, and a charming prospect over the gravel walk. I do not know a place in the country that is equal to Netherfield. You will not think of quitting it in a hurry, I hope, though you have but a short lease."

"Whatever I do is done in a hurry," replied he. "Therefore if I should resolve to quit Netherfield, I should probably be off in five minutes. At present, however, I consider myself as quite fixed here."

"That is exactly what I should have supposed of you," said Elizabeth.

"You begin to comprehend me, do you?" cried he, turning towards her.

"Oh yes—I understand you perfectly."

"I wish I might take this for a compliment; but to be so easily seen through I am afraid is pitiful."

"That is as it happens. It does not follow that a deep, intricate character is more or less estimable than such a one as yours."

"Lizzy," cried her mother. "Remember where you are, and do not run on in the wild manner that you are suffered to do at home."

"I did not know before that you were a studier of character," continued Mr. Bingley immediately. "It must be an amusing study."

"Yes, but intricate characters are the *most* amusing. They have at least that advantage."

Mr. Darcy spoke up at last. "The country can in general supply but a few subjects for such a study. In a country neighborhood you move in a very confined and unvarying society."

Elizabeth smiled. "But people themselves alter so much that there is something new to be observed in them forever."

"Yes, indeed," cried Mrs. Bennet, apparently offended by his manner of mentioning a country neighborhood. "I assure you there is quite as much of *that* going on in the country as in town."

Everybody was surprised, and Mr. Darcy, after looking at her for a moment, turned silently away. Mrs. Bennet, who fancied she had gained a complete victory over him, continued her triumph.

"I cannot see that London has any great advantage over the country, for my part, except the shops and public places. The country is a vast deal pleasanter, is it not, Mr. Bingley?"

"When I am in the country, I never wish to leave it," replied he. "And when I am in town it is pretty much the same. They have each their advantages, and I can be equally happy in either."

"Aye—that is because you have the right disposition. But that gentleman," Mrs. Bennet looked at Mr. Darcy, "seemed to think the country was nothing at all."

"Indeed, Mamma, you are mistaken," said Elizabeth, blushing for her mother. "You quite mistook Mr. Darcy. He only meant that there was not such a variety of people to be met with in the country as in the town, which you must acknowledge to be true."

"Certainly, my dear, nobody said there were. But as to not meeting with many people in this neighborhood, I believe there are few neighborhoods larger. I know we dine with four-and-twenty families."

Nothing but probable polite concern for Elizabeth seemed to enable Mr. Bingley to keep his countenance. His sister was less delicate and directed her eyes towards Mr. Darcy with a very expressive smile. Elizabeth, for the sake of saying something that might turn her mother's thoughts, now asked her if Charlotte Lucas had been at Longbourn.

"Yes, she called yesterday with her father. What an agreeable man Sir William is, Mr. Bingley, is not he? So much the man of fashion! So genteel and easy! He had always something to say to everybody. *That* is my idea of good breeding; and those persons who fancy themselves very important, and never open their mouths, quite mistake the matter."

"Did Charlotte dine with you?" Elizabeth tried distracting her once more.

"No, she would go home. I fancy she was wanted about the mince-pies. For my part, Mr. Bingley, I always keep servants that can do their own work; *my* daughters are brought up very differently. But everybody is to judge for themselves, and the Lucases are a very good sort of girls, I assure you. It is a pity they are not handsome! Lady Lucas herself has often said so and envied me Jane's beauty. I do not like to boast of my own child, but to be sure, Jane—one does not often see anybody better looking. It is what everybody says. I do not trust my own partiality. When she was only fifteen, there was a man at my brother Gardiner's in town so much in love with her that my sister-in-law was sure he would make her an offer before we came away. But he did not. Perhaps he thought her too young. However, he wrote some verses on her, and very pretty they were."

"And so ended his affection," snapped Elizabeth. Would her mother never cease to embarrass them all today? "There has been many a one, I fancy, overcome in the same way. I wonder who first discovered the efficacy of poetry in driving away love!"

"I have been used to consider poetry as the *food* of love," said Mr. Darcy.

Elizabeth turned toward him, expecting to find a knowing smile on his face. However, his gaze rested upon her with only its customary gravity. "Of a fine, stout, healthy love it may. Everything nourishes what is strong already. But if it be only a slight, thin sort of inclination, I am convinced that one good sonnet will starve it entirely away."

Mr. Darcy only smiled, and the general pause which ensued made Elizabeth tremble lest her mother should be exposing herself again. She longed to speak, but the shock of seeing Mr. Darcy smile made it impossible to think of a single word to say. His smile, so very rare, chased away the shadows that usually took up residence upon his countenance. He was nothing short of transformed. She could think of nothing but that she wished he would do so more often, and then wondered why such a thought should occur to her.

After a short silence, Mrs. Bennet began repeating her thanks to Mr. Bingley for his kindness to Jane, with an apology for troubling him also with Lizzy. Mr. Bingley was unaffectedly civil in his answer and forced his younger sister to be civil also and say what the occasion required. She performed her part indeed, though without much graciousness. But Mrs. Bennet was satisfied and soon afterwards ordered her carriage. Upon this signal, the youngest of her daughters put herself forward.

Lydia was a stout, well-grown girl of fifteen, with a fine complexion and good-humored countenance; a favorite with her mother, whose affection had brought her into public at an early age. She had high animal spirits and a sort of natural self-consequence, which the attention of the officers, to whom her uncle's good dinners and her own easy manners recommended her, had increased into assurance. She was very equal, therefore, to address Mr. Bingley on the subject of the ball, and abruptly reminded him of his promise, adding that it would be the most shameful thing in the world if he did not keep it. His answer to this sudden attack was delightful to their mother's ear.

"I am perfectly ready, I assure you, to keep my engagement, and when your sister is recovered, you shall, if you please, name the very day of the ball. But you would not wish to be dancing when she is ill."

Lydia declared herself satisfied. "Oh! Yes, it would be much better to wait till Jane is well, and by that time most likely Captain Carter would be at Meryton again."

Mrs. Bennet and her daughters then departed, and Elizabeth returned instantly to Jane, leaving her own and her relations' behavior to the remarks of the two ladies and Mr. Darcy. The latter of whom, however, could not be prevailed on to join in their censure of *her*, in spite of all Miss Bingley's witticisms on *fine eyes*.

* * * * *

The day passed much as the day before had done. Mrs. Hurst and Miss Bingley had spent some hours of the morning with the invalid, who continued, though slowly, to mend; and in the evening Elizabeth joined their party in the drawing room. The card table, however, did not appear. Mr. Darcy was writing, and Miss Bingley, seated near him, was watching the progress of his letter and repeatedly calling off his attention by messages to his sister. Mr. Hurst and Mr. Bingley were at piquet, and Mrs. Hurst was observing their game in between short naps.

Elizabeth took up some needlework and was sufficiently amused in attending to what passed between Mr. Darcy and his companion. The perpetual commendations of the lady, either on his handwriting, or on the evenness of his lines, or on the length of his letter, with the perfect unconcern with which her praises were received, formed a curious dialogue and was exactly in union with Elizabeth's opinion of each.

"How delighted Miss Darcy will be to receive such a letter!" said Miss Bingley.

He made no answer.

"You write uncommonly fast."

"You are mistaken. I write rather slowly."

"How many letters you must have occasion to write in the course of a year! Letters of business, too! How odious I should think them!"

"It is fortunate, then, that they fall to my lot instead of yours."

"Pray tell your sister that I long to see her."

"I have already told her so once by your desire."

"Tell your sister I am delighted to hear of her improvement on the harp; and pray let her know that I am quite in raptures with her beautiful little design for a table, and I think it infinitely superior to Miss Grantley's."

"Will you give me leave to defer your raptures till I write again? At present I have not room to do them justice."

"Oh! It is of no consequence. I shall see her in January. But do you always write such charming long letters to her, Mr. Darcy?"

"They are generally long; but whether always charming it is not for me to determine."

"It is a rule with me that a person who can write a long letter with ease cannot write ill."

Without further answering her, Mr. Darcy finished his letter.

When that business was over, he applied to Miss Bingley and Elizabeth for an indulgence of some music. Miss Bingley moved with some alacrity to the pianoforte. After a polite request that Elizabeth would lead the way, which the other as politely and more earnestly refused, Miss Bingley seated herself.

Mrs. Hurst sang with her sister, and while they were thus employed, Elizabeth could not help observing, as she turned over some music books that lay on the instrument, how frequently Mr. Darcy's eyes were fixed on her. She hardly knew how to suppose that she could be an object of admiration to so great a man, and yet that he should look at her because he disliked her was still more strange. She could only imagine at last, however, that she drew his notice because there was something more wrong and reprehensible, according to his ideas of right, than in any other person present.

* * * * *

After playing some Italian songs, Miss Bingley varied the charm by a lively Scotch air.

Soon afterwards, Darcy, drawing near Elizabeth, said to her, "Do not you feel a great inclination, Miss Elizabeth, to seize such an opportunity of dancing a reel?"

She smiled but made no answer. He repeated the question with some surprise at her silence.

"Oh!" said she. "I heard you before, but I could not immediately determine what to say in reply. You wanted me, I know, to say 'yes', that you might have the pleasure of despising my taste. But I always delight in overthrowing those kinds of schemes and cheating a person of their premeditated contempt. I have therefore made up my mind to tell you that I do not want to dance a reel at all—and now despise me if you dare."

"Indeed I do not dare." He smiled.

Elizabeth, perhaps having rather expected to affront him, seemed amazed at his gallantry. But there was a mixture of sweetness and archness in her manner which made it difficult for her to affront anybody, and Darcy had never been so bewitched by any woman as he was by her. He really believed that were it not for the inferiority of her connections, her fragile mortality as a human, and his immortal life as a vampire, he should be in some danger.

Miss Bingley must have seen or suspected enough to be jealous, and her great anxiety for the recovery of her dear friend Jane received some assistance from her desire to get rid of Elizabeth.

She often tried to provoke Darcy into disliking her guest by talking of their supposed marriage and planning his happiness in such an unnatural alliance.

As they walked together in the shrubbery the next day, Miss Bingley said, "I hope you will give your mother-in-law a few hints, when this desirable event takes place, as to the advantage of holding her tongue; and if you can compass it, do cure the younger girls of running after officers. And, if I may mention so delicate a subject, endeavor to check that little something bordering on conceit and impertinence which your lady possesses. And of course you must do something about her humanity as well, as that is sure to become quite an inconvenient temptation when next you grow thirsty with no willing volunteers nearby. Unless you have changed your mind and she is intended to become your new pet to supplant Mr. and Mrs. Hurst? Though I must warn you I am quite sure your lady's flavor will prove equal to her family's connections. Her sister's was, I assure you, not even half that of our usual fare."

He started, paused, and turned to stare in utter amazement at the vile creature at his side. To think that she had so little scruples as to partake of the very life force of a guest under her brother's very roof, and a very helpless, vulnerable guest at that! He could only hope that Jane's blood had been given without her express knowledge before or after the event, and that her present illness did not linger due to such a loss to Miss Bingley. Still worse was the thought that his own follies, his imprudent attention to the safety of Miss Bingley and her brother, had resulted in his being morally shackled to such a creature for all eternity for the sake of preventing future sins against humanity.

He would have to keep closer watch upon Miss Bingley during the remaining duration of the Bennet sisters' stay at Netherfield. He already had taken it upon himself to guard Bingley's door each night to ensure his friend would not be tempted to venture forth in the dark hours towards their room. Perhaps it would be simpler to stand guard at their door instead so as to protect them from all the vampires in the house at once.

He could only hope he would be able to withstand his own temptation sleeping within that room each night.

At length, he pulled himself from his thoughts and resumed walking, endeavoring to check his emotions. "Have you anything else to propose for my domestic felicity?"

"Oh! Yes. Do let the portraits of your uncle and aunt Phillips be placed in the gallery at Pemberley. Put them next to your great-uncle the judge. They are in the same profession, you know, only in different lines. As for your Elizabeth's picture, you must not have it taken, for what painter could do justice to those beautiful eyes?"

"It would not be easy, indeed, to catch their expression, but their color and shape, and the eyelashes, so remarkably fine, might be copied."

At that moment they were met from another walk by Mrs. Hurst and Miss Elizabeth herself.

"I did not know that you intended to walk," said Miss Bingley in some confusion, lest they had been overheard.

"You used us abominably ill, running away without telling us that you were coming out," answered Mrs. Hurst. Then taking the disengaged arm of Darcy, she left Miss Elizabeth to walk by herself. The path just admitted three.

Darcy felt their rudeness and immediately said, "This walk is not wide enough for our party. We had better go into the avenue."

But Miss Elizabeth, who did not seem to have the least inclination to remain with them, laughingly answered, "No, no; stay where you are. You are charmingly grouped and appear to uncommon advantage. The picturesque would be spoilt by admitting a fourth. Goodbye."

She then ran gaily off, apparently rejoicing as she rambled about in the hope of being at home again in a day or two. Miss Bennet had sent word that she was already so much recovered as to intend leaving her room for a couple of hours that evening.

He did not allow himself to examine the unhappiness that the impending loss of Miss Elizabeth's presence created within him. Any emotion with relation to her was not safe to dwell upon.

Chapter Seven

When the ladies removed after dinner, Elizabeth ran up to her sister, and seeing her well guarded from cold, attended her into the drawing room, where she was welcomed by her two friends with many professions of pleasure. Elizabeth had never seen them so agreeable as they were during the hour which passed before the gentlemen appeared. Their powers of conversation were considerable. They could describe an entertainment with accuracy, relate an anecdote with humor, and laugh at their acquaintance with spirit. Even Elizabeth felt herself drawn in by their charm.

But when the gentlemen entered, Jane was no longer the first object. Miss Bingley's eyes were instantly turned toward Mr. Darcy, and she had something to say to him before he had advanced many steps. He addressed himself to Miss Bennet with a polite congratulation. Mr. Hurst also made her a slight bow and said he was "very glad", but diffuseness and warmth remained for Mr. Bingley's salutation. He was full of joy and attention. The first half hour was spent in piling up the fire, lest she should suffer from the change of room, and she removed at his desire to the other side of the fireplace that she might be farther from the door. He then sat down by her and talked scarcely to anyone else. Elizabeth, at work on a book in the opposite corner, saw it all with great delight.

When tea was over, Mr. Hurst reminded his sister-in-law of the card table but in vain. She had obtained private intelligence that Mr. Darcy did not wish for cards, and Mr. Hurst soon found even his open petition rejected. She assured him that no one intended to play, and the silence of the whole party on the subject seemed to justify her. Mr.

42

Hurst had therefore nothing to do but to stretch himself on one of the sofas and go to sleep. Mr. Darcy took up a book; Miss Bingley did the same; and Mrs. Hurst, principally occupied in playing with her bracelets and rings in between yawns, joined now and then in her brother's conversation with Miss Bennet.

Miss Bingley's attention was quite as much engaged in watching Mr. Darcy's progress through his book as in reading her own, and she was perpetually either making some inquiry or looking at his page. She could not win him, however, to any conversation; he merely answered her question and read on. At length, quite exhausted by the attempt to be amused with her own book, which she had only chosen because it was the second volume of his, she gave a great yawn and said, "How pleasant it is to spend an evening in this way! I declare after all there is no enjoyment like reading! How much sooner one tires of anything than of a book! When I have a house of my own, I shall be miserable if I have not an excellent library."

No one made any reply. She then threw aside her book and cast her gaze round the room in quest for some amusement. When hearing her brother mentioning a ball to Miss Bennet, she turned suddenly towards him and said, "By the bye, Charles, are you really serious in meditating a dance at Netherfield? I would advise you, before you determine on it, to consult the wishes of the present party. I am much mistaken if there are not some among us to whom a ball would be rather a punishment than a pleasure."

"If you mean Darcy, he may go to bed, if he chooses, before it begins." Mr. Bingley grinned at his friend. "But as for the ball, it is quite a settled thing; and as soon as Nicholls has made white soup enough, I shall send round my cards."

"I should like balls infinitely better, if they were carried on in a different manner," replied Miss Bingley. "But there is something insufferably tedious in the usual process of such a meeting. It would surely be much more rational if conversation instead of dancing were made the order of the day."

"Much more rational, my dear Caroline, I dare say, but it would not be near so much like a ball," teased her brother.

Miss Bingley made no answer, and soon afterwards she got up and walked about the room. Her figure was elegant, and she walked well, but Mr. Darcy, at whom it was all aimed, was still inflexibly studious.

In the desperation of her feelings, she resolved on one effort more, and, turning to Elizabeth, said, "Miss Eliza Bennet, let me persuade you to follow my example and take a turn about the room. I assure you it is very refreshing after sitting so long in one attitude."

Elizabeth was surprised, but agreed to it immediately and allowed her hostess to take her hand, only to find that Miss Bingley's hand and arm were colder and harder than the marble columns they wound their way past. Miss Bingley was heedless of her surprise, for she had succeeded no less in the real object of her civility; Mr. Darcy looked up. He was as much awake to the novelty of attention in that quarter as Elizabeth herself could be, and unconsciously closed his book. From either the exertion of walking or the warmth of his attention, an answering warmth of life softened Miss Bingley's skin beneath Elizabeth's grip. Regardless, Elizabeth rested her hand upon Miss Bingley's arm only as much as the dictates of politeness required of her.

Mr. Darcy was directly invited to join their party, but he declined it. "I can imagine but two motives for your choosing to walk about the room together; either of which motives my joining you would interfere."

"What can he mean?" Miss Bingley was dying to know what could be his meaning, and asked Elizabeth whether she could at all understand him.

"Not at all," was her answer. "But depend upon it, he means to be severe on us, and our surest way of disappointing him will be to ask nothing about it."

Miss Bingley, however, was incapable of disappointing Mr. Darcy in anything, and persevered therefore in requiring an explanation of his two motives.

"I have not the smallest objection to explaining them," said he as soon as she allowed him to speak. "You either choose this method of passing the evening because you are in each other's confidence and have secret affairs to discuss, or because you are conscious that your figures appear to the greatest advantage in walking. If the first, I would be completely in your way, and if the second, I can admire you much better as I sit by the fire."

"Oh! Shocking!" cried Miss Bingley. "How shall we punish him for such a speech?"

"Tease him—laugh at him," replied Elizabeth. "Intimate as you are, you must know how it is to be done."

"Oh no, we must not laugh at Mr. Darcy."

"Mr. Darcy is not to be laughed at!" cried Elizabeth, coming to a stop before the gentleman in question. "What a shame! I dearly love a laugh. Follies and nonsense, whims and inconsistencies, *do* divert me, I own, and I laugh at them whenever I can. But these, I suppose, are precisely what you are without."

"No," said Mr. Darcy, looking up at her from his seat. "I have made no such pretension. I have faults enough, but they are not, I hope, of understanding. My temper I dare not vouch for. It is, I believe, too little yielding—certainly too little for the convenience of the world. I cannot forget the follies and vices of others so soon as I ought, nor their offenses against myself. My feelings are not puffed about with every attempt to move them. My temper would perhaps be called resentful. My good opinion, once lost, is lost forever."

"*That* is a failing indeed!" teased Elizabeth. "Implacable resentment *is* a shade in a character. But you have chosen your fault well. I really cannot *laugh* at it. You are safe from me."

"There is, I believe, in every disposition a tendency to some particular evil—a natural defect, which not even the best education can overcome." His stare became even more serious, as if begging her to understand some hidden meaning beneath his words. A challenge to her wit, no doubt. She would answer it.

"And *your* defect is to hate everybody."

He smiled. "And yours is willfully to misunderstand them."

He held her stare for some seconds, during which it seemed she was falling into some soft, dark abyss from which she feared she would wish never to be recovered. The gravity of his gaze pulled her toward him; she found herself actually leaning towards him, in danger of falling forward through the two feet separating them and into his arms, and struggling to remember why such an event would be disastrous.

"Do let us have a little music," cried Miss Bingley, tired of a conversation in which she had no share. "Louisa, you will not mind my waking Mr. Hurst?"

* * * * *

Elizabeth drew in a long breath, shook herself and turned away from him. Immediately he felt the sharp loss of the connection their gazes had just shared.

Who had glamoured whom?

Mrs. Hurst had not the smallest objection to her sister's proposal. The pianoforte was opened, and Darcy, after a few moments' recollection, was not sorry for it. He began to feel the danger of paying

Elizabeth too much attention, for it seemed that perhaps she had equal ability to cast an unnatural charm upon others when she so chose.

The sooner she and her sister removed from Netherfield, the better.

* * * * *

In consequence of an agreement between the sisters, Elizabeth wrote the next morning to their mother to beg that the carriage might be sent for them in the course of the day. But Mrs. Bennet, who had calculated on her daughters remaining at Netherfield till the following Tuesday, which would exactly finish Jane's week, could not bring herself to receive them with pleasure before. Her answer, therefore, was not propitious, at least not to Elizabeth's wishes, for she was impatient to get home. Against staying longer, however, Elizabeth was positively resolved—nor did she much expect it would be asked. On the contrary, fearful of being considered as intruding themselves needlessly long, she urged Jane to borrow Mr. Bingley's carriage immediately, and at length it was settled that their original design of leaving Netherfield that morning should be mentioned and the request made.

The communication excited many professions of concern, and enough was said of wishing them to stay at least till the following day to work on Jane; so till the morrow their going was deferred. Miss Bingley was then sorry that she had proposed the delay, for her jealousy and dislike of one sister much exceeded her affection for the other.

The master of the house heard with real sorrow that they were to go so soon, and repeatedly tried to persuade Miss Bennet that it would not be safe for her—that she was not enough recovered. But Jane was firm where she felt herself to be right.

* * * * *

To Mr. Darcy their going was welcome intelligence—Miss Elizabeth had been at Netherfield long enough. It was too difficult to pour the necessary weekly vial of blood into Bingley's wine at dinner with both the servants and her watchful eyes about, and it had been nearly a week since Bingley's last dose. Keeping up a mortal illusion upon their circle for Miss Elizabeth's sake was extremely tiring and grating upon his nerves. Additionally, she attracted him more than he liked—and Miss Bingley was uncivil to her, more teasing than usual to himself, and more than once had silently fought against the precarious illusion he continuously endeavored to hold around them. Miss Elizabeth's presence threatened to press Miss Bingley into unwisely revealing more than she should, and therefore risk all that their circle had collectively worked to build here. Therefore he wisely resolved to be particularly careful that no sign of admiration should *now* escape him, nothing that could elevate Miss Elizabeth with the hope of influencing his felicity to extend her stay; sensible that if such an idea had been suggested, his behavior during the last day must have material weight in confirming or crushing it. Steady to his purpose, he scarcely spoke ten words to her through the whole of Saturday, and though they were at one time left by themselves for half a tortorous hour, he adhered most conscientiously to his book and would not even look at her.

* * * * *

On Sunday after morning service, the separation, so agreeable to almost all, took place. Miss Bingley's civility to Elizabeth increased at last very rapidly, as well as her affection for Jane; and when they parted, after assuring the latter of the pleasure it would always give her to see her either at Longbourn or Netherfield and embracing her most tenderly, she even shook hands with the former. Elizabeth took leave of the whole party in the liveliest of spirits. Her only hesitation came in the moment when she began to climb into the carriage and found her hand assisted by the strength of another's. She looked down at the masculine hand cradling hers, to its owner's wrist and arm, and finally to its owner's face, only to find her gaze captured as well by Mr. Darcy. The expression upon his countenance, one of pained confusion and a question she could not make out, caused an answering pain of confusion within her. She had only long enough to wonder at his assistance, and to wonder equally at her reaction to it, when the moment passed. He released her hand, turned, and strode toward the house, the flexing of his hand the only indication of a reaction at all on his part.

By the time they reached their home, her racing pulse still had not recovered; nor had she managed to make out the meaning behind Mr. Darcy's unaccountable actions. But she was soon forced by needs from such thoughts, for Jane and she were not welcomed home very cordially by their mother. Mrs. Bennet wondered at their coming, and thought them very wrong to give so much trouble, and was sure Jane would have caught cold again. But their father, though very laconic in his expressions of pleasure, was really glad to see them; he had felt their importance in the family circle. The evening conversation, when they were all assembled, had lost much of its animation and almost all its sense by the absence of Jane and Elizabeth.

Chapter Eight

As they were at breakfast the next morning, Mr. Bennet said to his wife, "I hope, my dear, that you have ordered a good dinner today, because I have reason to expect an addition to our family party."

"Who do you mean, my dear? I know of nobody that is coming, I am sure, unless Charlotte Lucas should happen to call in—and I hope *my* dinners are good enough for her. I do not believe she often sees such at home."

"The person of whom I speak is a gentleman and a stranger."

Mrs. Bennet's eyes sparkled. "A gentleman and a stranger! It is Mr. Bingley, I am sure! Well, I am sure I shall be extremely glad to see Mr. Bingley. But—good Lord! How unlucky! There is not a bit of fish to be got today. Lydia, my love, ring the bell—I must speak to Hill this moment."

"It is *not* Mr. Bingley," said her husband. "It is a person whom I never saw in the whole course of my life."

This roused a general astonishment; and he had the pleasure of being eagerly questioned by his wife and his five daughters at once.

After amusing himself some time with their curiosity, he thus explained, "About a month ago I received a letter; and about a fortnight ago I answered it, for I thought it a case of some delicacy and requiring early attention. It is from my cousin, Mr. Collins, who, when I am dead, may turn you all out of this house as soon as he pleases."

"Oh!" cried his wife. "My dear, I cannot bear to hear that mentioned. Pray do not talk of that odious man. I do think it is the hardest thing in the world that your estate should be entailed away from your own children."

"It certainly is a most iniquitous affair," said Mr. Bennet. "And nothing can clear Mr. Collins from the guilt of inheriting Longbourn. But he has recently received ordination and a rectory to serve within, and wishes in some fashion to make amends to our girls for inheriting Longbourn upon his arrival here. At four o'clock, therefore, we may expect this peacemaking gentleman. He seems to be a most conscientious and polite young man, upon my word, and I doubt not will prove a valuable acquaintance, especially if his patroness Lady Catherine de Bourgh should be so indulgent as to let him come to us again."

"If he is disposed to make them any amends, I shall not be the person to discourage him," agreed Mrs. Bennet.

* * * * *

Mr. Collins was punctual to his time and was received with great politeness by the whole family. Mr. Bennet indeed said little. But the ladies were ready enough to talk, and Mr. Collins seemed neither in need of encouragement nor inclined to be silent himself. He was a tall, heavy-looking young man of five-and-twenty. His air was grave and stately, and his manners were very formal. He had not been long seated before he complimented Mrs. Bennet on having so fine a family of daughters; said he had heard much of their beauty, but that in this instance fame had fallen short of the truth; and added that he did not doubt her seeing them all in due time disposed of in marriage. This gallantry was not much to the taste of some of his hearers.

But Mrs. Bennet, who quarreled with no compliments, answered most readily. "You are very kind, I am sure, and I wish with all my heart it may prove so, for else they will be destitute enough. Things are settled so oddly."

"You allude, perhaps, to the entail of this estate."

"Ah! Sir, I do indeed. It is a grievous affair to my poor girls, you must confess. Not that I mean to find fault with *you*, for such things I know are all chance in this world. There is no knowing how estates will go when once they come to be entailed."

"I am very sensible, madam, of the hardship to my fair cousins, and could say much on the subject, but that I am cautious of appearing forward and precipitate. But I can assure the young ladies that I come prepared to admire them. At present I will not say more, but perhaps when we are better acquainted—"

He was interrupted by a summons to dinner, and the girls smiled to each other. They were not the only objects of Mr. Collins's admiration. The hall, the dining room, and all its furniture were examined and praised, and his commendation of everything would have touched Mrs. Bennet's heart but for the mortifying supposition of his viewing it all as his own future property. The dinner too in its turn was highly admired, and he begged to know to which of his fair cousins the excellence of its cooking was owing. But he was set right there by Mrs. Bennet, who assured him with some asperity that they were very well able to keep a good cook, and that her daughters had nothing to do in the kitchen. He begged pardon for having displeased her. In a softened tone she declared herself not at all offended, but he continued to apologize for about a quarter of an hour.

* * * * *

During dinner, Mr. Bennet scarcely spoke at all. But when the servants were withdrawn, he thought it time to have some conversation with his guest and therefore started a subject in which he expected him to shine by observing that he seemed very fortunate in his patroness. Lady Catherine de Bourgh's attention to his wishes and consideration for his comfort appeared very remarkable.

Mr. Bennet could not have chosen better. Mr. Collins was eloquent in her praise. The subject elevated him to more than his usual solemnity of manner, and with a most important aspect he protested that he had never in his life witnessed such behavior in a person of rank, such affability and condescension, as he had himself experienced from Lady Catherine. She had been graciously pleased to approve of both of the discourses which he had already had the honor of preaching before her. She had also asked him twice to dine at Rosings, and had sent for him only the Saturday before to make up her pool of quadrille in the evening. She had even condescended to advise him to marry as soon as he could, provided he chose with discretion, and had once paid him a visit in his humble parsonage, where she had perfectly approved all the alterations he had been making and had even vouchsafed to suggest some herself—some shelves in the closet upstairs.

"That is all very proper and civil, I am sure," said Mrs. Bennet. "And I dare say she is a very agreeable woman. It is a pity that great ladies in general are not more like her. Does she live near you, sir?"

"The garden in which stands my humble abode is separated only by a lane from Rosings Park, her ladyship's residence."

"I think you said she was a widow, sir? Has she any family?"

"She has only one daughter, the heiress of Rosings, and of very extensive property."

"Ah!" said Mrs. Bennet, shaking her head. "Then she is better off than many girls. And what sort of young lady is she? Is she handsome?"

"She is a most charming young lady indeed. She is unfortunately of a sickly constitution, which has prevented her from making that progress in many accomplishments which she could not have otherwise failed of. But she is perfectly amiable and often condescends to drive by my humble abode in her little phaeton and ponies. Her indifferent state of health unhappily prevents her being in town; and by that means, as I told Lady Catherine one day, has deprived the British court of its brightest ornaments. This is one of many of the little delicate compliments I often offer which are always acceptable to ladies. I have more than once observed to Lady Catherine that her charming daughter seemed born to be a duchess, and that the most elevated rank, instead of giving her consequence, would be adorned by her. These are the kind of little things which please her ladyship, and it is a sort of attention which I conceive myself peculiarly bound to pay."

"May I ask whether these pleasing attentions proceed from the impulse of the moment, or are the result of previous study?" asked Mr. Bennet, the hint of a smile at his mouth.

"Though I sometimes amuse myself with suggesting and arranging such little elegant compliments as may be adapted to ordinary occasions, I always wish to give them as unstudied an air as possible."

Mr. Bennet's expectations were fully answered. His cousin was as absurd as he had hoped, and he listened to him with the keenest enjoyment, maintaining at the same time the most resolute composure of countenance, and, except in an occasional glance at Elizabeth, requiring no partner in his pleasure.

By tea time, however, the dose had been enough, and Mr. Bennet was glad to take his guest into the drawing room again, and when tea was over, glad to invite him to read aloud to the ladies. Mr. Collins readily assented, and a book was produced. But on beholding it, for everything announced it to be from a circulating library, he started back, and begging pardon, protested that he never read novels. Kitty stared at him, and Lydia exclaimed. Other books were produced, and after some deliberation he chose Fordyce's Sermons.

Lydia gaped as he opened the volume, and before he had with very monotonous solemnity read three pages, she interrupted him with, "Do you know, Mamma, that my uncle Phillips talks of turning away Richard; and if he does, Colonel Forster will hire him. My aunt told me so herself on Saturday. I shall walk to Meryton tomorrow to hear more about it, and to ask when Mr. Denny comes back from town."

Lydia was bid by her two eldest sisters to hold her tongue.

But Mr. Collins, much offended, laid aside his book, and said, "I have often observed how little young ladies are interested by books of a serious stamp, though written solely for their benefit. It amazes me, I confess, for certainly there can be nothing so advantageous to them as instruction. But I will no longer importune my young cousin."

Then turning to Mr. Bennet, he offered himself as his antagonist at backgammon, and Mr. Bennet accepted the challenge. Mrs. Bennet and her daughters apologized most civilly for Lydia's interruption and promised that it should not occur again if he would resume his book. But Mr. Collins, after assuring them that he bore his young cousin no ill-will and should never resent her behavior as any affront, seated himself at another table with Mr. Bennet and prepared for backgammon.

* * * * *

Mr. Collins was not a sensible man, and the deficiency of nature had been but little assisted by education or society, the greatest part of his life having been spent under the guidance of an illiterate and miserly father. And though he belonged to one of the universities, he had merely kept the necessary terms without forming at it any useful acquaintance. The subjection in which his father had brought him up had given him originally great humility of manner. But it was now a good deal counteracted by the self-conceit of a weak head, living in retirement, and the consequential feelings of early and unexpected prosperity. A fortunate chance had recommended him to Lady Catherine de Bourgh when the living of Hunsford was vacant. And the respect which he felt for her high rank and his veneration for her as his patroness, mingling with a very good opinion of himself, of his authority as a clergyman, and his right as a rector, made him altogether a mixture of pride and obsequiousness, self-importance and humility.

Having now a good house and a very sufficient income, he intended to marry, and in seeking a reconciliation with the Longbourn family, he had a wife in view, as he meant to choose one of the daughters if he found them as handsome and amiable as they were represented by common report. This was his plan of amends, of atonement, for inheriting their father's estate, and he thought it an excellent one, full of eligibility and suitableness, and excessively generous and disinterested on his own part.

His plan did not vary on seeing them. Miss Bennet's lovely face confirmed his views and established all his strictest notions of what was due to seniority, and for the first evening she was his settled choice. The next morning, however, made an alteration, for in a quarter of an hour's tete-a-tete with Mrs. Bennet before breakfast, a conversation beginning with his parsonage house and leading naturally to the avowal of his hopes that a mistress might be found for it at Longbourn, produced from her amid very complaisant smiles and general encouragement a caution against the very Jane he had fixed on, and a recommendation for Elizabeth instead.

Mr. Collins had only to change from Jane to Elizabeth—and it was soon done—done while Mrs. Bennet was stirring the fire. Elizabeth, equally next to Jane in birth and beauty, succeeded her of course. Mrs. Bennet treasured up the hint and trusted that she might soon have two daughters married, and the man whom she could not bear to speak of the day before was now high in her good graces.

Lydia's intention of walking to Meryton was not forgotten; every sister except Mary agreed to go with her. Mr. Collins was to attend them at the request of Mr. Bennet, who was most anxious to get rid of him and have his library to himself; for thither Mr. Collins had followed him after breakfast, and there he would continue, nominally engaged with one of the largest folios in the collection, but really talking to Mr. Bennet with little cessation of his house and garden at Hunsford. Such doings discomposed Mr. Bennet exceedingly. In his library he had been always sure of leisure and tranquility, and though prepared, as he told Elizabeth, to meet with folly and conceit in every other room of the house, he was used to be free from them there. His civility, therefore, was most prompt in inviting Mr. Collins to join his daughters in their walk. And Mr. Collins, being in fact much better fitted for a walker than a reader, was extremely pleased to close his large book and go.

In pompous nothings on his side, and civil assents on that of his cousins, their time passed till they entered Meryton. The attention of the younger ones was then no longer to be gained by him. Their gazes were immediately wandering up the street in quest of the officers, and nothing less than a very smart bonnet indeed, or a really new muslin in a shop window, could recall them.

But the attention of every lady was soon caught by a young man whom they had never seen before, of most gentlemanlike appearance, walking with another officer on the other side of the way. The officer was the very Mr. Denny concerning whose return from London Lydia came to inquire, and he bowed as they passed. All were struck with the stranger's air, all wondered who he could be. Kitty and Lydia, determined if possible to find out, led the way across the street under pretense of wanting something in an opposite shop, and fortunately had just gained the pavement when the two gentlemen, turning back, had reached the same spot. Mr. Denny addressed them directly and entreated permission to introduce his friend, Mr. Wickham, who had returned with him the day before from town, and he was happy to say had accepted a commission in their corps. This was exactly as it should be, for the young man wanted only regimentals to make him completely charming. His appearance was greatly in his favor; he had all the best part of beauty, a fine countenance, a good figure, and very pleasing address, as well as a certain something about himself that naturally drew all to him.

The introduction was followed up on his side by a happy readiness of conversation—a readiness at the same time perfectly correct and unassuming. The whole party were still standing and talking together very agreeably when the sound of horses drew their notice, and Mr. Darcy and Mr. Bingley were seen riding down the street. On distinguishing the ladies of the group, the two gentlemen came directly towards them and began the usual civilities. Mr. Bingley was the principal spokesman, and Miss Bennet the principal object. He was then, he said, on his way to Longbourn on purpose to inquire after her. Mr. Darcy corroborated it with a bow and was beginning to determine not to fix his gaze on Elizabeth, when his eyes were suddenly arrested by the sight of the stranger. Elizabeth, happening to see the countenance of both as they looked at each other, was all astonishment at the effect of the meeting. Both changed color, one looked white, the other red. Mr. Wickham, after a few moments, touched his hat—a salutation which Mr. Darcy just deigned to return. What could be the meaning of it? It was impossible to imagine; it was impossible not to long to know.

In another minute, Mr. Bingley, but without seeming to have noticed what passed, took leave and rode on with his friend.

Mr. Denny and Mr. Wickham walked with the young ladies to the door of Mr. Phillip's house and then made their bows, in spite of Lydia's pressing entreaties that they should come in, and even in spite of Mrs. Phillips's throwing up the parlor window and loudly seconding the invitation.

Mrs. Phillips was always glad to see her nieces, and the two eldest, from their recent absence, were particularly welcome. She could provide no more information regarding Mr. Wickham other than that which Mr. Denny had already given. However, some of the other officers were to dine with the Phillips the next day, and their aunt promised to make her husband call on Mr. Wickham and give him an invitation also, if the family from Longbourn would come in the evening. This was agreed to, and Mrs. Phillips promised that they would have a nice, comfortable, noisy game of lottery tickets and a little bit of hot supper afterwards. The prospect of such delights was very cheering, and they parted in mutual good spirits.

As they walked home, Elizabeth related to Jane what she had seen pass between the two gentlemen. But though Jane would have defended either or both had they appeared to be in the wrong, she could no more explain such behavior than her sister.

Chapter Nine

As no objection was made to the young people's engagement with their aunt, and all Mr. Collins's scruples of leaving Mr. and Mrs. Bennet for a single evening during his visit were most steadily resisted, the coach conveyed him and his five cousins at a suitable hour to Meryton. The girls had the pleasure of hearing, as they entered the drawing room, that Mr. Wickham had accepted their uncle's invitation and was then in the house.

When this information was given and they had all taken their seats, Mr. Collins was at leisure to look around him and admire. He was so much struck with the size and furniture of the apartment that he declared he might almost have supposed himself in the small summer breakfast parlor at Rosings, a comparison that did not at first convey much gratification. In subsequently describing to her all the grandeur of Lady Catherine and her mansion, with occasional digressions in praise of his own humble abode and the improvements it was receiving, he was happily employed until the gentlemen joined them. He found in Mrs. Phillips a very attentive listener, whose opinion of his consequence increased with what she heard, and who was resolving to retail it all among her neighbors as soon as she could. To the girls, who could not listen to their cousin, and who had nothing to do but to wish for an instrument and examine their own indifferent imitations of china on the mantelpiece, the interval of waiting appeared very long. It was over at last, however. The gentlemen did approach, and when Mr. Wickham walked into the room, Elizabeth felt that she had neither been seeing him before, nor thinking of him since, with the smallest degree of unreasonable admiration. The officers of the militia were in general a very creditable, gentlemanlike set, and the best of them were of the present party. But Mr. Wickham was as far beyond them all in person, countenance, air, and walk, as *they* were superior to the broad-faced, stuffy Uncle Phillips, breathing port wine, who followed them into the room.

Mr. Wickham was the happy man towards whom almost every female eye was turned, and Elizabeth was the happy woman by whom he finally seated himself. The agreeable manner in which he immediately fell into conversation, though it was only on its being a wet night, made her feel that the commonest, dullest, most threadbare topic might be rendered interesting by the skill and indefinable charm of the speaker.

The card tables were soon placed. Mr. Wickham did not play at whist, and with ready delight was he received at the other table between Elizabeth and Lydia. At first there seemed danger of Lydia's engrossing him entirely, for she was a most determined talker. But being likewise extremely fond of lottery tickets, she soon grew too much interested in the game, too eager in making bets and exclaiming after prizes to have attention for anyone in particular. Allowing for the common demands of the game, Mr. Wickham was therefore at leisure to talk to Elizabeth, and she was very willing to hear him, though what she chiefly wished to hear she could not hope to be told—the history of his acquaintance with Mr. Darcy. She dared not even mention that gentleman.

Her curiosity, however, was unexpectedly relieved. Mr. Wickham began the subject himself. He inquired how far Netherfield was from Meryton, and after receiving her answer, asked in a hesitating manner how long Mr. Darcy had been staying there.

"About a month," said Elizabeth, and then, unwilling to let the subject drop, added, "He is a man of very large property in Derbyshire, I understand."

"Yes," replied Mr. Wickham. "His estate there is a noble one. A clear ten thousand per annum. You could not have met with a person more capable of giving you certain information on that head than myself, for I have been connected with his family in a particular manner from my infancy."

Elizabeth could not but look surprised.

"You may well be surprised, Miss Bennet, at such an assertion after seeing, as you probably might, the very cold manner of our meeting yesterday. Are you much acquainted with Mr. Darcy?"

"As much as I ever wish to be," cried Elizabeth very warmly. "I have spent four days in the same house with him, and I think him very disagreeable."

"I have no right to give *my* opinion as to his being agreeable or otherwise. I am not qualified to form one. I have known him too long and too well to be a fair judge. It is impossible for *me* to be impartial. But I believe your opinion of him would in general astonish—and perhaps you would not express it quite so strongly anywhere else. Here you are in your own family."

"Upon my word, I say no more *here* than I might say in any house in the neighborhood, except Netherfield. He is not at all liked in Hertfordshire. Everybody is disgusted with his pride. You will not find him more favorably spoken of by anyone."

After a short interruption, he said, "I cannot pretend to be sorry that he or that any man should not be estimated beyond their deserts; but with *him* I believe it does not often happen. The world is blinded by his fortune and consequence, or frightened by his high and imposing manners, and sees him only as he chooses to be seen."

"I should take him, even on *my* slight acquaintance, to be an ill-tempered man."

Mr. Wickham only shook his head.

At the next opportunity of speaking, he said, "I wonder whether he is likely to be in this country much longer."

"I do not at all know; but I heard nothing of his going away when I was at Netherfield. I hope your plans in favor of the militia will not be affected by his being in the neighborhood."

"Oh! No, it is not for *me* to be driven away by Mr. Darcy. If *he* wishes to avoid seeing *me*, he must go. We are not on friendly terms, and it always gives me pain to meet him. But I have no reason for avoiding him but what I might proclaim before all the world...a sense of very great ill-usage, and most painful regrets at his becoming what he has. His father, the late Mr. Darcy, was one of the best men that ever breathed and the truest friend I ever had, and I can never be in company with this Mr. Darcy without being grieved to the soul by a thousand tender recollections. His behavior to myself has been scandalous, but I verily believe I could forgive him anything and everything, rather than his disappointing the hopes and disgracing the memory of his father by what he has since become."

Elizabeth found the interest of the subject increase and listened with all her heart, but the delicacy of it prevented further inquiry.

Mr. Wickham began to speak on more general topics...Meryton, the neighborhood, the society, appearing highly pleased with all that he had yet seen and speaking of the latter with gentle but very intelligible gallantry.

"It was the prospect of constant society, and good society," he added, "which was my chief inducement to enter the shire. I knew it to be a most respectable, agreeable corps, and my friend Denny tempted me further by his account of their present quarters and the very great attentions and excellent acquaintances Meryton had procured them. Society, I own, is necessary to me. My spirits will not bear solitude. I *must* have employment and society. A military life is not what I was intended for, but circumstances have now made it eligible. The church *ought* to have been my profession—I was brought up for the church, and I should at this time have been in possession of a most valuable living, had it pleased the gentleman we were speaking of just now."

"Indeed!"

"Yes—the late Mr. Darcy bequeathed me the next presentation of the best living in his gift. He was my godfather and excessively attached to me. I cannot do justice to his kindness. He meant to provide for me amply, and thought he had done it, but when the living fell, it was given elsewhere."

"Good heavens!" cried Elizabeth. "But how could that be? How could his will be disregarded? Why did you not seek legal redress?"

"There was just such an informality in the terms of the bequest as to give me no hope from law. A man of honor could not have doubted the intention, but Mr. Darcy chose to doubt it—or to treat it as a merely conditional recommendation, and to assert that I had forfeited all claim to it by extravagance, imprudence—in short anything or nothing. Certain it is that the living became vacant two years ago, exactly as I was of an age to hold it, and that it was given to another man. And no less certain is it that I cannot accuse myself of having really done anything to deserve to lose it. I have a warm, unguarded temper, and I may have spoken my opinion *of* him, and *to* him, too freely. I can recall nothing worse. But the fact is that we are very different sort of men, if you may wish to call him that, and he hates me."

"This is quite shocking! He deserves to be publicly disgraced."

"Some time or other he *will* be—but it shall not be by *me*. Till I can forget his father, I can never defy or expose *him*."

Elizabeth honored him for such feelings and thought him handsomer than ever as he expressed them.

"But what," said she after a pause, "can have been his motive? What can have induced him to behave so cruelly?"

"A thorough, determined dislike of me—a dislike which I cannot but attribute in some measure to jealousy because his father loved me more than him. And yet still he might not have acted upon such an emotion had he better self-discipline, had he, in short, not become what he has…a monster of the most literal sort."

"A monster! Pray, do explain."

"Have you heard of the mythical vampire, an immortal creature that exists on the very life force, the blood, of others?"

She nodded. She had read a wonderfully dark gothic tale as a child about just such creatures of the night.

"This is what Mr. Darcy has become. He is nothing other than a vampire."

Elizabeth stared at him in shock. He must be jesting with her. Such creatures were mere myth, nothing more.

Mr. Wickham smiled. "You look amazed, which is understandable to be sure. Such creatures were only rumored to exist. Yet it is true. I have seen many of these monsters with my own eyes over the years, including the gentleman under discussion."

"But surely you jest," said Elizabeth. "While I have read of vampires, they were merely fictional stories meant to entertain. What I remember of them from the story, though, is that they are unable to walk about in daylight or enter sacred grounds."

"Ah, so I too once believed. Yet I have seen Mr. Darcy, and even others within the corps, drink human blood and perform physical feats I could never have believed had I not witnessed them myself. The only explanation may be that they, like many animal species in nature, have evolved over the years, adapting themselves to better seek their prey."

Elizabeth shuddered. "And there are vampires in the corps too!"

Mr. Wickham nodded. "Indeed. Though perhaps it should not be such a surprise, for where else would their blood thirst be quenched so easily as on a battlefield?"

Elizabeth did not know how to think upon such a story—whether Mr. Wickham were simply teasing her, or if any of what he claimed could be true. It seemed incredible. And yet her mind was filled with remembrances of past words and actions of Mr. Darcy, so many of which pointed to the veracity of Mr. Wickham's claims. Being a

61

vampire would certainly explain Mr. Darcy's general ill will towards assemblies and being forced to touch humans during the act of dancing.

Then other, stranger recollections reoccurred to her, though not of Mr. Darcy. She remembered her stay at Netherfield, walking with Miss Bingley, how hard and cold her hand and arm had been, the way her eyes had seemed to shine so unnaturally when the firelight reflected upon them just so. "Could Miss Bingley also be a vampire, by any chance?"

Mr. Wickham looked thoughtful. "I am not acquainted with her, so I could not say for sure. But it is entirely possible, especially if she was ever alone in Mr. Darcy's presence for long. A vampire need only drain a human dry, then give of their own blood to their victim in order to pass on their abominable condition."

Elizabeth remembered how often she and Jane had been alone with Miss Bingley and shuddered. "I had not thought Mr. Darcy so bad as this—though I have never liked him, I had not thought so very ill of him. I had supposed him to be despising his fellow man in general, but did not suspect him of such inhumanity as *this*." Could this be why she and so many others did not like him? Could they all have sensed, on some baser level of instinct, that the presence of Mr. Darcy represented real danger to themselves?

After a few minutes' reflection, she continued, "I *do* remember his boasting one day at Netherfield of the implacability of his resentments, of his having an unforgiving temper. Perhaps this is all due to the monster that now resides within him? His disposition as such must be dreadful."

"I will not trust myself on the subject," replied Wickham. "I can hardly be just to him."

Elizabeth was again deep in thought. Even if the bit about Mr. Darcy's being a vampire were only a jest, there was still the matter of his other actions against Mr. Wickham to contend with. After a time, she exclaimed, "To treat in such a manner the godson, the friend, the favorite of his father!" She could have added, "A young man, too, like *you*, whose very countenance may vouch for your being amiable"—but she contented herself with, "and one, too, who had probably been his companion from childhood, connected together, as I think you said, in the closest manner!"

"Indeed, which makes witnessing the recent changes in him all the more distressing. We were born in the same parish, within the same park; the greatest part of our youth was passed together as inmates of the same house, sharing the same amusements, objects of the same parental care. My father began life in the profession which your uncle, Mr. Phillips, appears to do so much credit to—but he gave up everything to be of use to the late Mr. Darcy and devoted all his time to the care of the Pemberley property. He was most highly esteemed by Mr. Darcy, a most intimate, confidential friend. Mr. Darcy often acknowledged himself to be under the greatest obligations to my father's active superintendence, and when, immediately before my father's death, Mr. Darcy gave him a voluntary promise of providing for me, I am convinced that he felt it to be as much a debt of gratitude to *him*, as of his affection to myself."

"How strange!" cried Elizabeth. "How abominable! I wonder that the very pride of this Mr. Darcy has not made him just to you! If from no better motive than that he should have been too proud to be dishonest—for dishonesty I must call it."

"It *is* wonderful," replied Wickham, "for almost all his actions may be traced to pride, and pride had often been his best friend even before his dark change. It has connected him nearer with virtue than with any other feeling. But we are none of us consistent, vampires or humans, and in his behavior to me there were stronger impulses even than pride."

"Can such abominable pride as his have ever done him good?"

"Yes. It has often led him to be liberal and generous, to give his money freely, to display hospitality, to assist his tenants, and relieve the poor. Family pride, and *filial* pride—for he is very proud of what his father was—have done this. Not to appear to disgrace his family, to degenerate from the popular qualities, or lose the influence of the Pemberley House by revealing his monstrous nature, is a powerful motive. He has also *brotherly* pride, which, with *some* brotherly affection, makes him a very kind and careful guardian of his sister, and you will hear him generally cried up as the most attentive and best of brothers."

"What sort of girl is Miss Darcy?"

He shook his head. "I wish I could call her amiable. It gives me pain to speak ill of a Darcy. But she is too much like her brother—very, very proud. And rumored to have experienced the dark change as well, though this is not known for sure of course. As a child, she was affectionate and pleasing, and extremely fond of me; and I have devoted hours and hours to her amusement. But she is nothing to me now. She is a handsome girl, about fifteen or sixteen, and, I understand, highly accomplished. Since her father's death, her home has been London, where a lady lives with her and superintends her education."

After many pauses and many trials of other subjects, Elizabeth could not help reverting once more to the first, and saying:

"I am astonished at his intimacy with Mr. Bingley! How can Mr. Bingley, who seems good humor itself, and is, I really believe, truly amiable, be in friendship with such a monster? Do you know Mr. Bingley?"

"Not at all."

"He is a sweet-tempered, amiable, charming man. He cannot know what Mr. Darcy is."

"Probably not; but Mr. Darcy can please where he chooses. Being a vampire ensures that he does not want for abilities. He can employ his dark arts of illusion to charm others and help him be a conversible companion if he thinks it worth his while. Among those who are his equals in human consequence, he is very different from what he is to the less prosperous. His pride never deserts him; but with the rich he is liberal minded, just, sincere, rational, honorable, and perhaps agreeable —allowing something for fortune and unnaturally enhanced figure."

The whist party soon afterwards breaking up, the players gathered round the other table, and Mr. Collins took his station between his cousin Elizabeth and Mrs. Phillips. The usual inquiries as to his success was made by the latter. It had not been very great; he had lost every point. But when Mrs. Phillips began to express her concern thereupon, he assured her with much earnest gravity that it was not of the least importance, that he considered the money as a mere trifle, and begged that she would not make herself uneasy.

"I know very well, madam," said he, "that when persons sit down to a card table, they must take their chances of these things, and happily I am not in such circumstances as to make five shillings any object. There are undoubtedly many who could not say the same, but thanks to Lady Catherine de Bourgh, I am removed far beyond the necessity of regarding little matters."

Mr. Wickham's attention was caught, and after observing Mr. Collins for a few moments, he asked Elizabeth in a low voice whether her relation was very intimately acquainted with the family of de Bourgh.

"Lady Catherine de Bourgh," she replied, "has very lately given him a living. I hardly know how Mr. Collins was first introduced to her notice, but he certainly has not known her long."

"You know of course that Lady Catherine de Bourgh and Lady Anne Darcy were sisters; consequently that she is aunt to the present Mr. Darcy."

"No, indeed, I did not. I knew nothing at all of Lady Catherine's connections. I never heard of her existence till the day before yesterday."

"Lady Catherine is aware of her nephew's monstrous nature. Yet her daughter, Miss de Bourgh, will have a very large fortune, and it is believed that she and her cousin will still unite the two estates. Should he change Miss de Bourgh into what he now is, this will also do what doctors have been unable to regarding her health, and make her finally well."

This information made Elizabeth almost smile as she thought of poor Miss Bingley. Vain indeed must be all her attentions, vain and useless her affection for his sister and her praise of himself, if he were already self-destined for another.

"Mr. Collins," said she, "speaks highly both of Lady Catherine and her daughter. But from some particulars that he has related of her ladyship, I suspect his gratitude misleads him, and that in spite of her being his patroness, she is an arrogant, conceited woman."

"I believe her to be both in a great degree," replied Mr. Wickham. "I have not seen her for many years, but I very well remember that I never liked her, and that her manners were dictatorial and insolent. She has the reputation of being remarkably sensible and clever. But I rather believe she derives part of her abilities from her rank and fortune, part from her authoritative manner, and the rest from the pride for her nephew, who chooses that everyone connected with him should have an understanding of the first class."

Elizabeth allowed that he had given a very rational account of it, and they continued talking together with mutual satisfaction till supper put an end to cards and gave the rest of the ladies their share of Mr. Wickham's attentions. There could be no conversation in the noise of Mrs. Phillips's supper party, but his manners recommended him to everybody. Whatever he said was said well, and whatever he did, done gracefully. Elizabeth went away with her head full of him. All the way home, she could think of nothing but of Mr. Wickham and of what he had told her. But there was not time for her even to mention his name as they went, for neither Lydia nor Mr. Collins were once silent. Lydia talked incessantly of lottery tickets, of the fish she had lost and the fish she had won. And Mr. Collins in describing the civility of Mr. and Mrs.

Phillips, protesting that he did not in the least regard his losses at whist, enumerating all the dishes at supper, and repeatedly fearing that he crowded his cousins, had more to say than he could well manage before the carriage stopped at Longbourn House.

Chapter Ten

The next day, Elizabeth related to Jane what had passed between Mr. Wickham and herself, not excluding Mr. Darcy's existence as a vampire. Jane listened with astonishment and concern. She knew not how to believe that Mr. Darcy could be so unnatural to humanity nor so unworthy of Mr. Bingley's regard, and yet it was not in her nature to question the veracity of a young man of such amiable appearance as Mr. Wickham. The possibility of his having endured such unkindness was enough to interest all her tender feelings, and nothing remained therefore to be done but to think well of them both, to defend the conduct of each, and throw into the account of accident or mistake whatever could not be otherwise explained.

"They have both," said she, "been deceived, I dare say, in some way or other, of which we can form no idea. Interested people have perhaps misrepresented each to the other. It is, in short, impossible for us to conjecture the causes or circumstances which may have alienated them, without actual blame on either side."

"Very true, indeed. And now, my dear Jane, what have you got to say on behalf of the interested people who have probably been concerned in the business? Do clear *them* too, or we shall be obliged to think ill of somebody."

"Laugh as much as you choose, but you will not laugh me out of my opinion. My dearest Lizzy, do but consider in what a disgraceful light it places Mr. Darcy, to be treating his father's favorite in such a manner, one whom his father had promised to provide for. And to be a vampire too! It is impossible. No man who had any value for his character could be capable of such actions. Can his most intimate friends be so excessively deceived in him? Oh! No."

"I can much more easily believe Mr. Bingley's being imposed on, than that Mr. Wickham should invent such a history as he gave me last night; names, facts, everything mentioned without ceremony. If it be not so, let Mr. Darcy contradict it. Besides, there was truth in his looks."

"It is difficult indeed—it is distressing. One does not know what to think."

"I beg your pardon; one knows exactly what to think. Mr. Darcy is quite obviously a monster. The only question remains as to whether he is a human monster, or one of the vampire variety."

But Jane could think with certainty on only one point—that Mr. Bingley, if he *had* been imposed on, would have much to suffer when the affair became public.

The two young ladies were summoned from the shrubbery, where this conversation passed, by the arrival of the very persons of whom they had been speaking. Mr. Darcy, Mr. Bingley and his sisters came to give their personal invitation for the long-expected ball at Netherfield, which was fixed for the following Tuesday. Elizabeth knew not how to act in the presence of a supposed vampire, though he appeared to be perfectly human even in the bright light of day.

The two ladies were delighted to see their dear friend again, called it an age since they had met, and repeatedly asked what she had been doing with herself since their separation. To the rest of the family they paid little attention, avoiding Mrs. Bennet as much as possible, saying not much to Elizabeth, and nothing at all to the others. Elizabeth watched Miss Bingley most carefully, searching for some repeat of the signs she had seen at Netherfield of abnormality…the skin like marble, the strange shine in her eyes, but saw only a too self-important girl eager to regain Jane's approbation. They were soon gone again, rising from their seats with an activity which took their brother and Mr. Darcy by surprise, and hurrying off as if eager to escape from Mrs. Bennet's civilities. Elizabeth was left quite confused as to whether Mr. Darcy and Miss Bingley were vampires or not, and vowed to study them both again for further proof at the ball.

The prospect of the Netherfield ball was extremely agreeable to every female of the family save Elizabeth, who was torn between anticipating further opportunity to converse with Mr. Wickham, and being in the close presence of two possible vampires again. Mrs. Bennet chose to consider it as given in compliment to her eldest daughter, and was particularly flattered by receiving the invitation from Mr. Bingley himself instead of a ceremonious card. Jane pictured to herself a happy evening in the society of her two friends and the attentions of their brother. And Elizabeth, upon reassuring herself that no vampire could cause anyone harm in such a public place, thought at last with pleasure of dancing a great deal with Mr. Wickham and of seeing a confirmation of everything in Mr. Darcy's look and behavior. The happiness anticipated by Catherine and Lydia depended less on any single event or any particular person, for though they each, like Elizabeth, meant to dance half the evening with Mr. Wickham, he was by no means the only partner who could satisfy them, and a ball was, at any rate, a ball. And even Mary could assure her family that she had no disinclination for it.

Elizabeth's spirits were so high on this occasion that, though she did not often speak unnecessarily to Mr. Collins, she could not help asking him whether he intended to accept Mr. Bingley's invitation, and if he did, whether he would think it proper to join in the evening's amusement. She was rather surprised to find that he entertained no scruple whatever on that head and was very far from dreading a rebuke either from the Archbishop or Lady Catherine de Bourgh by venturing to dance.

"I am by no means of the opinion, I assure you," said he, "that a ball of this kind, given by a young man of character, to respectable people, can have any evil tendency; and I am so far from objecting to dancing myself, that I shall hope to be honored with the hands of all my fair cousins in the course of the evening. I take this opportunity of soliciting yours, Miss Elizabeth, for the two first dances especially, a preference which I trust my cousin Jane will attribute to the right cause, and not to any disrespect for her."

Elizabeth felt herself completely taken in. She had fully proposed being engaged by Mr. Wickham for those very dances, and to have Mr. Collins instead! Her liveliness had never been worse timed. There was no help for it, however. Mr. Wickham's happiness and her own were perforce delayed a little longer, and Mr. Collins's proposal accepted with as good a grace as she could. She was not the better pleased with his gallantry from the idea it suggested of something more. It now first struck her that *she* was selected from among her sisters as worthy of being mistress of Hunsford Parsonage. The idea soon reached to conviction as she observed his increasing civilities toward herself and heard his frequent attempt at a compliment on her wit and vivacity.

And though more astonished than gratified herself by this effect of her charms, it was not long before her mother gave her to understand that the probability of their marriage was extremely agreeable to *her*. Elizabeth, however, did not choose to take the hint, being well aware that a serious dispute must be the consequence of any reply. Mr. Collins might never make the offer, and till he did, it was useless to quarrel about him.

If there had not been a Netherfield ball to prepare for and talk of, the younger Miss Bennets would have been in a very pitiable state at this time, for from the day of the invitation to the day of the ball, there was such a succession of rain as prevented their walking to Meryton once. No aunt, no officers, no news could be sought after—the very shoe-roses for Netherfield were got by proxy. Even Elizabeth might have found some trial of her patience in weather which totally suspended the improvement of her acquaintance with Mr. Wickham. And nothing less than a dance on Tuesday could have made such a gloomy Friday, Saturday, Sunday, and Monday endurable to Kitty and Lydia.

* * * * *

Till Elizabeth entered the drawing room at Netherfield and looked in vain for Mr. Wickham among the cluster of red coats there assembled, a doubt of his being present had never occurred to her. The certainty of meeting him had not been checked by any of those recollections that might not unreasonably have alarmed her. She had dressed with more than usual care and prepared in the highest spirits for the conquest of all that remained unsubdued of his heart, trusting that it was not more than might be won in the course of the evening. But in an instant arose the dreadful suspicion of his being purposely omitted for Mr. Darcy's pleasure in the Bingleys' invitation to the officers. Though this was not exactly the case, the absolute fact of his absence was pronounced by his friend Denny, to whom Lydia eagerly applied, and who told them that Wickham had been obliged to go to town on business the day before and was not yet returned, adding, with a significant smile, "I do not imagine his business would have called him away just now if he had not wanted to avoid a certain gentleman here."

This part of his intelligence, though unheard by Lydia, was caught by Elizabeth, and as it assured her that Mr. Darcy was not less answerable for Mr. Wickham's absence than if her first surmise had been just, every feeling of displeasure against the former was so sharpened by immediate disappointment that she could hardly reply with tolerable civility to the polite inquiries which he directly afterwards approached to make. Attendance, forbearance, patience with Mr. Darcy, was injury to Mr. Wickham. She was resolved against any sort of conversation with him, and turned away with a degree of ill-humor which she could not wholly surmount even in speaking to Mr. Bingley, whose blind partiality to such a being provoked her.

But Elizabeth was not formed for ill-humor; and though every prospect of her own was destroyed for the evening, it could not dwell long on her spirits. Having told all her griefs to Charlotte Lucas, whom she had not seen for a week, she was soon able to make a voluntary transition to the oddities of her cousin and to point him out to her particular notice. The first two dances, however, brought a return of distress; they were dances of mortification. Mr. Collins, awkward and solemn, apologizing instead of attending, and often moving wrong without being aware of it, gave her all the shame and misery which a disagreeable partner for a couple of dances can give. The moment of her release from him was ecstasy.

She danced next with an officer and had the refreshment of talking of Mr. Wickham and of hearing that he was universally liked. When those dances were over, she returned to Charlotte Lucas and was in conversation with her, when she found herself suddenly addressed by Mr. Darcy. He took her so much by surprise in his application for her hand that, without knowing what she did, she accepted him. He walked away again immediately, and she was left to fret over her own want of presence of mind.

Charlotte tried to console her. "I dare say you will find him very agreeable."

"Heaven forbid! *That* would be the greatest misfortune of all! To find agreeable one whom I am determined to hate! Do not wish me such an evil." She considered relating to Charlotte all that Mr. Wickham had told her, but the smallest lingering doubt of whether Mr. Darcy's immortal existence were only a jest held her back. There was the additional doubt as to whether Charlotte would believe her as well.

When the dancing recommenced, Mr. Darcy approached to claim her hand. Charlotte could not help cautioning her in a whisper not to be a simpleton and allow her fancy for Mr. Wickham to make her appear unpleasant in the eyes of a man ten times his consequence. If

71

only Charlotte could be trusted with the truth regarding such a creature! Yet she could not, so Elizabeth made no answer and took her place in the set, reading in her neighbors' looks their amazement in beholding her position across from Mr. Darcy. Her heart beat faster each time his cool hand touched hers as was required by the dance, for surely here was some proof of Mr. Wickham's claims against Mr. Darcy's unnatural state of being. Mere mortal men did not have hands so dry, cold and hard as marble as his were, especially during the physical exertion of a dance! The way his nearness made her heart hammer must be still more proof that her every instinct recognized in him the predator of humans.

They stood for some time without speaking a word, and she began to imagine that their silence was to last through the two dances. At first she was resolved not to break the silence, till suddenly fancying that obliging her partner to talk might eventually force him to reveal further hints of his true nature, she made some slight observation on the dance. He replied and was again silent. After a pause of some minutes, she addressed him a second time with, "It is *your* turn to say something now, Mr. Darcy. I talked about the dance, and *you* ought to make some sort of remark on the size of the room or the number of couples."

He smiled, his eyes uncommonly still as he stared down at her. "I assure you whatever you wish me to say will be said."

When she met his gaze for too long a moment, it seemed as if she were falling into some vast abyss from which she would never be recovered. Mr. Wickham described vampires has having special abilities over their human prey; could this be one of them? She averted her gaze. "Very well. That reply will do for the present. Perhaps by and by I may observe that private balls are much pleasanter than public ones. But *now* we may be silent."

"Do you talk by rule, then, while you are dancing?"

"Sometimes. One must speak a little, you know. It would look odd to be entirely silent for half an hour together; and yet for the advantage of *some*, conversation ought to be so arranged as that they may have the trouble of saying as little as possible."

"Are you consulting your own feelings in the present case, or do you imagine that you are gratifying mine?"

"Both," replied Elizabeth archly. "For I have always seen a great similarity in the turn of our minds. We are each of an unsocial, taciturn disposition, unwilling to speak unless we expect to say something that will amaze the whole room and be handed down to posterity with all the eclat of a proverb."

"This is no very striking resemblance of your own character, I am sure," said he. "How near it may be to *mine*, I cannot pretend to say. *You*think it a faithful portrait undoubtedly."

"I must not decide on my own performance."

He made no answer, and they were again silent till they had gone down the dance, when he asked her if she and her sisters did not very often walk to Meryton. She answered in the affirmative and, unable to resist the temptation, added, "When you met us there the other day, we had just been forming a new acquaintance."

The effect was immediate and exactly what she had wished for— what seemed to be possible confirmation of Mr. Wickham's claims. A deeper shade of cold hauteur overspread his features, but he said not a word, and in that forbidding silence, Elizabeth, though blaming herself for her own weakness, could not go on.

At length Mr. Darcy spoke, and in a constrained manner said, "Mr. Wickham is blessed with such happy manners as may ensure his *making* friends—whether he may be equally capable of *retaining* them is less certain."

"He has been so unlucky as to lose *your* friendship," replied Elizabeth with emphasis, "and in a manner which he is likely to suffer from all his life."

Mr. Darcy made no answer and seemed desirous of changing the subject. At that moment, Sir William Lucas appeared close to them, meaning to pass through the set to the other side of the room. But on perceiving Mr. Darcy, he stopped with a bow of superior courtesy to compliment him on his dancing and his partner.

"I have been most highly gratified indeed, my dear sir. Such very superior dancing is not often seen. It is evident that you belong to the first circles. Allow me to say, however, that your fair partner does not disgrace you, and that I must hope to have this pleasure often repeated, especially when a certain desirable event, my dear Eliza," glancing at her sister and Mr. Bingley, "shall take place. What congratulations will then flow in! I appeal to Mr. Darcy—but let me not interrupt you, sir. You will not thank me for detaining you from the bewitching converse of that young lady whose bright eyes are also upbraiding me."

The latter part of this address was scarcely heard by Mr. Darcy. But Sir William's allusion to his friend seemed to strike him forcibly, and his eyes were directed with a very serious expression towards Mr. Bingley and Jane, who were dancing together. Recovering himself shortly, however, he turned to his partner, his gaze once more capturing hers, and said, "Sir William's interruption has made me forget what we were talking of."

She could no longer think with any clarity, so lost was she within his strangely mesmorizing eyes. "I-I do not think we were speaking at all." One of his eyebrows arched, and the corners of his lips twitched. Mortification brought recollection to herself, and she was freed from his spell again. "What I mean to say is that Sir William could not have interrupted two people in the room who had less to say for themselves. We have tried two or three subjects already without success, and what we are to talk of next I cannot imagine."

"What think you of books?" said he, smiling.

"Books—oh! No. I am sure we never read the same, or not with the same feelings." For how could an immortal vampire such as he read with the same human thoughts, reactions, and emotions?

"I am sorry you think so; but if that be the case, there can at least be no want of subject. We may compare our different opinions."

"No—I cannot talk of books in a ballroom; my head is always full of something else." Especially while in the presence of a possible vampire.

"The present always occupies you in such scenes, does it?" said he with a look of doubt.

"Yes, always," she replied without knowing what she said, for her thoughts had wandered far from the subject, as soon afterwards appeared by her suddenly exclaiming, "I remember hearing you once say, Mr. Darcy, that you hardly ever forgave, that your resentment once created was unappeasable. You are very cautious, I suppose, as to its being created?"

"I am," said he with a firm voice.

"And never allow yourself to be blinded by prejudice or darker emotions?"

"I hope not."

"It is particularly incumbent on those who never change their opinion to be secure of judging properly at first."

"May I ask to what these questions tend?"

"Merely to the illustration of your character," said she, endeavoring to shake off her gravity. "I am trying to make it out."

"And what is your success?"

She shook her head. "I do not get on at all. I hear such different accounts of you as puzzle me exceedingly."

At that moment, the dance's steps brought them to within inches of each other. They were to part again, yet he stopped and held her there as well with the combined force of his gaze and her wish to hear his low reply of, "I can readily believe that reports may vary greatly with respect to me. However, I wish that you would not sketch my character at the present moment, as there is reason to fear that the performance would reflect no credit on either of us."

Her heart seemed to hammer at the base of her throat, making it difficult to reply. "But if I do not take your likeness now, I may never have another opportunity."

His gaze dropped to her throat for several long seconds, and her heart raced still faster. At last, he met her gaze again and coldly said, "I would by no means suspend any pleasure of yours."

He resumed the dance's steps, releasing her from his hold, and they went down the dance and parted in silence, on each side dissatisfied, though not to an equal degree, for in Mr. Darcy's breast there was a tolerable powerful feeling towards her which soon procured her pardon and directed all his anger against another.

Chapter Eleven

They had not long separated when Miss Bingley came towards her, and with an expression of civil disdain, accosted her with, "So, Miss Eliza, I hear you are quite delighted with George Wickham! Your sister has been talking to me about him and asking me a thousand questions; and I find that the young man quite forgot to tell you, among his other communication, that he was the son of old Wickham, the late Mr. Darcy's steward. However, let me recommend to you as a friend not to give implicit confidence to all his assertions, for as to Mr. Darcy's using him ill, it is perfectly false. On the contrary, he has always been remarkably kind to him, though George Wickham has treated Mr. Darcy in a most infamous manner. I do not know the particulars, but I know very well that Mr. Darcy is not in the least to blame, that he cannot bear to hear George Wickham mentioned, and that though my brother thought that he could not well avoid including him in his invitation to the officers, he was excessively glad to find that he had taken himself out of the way. His coming into the country at all is a most insolent thing, indeed, and I wonder how he could presume to do it. I pity you, Miss Eliza, for this discovery of your favorite's guilt, but really, considering his descent, one could not expect much better."

"His guilt and his descent appear by your account to be the same," said Elizabeth. "For I have heard you accuse him of nothing worse than of being the son of Mr. Darcy's steward, and of *that*, I can assure you, he informed me himself."

"I beg your pardon," replied Miss Bingley, turning away with a sneer. "Excuse my interference—it was kindly meant."

"Insolent girl!" said Elizabeth to herself. "You are much mistaken if you expect to influence me by such a paltry attack as this. I see nothing in it but your own willful ignorance and the malice of Mr. Darcy." She then sought her eldest sister, who had undertaken to make inquiries on the same subject of Mr. Bingley. Jane met her with a smile of such sweet complacency, a glow of such happy expression, as sufficiently marked how well she was satisfied with the occurrences of the evening. Elizabeth instantly read her feelings, and at that moment solicitude for Mr. Wickham, resentment against his enemies, and everything else gave way before the hope of Jane's being in the fairest way for happiness.

"I want to know," said she with a countenance no less smiling than her sister's, "what you have learnt about Mr. Wickham. But perhaps you have been too pleasantly engaged to think of any third person; in which case you may be sure of my pardon."

"No," replied Jane, "I have not forgotten him; but I have nothing satisfactory to tell you. Mr. Bingley does not know the whole of his history and is quite ignorant of the circumstances which have principally offended Mr. Darcy. But he will vouch for the good conduct, the probity, and honor of his friend, and is perfectly convinced that Mr. Wickham has deserved much less attention from Mr. Darcy than he has received. And I am sorry to say by his account as well as his sister's, Mr. Wickham is by no means a respectable young man. I am afraid he has been very imprudent and has deserved to lose Mr. Darcy's regard."

"Mr. Bingley does not know Mr. Wickham himself?"

"No; he never saw him till the other morning at Meryton."

"This account then is what he has received from Mr. Darcy. I am satisfied. But what does he say of the living?"

"He does not exactly recollect the circumstances, though he has heard them from Mr. Darcy more than once, but he believes that it was left to him *conditionally* only."

"I have not a doubt of Mr. Bingley's sincerity," said Elizabeth warmly. "But you must excuse my not being convinced by assurances only. Mr. Bingley's defense of his friend was a very able one, I dare say. But since he is unacquainted with several parts of the story and has learned the rest from that friend himself, I shall venture to still think of both gentlemen as I did before."

She then changed the discourse to one more gratifying to each, and on which there could be no difference of sentiment. Elizabeth listened with delight to the happy though modest hopes which Jane entertained of Mr. Bingley's regard, and said all in her power to heighten her confidence in it. On their being joined by Mr. Bingley himself, Elizabeth withdrew to Miss Lucas, to whose inquiry after the pleasantness of her last partner she had scarcely replied, before Mr. Collins came up to them and told her with great exultation that he had just been so fortunate as to make a most important discovery.

"I have found out," said he, "by a singular accident, that there is now in the room a near relation of my patroness. I happened to overhear the gentleman himself mentioning to the young lady who does the honors of the house the names of his cousin Miss de Bourgh, and of her mother Lady Catherine. How wonderfully these sort of things occur! Who would have thought of my meeting with a nephew of Lady Catherine de Bourgh in this assembly! I am most thankful that the discovery is made in time for me to pay my respects to him, which I am now going to do, and trust he will excuse my not having done it before. My total ignorance of the connection must plead my apology."

"You are not going to introduce yourself to Mr. Darcy!" cried Elizabeth in horror.

"Indeed I am. I shall entreat his pardon for not having done it earlier. I believe him to be Lady Catherine's nephew. It will be in my power to assure him that her ladyship was quite well yesterday se'nnight."

Elizabeth tried hard to dissuade him from such a scheme, assuring him that Mr. Darcy would consider his addressing him without introduction as an impertinent freedom rather than a compliment to his aunt; that it was not in the least necessary there should be any notice on either side; and that if it were, it must belong to Mr. Darcy, the superior in consequence, to begin the acquaintance. Mr. Collins listened to her with the determined air of following his own inclination, and when she ceased speaking, replied thus:

"My dear Miss Elizabeth, I have the highest opinion in the world of your excellent judgement in all matters within the scope of your understanding, but permit me to say that there must be a wide difference between the established forms of ceremony amongst the laity and those which regulate the clergy. For give me leave to observe that I consider the clerical office as equal in point of dignity with the highest rank in the kingdom—provided that a proper humility of behavior is at the same time maintained. You must therefore allow me to follow the dictates of my conscience on this occasion, which leads me to perform what I look on as a point of duty. Pardon me for neglecting to profit by your advice, which on every other subject shall be my constant guide, though in the case before us I consider myself more fitted by education and habitual study to decide on what is right than a young lady like yourself."

And with a low bow he left her to attack Mr. Darcy, whose reception of his advances she eagerly watched, and whose astonishment at being so addressed was very evident. Her cousin prefaced his speech with a solemn bow and, though she could not hear a word of it, she felt as if hearing it all, and saw in the motion of his lips the words "apology", "Hunsford", and "Lady Catherine de Bourgh". It vexed her to see him expose himself to such a being. Mr. Darcy was eyeing him with unrestrained wonder, yet when at last Mr. Collins allowed him time to speak, replied only with an air of distant civility. If only Mr. Collins could be so restrained! Mr. Collins, however, was not discouraged from speaking again, and Mr. Darcy's contempt seemed abundantly increasing with the length of his second speech, and at the end of it he only made him a slight bow and moved another way. Mr. Collins then returned to Elizabeth.

"I have no reason, I assure you," said he, "to be dissatisfied with my reception. Mr. Darcy seemed much pleased with the attention. He answered me with the utmost civility, and even paid me the compliment of saying that he was so well convinced of Lady Catherine's discernment as to be certain she could never bestow a favor unworthily. It was really a very handsome thought. Upon the whole, I am much pleased with him."

As Elizabeth had no longer any interest of her own to pursue, she turned her attention almost entirely on her sister and Mr. Bingley, and the train of agreeable reflections which her observations gave birth to made her perhaps almost as happy as Jane. She saw her in idea settled in that very house, in all the felicity which a marriage of true affection could bestow; and she felt capable, under such circumstances, of endeavoring even to like Mr. Bingley's two sisters. Her mother's thoughts she plainly saw were bent the same way, and she determined not to venture near her, lest she might hear too much. When they sat down to supper, therefore, she considered it a most unlucky perverseness which placed them within one of each other; and deeply was she vexed to find that her mother was talking to Lady Lucas freely, openly, and of nothing else but her expectation that Jane would soon be married to Mr. Bingley. It was an animating subject, and Mrs. Bennet seemed incapable of fatigue while enumerating the advantages of the match.

In vain did Elizabeth endeavor to check the rapidity of her mother's words or persuade her to describe her felicity in a less audible whisper. For, to her inexpressible vexation, she could perceive that the chief of it was overheard by Mr. Darcy, who sat opposite to them. Her mother only scolded her for being nonsensical.

"What is Mr. Darcy to me, pray, that I should be afraid of him? I am sure we owe him no such particular civility as to be obliged to say nothing *he* may not like to hear."

"For heaven's sake, madam, speak lower. What advantage can it be for you to offend Mr. Darcy? You will never recommend yourself to his friend by so doing!"

Nothing that she could say, however, had any influence. Her mother would talk of her views in the same intelligible tone. Elizabeth blushed and blushed again with shame and vexation. She could not help frequently glancing at Mr. Darcy, though every glance convinced her of what she dreaded; for though he was not always looking at her mother, she was convinced that his attention was invariably fixed by her. The expression of his face changed gradually from indignant contempt to a composed and steady gravity.

At length, however, Mrs. Bennet had no more to say, and Lady Lucas, who had been long yawning at the repetition of delights which she saw no likelihood of sharing, was left to the comforts of cold ham and chicken. Elizabeth now began to revive. But not long was the interval of tranquility; for when supper was over, singing was talked of, and she had the mortification of seeing Mary, after very little entreaty, preparing to oblige the company. By many significant looks and silent entreaties did she endeavor to prevent such a proof of complaisance, but in vain. Mary would not understand them; such an opportunity of exhibiting was delightful to her, and she began her song. Elizabeth's eyes were fixed on her with most painful sensations, and she watched her progress through the several stanzas with an impatience which was very ill rewarded at their close. For Mary, on receiving amongst the thanks of the table the hint of a hope that she might be prevailed on to favor them again, after the pause of half a minute began another. Mary's powers were by no means fitted for such a display; her voice was weak and her manner affected. Elizabeth was in agonies. She looked at Jane to see how she bore it, but Jane was very composedly talking to Mr. Bingley. She looked at his two sisters and saw them making signs of derision at each other, and at Mr. Darcy, who continued, however, imperturbably grave. She looked at her father to entreat his interference lest Mary should be singing all night.

He took the hint, and when Mary had finished her second song, said aloud, "That will do extremely well, child. You have delighted us long enough. Let the other young ladies have time to exhibit."

Mary, though pretending not to hear, was somewhat disconcerted; and Elizabeth, sorry for her and sorry for her father's speech, was afraid her anxiety had done no good, as Mr. Collins began another of his interminable speeches to all within the room on subjects no one could possibly care about.

To Elizabeth it appeared that had her family made an agreement to expose themselves as much as they could during the evening, it would have been impossible for them to play their parts with more spirit or finer success. Happy did she think it for Mr. Bingley and her sister that some of the exhibition had escaped his notice and that his feelings were not of a sort to be much distressed by the folly which he must have witnessed. That his two sisters and Mr. Darcy, however, should have such an opportunity of ridiculing her relations was bad enough, and she could not determine whether the silent contempt of the gentleman, or the insolent smiles of the ladies, were more intolerable.

The rest of the evening brought her little amusement. She was teased by Mr. Collins, who continued most perseveringly by her side, and though he could not prevail on her to dance with him again, put it out of her power to dance with others. In vain did she entreat him to stand up with somebody else, and offer to introduce him to any young lady in the room. He assured her that, as to dancing, he was perfectly indifferent to it, that his chief object was by delicate attentions to recommend himself to her, and that he should therefore make a point of remaining close to her the whole evening. There was no arguing upon such a project. She owed her greatest relief to her friend Miss Lucas, who often joined them and good-naturedly engaged Mr. Collins's conversation to herself.

She was at least free from the offense of Mr. Darcy's further notice. Though often standing within a very short distance of her, quite disengaged, he never came near enough to speak. She felt it to be the probable consequence of her allusions to Mr. Wickham and rejoiced in it.

The Longbourn party were the last of all the company to depart, and, by a maneuver of Mrs. Bennet, had to wait for their carriage a quarter of an hour after everybody else was gone, which gave them time to see how heartily they were wished away by some of the family.

When at length they arose to take leave, Mrs. Bennet was most pressingly civil in her hope of seeing the whole family soon at Longbourn, and addressed herself especially to Mr. Bingley to assure him how happy he would make them by eating a family dinner with them at any time without the ceremony of a formal invitation. Bingley was all grateful pleasure, and he readily engaged for taking the earliest opportunity of waiting on her after his return from London, whither he was obliged to go the next day for a short time.

Mrs. Bennet was perfectly satisfied and quitted the house under the delightful persuasion that, allowing for the necessary preparations of settlements, new carriages, and wedding clothes, she should undoubtedly see her daughter settled at Netherfield in the course of three or four months. Of having another daughter married to Mr. Collins, she thought with equal certainty and with considerable, though not equal, pleasure. Elizabeth was the least dear to her of all her children; and though the man and the match were quite good enough for *her*, the worth of each was eclipsed by Mr. Bingley and Netherfield.

Chapter Twelve

The next day opened a new scene at Longbourn. Mr. Collins made his declaration in form. Having resolved to do it without loss of time, as his leave of absence extended only to the following Saturday, and having no feelings of diffidence to make it distressing to himself even at the moment, he set about it in a very orderly manner with all the observances which he supposed a regular part of the business. On finding Mrs. Bennet, Elizabeth, and one of the younger girls together soon after breakfast, he addressed the mother in these words:

"May I hope, madam, for your interest with your fair daughter Elizabeth, when I solicit for the honor of a private audience with her in the course of this morning?"

Before Elizabeth had time for anything but a blush of surprise, Mrs. Bennet answered instantly, "Oh dear! Yes, certainly. I am sure Lizzy will be very happy—I am sure she can have no objection. Come, Kitty, I want you upstairs." And gathering her work together, she was hastening away, when Elizabeth called out:

"Dear madam, do not go. I beg you will not go. Mr. Collins must excuse me. He can have nothing to say to me that anybody need not hear. I am going away myself."

"No, no, nonsense, Lizzy. I desire you to stay where you are." And upon Elizabeth's seeming really, with vexed and embarrassed looks, about to escape, she added: "Lizzy, I *insist* upon your staying and hearing Mr. Collins."

Elizabeth would not oppose such an injunction—and a moment's consideration making her also sensible that it would be wisest to get it over as soon and as quietly as possible, she sat down again and tried to conceal by incessant employment the feelings which were divided between distress and diversion. Mrs. Bennet and Kitty walked off, and as soon as they were gone, Mr. Collins began.

"Believe me, my dear Miss Elizabeth, that your modesty, so far from doing you any disservice, rather adds to your other perfections. You would have been less amiable in my eyes had there *not* been this little unwillingness. But allow me to assure you that I have your respected mother's permission for this address. You can hardly doubt the purport of my discourse, however your natural delicacy may lead you to dissemble; my attentions have been too marked to be mistaken. Almost as soon as I entered the house, I singled you out as the companion of my future life. But before I am run away with by my feelings on this subject, perhaps it would be advisable for me to state my reasons for marrying—and, moreover, for coming into Hertfordshire with the design of selecting a wife, as I certainly did."

The idea of Mr. Collins, with all his solemn composure, being run away with by his feelings, made Elizabeth so near laughing that she could not use the short pause he allowed in any attempt to stop him further, and he continued:

"My reasons for marrying are, first, that I think it a right thing for every clergyman in easy circumstances, like myself, to set the example of matrimony in his parish; secondly, that I am convinced that it will add very greatly to my happiness; and thirdly—which perhaps I ought to have mentioned earlier, that it is the particular advice and recommendation of the very noble lady whom I have the honor of calling patroness. Twice has she condescended to give me her opinion on this subject; and it was but the very Saturday night before I left Hunsford that she said, 'Mr. Collins, you must marry. A clergyman like you must marry. Choose properly, choose a gentlewoman for *my* sake; and for your *own*, let her be an active, useful sort of person, not brought up high, but able to make a small income go a good way. This is my advice. Find such a woman as soon as you can, bring her to Hunsford, and I will visit her.' Allow me, by the way, to observe, my fair cousin, that I do not reckon the notice and kindness of Lady Catherine de Bourgh as among the least of the advantages in my power to offer. You will find her manners beyond anything I can describe; and your wit and vivacity, I think, must be acceptable to her, especially when tempered with the silence and respect which her rank will inevitably excite. Thus much for my general intention in favor of matrimony; it remains to be told why my views were directed towards Longbourn instead of my own neighborhood, where I can assure you there are many amiable young women. But the fact is that, being as I am to inherit this estate after the death of your honored father, I could not satisfy myself without resolving to choose a wife from among his daughters, that the loss to them might be as little as possible when the melancholy event takes place—which, however, may not be for several years. This has been my motive, my fair cousin, and I flatter myself it will not sink me in your esteem. And now nothing remains for me but to assure you in the most animated language of the violence of my affection. To fortune I am perfectly indifferent. On that head, I shall be uniformly silent; and you may assure yourself that no ungenerous reproach shall ever pass my lips when we are married."

It was absolutely necessary to interrupt him now.

"You are too hasty, sir," she cried. "You forget that I have made no answer. Accept my thanks for the compliment you are paying me, but it is impossible for me to do otherwise than to decline."

"I understand," replied Mr. Collins, with a formal wave of the hand, "that it is usual with young ladies to reject the addresses of the man whom they secretly mean to accept when he first applies for their favor; and that sometimes the refusal is repeated a second or even a third time."

"Upon my word, sir," cried Elizabeth, "your hope is a rather extraordinary one after my declaration. I do assure you that I am not one of those young ladies who are so daring as to risk their happiness on the chance of being asked a second time. I am perfectly serious in my refusal. You could not make *me* happy, and I am convinced that I am the last woman in the world who could make you so. Nay, were your friend Lady Catherine to know me, I am persuaded she would find me in every respect ill qualified for the situation."

"Were it certain that Lady Catherine would think so," said Mr. Collins very gravely—"but I cannot imagine that her ladyship would at all disapprove of you. And you may be certain when I have the honor of seeing her again, I shall speak in the very highest terms of your modesty, economy, and other amiable qualifications."

"Indeed, Mr. Collins, all praise of me will be unnecessary. I wish you very happy and very rich, and by refusing your hand, do all in my power to prevent your being otherwise. In making me the offer, you must have satisfied the delicacy of your feelings with regard to my family, and may take possession of Longbourn estate whenever it falls without any self-reproach. This matter may be considered, therefore, as finally settled." And rising as she thus spoke, she would have quitted the room, had Mr. Collins not thus addressed her:

"When I do myself the honor of speaking to you next on the subject, I shall hope to receive a more favorable answer than you have now given me; though I am far from accusing you of cruelty at present, because I know it to be the established custom of your sex to reject a man on the first application, and perhaps you have even now said as much to encourage my suit as would be consistent with the true delicacy of the female character."

"Really, Mr. Collins," cried Elizabeth with some warmth, "you puzzle me exceedingly. If what I have hitherto said can appear to you in the form of encouragement, I know not how to express my refusal in such a way as to convince you of its being one."

"You must give me leave to flatter myself, my dear cousin, that your refusal of my addresses is merely words of course. My reasons for believing it are briefly these: It does not appear to me that my hand is unworthy of your acceptance, or that the establishment I can offer would be any other than highly desirable. My situation in life, my connections with the family of de Bourgh, and my relationship to your own, are circumstances highly in my favor; and you should take it into further consideration that in spite of your manifold attractions, it is by no means certain that another offer of marriage may ever be made you. As I must therefore conclude that you are not serious in your rejection of me, I shall choose to attribute it to your wish of increasing my love by suspense, according to the usual practice of elegant females."

"I do assure you, sir, that I have no pretensions whatever to that kind of elegance which consists in tormenting a respectable man. I would rather be paid the compliment of being believed sincere. I thank you again and again for the honor you have done me in your proposals, but to accept them is absolutely impossible. My feelings in every respect forbid it. Can I speak plainer? Do not consider me now as an elegant female, intending to plague you, but as a rational creature speaking the truth from her heart."

"You are uniformly charming!" cried he with an air of awkward gallantry. "And I am persuaded that when sanctioned by the express authority of both your excellent parents, my proposals will not fail of being acceptable."

To such perseverance in willful self-deception Elizabeth would make no reply, and immediately and in silence withdrew, determined, if he persisted in considering her repeated refusals as flattering encouragement, to apply to her father, whose negative might be uttered in such a manner as to be decisive, and whose behavior at least could not be mistaken for the affectation and coquetry of an elegant female.

Mr. Collins was not left long to the silent contemplation of his successful love; for Mrs. Bennet, having dawdled about in the vestibule to watch for the end of the conference, no sooner saw Elizabeth open the door and with quick steps pass her towards the staircase, than she entered the breakfast room and congratulated both him and herself in warm terms on the happy prospect of their nearer connection. Mr. Collins received and returned these felicitations with equal pleasure and then proceeded to relate the particulars of their interview, with the result of which he trusted he had every reason to be satisfied, since the refusal which his cousin had steadfastly given him would naturally flow from her bashful modesty and the genuine delicacy of her character.

This information, however, startled Mrs. Bennet. She would have been glad to be equally satisfied that her daughter had meant to encourage him by protesting against his proposals, but she dared not believe it, and could not help saying so.

"But, depend upon it, Mr. Collins," she added, "that Lizzy shall be brought to reason. I will speak to her about it directly. She is a very headstrong, foolish girl, and does not know her own interest, but I will *make* her know it."

"Pardon me for interrupting you, madam," cried Mr. Collins. "But if she is really headstrong and foolish, I know not whether she would altogether be a very desirable wife to a man in my situation who naturally looks for happiness in the marriage state. If therefore she actually persists in rejecting my suit, perhaps it would be better not to force her into accepting me, because if liable to such defects of temper, she could not contribute much to my felicity."

"Sir, you quite misunderstand me," said Mrs. Bennet, alarmed. "Lizzy is only headstrong in such matters as these. In everything else she is as good-natured a girl as ever lived. I will go directly to Mr. Bennet, and we shall very soon settle it with her, I am sure."

She would not give him time to reply, but hurrying instantly to her husband, called out as she entered the library, "Oh! Mr. Bennet, you are wanted immediately; we are all in an uproar. You must come and make Lizzy marry Mr. Collins, for she vows she will not have him, and if you do not make haste he will change his mind and not have *her*."

Mr. Bennet raised his eyes from his book as she entered, and fixed them on her face with a calm unconcern which was not in the least altered by her communication.

"And what am I to do on the occasion? It seems a hopeless business."

"Speak to Lizzy about it yourself. Tell her that you insist upon her marrying him."

"Let her be called down. She shall hear my opinion."

Mrs. Bennet rang the bell, and Miss Elizabeth was summoned to the library.

"Come here, child," cried her father as she appeared. "I have sent for you on an affair of importance. I understand that Mr. Collins has made you an offer of marriage. Is it true?" Elizabeth replied that it was. "Very well—and this offer of marriage you have refused?"

"I have, sir."

"Very well. We now come to the point. Your mother insists upon your accepting it. Is it not so, Mrs. Bennet?"

"Yes, or I will never see her again."

"Then an unhappy alternative is before you, Elizabeth, for from this day you must be a stranger to one of your parents. Your mother will never see you again if you do *not* marry Mr. Collins, and I will never see you again if you *do*."

Elizabeth could not but smile at such a conclusion of such a beginning, but Mrs. Bennet, who had persuaded herself that her husband regarded the affair as she wished, was excessively disappointed.

Not yet, however, did Mrs. Bennet give up the point, in spite of her disappointment in her husband. She talked to Elizabeth again and again, coaxed and threatened her by turns. She endeavored to secure Jane in her interest; but Jane, with all possible mildness, declined interfering; and Elizabeth, sometimes with real earnestness, and sometimes with playful gaiety, replied to her attacks. Though her manner varied, however, her determination never did.

Mr. Collins, meanwhile, was meditating in solitude on what had passed. He thought too well of himself to comprehend on what motives his cousin could refuse him; and though his pride was hurt, he suffered in no other way. His regard for her was quite imaginary; and the possibility of her deserving her mother's reproach prevented his feeling any regret.

While the family was in this confusion, Charlotte Lucas came to spend the day with them. She was met in the vestibule by Lydia, who, flying to her, cried in a half whisper, "I am glad you are come, for there is such fun here! What do you think has happened this morning? Mr. Collins has made an offer to Lizzy, and she will not have him."

Charlotte hardly had time to answer before they were joined by Kitty, who came to tell the same news; and no sooner had they entered the breakfast room, where Mrs. Bennet was alone, than she likewise began on the subject, calling on Miss Lucas for her compassion and entreating her to persuade her friend Lizzy to comply with the wishes of all her family. "Pray do, my dear Miss Lucas," she added in a melancholy tone, "for nobody is on my side, nobody takes part with me. I am cruelly used, nobody feels for my poor nerves."

Charlotte's reply was spared by the entrance of Jane and Elizabeth.

"Aye, there she comes," continued Mrs. Bennet, "looking as unconcerned as may be, and caring no more for us than if we were at York, provided she can have her own way. But I tell you, Miss Lizzy— if you take it into your head to go on refusing every offer of marriage in this way, you will never get a husband at all—and I am sure I do not know who is to maintain you when your father is dead. I shall not be able to keep you—and so I warn you. I have done with you from this very day. I told you in the library, you know, that I should never speak to you again, and you will find me as good as my word. I have no pleasure in talking to undutiful children. Not that I have much pleasure, indeed, in talking to anybody. People who suffer as I do from nervous complaints can have no great inclination for talking. Nobody can tell what I suffer! But it is always so. Those who do not complain are never pitied."

Her daughters listened in silence to this effusion, sensible that any attempt to reason with her or soothe her would only increase the irritation. She talked on, therefore, without interruption from any of them, till they were joined by Mr. Collins, who entered the room with an air more stately than usual, and on perceiving whom, she said to the girls, "Now, I do insist upon it, that you, all of you, hold your tongues, and let me and Mr. Collins have a little conversation together."

Elizabeth passed quietly out of the room, Jane and Kitty followed, but Lydia stood her ground, determined to hear all she could; and Charlotte, detained first by the civility of Mr. Collins, whose inquiries after herself and all her family were very minute, and then by a little curiosity, satisfied herself with walking to the window and pretending not to hear. In a doleful voice Mrs. Bennet began the projected conversation: "Oh! Mr. Collins!"

"My dear madam," replied he, "let us be forever silent on this point. Far be it from me," he presently continued in a voice that marked his displeasure, "to resent the behavior of your daughter. Resignation to inevitable evils is the evil duty of us all; the peculiar duty of a young man who has been so fortunate as I have been in early preferment; and I trust I am resigned. You will not, I hope, consider me as showing any disrespect to your family, my dear madam, by thus withdrawing my pretensions to your daughter's favor, without having paid yourself and Mr. Bennet the compliment of requesting you to interpose your authority in my behalf. I have certainly meant well through the whole affair. My object has been to secure an amiable companion for myself, with due consideration for the advantage of all your family, and if my *manner* has been at all reprehensible, I here beg leave to apologize."

Chapter Thirteen

The discussion of Mr. Collins's offer was now nearly at an end, and Elizabeth had only to suffer from the uncomfortable feelings necessarily attending it, and occasionally from some peevish allusions of her mother. As for the gentleman himself, *his* feelings were chiefly expressed, not by embarrassment or dejection, or by trying to avoid her, but by stiffness of manner and resentful silence. He scarcely ever spoke to her, and the assiduous attentions which he had been so sensible of himself were transferred for the rest of the day to Miss Lucas, whose civility in listening to him was a seasonable relief to them all, and especially to her friend.

The morrow produced no abatement of Mrs. Bennet's ill-humor or ill health. Mr. Collins was also in the same state of angry pride. Elizabeth had hoped that his resentment might shorten his visit, but his plan did not appear in the least affected by it. He was always to have gone on Saturday, and to Saturday he meant to stay.

After breakfast, the girls walked to Meryton to inquire if Mr. Wickham were returned and to lament over his absence from the Netherfield ball. He joined them on their entering the town and attended them to their aunt's where his regret and vexation, and the concern of everybody, was well talked over. To Elizabeth, however, he voluntarily acknowledged that the necessity of his absence *had* been self-imposed.

"I found," said he, "as the time drew near that I had better not meet Mr. Darcy; that to be in the same room, the same party with him for so many hours together, might be more than I could bear, and that scenes might arise unpleasant to more than myself."

She highly approved his forbearance, and they had leisure for a full discussion of it, and for all the commendation which they civilly bestowed on each other, as Mr. Wickham and another officer walked back with them to Longbourn, and during the walk he particularly attended to her. His accompanying them was a double advantage; she felt all the compliment it offered to herself, and it was most acceptable as an occasion of introducing him to her father and mother.

Soon after their return, a letter was delivered to Miss Bennet; it came from Netherfield. The envelope contained a sheet of elegant, little, hot-pressed paper, well covered with a lady's fair, flowing hand. Elizabeth saw her sister's countenance change as she read it, and saw her dwelling intently on some particular passages. Jane recollected herself soon, and putting the letter away, tried to join with her usual cheerfulness in the general conversation; but Elizabeth felt an anxiety on the subject which drew off her attention even from Mr. Wickham. No sooner had he and his companion taken leave, than a glance from Jane invited her to follow her upstairs. When they had gained their own room, Jane, taking out the letter, said:

"This is from Caroline Bingley; what it contains has surprised me a good deal. The whole party have left Netherfield by this time, and are on their way to town—and without any intention of coming back again. You shall hear what she says."

She then read the first sentence aloud, which comprised the information of their having just resolved to follow their brother to town directly, and of their meaning to dine in Grosvenor Street, where Mr. Hurst had a house. The next was in these words: "I do not pretend to regret anything I shall leave in Hertfordshire, except your society, my dearest friend; but we will hope, at some future period, to enjoy many returns of that delightful intercourse we have known, and in the meanwhile may lessen the pain of separation by a very frequent and most unreserved correspondence. I depend on you for that." To these highflown expressions Elizabeth listened with all the insensibility of distrust; and though the suddenness of their removal surprised her, she saw nothing in it really to lament; it was not to be supposed that their absence from Netherfield would prevent Mr. Bingley's being there; and as to the loss of their society, she was persuaded that Jane must cease to regard it in the enjoyment of his.

"It is unlucky," said she, after a short pause, "that you should not be able to see your friends before they leave the country. But Mr. Bingley will not be detained in London by them."

"Caroline decidedly says that none of the party will return into Hertfordshire this winter. I will read it to you:"

"When my brother left us yesterday, he imagined that the business which took him to London might be concluded in three or four days; but as we are certain it cannot be so, and at the same time convinced that when Charles gets to town he will be in no hurry to leave it again, we have determined on following him thither, that he may not be obliged to spend his vacant hours in a comfortless hotel. Many of my acquaintances are already there for the winter; I wish that I could hear that you, my dearest friend, had any intention of making one of the crowd—but of that I despair. I sincerely hope your Christmas in Hertfordshire may abound in the gaieties which that season generally brings, and that your beaux will be so numerous as to prevent your feeling the loss of the three of whom we shall deprive you."

"It is evident by this," added Jane, "that he comes back no more this winter."

"It is only evident that Miss Bingley does not mean that he *should*."

"Why will you think so? It must be his own doing. He is his own master. But you do not know *all*. I will read you the passage which particularly hurts me. I will have no reserves from *you*.

"'Mr. Darcy is impatient to see his sister; and, to confess the truth, we are scarcely less eager to meet her again. I really do not think Georgiana Darcy has her equal for beauty, elegance, and accomplishments; and the affection she inspires in Louisa and myself is heightened into something still more interesting from the hope we dare entertain of her being hereafter our sister. My brother admires her greatly already; he will have frequent opportunity now of seeing her on the most intimate footing; her relations all wish the connection as much as his own; and a sister's partiality is not misleading me, I think, when I call Charles most capable of engaging any woman's heart. With all these circumstances to favor an attachment, and nothing to prevent it, am I wrong, my dearest Jane, in indulging the hope of an event which will secure the happiness of so many?'

"What do you think of *this* sentence, my dear Lizzy?" said Jane as she finished it. "Is it not clear enough? Does it not expressly declare that Caroline neither expects nor wishes me to be her sister; that she is perfectly convinced of her brother's indifference; and that if she suspects the nature of my feelings for him, she means most kindly to put me on my guard? Can there be any other opinion on the subject?"

"Yes, there can; for mine is totally different. Will you hear it?"

"Most willingly."

"You shall have it in a few words. Miss Bingley sees that her brother is in love with you, and wants him to marry Miss Darcy. She follows him to town in hope of keeping him there, and tries to persuade you that he does not care about you."

Jane shook her head.

"Indeed, Jane, you ought to believe me. No one who has ever seen you together can doubt his affection. Miss Bingley, I am sure, cannot. She is not such a simpleton. Could she have seen half as much love in Mr. Darcy for herself, she would have ordered her wedding clothes. But the case is this: We are not rich enough or grand enough for them; and she is the more anxious to get Miss Darcy for her brother, from the notion that when there has been *one* intermarriage, she may have less trouble in achieving a second; in which there is certainly some ingenuity, and I dare say it would succeed, if Miss de Bourgh were out of the way. But, my dearest Jane, you cannot seriously imagine that because Miss Bingley tells you her brother greatly admires Miss Darcy, he is in the smallest degree less sensible of *your* merit than when he took leave of you on Tuesday, or that it will be in her power to persuade him that, instead of being in love with you, he is very much in love with her friend."

"If we thought alike of Miss Bingley," replied Jane, "your representation of all this might make me quite easy. But I know the foundation is unjust. Caroline is incapable of willfully deceiving anyone; and all that I can hope in this case is that she is deceiving herself."

"That is right. You could not have started a more happy idea, since you will not take comfort in mine. Believe her to be deceived, by all means. You have now done your duty by her and must fret no longer."

"But, my dear sister, can I be happy, even supposing the best, in accepting a man whose sisters and friends are all wishing him to marry elsewhere?"

"You must decide for yourself," said Elizabeth. "And if, upon mature deliberation, you find that the misery of disobliging his two sisters is more than equivalent to the happiness of being his wife, I advise you by all means to refuse him."

"How can you talk so?" said Jane, faintly smiling. "You must know that though I should be exceedingly grieved at their disapprobation, I could not hesitate."

"I did not think you would; and that being the case, I cannot consider your situation with much compassion."

"But if he returns no more this winter, my choice will never be required. A thousand things may arise in six months!"

The idea of his returning no more Elizabeth treated with the utmost contempt. It appeared to her merely the suggestion of Caroline's interested wishes, and she could not for a moment suppose that those wishes, however openly or artfully spoken, could influence a young man so totally independent of everyone.

She represented to her sister as forcibly as possible what she felt on the subject, and had soon the pleasure of seeing its happy effect. Jane's temper was not desponding, and she was gradually led to hope, though the diffidence of affection sometimes overcame the hope, that Mr. Bingley would return to Netherfield and answer every wish of her heart.

They agreed that Mrs. Bennet should only hear of the departure of the family without being alarmed on the score of the gentleman's conduct. But even this partial communication gave her a great deal of concern, and she bewailed it as exceedingly unlucky that the ladies should happen to go away just as they were all getting so intimate together. After lamenting it at some length, however, she had the consolation that Mr. Bingley would be soon down again and dining at Longbourn, and the conclusion of all was the comfortable declaration that, though he had been invited only to a family dinner, she would take care to have two full courses.

* * * * *

The Bennets were engaged to dine with the Lucases, and again during the chief of the day was Miss Lucas so kind as to listen to Mr. Collins.

Elizabeth took an opportunity of thanking her. "It keeps him in good humor, and I am more obliged to you than I can express."

Charlotte assured her friend of her satisfaction in being useful, and that it amply repaid her for the little sacrifice of her time. This was very amiable, but Charlotte's kindness extended farther than Elizabeth had any conception of; its object was nothing else than to secure her from any return of Mr. Collins's addresses by engaging them towards herself. Such was Miss Lucas's scheme; and appearances were so favorable that, when they parted at night, she would have felt almost secure of success if he had not been to leave Hertfordshire so very soon.

But here Charlotte did injustice to the fire and independence of his character, for it led him to escape out of Longbourn House the next morning with admirable slyness and hasten to Lucas Lodge to throw himself at her feet. He was anxious to avoid the notice of his cousins from a conviction that if they saw him depart, they could not fail to conjecture his design, and he was not willing to have the attempt known till its success might be known likewise. For though feeling almost secure, and with reason, for Charlotte had been tolerably encouraging, he was comparatively diffident since the adventure of Wednesday. His reception, however, was of the most flattering kind. Charlotte perceived him from an upper window as he walked towards the house, and instantly set out to meet him accidentally in the lane. But little had she dared to hope that so much love and eloquence awaited her there.

In as short a time as Mr. Collins's long speeches would allow, everything was settled between them to the satisfaction of both, and as they entered the house he earnestly entreated her to name the day that was to make him the happiest of men. Though such a solicitation must be waived for the present, the lady felt no inclination to trifle with his happiness. The stupidity with which he was favored by nature must guard his courtship from any charm that could make a woman wish for its continuance, and Miss Lucas, who accepted him solely from the pure and disinterested desire of an establishment, cared not how soon that establishment was gained.

Sir William and Lady Lucas were speedily applied to for their consent, and it was bestowed with a most joyful alacrity. Mr. Collins's present circumstances made it a most eligible match for their daughter, to whom they could give little fortune, and his prospects of future wealth were exceedingly fair. Lady Lucas began directly to calculate, with more interest than the matter had ever excited before, how many years longer Mr. Bennet was likely to live. And Sir William gave it as his decided opinion that whenever Mr. Collins should be in possession of the Longbourn estate, it would be highly expedient that both he and his wife should make their appearance at St. James's. The whole family, in short, was properly overjoyed on the occasion. The younger girls formed hopes of coming out a year or two sooner than they might otherwise have done, and the boys were relieved from their apprehension of Charlotte's dying an old maid.

Charlotte herself was tolerably composed. She had gained her point and had time to consider it. Her reflections were in general satisfactory. Mr. Collins, to be sure, was neither sensible nor agreeable; his society was irksome, and his attachment to her must be imaginary.

But still he would be her husband. Without thinking highly either of men or matrimony, marriage had always been her object; it was the only provision for well-educated young women of small fortune, and however uncertain of giving happiness, must be their pleasantest preservative from want. This preservative she had now obtained; and at the age of twenty-seven, without having ever been handsome, she felt all the good luck of it. The least agreeable circumstance in the business was the surprise it must occasion to Elizabeth Bennet, whose friendship she valued beyond that of any other person. Elizabeth would wonder, and probably would blame her; and though her resolution was not to be shaken, her feelings must be hurt by such a disapprobation. She resolved to give her the information herself, and therefore charged Mr. Collins, when he returned to Longbourn to dinner, to drop no hint of what had passed before any of the family. A promise of secrecy was of course very dutifully given, but it could not be kept without difficulty, for the curiosity excited by his long absence burst forth in such very direct questions on his return as required some ingenuity to evade, and he was at the same time exercising great self-denial, for he was longing to publish his prosperous love.

As he was to begin his journey too early on the morrow to see any of the family, the ceremony of leave-taking was performed when the ladies moved for the night. Mrs. Bennet, with great politeness and cordiality, said how happy they should be to see him at Longbourn again whenever his engagements might allow him to visit them.

"My dear madam," he replied, "this invitation is particularly gratifying, because it is what I have been hoping to receive; and you may be very certain that I shall avail myself of it as soon as possible."

They were all astonished, and Mr. Bennet, who could by no means wish for so speedy a return, immediately said, "But is there not danger of Lady Catherine's disapprobation here, my good sir? You had better neglect your relations than run the risk of offending your patroness."

"My dear sir," replied Mr. Collins, "I am particularly obliged to you for this friendly caution, and you may depend upon my not taking so material a step without her ladyship's concurrence."

"You cannot be too much upon your guard. Risk anything rather than her displeasure; and if you find it likely to be raised by your coming to us again, which I should think exceedingly probable, stay quietly at home, and be satisfied that we shall take no offence."

"Believe me, my dear sir, my gratitude is warmly excited by such affectionate attention; and depend upon it, you will speedily receive from me a letter of thanks for this, and for every other mark of your regard during my stay in Hertfordshire. As for my fair cousins, though my absence may not be long enough to render it necessary, I shall now take the liberty of wishing them health and happiness, not excepting my cousin Elizabeth."

With proper civilities the ladies then withdrew; all of them equally surprised that he meditated a quick return. Mrs. Bennet wished to understand by it that he thought of paying his addresses to one of her younger girls, and Mary might have been prevailed on to accept him. She rated his abilities much higher than any of the others; there was a solidity in his reflections which often struck her, and though by no means so clever as herself, she thought that if encouraged to read and improve himself by such an example as hers, he might become a very agreeable companion. But on the following morning, every hope of this kind was done away with. Miss Lucas called soon after breakfast, and in a private conference with Elizabeth related the event of the day before.

The possibility of Mr. Collins's fancying himself in love with her friend had once occurred to Elizabeth within the last day or two. But that Charlotte could encourage him seemed almost as far from possibility as she could encourage him herself, and her astonishment was consequently so great as to overcome at first the bounds of decorum, and she could not help crying out:

"Engaged to Mr. Collins! My dear Charlotte—impossible!"

The steady countenance which Charlotte had commanded in telling her story gave way to a momentary confusion here on receiving so direct a reproach. Though, as it was no more than she expected, she soon regained her composure and calmly replied:

"Why should you be surprised, my dear Eliza? Do you think it incredible that Mr. Collins should be able to procure any woman's good opinion because he was not so happy as to succeed with you?"

But Elizabeth had now recollected herself, and making a strong effort for it, was able to assure with tolerable firmness that the prospect of their relationship was highly grateful to her, and that she wished her all imaginable happiness.

"I see what you are feeling," replied Charlotte. "You must be surprised, very much surprised—so lately as Mr. Collins was wishing to marry you. But when you have had time to think it over, I hope you will be satisfied with what I have done. I am not romantic, you know; I never was. I ask only a comfortable home; and considering Mr. Collins's character, connection, and situation in life, I am convinced that my chance of happiness with him is as fair as most people can boast on entering the marriage state."

Elizabeth quietly answered "undoubtedly", and after an awkward pause, they returned to the rest of the family. Charlotte did not stay much longer, and Elizabeth was then left to reflect on what she had heard. It was a long time before she became at all reconciled to the idea of so unsuitable a match. The strangeness of Mr. Collins's making two offers of marriage within three days was nothing in comparison of his being now accepted. She had always felt that Charlotte's opinion of matrimony was not exactly like her own, but she had not supposed it to be possible that, when called into action, she would have sacrificed every better feeling to worldly advantage. Charlotte the wife of Mr. Collins was a most humiliating picture! And to the pang of a friend disgracing herself and sunk in her esteem was added the distressing conviction that it was impossible for that friend to be tolerably happy in the lot she had chosen.

Chapter Fourteen

Elizabeth was sitting with her mother and sisters, reflecting on what she had heard and doubting whether she was authorized to mention it, when Sir William Lucas himself appeared, sent by his daughter, to announce her engagement to the family. With many compliments to them, and much self-congratulation on the prospect of a connection between the houses, he unfolded the matter—to an audience not merely wondering, but incredulous. For Mrs. Bennet, with more perseverance than politeness, protested he must be entirely mistaken.

And Lydia, always unguarded and often uncivil, boisterously exclaimed, "Good Lord! Sir William, how can you tell such a story? Do not you know that Mr. Collins wants to marry Lizzy?"

Nothing less than the complaisance of a courtier could have borne without anger such treatment; but Sir William's good breeding carried him through it all. And though he begged leave to be positive as to the truth of his information, he listened to all their impertinence with the most forbearing courtesy.

Elizabeth, feeling it incumbent on her to relieve him from so unpleasant a situation, now put herself forward to confirm his account by mentioning her prior knowledge of it from Charlotte herself. She endeavored to put a stop to the exclamations of her mother and sisters by the earnestness of her congratulations to Sir William, in which she was readily joined by Jane, and by making a variety of remarks on the happiness that might be expected from the match, the excellent character of Mr. Collins, and the convenient distance of Hunsford from London.

Mrs. Bennet was in fact too much overpowered to say a great deal while Sir William remained, but no sooner had he left them than her feelings found a rapid vent. In the first place, she persisted in disbelieving the whole of the matter. Secondly, she was very sure that Mr. Collins had been taken in. Thirdly, she trusted that they would never be happy together, and fourthly, that the match might be broken off. Two inferences, however, were plainly deduced from the whole: one, that Elizabeth was the real cause of the mischief; and the other that she herself had been barbarously misused by them all. And on these two points she principally dwelt during the rest of the day. Nothing could console and nothing could appease her. Nor did that day wear out her resentment. A week elapsed before she could see Elizabeth without scolding her, a month passed away before she could speak to Sir William or Lady Lucas without being rude, and many months were gone before she could at all forgive their daughter.

Mr. Bennet's emotions were much more tranquil on the occasion, and such as he did experience he pronounced to be of a most agreeable sort. For it gratified him, he said, to discover that Charlotte Lucas, whom he had been used to think tolerably sensible, was as foolish as his wife, and more foolish than his daughter!

Jane confessed herself a little surprised at the match, but she said less of her astonishment than of her earnest desire for their happiness; nor could Elizabeth persuade her to consider it as improbable. Kitty and Lydia were far from envying Miss Lucas, for Mr. Collins was only a clergyman, and it affected them in no other way than as a piece of news to spread at Meryton.

Lady Lucas could not be insensible of triumph on being able to retort on Mrs. Bennet the comfort of having a daughter well married, and she called at Longbourn rather oftener than usual to say how happy she was, though Mrs. Bennet's sour looks and ill-natured remarks might have been enough to drive happiness away.

Between Elizabeth and Charlotte there was a restraint which kept them mutually silent on the subject, and Elizabeth felt persuaded that no real confidence could ever subsist between them again. Her disappointment in Charlotte made her turn with fonder regard to her elder sister, of whose rectitude and delicacy she was sure her opinion could never be shaken, and for whose happiness she grew daily more anxious, as Mr. Bingley had now been gone a week and nothing more was heard of his return.

Jane had sent Caroline an early answer to her letter and was counting the days till she might reasonably hope to hear again. The promised letter of thanks from Mr. Collins arrived on Tuesday, addressed to their father and written with all the solemnity of gratitude which a twelvemonth's abode in the family might have prompted. After discharging his conscience on that head, he proceeded to inform them, with many rapturous expressions, of his happiness in having obtained the affection of their amiable neighbor, Miss Lucas, and then explained that it was merely with the view of enjoying her society that he had been so ready to close with their kind wish of seeing him again at Longbourn, whither he hoped to be able to return on Monday fortnight. For Lady Catherine, he added, so heartily approved his marriage that she wished it to take place as soon as possible, which he trusted would be an unanswerable argument with his amiable Charlotte to name an early day for making him the happiest of men.

Mr. Collins's return into Hertfordshire was no longer a matter of pleasure to Mrs. Bennet. On the contrary, she was as much disposed to complain of it as her husband. It was very strange that he should come to Longbourn instead of to Lucas Lodge; it was also very inconvenient and exceedingly troublesome. She hated having visitors in the house while her health was so indifferent, and lovers were of all people the most disagreeable. Such were the gentle murmurs of Mrs. Bennet, and they gave way only to the greater distress of Mr. Bingley's continued absence.

Neither Jane nor Elizabeth were comfortable on this subject. Day after day passed away without bringing any other tidings of him than the report which shortly prevailed in Meryton of his coming no more to Netherfield the whole winter; a report which highly incensed Mrs. Bennet, and which she never failed to contradict as a most scandalous falsehood.

Even Elizabeth began to fear—not that Bingley was indifferent—but that his sisters would be successful in keeping him away. Unwilling as she was to admit an idea so destructive of Jane's happiness, and so dishonorable to the stability of her lover, she could not prevent its frequently occurring. The united efforts of his two unfeeling sisters and of his overpowering immortal friend, assisted by the attractions of Miss Darcy and the amusements of London might be too much, she feared, for the strength of his attachment.

As for Jane, *her* anxiety under this suspense was, of course, more painful than Elizabeth's, but whatever she felt she was desirous of concealing, therefore between herself and Elizabeth the subject was never alluded to. But as no such delicacy restrained her mother, an hour seldom passed in which she did not talk of Mr. Bingley, express her impatience for his arrival, or even require Jane to confess that if he did not come back she would think herself very ill used. It needed all Jane's steady mildness to bear these attacks with tolerable tranquility.

Mr. Collins returned most punctually on Monday fortnight, but his reception at Longbourn was not quite so gracious as it had been on his first introduction. He was too happy, however, to need much attention; and luckily for the others, the business of love-making relieved them from a great deal of his company. The chief of every day was spent by him at Lucas Lodge, and he sometimes returned to Longbourn only in time to make an apology for his absence before the family went to bed.

Mrs. Bennet was really in a most pitiable state. The very mention of anything concerning the match threw her into an agony of ill-humor, and wherever she went she was sure of hearing it talked of. The sight of Miss Lucas was odious to her. As her successor in that house, she regarded her with jealous abhorrence. Whenever Charlotte came to see them, she concluded her to be anticipating the hour of possession, and whenever she spoke in a low voice to Mr. Collins, was convinced that they were talking of the Longbourn estate and resolving to turn herself and her daughters out of the house as soon as Mr. Bennet were dead.

She complained bitterly of all this to her husband. "Indeed, Mr. Bennet, it is very hard to think that Charlotte Lucas should ever be mistress of this house, that I should be forced to make way for *her*, and live to see her take her place in it!"

"My dear, do not give way to such gloomy thoughts. Let us hope for better things. Let us flatter ourselves that I may be the survivor."

* * * * *

Miss Bingley's letter arrived and put an end to doubt. The very first sentence conveyed the assurance of their being all settled in London for the winter, and concluded with her brother's regret at not having had time to pay his respects to his friends in Hertfordshire before he left the country.

Hope was over, entirely over. When Jane could attend to the rest of the letter, she found little except the professed affection of the writer that could give her any comfort. Miss Darcy's praise occupied the chief of it. Her many attractions were again dwelt on, and Caroline boasted joyfully of their increasing intimacy and ventured to predict the accomplishment of the wishes which had been unfolded in her former letter. She wrote also with great pleasure of her brother's being an inmate of Mr. Darcy's house, and mentioned with raptures some plans of the latter with regard to new furniture.

Elizabeth, to whom Jane very soon communicated the chief of all this, heard it in silent indignation. Her heart was divided between concern for her sister and resentment against all others. To Caroline's assertion of her brother's being partial to Miss Darcy she paid no credit. That he was really fond of Jane, she doubted no more than she had ever done. And much as she had always been disposed to like him, she could not think without anger, hardly without contempt, on that easiness of temper, that want of proper resolution, which now made him the slave of his designing friends and led him to sacrifice his own happiness to the caprice of their inclination. Had his own happiness, however, been the only sacrifice, he might have been allowed to sport with it in whatever manner he thought best, but her sister's was involved in it, as she thought he must be sensible himself. It was a subject, in short, on which reflection would be long indulged and must be unavailing. She could think of nothing else. And yet, whether Mr. Bingley's regard had really died away or were suppressed by his friends' interference; whether he had been aware of Jane's attachment or it had escaped his observation; whatever were the case, though her opinion of him must be materially affected by the difference, her sister's situation remained the same, her peace equally wounded.

A day or two passed before Jane had courage to speak of her feelings to Elizabeth. But at last, on Mrs. Bennet's leaving them together after a longer irritation than usual about Netherfield and its master, she could not help giving vent to her emotions.

"Oh, that my dear mother had more command over herself! She can have no idea of the pain she gives me by her continual reflections on him. But I will not repine. It cannot last long. He will be forgot, and we shall all be as we were before."

Elizabeth looked at her sister with incredulous solicitude, but said nothing.

"You doubt me," cried Jane, slightly coloring. "Indeed, you have no reason. He may live in my memory as the most amiable man of my acquaintance, but that is all. I have nothing either to hope or fear, and nothing to reproach him with. Thank God! I have not *that* pain. A little time, therefore—I shall certainly try to get the better."

With a stronger voice she soon added, "I have this comfort immediately, that it has not been more than an error of fancy on my side, and that it has done no harm to anyone but myself."

"My dear Jane!" exclaimed Elizabeth. "You are too good. Your sweetness and disinterestedness are really angelic. I do not know what to say to you. I feel as if I had never done you justice or loved you as you deserve."

Jane eagerly disclaimed all extraordinary merit and threw back the praise on her sister's warm affection.

"Nay, this is not fair," said Elizabeth. "*You* wish to think all the world respectable and are hurt if I speak ill of anybody. I only want to think *you* perfect, and you set yourself against it. Do not be afraid of my running into any excess, of my encroaching on your privilege of universal goodwill. You need not. There are few people whom I really love, and still fewer of whom I think well. The more I see of the world, the more am I dissatisfied with it. Every day confirms my belief of the inconsistency of all human characters, and of the little dependence that can be placed on the appearance of merit or sense. I have met with two instances lately. One I will not mention; the other is Charlotte's marriage. It is unaccountable! In every view it is unaccountable!"

"My dear Lizzy, do not give way to such feelings as these. They will ruin your happiness. You do not make allowance enough for difference of situation and temper. Consider Mr. Collins's respectability and Charlotte's steady, prudent character. Remember that she is one of a large family; that as to fortune, it is a most eligible match; and be ready to believe, for everybody's sake, that she may feel something like regard and esteem for our cousin."

"To oblige you, I would try to believe almost anything, but no one else could be benefited by such a belief as this. For were I persuaded that Charlotte had any regard for him, I should only think worse of her understanding than I now do of her heart. My dear Jane, Mr. Collins is a conceited, pompous, narrow minded, silly man. You know he is, as well as I do, and you must feel as I do that the woman who married him cannot have a proper way of thinking. You shall not defend her, though it is Charlotte Lucas. You shall not, for the sake of one individual, change the meaning of principle and integrity, nor endeavor to persuade yourself or me that selfishness is prudence and insensibility of danger is security for happiness."

"I must think your language too strong in speaking of both," replied Jane. "And I hope you will be convinced of it by seeing them happy together. But enough of this. You alluded to something else. You mentioned *two* instances. I cannot misunderstand you, but I entreat you, dear Lizzy, not to pain me by thinking *that person* to blame, and saying your opinion of him is sunk. We must not be so ready to fancy ourselves intentionally injured. We must not expect a lively young man to be always so guarded and circumspect. It is very often nothing but our own vanity that deceives us. Women fancy admiration means more than it does."

"And men take care that they should."

"If it is designedly done, they cannot be justified. But I have no idea of there being so much design in the world as some persons imagine."

"I am far from attributing any part of Mr. Bingley's conduct to design," said Elizabeth. "But without scheming to do wrong, or to make others unhappy, there may be error, and there may be misery. Thoughtlessness, want of attention to other people's feelings, and want of resolution will do the business."

"And do you impute it to either of those?"

"Yes, to the last. But if I go on, I shall displease you by saying what I think of persons you esteem. Stop me whilst you can."

"You persist, then, in supposing his sisters influence him?"

"Yes, in conjunction with his monster of a friend."

"I cannot believe it. Why should they try to influence him? They can only wish his happiness; and if he is attached to me, no other woman can secure it."

"Your first position is false. They may wish many things besides his happiness. They may wish his increase of wealth and consequence. They may wish him to marry a girl who has all the importance of money, great connections, and pride."

"Beyond a doubt, they *do* wish him to choose Miss Darcy," replied Jane. "But this may be from better feelings than you are supposing. They have known her much longer than they have known me. No wonder if they love her better. But whatever may be their own wishes, it is very unlikely they should have opposed their brother's. What sister would think herself at liberty to do it, unless there were something very objectionable? If they believed him attached to me, they would not try to part us; if he were so, they could not succeed. By supposing such an affection, you make everybody acting unnaturally and wrong, and me most unhappy. Do not distress me by the idea. I am not ashamed of having been mistaken—or, at least, it is light, it is nothing in comparison of what I should feel in thinking ill of him or his sisters. Let me take it in the best light, in the light in which it may be understood."

Elizabeth could not oppose such a wish, and from this time Mr. Bingley's name was scarcely ever mentioned between them.

Mrs. Bennet still continued to wonder and repine at his returning no more, and though a day seldom passed in which Elizabeth did not account for it clearly, there was little chance of her ever considering it with less perplexity. Her daughter endeavored to convince her of what she did not believe herself, that his attentions to Jane had been merely the effect of a common and transient liking which ceased when he saw her no more. But though the probability of the statement was admitted at the time, she had the same story to repeat every day. Mrs. Bennet's best comfort was that Mr. Bingley must be down again in the summer.

Mr. Bennet treated the matter differently, saying one day, "So, Lizzy, your sister is crossed in love, I find. I congratulate her. Next to being married, a girl likes to be crossed a little in love now and then. It is something to think of, and it gives her a sort of distinction among her companions. Now is your turn. Here are officers enough in Meryton to disappoint all the young ladies in the country. Let Wickham be *your* man. He is a pleasant fellow and would jilt you creditably. And it is a comfort to think that whatever of that kind may befall you, you have an affectionate mother who will make the most of it."

Mr. Wickham's society was of material service in dispelling the gloom which the late perverse occurrences had thrown on many of the Longbourn family. They saw him often, and to his other recommendations was now added that of general unreserve. The whole of what Elizabeth had already heard, all that he had suffered from him and his claims on Mr. Darcy, excepting that he was a vampire, was now openly acknowledged and publicly canvassed. Everybody was pleased to know how much they had always disliked Mr. Darcy before they had known anything of the matter.

Only the darkest secrets of Mr. Darcy's monstrous predatory nature were reserved for Elizabeth's knowledge alone, which Mr. Wickham discussed with her at length when opportunity for private conversation was allowed. From these conversations, she learned a great deal more than she could have ever imagined about vampires. Contrary to many of the old legends, they were entirely capable of withstanding direct sunlight and proximity to religious places and items without harm. Nor had garlic any affect on them, though they were entirely susceptible to being staked through the heart, decapitation, or fire. Otherwise, their immortal bodies merely needed fresh infusions of human blood once a week to keep them sane and at full strength. They were also able to glamour others into seeing them as normal humans of great charm and attraction. The more Mr. Wickham spoke so matter-of-factly about such creatures, the more Elizabeth began to feel the absolute veracity of his words, and she faithfully relayed all to Jane at the earliest of opportunities for private discussion.

Jane was the only person who could suppose there might be any extenuating circumstances in the case, unknown to the society of Hertfordshire or Mr. Wickham. Her mild and steady candor always pleaded for allowances and urged the possibility of mistakes and fanciful imagination—but by everybody else Mr. Darcy was condemned as the worst of men.

So too in Elizabeth's mind, Mr. Darcy was condemned as the worst of monsters.

Chapter Fifteen

After a week spent in professions of love and schemes of felicity, Mr. Collins was called from his amiable Charlotte by the arrival of Saturday. The pain of separation, however, might be alleviated on his side by preparations for the reception of his bride, as he had reason to hope that shortly after his return into Hertfordshire, the day would be fixed that was to make him the happiest of men. He took leave of his relations at Longbourn with as much solemnity as before, wished his fair cousins health and happiness again, and promised their father another letter of thanks.

On the following Monday, Mrs. Bennet had the pleasure of receiving her brother and his wife, who came as usual to spend Christmas at Longbourn. Mr. Gardiner was a sensible, gentlemanlike man, greatly superior to his sister in nature as well as education. The Netherfield ladies would have had difficulty in believing that a man who lived by trade and within view of his own warehouses could have been so well-bred and agreeable. Mrs. Gardiner, who was several years younger than Mrs. Bennet and Mrs. Phillips, was an amiable, intelligent, elegant woman, and a great favorite with all her Longbourn nieces. Between the two eldest and herself especially, there subsisted a particular regard. They had frequently been staying with her in town.

The first part of Mrs. Gardiner's business on her arrival was to distribute her presents and describe the newest fashions. When this was done she had a less active part to play. It became her turn to listen. Mrs. Bennet had many grievances to relate and much to complain of. They had all been very ill-used since she last saw her sister. Two of her girls had been upon the point of marriage, and after all there was nothing in it.

"I do not blame Jane," she continued. "For Jane would have got Mr. Bingley if she could. But Lizzy! Oh, sister! It is very hard to think that she might have been Mr. Collins's wife by this time had it not been for her own perverseness. He made her an offer in this very room, and she refused him. The consequence of it is that Lady Lucas will have a daughter married before I have, and that the Longbourn estate is just as much entailed as ever. The Lucases are very artful people indeed, sister. They are all for what they can get. I am sorry to say it of them, but so it is. It makes me very nervous and poorly, to be thwarted so in my own family, and to have neighbors who think of themselves before anybody else. However, your coming just at this time is the greatest of comforts, and I am very glad to hear what you tell us of long sleeves."

Mrs. Gardiner, to whom the chief of this news had been given before in the course of Jane and Elizabeth's correspondence with her, made her sister a slight answer, and, in compassion to her nieces, turned the conversation.

When alone with Elizabeth afterwards, she spoke more on the subject. "It seems likely to have been a desirable match for Jane. I am sorry it went off. But these things happen so often! A young man, such as you describe Mr. Bingley, so easily falls in love with a pretty girl for a few weeks, and when accident separates them, so easily forgets her, that these sort of inconsistencies are very frequent."

"An excellent consolation in its way," said Elizabeth. "But it will not do for *us*. We do not suffer by *accident*. It does not often happen that the interference of friends will persuade a young man of independent fortune to think no more of a girl whom he was violently in love with only a few days before."

"But that expression of 'violently in love' is so hackneyed, so doubtful, so indefinite, that it gives me very little idea. It is as often applied to feelings which arise from a half hour's acquaintance, as to a real, strong attachment. Pray, how violent was Mr. Bingley's love?"

"I never saw a more promising inclination. He was growing quite inattentive to other people and wholly engrossed by her. Every time they met, it was more decided and remarkable. At his own ball he offended two or three young ladies by not asking them to dance, and I spoke to him twice myself without receiving an answer. Could there be finer symptoms? Is not general incivility the very essence of love?"

"Oh, yes! Of that kind of love which I suppose him to have felt. Poor Jane! I am sorry for her, because with her disposition, she may not get over it immediately. It had better have happened to *you*, Lizzy. You would have laughed yourself out of it sooner. But do you think she would be prevailed upon to go back with us? Change of scene might be of service—and perhaps a little relief from home may be as useful as anything."

Elizabeth was exceedingly pleased with this proposal and felt persuaded of her sister's ready acquiescence.

Mrs. Gardiner added, "I hope that no consideration with regard to this young man will influence her. We live in so different a part of town, all our connections are so different, and as you well know, we go out so little that it is very improbable that they should meet at all, unless he really comes to see her."

"And *that* is quite impossible; for he is now in the custody of his friend, and Mr. Darcy would no more suffer him to call on Jane in such a part of London! My dear aunt, how could you think of it? Mr. Darcy may perhaps have *heard* of such a place as Gracechurch Street, but he would hardly think a month's ablution enough to cleanse him from its impurities were he once to enter it. And depend upon it, Mr. Bingley never stirs without him."

Mrs. Gardiner laughed at such teasing. "So much the better. I hope they will not meet at all. But does not Jane correspond with his sister? *She* will not be able to help calling."

Elizabeth shook her head. "She will drop the acquaintance entirely."

But in spite of the certainty with which Elizabeth affected to place this point, she felt a solicitude on the subject which convinced her that she did not consider it entirely hopeless. It was possible, and sometimes she thought it probable, that his affection might be reanimated and the influence of his friends successfully combated by the more natural influence of Jane's attractions.

Jane accepted her aunt's invitation with pleasure, and the Bingleys were not otherwise in her thoughts at the same time than as she hoped by Caroline's not living in the same house with her brother, she might occasionally spend a morning with her without any danger of seeing him.

The Gardiners stayed a week at Longbourn, and what with the Phillipses, the Lucases, and the officers, there was not a day without engagement. Mrs. Bennet had so carefully provided for the entertainment of her brother and sister that they did not once sit down to a family dinner. When the engagement was for home, some of the officers always made part of it—of which officers Mr. Wickham was sure to be one. On these occasions, Mrs. Gardiner, rendered suspicious by Elizabeth's warm commendation, narrowly observed them both. Without supposing them, from what she saw, to be very seriously in love, their preference for each other was plain enough to make her a little uneasy. She resolved to speak to Elizabeth on the subject before she left Hertfordshire and represent to her the imprudence of encouraging such an attachment.

To Mrs. Gardiner, Mr. Wickham had one means of affording pleasure unconnected with his general powers. About ten or a dozen years ago, before her marriage, she had spent a considerable time in that very part of Derbyshire to which he belonged. They had, therefore, many acquaintances in common. And though Mr. Wickham had been little there since the death of Mr. Darcy's father, it was yet in his power to give her fresher intelligence of her former friends than she had been in the way of procuring.

Mrs. Gardiner had seen Pemberley and known the late Mr. Darcy by character perfectly well. Here consequently was an inexhaustible subject of discourse. In comparing her recollection of Pemberley with the minute description which Mr. Wickham could give, and in bestowing her tribute of praise on the character of its late possessor, she was delighting both him and herself. On being made acquainted with the present Mr. Darcy's treatment of him, she tried to remember some of that gentleman's reputed disposition when quite a lad which might agree with it, and was confident at last that she recollected having heard Mr. Fitzwilliam Darcy formerly spoken of as a very proud, ill-natured boy.

Mrs. Gardiner's caution to Elizabeth was punctually and kindly given on the first favorable opportunity of speaking to her alone.

After honestly telling her what she thought, she thus went on, "You are too sensible a girl, Lizzy, to fall in love merely because you are warned against it. Therefore, I am not afraid of speaking openly. Seriously, I would have you be on your guard. Do not involve yourself or endeavor to involve him in an affection which the want of fortune would make so very imprudent. I have nothing to say against *him*. He is a most interesting young man, and if he had the fortune he ought to have, I should think you could not do better. But as it is, you must not let your fancy run away with you. You have sense, and we all expect you to use it. Your father would depend on *your* resolution and good conduct, I am sure. You must not disappoint your father."

"My dear aunt, this is being serious indeed." Elizabeth smiled.

"Yes, and I hope to engage you to be serious likewise."

"Well, then, you need not be under any alarm. I will take care of myself, and of Mr. Wickham too. He shall not be in love with me if I can prevent it."

"Elizabeth, you are not serious now."

Elizabeth struggled to check her smile. "I beg your pardon, I will try again. At present I am not in love with Mr. Wickham. No, I certainly am not. But he is, beyond all comparison, the most agreeable man I ever saw, especially when I am in his actual presence. Still, if he becomes really attached to me—well, I believe it will be better that he should not. I do see the imprudence of it. Oh! That abominable Mr. Darcy! If not for his actions against Mr. Wickham..."

Elizabeth sighed. "But such as things now stand for Mr. Wickham, the truth must be faced. My father's opinion of me does me the greatest honor, and I should be miserable to forfeit it. And yet, my father *is* partial to Mr. Wickham regardless of his present circumstances."

Mrs. Gardiner frowned and leaned forward, her lips parting as if to restate her warnings.

Elizabeth shook her head and held up a hand to stay her aunt's arguments. "My dear aunt, rest assured that I should be very sorry to be the means of making any of you unhappy. But since we see every day that where there is affection, young people are seldom withheld by immediate want of fortune from entering into engagements with each other, how can I promise to be wiser than so many of my fellow creatures if I am tempted? Or how am I even to know that it would be wisdom to resist? All that I can promise you, therefore, is not to be in a hurry. I will not be in a hurry to believe myself his first object. When I am in company with him, I will not be wishing. In short, I will do my best."

"Perhaps it will be as well if you discourage his coming here so very often. At least, you should not *remind* your mother of inviting him."

"As I did the other day," said Elizabeth with a conscious smile. "Very true, it will be wise of me to refrain from *that*. But do not imagine that he is always here so often. It is on your account that he has been so frequently invited this week. You know my mother's ideas as to the necessity of constant company for her friends. But really, and upon my honor, I will try to do what I think to be the wisest. And now I hope you are satisfied."

Her aunt assured her that she was, and Elizabeth having thanked her for the kindness of her hints, they parted, a wonderful instance of advice being given on such a point without being resented.

Mr. Collins returned into Hertfordshire soon after it had been quitted by the Gardiners and Jane. But as he took up his abode with the Lucases, his arrival was no great inconvenience to Mrs. Bennet. His marriage was now fast approaching, and she was at length so far resigned as to think it inevitable, and even repeatedly to say in an ill-natured tone, that she "*wished* they might be happy". Thursday was to be the wedding day, and on Wednesday Miss Lucas paid her farewell visit. When Charlotte rose to take leave, Elizabeth, ashamed of her mother's ungracious and reluctant good wishes, and sincerely affected herself, accompanied her out of the room.

As they went downstairs together, Charlotte said, "I shall depend on hearing from you very often, Eliza."

"*That* you certainly shall."

"And I have another favor to ask you. Will you come and see me?"

"We shall often meet, I hope, in Hertfordshire."

"I am not likely to leave Kent for some time. Promise me, therefore, to come to Hunsford. My father and Maria are coming to me in March. I hope you will consent to be of the party. Indeed, Eliza, you will be as welcome as either of them."

Elizabeth could not refuse, though she foresaw little pleasure in the visit.

The wedding took place. The bride and bridegroom set off for Kent from the church door, and everybody had as much to say and hear on the subject as usual. Elizabeth soon heard from her friend, and their correspondence was as regular and frequent as it had ever been. That it should be equally unreserved was impossible. Elizabeth could never address her without feeling that all the comfort of intimacy was over, and though determined not to slacken as a correspondent, it was for the sake of what had been rather than what was. Charlotte's first letters were received with a good deal of eagerness. There could not but be curiosity to know how she would speak of her new home, how she would like Lady Catherine, and how happy she would dare pronounce herself to be. Although when the letters were read, Elizabeth felt that

Charlotte expressed herself on every point exactly as she might have foreseen. She wrote cheerfully, seemed surrounded with comforts, and mentioned nothing which she could not praise. The house, furniture, neighborhood, and roads were all to her taste, and Lady Catherine's behavior was most friendly and obliging. It was Mr. Collins's picture of Hunsford and Rosings rationally softened, and Elizabeth perceived that she must wait for her own visit there to know the rest.

Jane had already written a few lines to her sister to announce their safe arrival in London, and when she wrote again, Elizabeth hoped it would be in her power to say something of the Bingleys. Her impatience for this second letter was as well rewarded as impatience generally is. Jane had been a week in town without either seeing or hearing from Caroline. She accounted for it, however, by supposing that her last letter to her friend from Longbourn had by some accident been lost.

Jane's letter continued:

"My aunt is going tomorrow into that part of the town, and I shall take the opportunity of calling in Grosvenor Street."

She wrote again when the visit was paid and she had seen Miss Bingley.

"I did not think Caroline in spirits, but she was very glad to see me and reproached me for giving her no notice of my coming to London. I was right, therefore; my last letter had never reached her. I inquired after their brother, of course. He was well, but so much engaged with Mr. Darcy that they scarcely ever saw him. I found that Miss Darcy was expected to dinner. I wish I could see her. My visit was not long, as Caroline and Mrs. Hurst were going out. I dare say I shall see them soon here."

Elizabeth shook her head over this letter. It convinced her that accident only could reveal to Mr. Bingley her sister's being in town.

Four weeks passed away, and Jane saw nothing of him. She endeavored to persuade herself that she did not regret it, but she could no longer be blind to Miss Bingley's inattention. After waiting at home every morning for a fortnight, and inventing every evening a fresh excuse for her, the visitor did at last appear. But the shortness of her stay, and yet more, the alteration of her manner would allow Jane to deceive herself no longer. The letter which she wrote on this occasion to her sister will prove what she felt.

"My dearest Lizzy will, I am sure, be incapable of triumphing in her better judgement at my expense when I confess myself to have been entirely deceived in Miss Bingley's regard for me. But, my dear sister, though the event has proved you right, do not think me obstinate if I still assert that, considering what her behavior was, my confidence was as natural as your suspicion. I do not at all comprehend her reason for wishing to be intimate with me. But if the same circumstances were to happen again, I am sure I should be deceived again.

Caroline did not return my visit till yesterday, and not a note, not a line, did I receive in the meantime. When she did come, it was very evident that she had no pleasure in it. She made a slight, formal apology for not calling before, said not a word of wishing to see me again, and was in every respect so altered a creature that when she went away I was perfectly resolved to continue the acquaintance no longer.

I pity, though I cannot help blaming her. She was very wrong in singling me out as she did. I can safely say that every advance to intimacy began on her side. But I pity her, because she must feel that she has been acting wrong, and because I am very sure that anxiety for her brother is the cause of it. I need not explain myself farther. Though *we* know this anxiety to be quite needless, yet if she feels it, it will easily account for her behavior to me. And so deservedly dear as he is to his sister, whatever anxiety she must feel on his behalf is natural and amiable. I cannot but wonder, however, at her having any such fears now, because, if he had at all cared about me, we must have met long ago. He knows of my being in town, I am certain, from something she said herself; and yet it would seem, by her manner of talking, as if she wanted to persuade herself that he is really partial to Miss Darcy.

I cannot understand it. If I were not afraid of judging harshly, I should be almost tempted to say that there is a strong appearance of duplicity in all this. But I will endeavor to banish every painful thought and think only of what will make me happy —your affection, and the invariable kindness of my dear uncle and aunt. Let me hear from you very soon. Miss Bingley said something of his never returning to Netherfield again, of giving up the house, but not with any certainty. We had better not mention it. I am extremely glad that you have such pleasant accounts from our friends at Hunsford. Pray go to see them with

116

Sir William and Maria. I am sure you will be very comfortable there.

Yours, etc."

This letter gave Elizabeth some pain. But her spirits returned as she considered that Jane would no longer be duped by the sister at least. All expectation from the brother was now absolutely over. She would not even wish for a renewal of his attentions. His character sunk on every review of it. As a punishment for him, as well as a possible advantage to Jane, she seriously hoped he might really soon marry Mr. Darcy's sister, as by Mr. Wickham's account, she would make him abundantly regret what he had thrown away.

Mrs. Gardiner about this time reminded Elizabeth of her promise concerning Mr. Wickham and required information. Elizabeth had such to send as might rather give contentment to her aunt than to herself. His apparent partiality had subsided. His attentions were over; he was the admirer of someone else. Elizabeth was watchful enough to see it all, but she could see it and write of it without material pain. Her heart had been but slightly touched, and her vanity was satisfied with believing that *she* would have been his only choice had fortune permitted it. The sudden acquisition of ten thousand pounds was the most remarkable charm of Miss King, the young lady to whom he was now rendering himself agreeable. But Elizabeth, less clear sighted perhaps in this case than in Charlotte's, did not quarrel with him for his wish of independence. Nothing, on the contrary, could be more natural. And while she was able to suppose that it cost him a few struggles to relinquish her, she was also ready to allow it a wise and desirable measure for both, and could very sincerely wish him happy.

All this was acknowledged to Mrs. Gardiner; and after relating the circumstances, she thus went on:

"I am now convinced, my dear aunt, that I have never been much in love. For had I really experienced that pure and elevating passion, I should at present detest his very name and wish him all manner of evil. But my feelings are not only cordial towards *him*, they are even impartial towards Miss King. I cannot find out that I hate her at all, or that I am in the least unwilling to think her a very good sort of girl. There can be no love in all this. My watchfulness has been effectual. And though I certainly should be a more interesting object to all my acquaintances were I distractedly in love with him, I cannot say that I regret my comparative insignificance. Importance may sometimes be purchased too dearly. Kitty and Lydia take his defection much more to heart than I do. They are young in the ways of the world, and not yet open to the mortifying conviction that handsome young men must have something to live on as well as the plain."

Chapter Sixteen

With no greater events than these in the Longbourn family, and otherwise diversified by little beyond the walks to Meryton, sometimes dirty and sometimes cold, did January and February pass away. March was to take Elizabeth to Hunsford. She had not at first thought very seriously of going thither. But Charlotte, she soon found, was depending on the plan, and she gradually learned to consider it herself with greater pleasure as well as greater certainty. Absence had increased her desire of seeing Charlotte again and weakened her disgust of Mr. Collins. There was novelty in the scheme, and as home could not be faultless with such a mother and such uncompanionable sisters, a little change was not unwelcome for its own sake. The journey would moreover give her a peep at Jane. In short, as the time drew near, she would have been very sorry for any delay. Everything, however, went on smoothly and was finally settled according to Charlotte's first sketch. She was to accompany Sir William and his second daughter. The improvement of spending a night in London was added in time, and the plan became as perfect as a plan could be.

The only pain was in leaving her father, who would certainly miss her, and who, when it came to the point, so little liked her going that he told her to write to him and almost promised to answer her letter.

The farewell between herself and Mr. Wickham was perfectly friendly, on his side even more. His present pursuit could not make him forget that Elizabeth had been the first to excite and to deserve his attention, the first to listen and to pity, the first to be admired; and in his manner of bidding her adieu, wishing her every enjoyment, reminding her of what she was to expect in Lady Catherine de Bourgh, and trusting their opinion of her—their opinion of everybody—would always coincide, there was a solicitude, an interest which she felt must ever attach her to him with a most sincere regard. She parted from him convinced that, whether married or single, he must always be her model of the amiable and pleasing.

Her fellow travelers the next day were not of a kind to make her think him less agreeable. Sir William Lucas and his daughter Maria, a good-humored girl but as empty-headed as himself, had nothing to say that could be worth hearing, and were listened to with about as much delight as the rattle of the chaise. Elizabeth loved absurdities, but she had known Sir William's too long. He could tell her nothing new of the wonders of his presentation and knighthood, and his civilities were worn out, like his information.

It was a journey of only twenty-four miles, and they began it so early as to be in Gracechurch Street by noon. As they drove to Mr. Gardiner's door, Jane was at a drawing room window watching their arrival. Wen they entered the passage she was there to welcome them, and Elizabeth, looking earnestly in her face, was pleased to see it healthful and lovely as ever. On the stairs were a troop of little boys and girls whose eagerness for their cousin's appearance would not allow them to wait in the drawing room, and whose shyness, as they had not seen her for a twelvemonth, prevented their coming lower. All was joy and kindness. The day passed most pleasantly away, the morning in bustle and shopping, and the evening at one of the theatres.

Elizabeth then contrived to sit by her aunt so that they might converse with ease before the play's beginning. Their first subject was her sister, and she was more grieved than astonished to hear, in reply to her minute inquiries, that though Jane always struggled to support her spirits, there were periods of dejection. It was reasonable, however, to hope that they would not continue long. In hushed murmurs concealed from others beneath the gathering's general noise, Mrs. Gardiner gave her the particulars also of Miss Bingley's visit in Gracechurch Street, and repeated conversations occurring at different times between Jane and herself which proved that the former had, from her heart, given up the acquaintance.

Mrs. Gardiner then rallied her niece on Mr. Wickham's desertion and complimented her on bearing it so well. She added, "But my dear Elizabeth, what sort of girl is Miss King? I should be sorry to think our friend mercenary."

"Pray, my dear aunt, what is the difference in matrimonial affairs between the mercenary and the prudent motive? Where does discretion end and avarice begin? Last Christmas you were afraid of his marrying me because it would be imprudent, and now, because he is trying to get a girl with only ten thousand pounds, you want to find out that he is mercenary."

"If you will only tell me what sort of girl Miss King is, I shall know what to think."

"She is a very good kind of girl, I believe. I know no harm of her."

"But he paid her not the smallest attention till her grandfather's death made her mistress of this fortune."

"No. Why should he? If it were not allowable for him to gain *my* affections because I had no money, what occasion could there be for making love to a girl whom he did not care about and who was equally poor?"

"But there seems an indelicacy in directing his attentions towards her so soon after this event."

"A man in distressed circumstances has not time for all those elegant decorums which other people may observe. If *she* does not object to it, why should *we*?"

"*Her* not objecting does not justify *him*. It only shows her being deficient in something herself—sense or feeling."

"Well!" cried Elizabeth amid quiet laughter. "Have it as you choose. *He* shall be mercenary, and *she* shall be foolish."

"No, Lizzy, that is what I do *not* choose. I should be sorry, you know, to think ill of a young man who has lived so long in Derbyshire."

"Oh! If that is all, I have a very poor opinion of young men who live in Derbyshire, and their intimate friends who live in Hertfordshire are not much better. I am sick of them all. Thank Heaven I am going tomorrow where I shall find a man who has not one agreeable quality, who has neither manner nor sense to recommend him. Stupid men are the only ones worth knowing after all."

Mrs. Gardiner shook her head at her niece's teasing and returned it in kind. "Take care, Lizzy. That speech savors strongly of disappointment."

The start of the play brought an end to their conversation.

Before they were separated by the play's conclusion, Elizabeth had the unexpected happiness of an invitation to accompany her uncle and aunt on a tour of pleasure which they proposed taking in the summer.

"We have not determined how far it shall carry us," said Mrs. Gardiner. "But, perhaps, to the Lakes."

No scheme could have been more agreeable to Elizabeth, and her acceptance of the invitation was most ready and grateful. "Oh, my dear, dear aunt, what delight! What felicity! You give me fresh life and vigor. Adieu to disappointment and spleen. What are young men to rocks and mountains?"

Every object in the next day's journey was new and interesting to Elizabeth, and her spirits were in a state of enjoyment, for she had seen her sister looking so well as to banish all fear for her health, and the prospect of her northern tour was a constant source of delight.

When they left the high road for the lane to Hunsford, every eye was in search of the Parsonage, and every turning expected to bring it in view. The palings of Rosings Park was their boundary on one side. Elizabeth smiled at the recollection of all that she had heard of its inhabitants.

At length the Parsonage was discernible. The garden sloping to the road, the house standing in it, the green pales, and the laurel hedge, everything declared they were arriving. Mr. Collins and Charlotte appeared at the door, and the carriage stopped at the small gate which led by a short gravel walk to the house, amidst the nods and smiles of the whole party. In a moment they were all out of the chaise, rejoicing at the sight of each other. Mrs. Collins welcomed her friend with the liveliest pleasure, and Elizabeth was more and more satisfied with coming when she found herself so affectionately received. She saw instantly that her cousin's manners were not altered by his marriage. His formal civility was just what it had been, and he detained her some minutes at the gate to hear and satisfy his inquiries after all her family. They were then, with no other delay than his pointing out the neatness of the entrance, taken into the house. As soon as they were in the parlor, he welcomed them a second time with ostentatious formality to his humble abode and punctually repeated all his wife's offers of refreshment before leading them on a tour of his garden.

From his garden, Mr. Collins would have led them round his two meadows as well. But the ladies, not having shoes to encounter the remains of a white frost, turned back. While Sir William accompanied him, Charlotte took her sister and friend over the house, extremely well pleased probably to have the opportunity of showing it without her husband's help. It was rather small but well built and convenient, and everything was fitted up and arranged with a neatness and consistency of which Elizabeth gave Charlotte all the credit. When Mr. Collins could be forgotten, there was really an air of great comfort throughout, and by Charlotte's evident enjoyment of it, Elizabeth supposed he must be often forgotten.

She had already learned that Lady Catherine was still in the country. It was spoken of again while they were at dinner.

Mr. Collins, joining into the conversation, observed, "Yes, Miss Elizabeth, you will have the honor of seeing Lady Catherine de Bourgh on the ensuing Sunday at church, and I need not say you will be delighted with her. She is all affability and condescension, and I doubt not but you will be honored with some portion of her notice when service is over. I have scarcely any hesitation in saying she will include you and my sister Maria in every invitation with which she honors us during your stay here. Her behavior to my dear Charlotte is charming. We dine at Rosings twice every week, and are never allowed to walk home. Her ladyship's carriage is regularly ordered for us."

"Lady Catherine is a very respectable, sensible woman indeed," added Charlotte. "And a most attentive neighbor."

"Very true, my dear, that is exactly what I say," Mr. Collins agreed. "She is the sort of woman whom one cannot regard with too much deference."

The evening was spent chiefly in talking over Hertfordshire news and telling again what had already been written. When it closed, Elizabeth, in the solitude of her chamber, had to meditate upon Charlotte's degree of contentment to understand her address in guiding, and composure in bearing with, her husband, and to acknowledge that it was all done very well. She had also to anticipate how her visit would pass, the quiet tenor of their usual employments, the vexatious interruptions of Mr. Collins, and the gaieties of their intercourse with Rosings. A lively imagination soon settled it all.

About the middle of the next day, as she was in her room getting ready for a walk, a sudden noise below seemed to speak the whole house in confusion. After listening a moment, she heard somebody running upstairs in a violent hurry and calling loudly after her.

She opened the door and met Maria in the landing place, who, breathless with agitation, cried out, "Oh, my dear Eliza! Pray make haste and come into the dining room, for there is such a sight to be seen! I will not tell you what it is. Make haste, and come down this moment."

Elizabeth asked questions in vain. Maria would tell her nothing more, and down they ran into the dining room, which fronted the lane, in quest of this wonder.

It was two ladies stopping in a low phaeton at the garden gate.

"Is this all?" cried Elizabeth. "I expected at least that the pigs were got into the garden, and here is nothing but Lady Catherine and her daughter."

"La!" said Maria, quite shocked at the mistake. "My dear, it is not Lady Catherine. The old lady is Mrs. Jenkinson, who lives with them. The other is Miss de Bourgh. Only look at her. She is quite a little creature. Who would have thought that she could be so thin and small?"

"She is abominably rude to keep Charlotte out of doors in all this wind. Why does she not come in?"

"Oh, Charlotte says she hardly ever does. It is the greatest of favors when Miss de Bourgh comes in."

"I like her appearance," said Elizabeth, struck with other ideas. "She looks sickly and cross. Yes, she will do for him very well. She will make him a very proper wife." And if, as Mr. Wickham had suggested, Mr. Darcy did indeed turn such a small and fragile person into a vampire like himself, she still could certainly do no one any harm.

Mr. Collins and Charlotte were both standing at the gate in conversation with the ladies; and Sir William, to Elizabeth's high diversion, was stationed in the doorway in earnest contemplation of the greatness before him and constantly bowing whenever Miss de Bourgh looked that way. Elizabeth found that she must cover her mouth to stifle a laugh.

At length there was nothing more to be said. The ladies drove on, and the others returned into the house. Mr. Collins no sooner saw the two girls at the window than he began to congratulate them on their good fortune, which Charlotte explained by letting them know that the whole party was asked to dine at Rosings the next day.

Though Elizabeth said nothing, she wondered if imagining tomorrow's dinner party would provide more entertainment than the actual event itself might provide. From Mr. Wickham's stories and warnings, Elizabeth expected Lady Catherine to be quite dull. She could only hope that her imagination might aide her equally well in getting her through what would surely be a long evening indeed.

Chapter Seventeen

Mr. Collins's triumph, in consequence of this invitation, was complete. The power of displaying the grandeur of his patroness to his wondering visitors, and of letting them see her civility towards himself and his wife, was exactly what he had wished for. That an opportunity of doing it should be given so soon was such an instance of Lady Catherine's condescension as he knew not how to admire enough.

"I confess," said he, "that I should not have been at all surprised by her ladyship's asking us on Sunday to drink tea and spend the evening at Rosings. I rather expected, from my knowledge of her affability, that it would happen. But who could have foreseen such an attention as this? Who could have imagined that we should receive an invitation to dine there so immediately after your arrival!"

"I am the less surprised at what has happened," replied Sir William, "from that knowledge of what the manners of the great really are, which my situation in life has allowed me to acquire. About the court, such instances of elegant breeding are not uncommon."

Scarcely anything was talked of the whole day or next morning but their visit to Rosings. Mr. Collins was carefully instructing them in what they were to expect, that the sight of such rooms, so many servants, and so splendid a dinner might not wholly overpower them.

When the ladies were separating for the toilette, he said to Elizabeth, "Do not make yourself uneasy, my dear cousin, about your apparel. Lady Catherine is far from requiring that elegance of dress in us which becomes herself and her daughter. I would advise you merely to put on whatever of your clothes is superior to the rest—there is no occasion for anything more. Lady Catherine will not think the worse of you for being simply dressed. She likes to have the distinction of rank preserved."

Elizabeth swallowed the urge to reply for fear of exactly what her response might be.

While they were dressing, he came two or three times to their different doors to recommend their being quick, as Lady Catherine very much objected to being kept waiting for her dinner. Such formidable accounts of her ladyship, and her manner of living, quite frightened Maria Lucas who had been little used to company, and she looked forward to her introduction at Rosings with as much apprehension as her father had done to his presentation at St. James's.

As the weather was fine, they had a pleasant walk of about half a mile across the park. Every park has its beauty and its prospects, and Elizabeth saw much to be pleased with, though she could not be in such raptures as Mr. Collins expected the scene to inspire, and was but slightly affected by his enumeration of the windows in front of the house and his relation of what the glazing altogether had originally cost Sir Lewis de Bourgh.

When they ascended the steps to the hall, Maria's alarm was every moment increasing, and even Sir William did not look perfectly calm. Elizabeth's courage did not fail her. She had heard nothing of Lady Catherine that spoke her awful from any extraordinary talents or miraculous virtue, and the mere stateliness of money or rank she thought she could witness without trepidation.

From the entrance hall, of which Mr. Collins pointed out with a rapturous air the fine proportion and the finished ornaments, they followed the servants through an antechamber to the room where Lady Catherine, her daughter, and Mrs. Jenkinson were sitting. Her ladyship, with great condescension, arose to receive them. As Mrs. Collins had settled it with her husband that the office of introduction should be hers, it was performed in a proper manner without any of those apologies and thanks which he would have thought necessary.

In spite of having been at St. James's, Sir William was so completely awed by the grandeur surrounding him that he had but just courage enough to make a very low bow and take his seat without saying a word. His younger daughter, frightened almost out of her senses, sat on the edge of her chair, not knowing which way to look. However, Elizabeth found herself quite equal to the scene and could observe the three ladies before her composedly. Lady Catherine was a tall, large woman with strongly-marked features which might once have been handsome. Her air was not conciliating, nor was her manner of receiving them such as to make her visitors forget their inferior rank. She was not rendered formidable by silence. Whatever she said was spoken in so authoritative a tone as marked her self-importance and brought Mr. Wickham immediately to Elizabeth's mind; and from the observation of the day altogether, she believed Lady Catherine to be exactly what he represented.

After examining the mother in whose countenance and deportment she soon found some resemblance of Mr. Darcy, she turned her eyes on the daughter and could almost have joined in Maria's astonishment at her being so thin and so small. There was neither in figure nor face any likeness between the ladies. Miss de Bourgh was pale and sickly. Her features, though not plain, were insignificant. And she spoke very little, except in a low voice, to Mrs. Jenkinson, in whose appearance there was nothing remarkable, and who was entirely engaged in listening to what she said and placing a screen in the proper direction before her eyes.

After sitting a few minutes, they were all sent to one of the windows to admire the view, Mr. Collins attending them to point out its beauties, and Lady Catherine kindly informing them that it was much better worth looking at in the summer. At that moment, a side door opened to admit the unexpected early arrival of none other than Mr. Darcy and a man who soon was introduced as Lady Catherine's second nephew Colonel Fitzwilliam.

Colonel Fitzwilliam, who led the way, was about thirty, not handsome, but in person and address most truly the gentleman. But as he was standing beside his cousin, Elizabeth found it difficult to observe him more closely. Her gaze was of a mind of its own and determined to dwell principally on the cousin she knew too much of for comfort.

Though Mr. Darcy stared at Elizabeth for a long moment immediately upon his arrival within the room, he soon turned his unsettling attention elsewhere and looked just as he had been used to look in Hertfordshire. He paid his compliments with his usual reserve to Mrs. Collins, and whatever might be his feelings toward her friend, met her with every appearance of composure. Elizabeth merely curtseyed to him without saying a word. Once she recovered from the shock of his arrival, she began to anticipate the amusement of seeing how hopeless Miss Bingley's designs on him were by his behavior toward his cousin Miss de Bourgh, for whom he was evidently destined.

They were all soon called to dinner, and Elizabeth considered it a great misfortune to have been seated at Mr. Darcy's right. Enduring his presence in the same room after so long an absence was difficult enough without the addition of such proximity.

At length, his civility was so far awakened as to inquire of Elizabeth after the health of her family.

She managed to answer him in the usual way, and after a moment's pause, added, "My eldest sister has been in town these three months. Have you never happened to see her there?"

She was perfectly sensible that he never had, but she wished to see whether he would betray any consciousness of what had passed between the Bingleys and Jane.

A slight frown deepened the corners of his mouth as he answered, "I have not been so fortunate as to meet Miss Bennet there."

At which point, the subject could be pursued no further, as Lady Catherine began her inquisition as to how many sisters Elizabeth had, whether they were older or younger than herself, whether any of them were likely to be married, whether they were handsome, where they had been educated, what carriage her father kept, and what had been her mother's maiden name?

Elizabeth felt all the impertinence of her questions but answered them very composedly, though the interrogation proceeded so rapidly without pause that she had not time to take even one sip of her soup.

The table fell into complete silence as the questions continued. To her left, Mr. Darcy grew so still that Elizabeth was reminded yet again of Mr. Wickham's stories regarding him. He seemed not even to breathe as he stared at his aunt.

Lady Catherine ignored him entirely, her sharp, beady gaze fixed upon Elizabeth as she observed, "Your father's estate is entailed on Mr. Collins, I think. For your sake," turning to Charlotte, "I am glad of it; but otherwise I see no occasion for entailing estates from the female line. It was not thought necessary in Sir Lewis de Bourgh's family. Do you play and sing, Miss Bennet?"

"A little."

"Oh! Then some time or other we shall be happy to hear you. Our instrument is a capital one, probably superior to your own. You shall try it some day. Do your sisters play and sing?"

"One of them does."

"Why did not you all learn? You ought all to have learned. The Miss Webbs all play, and their father has not so good an income as yours. Do you draw?"

"No, not at all."

"What, none of you?"

"Not one."

"That is very strange. But I suppose you had no opportunity. Your mother should have taken you to town every spring for the benefit of masters."

"My mother would have had no objection, but my father hates London."

"Has your governess left you?"

"We never had any governess."

"No governess! How was that possible? Five daughters brought up at home without a governess! I never heard of such a thing. Your mother must have been quite a slave to your education."

Elizabeth could hardly help smiling as she assured her that had not been the case.

"Then who taught you? Who attended to you? Without a governess, you must have been neglected."

"We were always encouraged to read and had all the masters that were necessary. Those who chose to be idle certainly might."

"Aye, no doubt; but that is what a governess will prevent, and if I had known your mother, I should have advised her most strenuously to engage one. I always say that nothing is to be done in education without steady and regular instruction, and nobody but a governess can give it. It is wonderful how many families I have been the means of supplying in that way. I am always glad to get a young person well placed out. Four nieces of Mrs. Jenkinson are most delightfully situated through my means; and it was but the other day that I recommended another young person, who was merely accidentally mentioned to me, and the family are quite delighted with her. Are any of your younger sisters out, Miss Bennet?"

"Yes, ma'am, all."

"All! What, all five out at once? Very odd! And you only the second. The younger ones out before the elder ones are married! Your younger sisters must be very young?"

"Yes, my youngest is not sixteen. Perhaps *she* is full young to be much in company. But really, ma'am, I think it would be very hard upon younger sisters to not have their share of society and amusement because the elder may not have the means or inclination to marry early. The last born has as good a right to the pleasures of youth as the first. And to be kept back on *such* a motive! I think it would not be very likely to promote sisterly affection or delicacy of mind."

"Upon my word," said her ladyship. "You give your opinion very decidedly for so young a person. Pray, what is your age?"

"With three younger sisters grown up," replied Elizabeth, smiling, "your ladyship can hardly expect me to own it."

Lady Catherine seemed quite astonished at not receiving a direct answer, and Elizabeth suspected herself to be the first creature who had ever dared to trifle with so much dignified impertinence.

To her left, she saw Mr. Darcy turn white, his mouth setting in restrained displeasure of some sort, perhaps in response to Elizabeth's refusal to answer his esteemed aunt.

Still, at least she was allowed a moment's peace in order to eat her soup at last.

When dinner was completed, they all adjourned to the drawing room, where there was little to be done but to hear Lady Catherine talk, which she did without any intermission till coffee came in, delivering her opinion on every subject in so decisive a manner as proved that she was not used to having her judgement controverted. She inquired into Charlotte's domestic concerns familiarly and minutely, gave her a great deal of advice as to the management of them all, told her how everything ought to be regulated in so small a family as hers, and instructed her as to the care of her cows and her poultry. Elizabeth found that nothing was beneath this great lady's attention which could furnish her with an occasion of dictating to others.

Elizabeth had the good fortune to be seated farthest from Lady Catherine and next to Colonel Fitzwilliam who, in contrast to his aunt and cousin, turned out to be quite a pleasure to converse with. Colonel Fitzwilliam seemed really glad to see them. Anything was a welcome relief to him at Rosings, and Mrs. Collins's friend seemed to have caught his fancy very much. He talked so agreeably of Kent and Hertfordshire, of traveling and staying at home, of new books and music, that Elizabeth had never been half so well entertained. They conversed with so much spirit and flow as to draw the attention of Lady Catherine herself, as well as of Mr. Darcy. *His* eyes had been soon and repeatedly turned towards them with a look of curiosity.

Her ladyship shared the feeling, which was more openly acknowledged after a while, for she did not scruple to call out, "What is

130

that you are saying, Fitzwilliam? What is it you are talking of? What are you telling Miss Bennet? Let me hear what it is."

"We are speaking of music, madam," said he when no longer able to avoid a reply.

"Of music! Then pray speak aloud. It is of all subjects my delight. I must have my share in the conversation if you are speaking of music. There are few people in England, I suppose, who have more true enjoyment of music than myself, or a better natural taste. If I had ever learned, I should have been a great proficient. And so would Anne, if her health had allowed her to apply. I am confident that she would have performed delightfully. Elizabeth, you spoke of your proficiency at dinner; demonstrate for us now."

Elizabeth protested, not from false modesty, but from fear of embarrassment. Her proficiency at the pianoforte was by no means high enough to secure the good esteem of more than her friend Mrs. Collins in such society as was held within this room. Yet Lady Catherine, as in all things, would not be denied, and assisted by Mr. Collins, succeeded in their enjoined demands to hear her play.

However, no sooner had Elizabeth's fingers begun to stumble over the keys than Lady Catherine proceeded to speak over the music by asking, "How does Georgiana get on, Darcy?"

Mr. Darcy spoke of his sister's proficiency with a mixture of affectionate praise and some embarrassment, possibly from his aunt's rudeness.

"I am very glad to hear such a good account of her," said Lady Catherine. "And pray tell her from me that she cannot expect to excel if she does not practice a good deal."

"I assure you, madam, that she does not need such advice. She practices constantly."

"So much the better. It cannot be done too much, and when I next write to her, I shall charge her not to neglect it on any account. I often tell young ladies that no excellence in music is to be acquired without constant practice. Mrs. Collins, though she has no instrument, is very welcome, as I have often told her, to come to Rosings every day and play on the pianoforte in Mrs. Jenkinson's room. She would be in nobody's way, you know, in that part of the house."

Mr. Darcy looked a little ashamed of his aunt's ill-breeding and made no answer other than to walk away from her, and making with his usual deliberation towards the pianoforte, stationed himself so as to command a full view of the fair performer's countenance.

Elizabeth saw what he was doing, and at the first convenient pause, turned to him with an arch smile and said, "You mean to frighten me, Mr. Darcy, by coming in all this state to hear me? I will not be alarmed though your sister *does* play so well. There is a stubbornness about me that never can bear to be frightened at the will of others. My courage always rises at every attempt to intimidate me."

Colonel Fitzwilliam joined them and drew a chair near her.

"I shall not say you are mistaken," replied Mr. Darcy, "because you could not really believe me to entertain any design of alarming you. I have had the pleasure of your acquaintance long enough to know that you find great enjoyment in occasionally professing opinions which in fact are not your own."

Elizabeth could not help but laugh heartily at this picture of herself and said to Colonel Fitzwilliam, "Your cousin will give you a very pretty notion of me and teach you not to believe a word I say. I am particularly unlucky in meeting with one so able to expose my real character in a part of the world where I had hoped to pass myself off with some degree of credit. Indeed, Mr. Darcy, it is very ungenerous of you to mention all that you knew to my disadvantage in Hertfordshire —and, give me leave to say, very impolitic too—for it is provoking me to retaliate, and such things may come out as will shock your relations to hear."

He grew still in that particular way he had, his gaze studying every inch of her expression before he replied, "I am not afraid of you."

Was he fearful that she knew his secret and might reveal it to his cousin? But this would mean that Colonel Fitzwilliam knew nothing of his cousin's changed nature. Impossible. He must only be wondering whether she knew of his secret at all.

"Pray let me hear what you have to accuse him of," cried Colonel Fitzwilliam. "I should like to know how he behaves among strangers."

Though she spoke to Colonel Fitzwilliam, she could not manage to turn her gaze away from Mr. Darcy's eyes. "You shall hear then—but prepare yourself for something very dreadful. The first time of my ever seeing him in Hertfordshire, you must know, was at a ball—and at this ball, what do you think he did? He danced only four dances, though gentlemen were scarce, and, to my certain knowledge, more than one young lady was sitting down in want of a partner. Mr. Darcy, you cannot deny the fact."

Colonel Fitzwilliam laughed in shock and shook his head in obvious disgust.

132

Mr. Darcy's eyes darkened with something akin to pain or regret, she knew not which or why. After some hesitation, he said, "I had not at that time the honor of knowing any lady in the assembly beyond my own party."

Whatever the expression within his eyes, the answering discomfort it produced in her drove her to lighten the conversation. She forced a smile. "True. And nobody can ever be introduced in a ballroom. Well, Colonel Fitzwilliam, what do I play next? My fingers await your orders."

"Perhaps I should have judged better had I sought an introduction," murmured Mr. Darcy. "But I am ill-qualified to recommend myself to strangers."

She was tempted to turn the conversation to one less obviously painful to him. But the earnestness in his gaze, in his tone and words, paired with the utterly nonsensical excuse he provided, pushed her to continue on.

Still addressing Colonel Fitzwilliam, she said, "Shall we ask your cousin the reason for this? Shall we ask Mr. Darcy why a man of sense and education, and who has lived in the world, is ill qualified to recommend himself to strangers?"

"I can answer your question without applying to him," replied Colonel Fitzwilliam. "It is because he will not give himself the trouble."

Mr. Darcy grew completely still again, his dark gaze unwavering from her own. "I certainly have not the talent which some people possess of conversing easily with those I have never seen before. I cannot catch their tone of conversation, or appear interested in their concerns, as I often see done."

"My fingers do not move over this instrument in the masterly manner which I see so many women's do," replied she without hesitation. "They have not the same force or rapidity, and do not produce the same expression. But then I have always supposed it to be my own fault—because I will not take the trouble of practicing. It is not that I do not believe *my* fingers as capable as any other woman's of superior execution."

At last, the corners of Mr. Darcy's mouth rose into a partial smile. "You are perfectly right. You have employed your time much better. No one admitted to the privilege of hearing you can think anything wanting. We neither of us enjoy performing to strangers."

Here they were interrupted by Lady Catherine, who called out to know what they were talking of. Elizabeth immediately began playing again.

Lady Catherine approached, and, after listening for a few minutes, said to Mr. Darcy, "Miss Bennet would not play at all amiss if she practiced more and could have the advantage of a London master. She has a very good notion of fingering, though her taste is not equal to Anne's. Anne would have been a delightful performer, had her health allowed her to learn."

Elizabeth looked at Mr. Darcy to see how cordially he assented to his cousin's praise. But neither at that moment nor at any other could she discern any symptom of love. And from the whole of his behavior to Miss de Bourgh she derived this comfort for Miss Bingley, that he might have been just as likely to marry *her*, had she been his relation.

Lady Catherine continued her remarks on Elizabeth's performance, mixing with them many instructions on execution and taste. Elizabeth received them with all the forbearance of civility, and, at the request of the gentlemen, remained at the instrument till her ladyship's carriage was ready to take them all home.

Chapter Eighteen

Elizabeth was sitting by herself the next morning and writing to Jane while the others were gone on business into the village, when she was startled by a ring at the door, the certain signal of a visitor. As she had heard no carriage, she thought it not unlikely to be Lady Catherine. Under that apprehension, she was putting away her half-finished letter that she might escape all impertinent questions, when the door opened, and, to her very great surprise, Mr. Darcy, and Mr. Darcy only, entered the room.

He seemed astonished too on finding her alone and apologized for his intrusion by letting her know that he had understood all the ladies were to be within. At first, no little amount of alarm passed through her at the thought of being alone with him as she remembered all of Mr. Wickham's claims regarding Mr. Darcy's monstrous side. After a moment, however, she also recalled that the maid must be close by and aware of Mr. Darcy's arrival. So too had Mr. Darcy always shown great restraint upon the darker side of his nature while in her company. Thus reassured of her probable safety, she was able to smile and be polite once more.

They then sat down, and when her inquiries after Rosings were made, seemed in danger of sinking into total silence. It was absolutely necessary, therefore, to think of something, and in this emergence recollecting *when* she had seen him last in Hertfordshire, and feeling curious to know what he would say on the subject of their hasty departure, she observed:

"How very suddenly you all quitted Netherfield last November, Mr. Darcy! It must have been a most agreeable surprise to Mr. Bingley to see you all after him so soon. For, if I recollect right, he went but the day before. He and his sisters were well, I hope, when you left London?"

"Perfectly so, I thank you."

She found that she was to receive no other answer, and, after a short pause added, "I think I have understood that Mr. Bingley has not much idea of ever returning to Netherfield again?"

"I have never heard him say so, but it is probable that he may spend very little of his time there in the future. He has many friends and is at a time of life when friends and engagements are continually increasing."

"If he means to be but little at Netherfield, it would be better for the neighborhood that he should give up the place entirely, for then we might possibly get a settled family there. But perhaps Mr. Bingley did not take the house so much for the convenience of the neighborhood as for his own, and we must expect him to keep it or quit it on the same principle."

"I should not be surprised if he were to give it up as soon as any eligible purchase offers."

Elizabeth made no answer. She was afraid of talking longer of his friend, and having nothing else to say, was now determined to leave the trouble of finding a subject to him.

He took the hint and soon began with, "This seems a very comfortable house. Lady Catherine, I believe, did a great deal to it when Mr. Collins first came to Hunsford."

"I believe she did—and I am sure she could not have bestowed her kindness on a more grateful object." She smiled.

"Mr. Collins appears to be very fortunate in his choice of a wife, and it must be very agreeable for her to be settled within so easy a distance of her own family and friends."

"An easy distance, do you call it? It is nearly fifty miles." Surely he was jesting?

"And what is fifty miles of good road? Little more than half a day's journey. Yes, I call it a *very* easy distance." The corners of his mouth softened into nearly a smile.

"I should never have considered the distance as one of the *advantages* of the match. I should never have said Mrs. Collins was settled *near* her family."

She had hoped that start of a smile would form into a fully fledged one at her continued teasing. Instead, his expression turned watchful.

"It is a proof of your own attachment to Hertfordshire. Anything beyond the very neighborhood of Longbourn, I suppose, would appear far."

He must be supposing her to be thinking of Jane and Netherfield. She blushed as she answered, "I do not mean to say that a woman may not be settled too near her family. The far and the near must be relative, and depend on many varying circumstances. Where there is fortune to make the expenses of traveling unimportant, distance becomes no evil. But that is not the case *here*. Mr. and Mrs. Collins have a comfortable income, but not such a one as will allow for frequent journeys—and I am persuaded my friend would not call herself *near* her family under less than *half* the present distance."

Mr. Darcy drew his chair a little towards her, and said, "*You* cannot have a right to such very strong local attachment. *You* cannot have been always at Longbourn."

Surprised, Elizabeth searched his countenance for meaning.

The gentleman experienced some change of feeling; he drew back his chair, took a newspaper from the table, and glancing over it, said in a colder voice, "Are you pleased with Kent?"

A short dialogue on the subject of the country ensued, on either side calm and concise—and soon put an end to by the entrance of Charlotte and her sister just returned from their walk. The tete-a-tete surprised them. Mr. Darcy related the mistake which had occasioned his intruding on Miss Bennet, and after sitting a few minutes longer without saying much to anybody, went away.

"What can be the meaning of this?" said Charlotte as soon as he was gone. "My dear, Eliza, he must be in love with you, or he would never have called on us in this familiar way."

But when Elizabeth told of his silence, it did not seem very likely even to Charlotte's wishes to be the case. After various conjectures, they could at last only suppose his visit to proceed from the difficulty of finding anything to do, which was the more probable from the time of year. All field sports were over. Within doors there was Lady Catherine, books, and a billiard table.

But gentlemen cannot always be within doors, and in the nearness of the Parsonage, or the pleasantness of the walk to it, or of the people who lived in it, the two cousins found a temptation from this period of walking thither almost every day. They called at various times of the morning, sometimes separately, sometimes together, and now and then accompanied by their aunt. It was plain to them all that Colonel

Fitzwilliam came because he had pleasure in their society, a persuasion which of course recommended him still more. Elizabeth was reminded by her own satisfaction in being with Colonel Fitzwilliam, as well as by his evident admiration of her, of her former favorite George Wickham. And though in comparing them she saw there was less captivating softness in Colonel Fitzwilliam's manners, she believed he might have the best informed mind.

But why Mr. Darcy came so often to the Parsonage it was more difficult to understand. It could not be for society, as he frequently sat there ten minutes together without opening his lips. And when he did speak, it seemed the effect of necessity rather than of choice—a sacrifice to propriety, not a pleasure to himself. He seldom appeared really animated, which Elizabeth privately attributed of course to his being a vampire, a secret she continued to withhold from her friend.

Mrs. Collins knew not what to make of him. Colonel Fitzwilliam's occasionally laughing at his cousin's stupidity proved that he was generally different, which her own knowledge of him could not have told her. As she would like to have believed this change the effect of love, and the object of that love her friend Eliza, she set herself seriously to work to find it out. She watched Mr. Darcy whenever they were at Rosings and whenever he came to Hunsford, but without much success. He certainly looked at her friend a great deal, but the expression of that look was disputable. It was an earnest, steadfast gaze, but she often doubted whether there were much admiration in it, and sometimes it seemed nothing but absence of mind.

She had once or twice suggested to Elizabeth the possibility of his being partial to her, but Elizabeth always laughed at the idea. And Mrs. Collins did not think it right to press the subject from the danger of raising expectations which might only end in disappointment. In her kind schemes for Elizabeth, she sometimes planned her marrying Colonel Fitzwilliam instead. He was beyond comparison the most pleasant man. He certainly admired her, and his situation in life was most eligible. But to counterbalance these advantages, Mr. Darcy had considerable patronage in the church, and his cousin could have none at all.

More than once did Elizabeth, in her ramble within the park, unexpectedly meet Mr. Darcy. At first, she felt all the perverseness of the mischance that should bring him where no one else was brought, and to prevent its ever happening again, took care to inform him that it was a favorite haunt of hers. How it could occur a second time, therefore, was very odd! Yet it did, and even a third, and from that point she began to take great care in only walking within Charlotte's view from her parlor windows at the Parsonage.

These unexpected meetings seemed like willful ill-nature, or a voluntary penance, for on these occasions it was not merely a few formal inquiries and an awkward pause and then away, but he actually thought it necessary to turn back and walk with her. He never said a great deal, nor did she give herself the trouble of talking much. But it struck her in the course of their third reconnoiter that he was asking some odd, unconnected questions—about her pleasure in being at Hunsford, her love of solitary walks, and her opinion of Mr. and Mrs. Collins's happiness. Still, in spite of the odd questions he sometimes posed, it was amusing to find that two people could manage to walk in a somewhat companionable state together despite having so little to say to one another. Anyone else would have insisted upon chattering about anything and everything possible, thus marring the simple beauty of the park and all its natural sounds. Mr. Darcy's questions were so far apart in their appearances that they never failed to startle her, and seemed almost to have been involuntarily voiced thoughts on their speaker's part.

More surprisingly, Mr. Darcy's silences were not always of a dark and unhappy nature. She often found him partially smiling at times, when he wasn't bearing his usual thoughtful frown. And there was a certain peace in their shared silences that was not often found at Longbourn, which afforded her mind the opportunity to reflect deeper upon her thoughts with the ease with which she was used to only finding upon her solitary walks at home.

In short, after yet another of these unexpected meetings, she found that she could not quite regret having to share her walks with someone as quiet and understanding of the value of silence as Mr. Darcy.

She was engaged one day as she walked in perusing Jane's last letter and dwelling on some passages which proved that Jane had not written in spirits, when, instead of being again surprised by Mr. Darcy, she saw on looking up that Colonel Fitzwilliam was meeting her.

Putting away the letter immediately and forcing a smile to cover her disappointment, for now she would be forced to display her wit through lively conversation, she said, "I did not know before that you ever walked this way."

"I have been making the tour of the park, as I generally do every year, and intend to close it with a call at the Parsonage. Are you going much farther?"

"No, I should have turned in a moment."

And accordingly she did turn, and they walked towards the Parsonage together.

"Do you certainly leave Kent on Saturday?" said she.

"Yes, if Darcy does not put it off again. But I am at his disposal. He arranges the business just as he pleases."

Thus all of Charlotte's kind hopes for her and Colonel Fitzwilliam must be ended. Yet Elizabeth found that, as with Mr. Wickham, she was not pained in the least at the loss of such hopes. Colonel Fitzwilliam was simply another gentleman who proved to be of great wit, charm, and entertaining to converse with, and nothing more.

She smiled. "And if not able to please himself in the arrangement, he has at least pleasure in the great power of choice. I do not know anybody who seems more to enjoy the power of doing what he likes than Mr. Darcy."

"He likes to have his own way very well," replied Colonel Fitzwilliam with a laugh. "But so we all do. It is only that he has better means of having it than many others because he is rich and many others are poor. I speak feelingly. A younger son, you know, must be inured to self-denial and dependence."

"In my opinion, the younger son of an earl can know very little of either. Now seriously, what have you ever known of self-denial and dependence? When have you been prevented by want of money from going wherever you chose or procuring anything you had a fancy for?"

He laughed again. "These are home questions—and perhaps I cannot say that I have experienced many hardships of that nature. But in matters of greater weight, I may suffer from want of money. Younger sons cannot marry where they like."

"Unless where they like women of fortune, which I think they very often do."

"Our habits of expense make us too dependent, and there are not many in my rank of life who can afford to marry without some attention to money."

"Is this," thought Elizabeth, "meant for me?" She colored at the idea, but recovering herself, said in a lively tone, "And pray, what is the usual price of an earl's younger son? Unless the elder brother is very sickly, I suppose you would not ask above fifty thousand pounds."

He answered her in the same style, and the subject dropped.

To interrupt a silence which might make him fancy her affected with what had passed, she soon afterwards said, "I imagine your cousin brought you down with him chiefly for the sake of having someone at his disposal. I wonder he does not marry to secure a lasting convenience of that kind. But perhaps his sister does as well for the present, and as she is under his sole care, he may do what he likes with her." She was of course alluding to Mr. Darcy's monstrous nature and its resulting dietary needs, and wondering if Colonel Fitzwilliam was acquainted with such secret knowledge of his cousin.

"No," said Colonel Fitzwilliam. "That is an advantage which he must divide with me. I am joined with him in the guardianship of Miss Darcy."

She studied him from the corner of her eye. Could he mean that he too was a vampire? Oh, surely not, for if so, she would have sensed that great pull of unsettling gravity that always drew her towards Mr. Darcy when in his presence. No, Colonel Fitzwilliam must be referring to something else. But why would Miss Darcy have need of not one but two guardians? Could it be possible that Mr. Wickham's fears for Miss Darcy had a foundation, and that Mr. Darcy had committed an even more heinous crime in passing on his dark nature to his sister as well? Could she be a young, blood thirsty vampire in need of two guardians to keep her inhuman behavior in hand?

"Are you indeed?" She fought to maintain a light tone. "And pray what sort of guardians do you make? Does your charge give you much trouble? Young ladies of her age are sometimes a little difficult to manage, and if she has the true Darcy spirit, she may like to have her own way."

As she spoke she observed him looking at her earnestly, and the sharp manner in which he immediately asked her why she supposed Miss Darcy likely to give them any uneasiness, convinced her that she had somehow or other got pretty near the truth. Miss Darcy, a vampire as well! And most probably at the hands of her own brother!

Cold chills spread over her skin, forcing her to suppress a shudder of horror. She swallowed and with great difficulty said, "You need not be frightened. I never heard any harm of her, and I dare say she is one of the most tractable creatures in the world. She is a very great favorite with some ladies of my acquaintance, Mrs. Hurst and Miss Bingley. I think I have heard you say that you know them."

"I know them a little. Their brother is a pleasant gentlemanlike man—he is a great friend of Darcy's."

"Oh! Yes," said Elizabeth drily. "Mr. Darcy is uncommonly kind to Mr. Bingley and takes a prodigious deal of care of him."

"Care of him! Yes, I really believe Darcy *does* take care of him in those points where he most wants care. From something that he told me in our journey hither, I have reason to think Bingley very much indebted to him. But I ought to beg his pardon, for I have no right to suppose that Bingley was the person meant. It was all conjecture."

"What is it you mean?"

"It is a circumstance which Darcy could not wish to be generally known, because if it were to get round to the lady's family, it would be an unpleasant thing."

"You may depend upon my not mentioning it."

"And remember that I have not much reason for supposing it to be Bingley. What he told me was merely this: that he congratulated himself on having lately saved a friend from the inconveniences of a most imprudent marriage, but without mentioning names or any other particulars. I only suspected it to be Bingley from believing him the kind of young man to get into a scrape of that sort, and from knowing them to have been together the whole of last summer."

"Did Mr. Darcy give you reasons for this interference?"

"I understood that there were some very strong objections against the lady."

"And what arts did he use to separate them?"

"He did not talk to me of his own arts," said Colonel Fitzwilliam, smiling. "He only told me what I have now told you."

Elizabeth made no answer and walked on, her heart swelling with indignation. It was exactly as she had expected.

After watching her a little, Fitzwilliam asked her why she was so thoughtful.

"I am thinking of what you have been telling me," said she. "Your cousin's conduct...does not suit my feelings. Why was he to be the judge?"

"You are rather disposed to call his interference officious?"

"I do not see what right Mr. Darcy had to decide on the propriety of his friend's inclination, or why, upon his own judgement alone, he was to determine and direct in what manner his friend was to be happy. But," she continued, recollecting herself, "as we know none of the particulars, it is not fair to condemn him. It is not to be supposed that there was much affection in the case."

"That is not an unnatural surmise. But it is a sad lessening of the honor of my cousin's triumph."

This was spoken jestingly; but it appeared to her so just a picture of Mr. Darcy that she would not trust herself with an answer, and therefore, abruptly changing the conversation, talked on indifferent matters until they reached the Parsonage. There, shut into her own room as soon as their visitor left them, she could think without interruption of all that she had heard.

It was not to be supposed that any other people could be meant than those with whom she was connected. There could not exist in the world *two* men over whom Mr. Darcy could have such boundless influence. That he had been concerned in the measures taken to separate Mr. Bingley and Jane she had never doubted. But she had always attributed to Miss Bingley the principal design and arrangement of them. If his own vanity, however, did not mislead him, *he* was the cause, his pride and caprice were the cause of all that Jane had suffered, and still continued to suffer. He had ruined for a while every hope of happiness for the most affectionate, generous heart in the world, and no one could say how lasting an evil he might have inflicted.

"There were some very strong objections against the lady," were Colonel Fitzwilliam's words. And those strong objections probably were her having one uncle who was a country attorney, and another who was in business in London.

"To Jane herself," she exclaimed to the empty room, "there could be no possibility of objection; all loveliness and goodness as she is! Her understanding excellent, her mind improved, and her manners captivating. Neither could anything be urged against my father, who, though with some peculiarities, has abilities Mr. Darcy himself need not disdain, and respectability which he will probably never reach." When she thought of her mother, her confidence gave way a little. But she would not allow that any objections *there* had material weight with Mr. Darcy, whose pride, she was convinced, would receive a deeper wound from the want of importance in his friend's connections than from their want of sense. She was quite decided at last that he had been partly governed by this worst kind of pride, and partly by the wish of retaining Mr. Bingley for his sister.

The agitation and tears which the subject occasioned brought on a headache, and it grew so much worse towards the evening that, added to her unwillingness to see Mr. Darcy, it determined her not to attend her cousins to Rosings, where they were engaged to drink tea. Mrs. Collins, seeing that she was really unwell, did not press her to go and as much as possible prevented her husband from pressing her. But Mr. Collins could not conceal his apprehension of Lady Catherine's being rather displeased by her staying at home.

Chapter Nineteen

When they were gone, Elizabeth chose for her employment the examination of all the letters which Jane had written to her since her being in Kent. They contained no actual complaint, nor was there any revival of past occurrences or any communication of present suffering. But in all, and in almost every line of each, there was a want of that cheerfulness which had been used to characterize her style, and which, proceeding from the serenity of a mind at ease with itself and kindly disposed towards everyone, had been scarcely ever clouded. Elizabeth noticed every sentence conveying the idea of uneasiness, with an attention which it had hardly received on the first perusal. Mr. Darcy's shameful boast of what misery he had been able to inflict gave her a keener sense of her sister's sufferings.

As if nature itself felt her pain, the heavy clouds that had been gathering all day gave way to a downpour. The pattering of the raindrops against the windows usually gave her great pleasure with their soothing rhythms. Yet they offered no happiness today. Consolation could only come from the thought that Mr. Darcy's visit to Rosings was to end on the day after the next—and a still greater consolation came from the fact that in less than a fortnight she should herself be with Jane again and enabled to contribute to the recovery of her spirits by all that affection could do.

While attempting to settle her mind with such reassurances, she was suddenly roused by the sound of the doorbell, and to her utter amazement she saw Mr. Darcy walk into the room, his hair and clothing dripping from the rain.

In a hurried manner he immediately began an inquiry after her health, imputing his visit to a wish of hearing that she were better. She answered him with cold civility. He sat down for a few moments, and then getting up, walked about the room. Elizabeth was surprised but said not a word.

After a silence of several minutes, he came towards her in an agitated manner, and thus began, "In vain I have struggled. It will not do. My feelings will not be repressed. You must allow me to tell you how ardently I admire and love you."

Elizabeth's astonishment was beyond expression. She stared, colored, doubted, and was silent.

This he considered sufficient encouragement to continue. "I know this is wrong, that what I feel and hope is wrong and goes against all reason, against my very character. I have struggled for months now against such feelings. But I can bear the torment no longer. I came to Rosings only to see you, to tell you that it no longer matters...the degradation and inferiority of your birth, your family, your want of connections, nor any other obstacle that stands between us. Against my better judgement, I love you. I must ask for your hand in marriage."

As he spoke with eyes both softened and darkened by the tormented love he professed to feel, in spite of her deeply-rooted dislike, she could not be insensible to the compliment of such a man's affection. And though her intentions did not vary for an instant, she was at first sorry for the pain he was to receive, till roused to resentment by his subsequent language, she lost all compassion in anger. She tried, however, to compose herself to answer him with patience when he should have done, for after all, he was supposedly a vampire of boundless strength and speed, and she was but a mortal who could be crushed in an instant if he so chose.

Upon his conclusion wherein he expressed his hope for her hand, however, she could easily see that he had no doubt of a favorable answer. He *spoke* of apprehension and anxiety, but his countenance expressed real security, and, too, he had yet to admit to his immortal state of existence, as if he had no intention of revealing the truth even to the woman he professed to love.

Such a circumstance could only exasperate farther, and when he ceased speaking, the color rose into her cheeks, and she said, "In such cases as this, it is, I believe, the established mode to express a sense of obligation for the sentiments avowed, however unequally they may be returned. It is natural that obligation should be felt, and if I could *feel*

146

gratitude, I would now thank you. But I cannot—I have never desired your good opinion, and you have certainly bestowed it most unwillingly. I am sorry to have occasioned pain to anyone. It has been most unconsciously done, however, and I hope will be of short duration. The feelings which you tell me have long prevented the acknowledgment of your regard can have little difficulty in overcoming it after this explanation."

Mr. Darcy, who was leaning against the mantelpiece with his eyes fixed on her face, seemed to catch her words with no less resentment than surprise. His complexion became pale with anger, and the disturbance of his mind was visible in every feature. He was struggling for the appearance of composure, and would not allow himself to speak till he believed himself to have attained it. The pause was to Elizabeth's feelings dreadful.

At length, with a voice of forced calmness, he took three steps closer to her and said, "And this is all the reply which I am to have the honor of expecting! I might wish to be informed why, with so little endeavor at civility, I am thus rejected."

Forgetting herself in her fury, she took a step closer to him. "I might as well inquire why with so evident a desire of offending and insulting me, you chose to tell me that you liked me against your will, against your reason, and even against your character? Was not this some excuse for incivility, if I *was* uncivil? But I have other provocations. You know I have."

"Such as?"

"Had not my feelings decided against you—had they been indifferent, or had they even been favorable, do you think that any consideration would tempt me to accept a vile monster who has been the means of ruining, perhaps forever, the happiness of a most beloved sister?"

As she pronounced these words, Mr. Darcy changed color. But the emotion was short, and he listened without attempting to interrupt her while she continued.

"I have every reason in the world to think ill of you. No motive can excuse the unjust and ungenerous part you acted *there*. You dare not, you cannot deny, that you have been the principal, if not the only means of dividing them from each other—of exposing one to the censure of the world for caprice and instability, and the other to its derision for disappointed hopes, and involving them both in misery of the acutest kind."

147

She paused and saw with no slight indignation that he was listening with an air which proved him wholly unmoved by any feeling of remorse. What monstrous indifference to human emotions was thus on display! Had he no heart left in that immortal body of his?

"Can you deny that you have done it?" repeated she.

With assumed tranquility he then replied, "I have no wish of denying that I did everything in my power to separate my friend from your sister, or that I rejoice in my success. Towards *him* I have been kinder than towards myself."

Her hands fisted; she stepped closer to him. Cold droplets of rain fell from his hair to her cheek and nose, barely noticed.

"But it is not merely this affair on which my dislike is founded," continued she. "Long before it had taken place my opinion of you was decided. Your character was unfolded in the recital which I received many months ago from Mr. Wickham. On this subject, what can you have to say? In what imaginary act of friendship can you here defend yourself? Or under what misrepresentation can you here impose upon others?"

His color further lessened till all resemblance of human health had at last left him. He closed the distance between them with one final step and said through clenched teeth, "You take an eager interest in that gentleman's concerns."

"Who that knows what his misfortunes have been can help feeling an interest in him?" His nearness had at last succeeded in making her tremble, though she knew not whether such a reaction proceeded from fear, fury, or something else that made her heart race.

"His misfortunes!" hissed Mr. Darcy. "Oh yes, his misfortunes have been great indeed."

"And at your infliction," cried Elizabeth with energy. "You have reduced him to his present state of poverty—comparative poverty. You have withheld the advantages which you must know to have been designed for him. You have deprived the best years of his life of that independence which was no less his due than his dessert. You have done all this! And yet you can treat the mention of his misfortune with contempt and ridicule. And this is making no mention of certain other dark, amoral aspects of your changed nature."

At her final accusation, she watched his face most carefully and noted the rapid succession of first surprise, then resignation, followed closely by fury. "He told you everything?"

"He told me what you are, and I have learned of what you have done to your sister as well." She was surprised to discover a deep yearning within her to hear his denial.

Instead, she had just enough time to hear his quick indrawn breath through parted lips and to see a hint of two sharp teeth before he turned away. Fangs.

It was true. All of it. He was a vampire. He had turned his sister, of whose protection he was responsible, into a vampire as well. All that he was reputed to have done against Mr. Wickham...it was all true.

She took a stumbling step backward, reaching for the table to brace a hand against.

A single drop of rain splashed against her cheek. She looked up. He had closed the distance between them, and she hadn't heard a sound. Yet he did not touch her or attempt to.

He did not have to in order to make her tremble before him. But what she had once told him at Rosings was also the truth...she did not take kindly to anyone's attempts to frighten her, and she would not allow him to do so now. Resolutely, she raised her chin and met his gaze, so dark now she did not know how she could have ever wondered at Mr. Wickham's warnings regarding him.

"And this is your opinion of me!" murmured he, his cool breath whispering over her forehead. "This is the estimation in which you hold me! I thank you for explaining it so fully. My faults, according to this calculation, are heavy indeed! But perhaps," he paused, his gaze searching over her face before lingering at her lips, "these offenses might have been overlooked if not for your prejudice against my kind and had not your pride been hurt by my honest confession of the scruples that had long prevented my forming any serious design. These bitter accusations might have been suppressed had I, with greater policy, concealed my struggles and flattered you into the belief of my being impelled by unqualified, unalloyed inclination; by reason, by reflection, by everything. But disguise of every sort is my abhorrence, which I endeavor to avoid when at all possible. Nor am I ashamed of the feelings I related. They were natural and just. Could you expect me to rejoice in the inferiority of your connections? To congratulate myself on the hope of relations, whose condition in life is so decidedly beneath my own?"

Prejudiced? She? How utterly ridiculous! If his actions had been right and good towards others, she would not care one whit that he was a vampire.

149

Elizabeth felt herself growing more angry every moment, yet she tried to the utmost to speak with composure when she said, "You are mistaken, Mr. Darcy, if you suppose that the mode of your declaration affected me in any other way than as it spared the concern which I might have felt in refusing you had you behaved in a more *gentlemanlike* manner."

She saw him start at this, but he said nothing, and she continued.

"However, being what you are, you could not have made the offer of your hand in any possible way that would have tempted me to accept it."

"Because I am a vampire," murmured he.

"No, sir."

Again his astonishment was obvious as he looked at her with an expression of mingled incredulity and confusion.

She went on. "From the very beginning—from the first moment, I may almost say—of my acquaintance with you, your manners, your arrogance, your conceit, and your selfish disdain of the feelings of others, were such as to form the groundwork of disapprobation on which succeeding events have built so immovable a dislike. I had not known you a month before I felt that you were the last creature in the world whom I could ever be prevailed on to marry."

He searched her eyes, and the pain in them was nearly enough to be the undoing of her anger, which never lasted long anyways. His head inclined towards her, and she found herself leaning towards him, on the verge of needing to brace her hands on his chest to prevent falling over, before he drew in a breath and spoke.

"You have said quite enough, madam. I perfectly comprehend your feelings, and have now only to be ashamed of what my own have been. Forgive me for having taken up so much of your time, and accept my best wishes for your health and happiness."

And with these words he turned and left the room in a blur, at one moment there before her, the next outside on his horse riding away in the rain as fast as the animal could carry him.

The tumult of her mind was now painfully great. She knew not how to support herself, and from actual weakness sat down and cried in the growing darkness for half an hour. Her astonishment, as she reflected on what had passed, was increased by every review of it. That she should receive an offer of marriage from Mr. Darcy, who had just moments ago all but admitted that he was a vampire! That he, with his black heart, should have managed to be in love with her for so many months! So much in love as to wish to marry her in spite of all the objections which had made him prevent his friend's marrying her sister, and which must appear at least with equal force in his own case—was almost incredible! It was gratifying to have inspired unconsciously so strong an affection, even in one who enjoyed the bliss of an eternal life in return for others' sacrifices of precious blood. Yet even that could perhaps be overlooked, if such sacrifices were willingly given, had he not been found so wanting, so deficient in human character and actions towards others. But his pride, his abominable pride—his shameless avowal of what he had done with respect to Jane and his uncaring lack of refute to the charge of his turning his sister into a vampire—his unpardonable assurance in acknowledging, though he could not justify it, and the cold, unfeeling manner in which he had mentioned Mr. Wickham, his monstrous cruelty towards whom he had not attempted to deny, soon overcame the pity which the consideration of his attachment had for a moment excited. She continued in very agitated reflections till the sound of Lady Catherine's carriage made her feel how unequal she was to encounter Charlotte's observation, and hurried her away to her room.

Chapter Twenty

Elizabeth awoke the next morning to the same thoughts and meditations which had at length closed her eyes. She could not yet recover from the surprise of what had happened. It was impossible to think of anything else. Totally indisposed for employment, she resolved soon after breakfast to indulge herself in air and exercise. She was proceeding directly to her favorite walk, when the recollection of Mr. Darcy's sometimes coming there stopped her, and instead of entering the park, she turned up the lane, which led farther from the turnpike-road. The park paling was still the boundary on one side, and she soon passed one of the gates into the ground.

After walking two or three times along that part of the lane, she was tempted, by the pleasantness of the morning, to stop at the gates and look into the park. The five weeks which she had now passed in Kent had made a great difference in the country, and every day was adding to the verdure of the early trees. She was on the point of continuing her walk when she caught a glimpse of a gentleman within the sort of grove which edged the park. He was moving that way, and fearful of its being Mr. Darcy, she was directly retreating.

But the person who advanced was now near enough to see her, and stepping forward with eagerness, pronounced her name.

She had turned away; but on hearing herself called, though in a voice which proved it to be Mr. Darcy, she moved again towards the gate.

He had by that time reached it also, and, holding out a letter, which she instinctively took, said, with a look of haughty composure, "I have been walking in the grove some time in the hope of meeting you. Will you do me the honor of reading that letter?" And then, with a slight bow, he turned again into the plantation and was soon out of sight.

With no expectation of pleasure, but with the strongest curiosity, Elizabeth opened the letter, and, to her still increasing wonder, perceived an envelope containing two sheets of letter-paper, written quite through, in a very close hand. The envelope itself was likewise full. Pursuing her way along the lane, she then began it. It was dated from Rosings, at eight o'clock in the morning, and was as follows:

"Be not alarmed, madam, on receiving this letter, by the apprehension of its containing any repetition of those sentiments or renewal of those offers which were last night so disgusting to you. I write without any intention of paining you or humbling myself by dwelling on wishes which, for the happiness of both, cannot be too soon forgotten. The effort which the formation and the perusal of this letter must occasion should have been spared, had not my character required it to be written and read. You must, therefore, pardon the freedom with which I demand your attention. Your feelings, I know, will bestow it unwillingly, but I demand it of your justice.

"Three offenses of a very different nature, and by no means of equal magnitude, you last night laid to my charge. The first mentioned was that, regardless of the sentiments of either, I had detached Mr. Bingley from your sister. The second, that I have inflicted upon my sister that which I suffer from. And the third, that I had, in defiance of various claims, in defiance of honor and humanity, ruined the immediate prosperity and blasted the prospects of Mr. Wickham. To willfully and wantonly have thrown off the companion of my youth, the acknowledged favorite of my father, a young man who had scarcely any other dependence than on our patronage, and who had been brought up to expect its exertion, would be a depravity to which the separation of two young persons, whose affection could be the growth of only a few weeks, could bear no comparison. But from the severity of that blame which was last night so liberally bestowed, respecting each circumstance, I shall hope to be in the future secured, when the following account of my actions and their motives has been read. If in the explanation of them, which is due to myself, I am under the necessity of relating feelings which may be offensive to yours, I can only say that I am sorry.

The necessity must be obeyed, and further apology would be absurd.

"I had not been long in Hertfordshire before I saw, in common with others, that Bingley preferred your elder sister to any other young woman in the country. But it was not till the evening of the dance at Netherfield that I had any apprehension of his feeling a serious attachment. I had often seen him in love before. At that ball, while I had the honor of dancing with you, I was first made acquainted by Sir William Lucas's accidental information that Bingley's attentions to your sister had given rise to a general expectation of their marriage. He spoke of it as a certain event, of which the time alone could be undecided. From that moment I observed my friend's behavior attentively, and I could then perceive that his partiality for Miss Bennet was beyond what I had ever witnessed in him.

"Your sister I also watched. Her look and manners were open, cheerful, and engaging as ever, but without any symptom of peculiar regard, and I remained convinced from the evening's scrutiny that though she received his attentions with pleasure, she did not invite them by any participation of sentiment. If *you* have not been mistaken here, *I* must have been in error. Your superior knowledge of your sister must make the latter probable. If it be so, if I have been misled by such error to inflict pain on her, your resentment has not been unreasonable. But I shall not scruple to assert that the serenity of your sister's countenance and air was such as might have given the most acute observer a conviction that, however amiable her temper, her heart was not likely to be easily touched. That I was desirous of believing her indifferent is certain—but I will venture to say that my investigation and decisions are not usually influenced by my hopes or fears. I did not believe her to be indifferent because I wished it. I believed it on impartial conviction, as truly as I wished it in reason.

"My objections to the marriage were not merely those which I last night acknowledged to have the utmost force of passion to put aside in my own case. The want of connection could not be so great an evil to my friend as to me. But there were other causes of repugnance, causes which, though still existing, and existing to an equal degree in both instances, I had myself endeavored to forget because they were not immediately before me. These causes must be stated, though briefly. The situation of your mother's family, though objectionable, was nothing in comparison to that total want of propriety so frequently, so almost uniformly betrayed by herself, by your three younger sisters, and occasionally even by your father, made most especially apparent at the Netherfield ball. Pardon me. It pains me to offend you. But amidst your concern for the defects of your nearest relations, and your displeasure at this representation of them, let it give you consolation to consider that equal praise must be bestowed upon you and your elder sister for your conduct, sense and disposition. There is the additional, and no less great, consideration that your sister's temperament, so cheerful and free of care, could not make the knowledge of Bingley's immortality a comfortable one for her to bear. For it is true... Bingley, through the act of a great accident for which I take full though indirect blame, is a vampire like myself, though he was not made aware of his changed existence until after he removed from Netherfield to London. Such knowledge was previously kept from him by myself and his sister Miss Bingley in an endeavor to protect his equally cheerful and carefree temperament for as long as the situation made permissible.

"The part which I acted is now to be explained. His sisters' uneasiness had been equally excited with my own at that final evening in Hertfordshire; our coincidence of feeling was soon discovered, and, alike sensible that no time was to be lost in detaching their brother before his growing emotions could cause a loss of control on his part and unknowingly endanger your sister's life, we shortly resolved on joining him directly in London. We accordingly went—and there I readily engaged in the office of revealing the dark truth of Bingley's change and pointing out to my friend the certain evils of such a choice as marriage to a vulnerable human. I described and enforced them earnestly.

"But however this remonstrance might have staggered or delayed his determination, I do not suppose that it would ultimately have prevented the marriage, had it not been seconded by the assurance that I hesitated not in giving of your sister's indifference. He wanted to believe she returned his affection with sincere, if not with equal regard, and hoped that perhaps she could learn to love even his immortal differences. But Bingley has great natural modesty with a stronger dependence on my judgement than on his own. To convince him, therefore, that he

155

had deceived himself was no very difficult point. To persuade him against returning into Hertfordshire, when that conviction had been given, was scarcely the work of a moment. I cannot blame myself for having done thus much to save your sister's life.

"There is but one part of my conduct in the whole affair on which I do not reflect with satisfaction. It is that I condescended to adopt the measures of art so far as to conceal from him your sister's being in town. I knew it myself, as it was known to Miss Bingley, but her brother is even yet ignorant of it. That they might have met without ill consequence is perhaps probable. But his regard did not appear to me enough extinguished for him to see her without some danger. Perhaps this concealment, this disguise was beneath me. It is done, however, and it was done for the best. On this subject I have nothing more to say, no other apology to offer. If I have wounded your sister's feelings, it was unknowingly done and though the motives which governed me may to you appear insufficient, I have not yet learnt to condemn them.

"With respect to that other, more weighty accusation of having injured Mr. Wickham and further, to ending my own sister's mortal existence, I can only refute both by laying before you the whole of his connection with my family. Of what he has *particularly* accused me I am ignorant. But of the truth of what I shall relate, I can summon more than one witness of undoubted veracity.

"Mr. Wickham is the son of a very respectable man who had for many years the management of all the Pemberley estates, and whose good conduct in the discharge of his trust naturally inclined my father to be of service to him, and on George Wickham, who was his godson, his kindness was therefore liberally bestowed. My father supported him at school, and afterwards at Cambridge—most important assistance, as his own father, always poor from the extravagance of his wife, would have been unable to give him a gentleman's education. My father was not only fond of this young man's society, whose manner were always engaging. He had also the highest opinion of him, and hoping the church would be his profession, intended to provide for him in it. As for myself, it is many, many years since I first began to think of him in a very different manner. The vicious propensities—the want of principle, which he was careful to guard from the knowledge of his best friend, could not escape the observation of a young man of nearly the same age with himself, and who had opportunities of seeing him in unguarded moments, which Mr. Darcy could not have. Here again I shall give you pain ——to what degree you only can tell. But whatever may be the sentiments which Mr. Wickham has created, a suspicion of their nature shall not prevent me from unfolding his real character—it adds even another motive.

"My excellent father died about five years ago. His attachment to Mr. Wickham was to the last so steady that in his will he particularly recommended it to me to promote his advancement in the best manner that his profession might allow ——and if he took orders, desired that a valuable family living might be his as soon as it became vacant. There was also a legacy of one thousand pounds. His own father did not long survive mine, and within half a year from these events, Mr. Wickham wrote to inform me that, having finally resolved against taking orders, he hoped I should not think it unreasonable for him to expect some more immediate pecuniary advantage, in lieu of the preferment, by which he could not be benefited. He had some intention, he added, of studying law, and I must be aware that the interest of one thousand pounds would be a very insufficient support therein. I rather wished than believed him to be sincere. But at any rate, I was perfectly ready to accede to his proposal. I knew that Mr. Wickham ought not to be a clergyman. The business was therefore soon settled—he resigned all claim to assistance in the church, were it possible that he could ever be in a situation to receive it, and accepted in return three thousand pounds. All connection between us seemed now dissolved. I thought too ill of him to invite him to Pemberley or admit his society in town.

"In town I believe he chiefly lived, but his studying the law was a mere pretence, and being now free from all restraint, his life was one of idleness and dissipation. It is during this period that I believe he was turned into a vampire. For about three years I heard little of him. But on the decease of the incumbent of the living which had been designed for him, he applied to me again by letter for the presentation. His circumstances, he assured me, were exceedingly bad, and I had no difficulty in believing it. He had found the law a most unprofitable study and was now absolutely resolved on being ordained, if I would present him to the living in question—of which he trusted there could be little doubt, as he was well assured that I had no other person to provide for, and I could not have forgotten my revered father's intentions. You will hardly blame me for refusing to comply with this entreaty, or for resisting every repetition to it. His resentment was in proportion to the distress of his circumstances—and he was doubtless as violent in his abuse of me to others as in his reproaches to myself. After this period every appearance of acquaintance was dropped. How he lived I know not. But last summer he was again most painfully obtruded on my notice.

"I must now mention a circumstance which I would wish to forget myself, and which no obligation less than the present should induce me to unfold to any human being. Having said thus much, I feel no doubt of your secrecy. My sister, who is more than ten years my junior, was left to the guardianship of my mother's nephew, Colonel Fitzwilliam, and myself. About a year ago, she was taken from school and an establishment formed for her in London. And last summer she went with the lady who presided over it to Ramsgate. Thither also went Mr. Wickham, undoubtedly by design, for there proved to have been a prior acquaintance between him and Mrs. Younge, in whose character we were most unhappily deceived, for we later learned that she was the actual maker of Wickham's immortal change. By her connivance and aid, he so far recommended himself to Georgiana, whose affectionate heart retained a strong impression of his kindness to her as a child, that she was persuaded to believe herself in love and to consent to an elopement. She was then but fifteen, and he quickly made her like himself. I joined them unexpectedly a day or two before the intended elopement, where Georgiana, unable to support the idea of grieving and offending a brother whom she almost looked up to as a father, acknowledged the whole to me. During the course of such an emotional reveal, and unknowing of her changed nature, she lost control and drained me of almost all my blood to the very brink of death.

"Mr. Wickham discovered me lying there near death. Only a wish for revenge impelled him to give me his cursed blood, thus changing me into one of his kind so that I too might be forced to endure an eternity of darkness and unholy thirst. You may imagine what I felt upon waking to the horror of this new existence and his gloating explanation of it all. Only the

158

responsibility of my sister's care prevented me from ending my life then and there. And only a regard for my sister's credit and feelings prevented any public exposure. But such proved unnecessary. Once I made it clear to Mr. Wickham that he would never see a single pound of my sister's fortune, which is thirty thousand pounds, and secured in his knowledge that he had at least exacted revenge upon my entire remaining family, Mr. Wickham left the place immediately and Mrs. Younge was of course removed from her charge.

"Yet his act of revenge did not stop there, for two weeks later while I was outside conversing with my steward, Bingley and Miss Bingley paid an unexpected visit to Pemberley, and my sister once again lost control. Faced with the decision to either let them die or change them, I gave them my immortal blood and assumed responsibility for them. Upon reflection, perhaps this was a faulty decision, but at the time, I only desired to save them from death. Miss Bingley was too quick minded and therefore received full explanation of her change, which she has not seemed too perturbed by, for the heightened abilities of our kind apparently appeal to her temperament. However, it was her strong wish that Bingley not be told of his change until absolute necessity must force the truth, and for this mistake I take full responsibility for agreeing to, as while it offered a temporary respite for his mind, the revelation of it has since caused the much feared despair in my friend from which he has yet to recover.

"This, madam, is a faithful narrative of every event in which we have been concerned together, and if you do not absolutely reject it as false, you will, I hope, acquit me henceforth of cruelty towards Mr. Wickham and my sister. I know not in what manner under what form of falsehood he had imposed on you. But his success is not perhaps to be wondered at. Ignorant as you previously were of everything concerning either, detection could not be in your power, and suspicion certainly not in your inclination.

"You may possibly wonder why all this was not told you last night. But I was not then master enough of myself to know what could or ought to be revealed. For the truth of everything here related, I can appeal more particularly to the testimony of Colonel Fitzwilliam who, from our near relationship and constant intimacy, and, still more, as one of the executors of my father's will, has been unavoidably acquainted with every particular of these transactions. If your abhorrence of *me* should make *my* assertions valueless, you cannot be prevented by the same cause from confiding in my cousin. And that there may be the possibility of consulting him, I shall endeavor to find some opportunity of putting this letter in your hands in the course of the morning. I will only add, God bless you.

"FITZWILLIAM DARCY"

Chapter Twenty-one

If Elizabeth, when Mr. Darcy gave her the letter, did not expect it to contain a renewal of his offers, she had formed no expectation at all of its contents. But such as they were, it may well be supposed how eagerly she went through them, and what a contrariety of emotion they excited. Her feelings as she read were scarcely to be defined. With amazement did she first understand that he believed any apology to be in his power. And steadfastly was she persuaded that he could have no explanation to give which a just sense of shame would not conceal. With a strong prejudice against everything he might say, she began his account of what had happened at Netherfield. She read with an eagerness which hardly left her power of comprehension, and from impatience of knowing what the next sentence might bring, was incapable of attending to the sense of the one before her eyes. His belief of her sister's insensibility she instantly resolved to be false, and his account of the real, the worst objections to the match, made her too angry to have any wish of doing him justice. To believe that her good sister Jane would not continue to love Bingley in spite of his accidentally changed situation in life was utter nonsense.

But when this subject was succeeded by his account of Mr. Wickham—when she read with somewhat clearer attention a relation of events which, if true, must overthrow every cherished opinion of his worth, and which bore so alarming an affinity to his own history of himself—her feelings were yet more acutely painful and more difficult for definition. Astonishment, apprehension, and even horror oppressed her. She wished to discredit it entirely, repeatedly exclaiming, "This must be false! This cannot be! This must be the grossest falsehood!"

And when she had gone through the whole letter, though scarcely knowing anything of the last page or two, she put it hastily away, protesting that she would not regard it, that she would never look at it again.

In this perturbed state of mind, with thoughts that could rest on nothing, she walked on. But it would not do. In half a minute the letter was unfolded again, and collecting herself as well as she could, she again began the mortifying perusal of all that related to Mr. Wickham, and commanded herself so far as to examine the meaning of every sentence. The account of his connection with the Pemberley family was exactly what he had related himself, and the kindness of the late Mr. Darcy, though she had not before known its extent, agreed equally well with his own words. So far each recital confirmed the other. But when she came to the will, the difference was great. What Mr. Wickham had said of the living was fresh in her memory, and as she recalled his very words, it was impossible not to feel that there was gross duplicity on one side or the other. For a few moments, she flattered herself that her wishes did not err. But when she read and re-read with the closest attention the particulars immediately following of Mr. Wickham's resigning all pretensions to the living, of his receiving in lieu so considerable a sum as three thousand pounds, of his being changed into a vampire, again was she forced to hesitate. She put down the letter, weighed every circumstance with what she meant to be impartiality, deliberated on the probability of each statement, but with little success. On both sides it was only assertion. Again she read on. But every line proved more clearly that the affair, which she had believed it impossible that any contrivance could so represent as to render Mr. Darcy's conduct in it less than infamous, was capable of a turn which must make him entirely blameless throughout the whole.

The extravagance and general profligacy which he scrupled not to lay at Mr. Wickham's charge exceedingly shocked her, the more so as she could bring no proof of its injustice. She had never heard of him before his entrance into the militia, in which he had engaged at the persuasion of the young man who, on meeting him accidentally in town, had there renewed a slight acquaintance. Of his former way of life nothing had been known in Hertfordshire but what he told himself. Of the abilities and characteristics of vampires, he was too well informed to be a mere observer. As to his real character, had information been in her power, she had never felt a wish of inquiring. His countenance, voice, and manner had established him at once in the possession of every virtue. She tried to recollect some instance of goodness, some distinguished trait of integrity or benevolence, that might rescue him from the attacks of Mr. Darcy; or at least, by the predominance of virtue, atone for those casual errors under which she would endeavor to class what Mr. Darcy had described as the idleness and vice of many years' continuance. But no such recollection befriended her. She could see him instantly before her, in every charm of air and address. But she could remember no more substantial good than what she had felt while in his presence, now most probably due to vampire abilities of attraction, and the general approbation of the neighborhood and the regard which those same powers had gained him in the militia. After pausing on this point a considerable while, she once more continued to read. But, alas! The story which followed of his designs on Miss Darcy received some confirmation from what had passed between Colonel Fitzwilliam and herself only the morning before. And at last she was referred for the truth of every particular to Colonel Fitzwilliam himself, from whom she had previously received the information of his near concern in all his cousin's affairs, and whose character she had no reason to question. At one time she had almost resolved on applying to him, but the idea was checked by the awkwardness of the application, and at length wholly banished by the conviction that Mr. Darcy would never have hazarded such a proposal if he had not been well assured of his cousin's corroboration.

She perfectly remembered everything that had passed in conversation between Mr. Wickham and herself in their first evening at Mr. Phillips's. Many of his expressions were still fresh in her memory. She was *now* struck with the impropriety of such communications to a stranger, and wondered it had escaped her before. She saw the indelicacy of putting himself forward as he had done, and the inconsistency of his professions with his conduct. She remembered that he had boasted of having no fear of seeing Mr. Darcy—that Mr. Darcy might leave the country, but that *he* should stand his ground—yet he had avoided the Netherfield ball the very next week. She remembered also that, till the Netherfield family had quitted the country, he had told his story to no one but herself. But after their removal it had been everywhere discussed and he had then no reserves, no scruples in sinking Mr. Darcy's character, though he had assured her that respect for the father would always prevent his exposing the son.

How differently did everything now appear in which he was concerned! His attentions to Miss King were now the consequence of views solely and hatefully mercenary, and the mediocrity of her fortune proved no longer the moderation of his wishes but his eagerness to grasp at anything. His behavior to herself could now have had no tolerable motive. He had either been deceived with regard to her fortune or had been gratifying his vanity by encouraging the preference which she believed she had most incautiously shown. Every lingering struggle in his favor grew fainter and fainter. In farther justification of Mr. Darcy, she could not but allow that Mr. Bingley, when questioned by Jane, had long ago asserted his blamelessness in the affair; that proud and repulsive as were his manners, she had never, in the whole course of their acquaintance—an acquaintance which had latterly brought them much together and given her a sort of intimacy with his ways—seen anything that betrayed him to be unprincipled or unjust, anything that spoke him of irreligious or immoral habits; that among his own connections he was esteemed and valued; that even Wickham had allowed him merit as a brother, and that she had often heard him speak so affectionately of his sister as to prove him capable of *some* amiable feeling; that had his actions been what Mr. Wickham represented them, so gross a violation of everything right could hardly have been concealed from the world; and that friendship between a person capable of it, and such an amiable man as Mr. Bingley, was incomprehensible.

She grew absolutely ashamed of herself. Of neither Mr. Darcy nor Mr. Wickham could she think without feeling she had been blind, partial, prejudiced, absurd.

"How despicably I have acted!" cried she. "I, who have prided myself on my discernment! I, who have valued myself on my abilities! Who have often disdained the generous candor of my sister, and gratified my vanity in useless or blamable mistrust! How humiliating is this discovery! Yet, how just a humiliation! Had I been in love with Mr. Wickham, I could not have been more wretchedly blind! But vanity, not love, has been my folly. Pleased with the preference of one, and offended by the neglect of the other on the very beginning of our acquaintance, I have courted prepossession and ignorance and driven reason away where either were concerned. Till this moment I never knew myself."

Worse, an intolerable sensation in the depths of her heart told her just how little she had known herself, for it hinted that all her disapprobation of Mr. Darcy had merely been a type of mask to shield herself from her real, true feelings towards him, feelings which she had yet to experience for any other man and which she was still not wholly comfortable in giving name to. But such thoughts were intolerable. Far better to think upon safer matters.

From herself to Jane, from Jane to Mr. Bingley, her thoughts were in a line which soon brought to her recollection that Mr. Darcy's explanation *there* had appeared very insufficient, and she read it again. Widely different was the effect of a second perusal. How could she deny that credit to his assertions in one instance which she had been obliged to give in the other? He declared himself to be totally unsuspicious of her sister's attachment, and she could not help remembering what Charlotte's opinion had always been towards Jane's hidden feelings. Neither could she deny the justice of his description of Jane. She felt that Jane's feelings, though fervent, were little displayed, and that there was a constant complacency in her air and manner not often united with great sensibility.

When she came to that part of the letter in which her family was mentioned in terms of such mortifying yet merited reproach, her sense of shame was severe. The justice of the charge struck her too forcibly for denial, and the circumstances to which he particularly alluded as having passed at the Netherfield ball, and as confirming all his first disapprobation, could not have made a stronger impression on his mind than on hers.

The compliment to herself and her sister was not unfelt. It soothed, but it could not console her for the contempt which had thus been self-attracted by the rest of her family. And as she considered that Jane's disappointment had in fact been the work of her nearest relations, and reflected how materially the credit of both must be hurt by such impropriety of conduct, she felt depressed beyond anything she had ever known before.

After wandering along the lane for two hours, giving way to every variety of thought, reconsidering events, determining probabilities, and reconciling herself as well as she could to a change so sudden and so important both in her mind and her heart, fatigue and a recollection of her long absence made her at length return home. She entered the house with the wish of appearing cheerful as usual and the resolution of repressing such reflections as must make her unfit for conversation.

She was immediately told that the two gentlemen from Rosings had each called during her absence...Mr. Darcy, only for a few minutes, to take leave—but that Colonel Fitzwilliam had been sitting with them at least an hour, hoping for her return, and almost resolving to walk

165

after her till she could be found. Elizabeth could but just *affect* concern in missing him; she really rejoiced at it. Colonel Fitzwilliam was no longer an object. She could think only of her letter and all that she had learned of Mr. Wickham, Mr. Bingley and his sister, Miss Darcy, her own family…and of Mr. Darcy, who as it turned out was so much more a man than a monster after all, despite his eternally changed circumstances. A man whom she had every cause to fear she was in great danger of falling in love with.

The two gentlemen left Rosings the next morning. Mr. Collins, having been in waiting near the lodges to make them his parting obeisance, was able to bring home the pleasing intelligence of their appearing in very good health and in as tolerable spirits as could be expected after the melancholy scene so lately gone through at Rosings. To Rosings he then hastened to console Lady Catherine and her daughter, and on his return brought back with great satisfaction a message from her ladyship importing that she felt herself so dull as to make her very desirous of having them all to dine with her.

Elizabeth could not see Lady Catherine without recollecting that, had she chosen it, she might by this time have been presented to her as her future niece. Nor could she think without a smile of what her ladyship's indignation would have been. "What would she have said? How would she have behaved?" were questions with which she amused herself.

Their first subject was the diminution of the Rosings party. "I assure you, I feel it exceedingly," said Lady Catherine. "I believe no one feels the loss of friends so much as I do. But I am particularly attached to these young men, and know them to be so much attached to me! They were excessively sorry to go! But so they always are. The dear Colonel rallied his spirits tolerably till just at last. But Darcy seemed to feel it most acutely, more, I think, than last year. His attachment to Rosings certainly increases."

Mr. Collins had a compliment and an allusion to throw in here, which were kindly smiled on by the mother and daughter.

Lady Catherine observed after dinner that Miss Bennet seemed out of spirits, and immediately accounted for it herself by supposing that she did not like to go home again so soon. She had many questions to ask respecting their journey, and as she did not answer them all herself, attention was necessary, which Elizabeth believed to be lucky for her. Otherwise with a mind so occupied, she might have forgotten where

166

she was. Reflection must be reserved for solitary hours. Whenever she was alone, she gave way to it as the greatest relief, and not a day went by without a solitary walk in which she might indulge in all the delight of unpleasant recollections.

Mr. Darcy's letter she was in a fair way of soon knowing by heart. She studied every sentence, and her feelings towards its writer were at times widely different. When she remembered the style of his address, she was still full of indignation. But when she considered how unjustly she had condemned and upbraided him, her anger was turned against herself, and his disappointed feelings became the object of compassion. His attachment excited gratitude and other, less easily defined feelings, his general character respect. But she held no hope for seeing him again, for in her own past behavior there was a constant source of vexation and regret, and in the unhappy defects of her family, a subject of yet heavier chagrin. They were hopeless of remedy. Her father, contented with laughing at them, would never exert himself to restrain the wild giddiness of his youngest daughters. And her mother, with manners so far from right herself, was entirely insensible of the evil. Elizabeth had frequently united with Jane in an endeavor to check the imprudence of Catherine and Lydia. But while they were supported by their mother's indulgence, what chance could there be of improvement? Catherine, weak-spirited, irritable, and completely under Lydia's guidance, had been always affronted by their advice. And Lydia, self-willed and careless, would scarcely give them a hearing. They were ignorant, idle, and vain. While there was an officer in Meryton, they would flirt with him, and while Meryton was within a walk of Longbourn, they would be going there forever.

Anxiety on Jane's behalf was another prevailing concern, and Mr. Darcy's explanation, by restoring Mr. Bingley to all her former good opinion, heightened the sense of what Jane had lost. His affection was proved to have been sincere and his conduct cleared of all blame, unless any could be attached to the implicitness of his confidence in his friend. How grievous then was the thought that, of a situation so desirable in almost every respect and so promising for happiness, Jane had been deprived by the folly and indecorum of her own family! When to these recollections was added the development of Mr. Wickham's character, it may be easily believed that the happy spirits which had seldom been depressed before were now so much affected as to make it almost impossible for her to appear tolerably cheerful.

167

Their engagements at Rosings were as frequent during the last week of her stay as they had been at first. The very last evening was spent there. Her ladyship again inquired minutely into the particulars of their journey, gave them directions as to the best method of packing, and was so urgent on the necessity of placing gowns in the only right way that Maria thought herself obliged, on her return, to undo all the work of the morning and pack her trunk afresh.

When they parted, Lady Catherine with great condescension wished them a good journey and invited them to come to Hunsford again next year, and Miss de Bourgh exerted herself so far as to curtsey and hold out her hand to both.

Chapter Twenty-two

On Saturday morning Elizabeth and Mr. Collins met for breakfast a few minutes before the others appeared. He took the opportunity of paying the parting civilities which he deemed indispensably necessary.

"I know not, Miss Elizabeth, whether Mrs. Collins has yet expressed her sense of your kindness in coming to us. But I am very certain you will not leave the house without receiving her thanks for it. The favor of your company has been much felt, I assure you. We know how little there is to tempt anyone to our humble abode. Our plain manner of living, our small rooms and few domestics, and the little we see of the world, must make Hunsford extremely dull to a young lady like yourself. But I hope you will believe us grateful for the condescension, and that we have done everything in our power to prevent your spending your time unpleasantly."

Elizabeth was eager with her thanks and assurances of happiness. She had spent six weeks with great enjoyment; and the pleasure of being with Charlotte, and the kind attentions she had received, must make *her* feel the obliged.

Mr. Collins was gratified, and with a more smiling solemnity replied, "You may, in fact, carry a very favorable report of us into Hertfordshire, my dear cousin. I flatter myself at least that you will be able to do so. Lady Catherine's great attentions to Mrs. Collins you have been a daily witness of. And altogether I trust it does not appear that your friend has drawn an unfortunate—but on this point it will be as well to be silent. Only let me assure you, my dear Miss Elizabeth, that I can from my heart most cordially wish you equal felicity in marriage. My dear Charlotte and I have but one mind and one way of thinking.

There is in everything a most remarkable resemblance of character and ideas between us. We seem to have been designed for each other."

Elizabeth could safely say that it was a great happiness where that was the case, and with equal sincerity could add that she firmly believed and rejoiced in his domestic comforts. She was not sorry, however, to have the recital of them interrupted by the lady from whom they sprang. Poor Charlotte! It was melancholy to leave her to such society! But she had chosen it with her eyes open, and though evidently regretting that her visitors were to go, she did not seem to ask for compassion. Her home and her housekeeping, her parish and her poultry, and all their dependent concerns, had not yet lost their charms.

At length the chaise arrived, the trunks were fastened on, the parcels placed within, and it was pronounced to be ready. After an affectionate parting between the friends, Elizabeth was attended to the carriage by Mr. Collins, and as they walked down the garden he was commissioning her with his best respects to all her family, not forgetting his thanks for the kindness he had received at Longbourn in the winter, and his compliments to Mr. and Mrs. Gardiner, though unknown. He then handed her in, Maria followed, and the door was on the point of being closed, when he suddenly reminded them with some consternation that they had hitherto forgotten to leave any message for the ladies at Rosings.

"But," he added, "you will of course wish to have your humble respects delivered to them, with your grateful thanks for their kindness to you while you have been here."

Elizabeth made no objection; the door was then allowed to be shut, and the carriage drove off.

"Good gracious!" cried Maria after a few minutes' silence. "It seems but a day or two since we first came! And yet how many things have happened!"

"A great many indeed," said her companion with a deep and painful sigh.

"We have dined nine times at Rosings, besides drinking tea there twice! How much I shall have to tell!"

Elizabeth added privately, "And how much I shall have to conceal!"

Their journey was performed without much conversation or any alarm, and within four hours of their leaving Hunsford they reached Mr. Gardiner's house, where they were to remain a few days.

Jane looked well, and Elizabeth had little opportunity of studying her spirits amidst the various engagements which the kindness of her aunt had reserved for them. But Jane was to go home with her, and at Longbourn there would be leisure enough for observation. As to Mr. Darcy's proposals, she decided to keep all a secret in fear that, if she once entered on the subject, she would be hurried into repeating something of Mr. Bingley's dark circumstances which might only grieve her sister further. While Jane's openness of heart would certainly allow her to continue to regard Mr. Bingley with equal affection after learning that he was a vampire, there seemed no point in revealing such a painful truth for Jane to dwell upon when her union with Mr. Bingley was now an improbability.

She was now, on being settled at home, at leisure to observe the real state of her sister's spirits. Jane was not happy. She still cherished a very tender affection for Mr. Bingley. Having never even fancied herself in love before, her regard had all the warmth of first attachment and, from her age and disposition, greater steadiness than most first attachments often boast. And so fervently did she value his remembrance and prefer him to every other man, that all her good sense and all her attention to the feelings of her friends were requisite to check the indulgence of those regrets which must have been injurious to her own health and their tranquility.

"Well, Lizzy," said Mrs. Bennet one day, "what is your opinion *now* of this sad business of Jane's? For my part, I am determined never to speak of it again to anybody. I told my sister Phillips so the other day. But I cannot find out that Jane saw anything of him in London. Well, he is a very undeserving young man, and I do not suppose there's the least chance in the world of her ever getting him now. There is no talk of his coming to Netherfield again in the summer, and I have inquired of everybody, too, who is likely to know."

"I do not believe he will ever live at Netherfield any more," agreed Elizabeth.

"Oh well! It is just as he chooses. Nobody wants him to come. Though I shall always say he used my daughter extremely ill, and if I was her, I would not have put up with it. Well, my comfort is that I am sure Jane will die of a broken heart, and then he will be sorry for what he has done."

But as Elizabeth could not receive comfort from any such expectation, she made no answer.

"Well, Lizzy," continued her mother soon afterwards, "and so the Collinses live very comfortable, do they? Well, well, I only hope it will last. And what sort of table do they keep? Charlotte is an excellent manager, I dare say. If she is half as sharp as her mother, she is saving enough. There is nothing extravagant in *their* housekeeping, I dare say."

"No, nothing at all."

"A great deal of good management, depend upon it. Yes, yes. *They* will take care not to outrun their income. *They* will never be distressed for money. Well, much good may it do them! And so, I suppose, they often talk of having Longbourn when your father is dead. They look upon it as quite their own, I dare say, whenever that happens."

"It was a subject which they could not mention before me."

"No, it would have been strange if they had. But I make no doubt they often talk of it between themselves. Well, if they can be easy with an estate that is not lawfully their own, so much the better. I should be ashamed of having one that was only entailed on me."

The first week of their return was soon gone. The second began. It was the last of the regiment's stay in Meryton, and all the young ladies in the neighborhood were drooping apace. The dejection was almost universal. The elder Miss Bennets alone were still able to eat, drink, sleep and pursue the usual course of their employments. Very frequently were they reproached for this insensibility by Kitty and Lydia, whose own misery was extreme, and who could not comprehend such hard heartedness in any of the family.

"Good Heaven! What is to become of us? What are we to do?" would they often exclaim in the bitterness of woe. "How can you be smiling so, Lizzy?"

Their affectionate mother shared all their grief. She remembered what she had herself endured on a similar occasion, five-and-twenty years ago.

"I am sure I cried for two days together when Colonel Miller's regiment went away," said she. "I thought I should have broken my heart."

"I am sure I shall break *mine*," said Lydia.

"If one could but go to Brighton!" observed Mrs. Bennet.

"Oh, yes!" agreed Lydia. "If one could but go to Brighton! But Papa is so disagreeable."

"A little sea bathing would set me up forever." Mrs. Bennet sat back with a wistful sigh.

"And my aunt Phillips is sure it would do *me* a great deal of good," added Kitty.

Such were the kind of lamentations resounding perpetually through Longbourn House. Elizabeth tried to be diverted by them, but all sense of pleasure was lost in shame. She felt anew the justice of Mr. Darcy's objections, and never had she been so much disposed to pardon his interference in the views of his friend.

But the gloom of Lydia's prospect was shortly cleared away, for she received an invitation from Mrs. Forster, the wife of the colonel of the regiment, to accompany her to Brighton. This invaluable friend was a very young woman and very lately married. A resemblance in good humor and good spirits had recommended her and Lydia to each other, and out of their three months' acquaintance they had been intimate two.

The rapture of Lydia on this occasion, her adoration of Mrs. Forster, the delight of Mrs. Bennet, and the mortification of Kitty, are scarcely to be described. Wholly inattentive to her sister's feelings, Lydia flew about the house in restless ecstasy, calling for everyone's congratulations and laughing and talking with more violence than ever, whilst the luckless Kitty continued in the parlor repining at her fate in terms as unreasonable as her accent was peevish.

"I cannot see why Mrs. Forster should not ask *me* as well as Lydia," wailed she. "Though I am *not* her particular friend, I have just as much right to be asked as she has, and more too, for I am two years older."

In vain did Elizabeth attempt to make her reasonable and Jane to make her resigned. As for Elizabeth herself, this invitation was so far from exciting in her the same feelings as in her mother and Lydia that she considered it the death warrant of all possibility of common sense for the latter. Detestable as such a step must make her were it known, she could not help secretly advising her father not to let Lydia go. She represented to him all the improprieties of Lydia's general behavior, the little advantage she could derive from the friendship of such a woman as Mrs. Forster, and the probability of her being yet more imprudent with such a companion at Brighton, where the temptations must be greater than at home.

He heard her attentively, and then said, "Lydia will never be easy until she has exposed herself in some public place or other, and we can never expect her to do it with so little expense or inconvenience to her family as under the present circumstances."

"If you were aware of the very great disadvantage to us all which must arise from the public notice of Lydia's unguarded and imprudent manner—nay, which has already arisen from it, I am sure you would judge differently in the affair."

"Already arisen?" repeated Mr. Bennet. "What, has she frightened away some of your lovers? Poor little Lizzy! But do not be cast down. Such squeamish youths as cannot bear to be connected with a little absurdity are not worth a regret. Come, let me see the list of pitiful fellows who have been kept aloof by Lydia's folly."

"Indeed you are mistaken. I have no such injuries to resent. It is not of particular, but of general evils, which I am now complaining. Our importance, our respectability in the world must be affected by the wild volatility, the assurance and disdain of all restraint which mark Lydia's character. Excuse me, for I must speak plainly. If you, my dear father, will not take the trouble of checking her exuberant spirits and teaching her that her present pursuits are not to be the business of her life, she will soon be beyond the reach of amendment. Her character will be fixed, and she will, at sixteen, be the most determined flirt that ever made herself or her family ridiculous. In this danger Kitty also is comprehended. She will follow wherever Lydia leads. Vain, ignorant, idle, and absolutely uncontrolled! Oh! My dear father, can you suppose it possible that they will not be censured and despised wherever they are known, and that their sisters will not be often involved in the disgrace?"

Mr. Bennet saw that her whole heart was in the subject and affectionately took her hand. "Do not make yourself uneasy, my love. Wherever you and Jane are known you must be respected and valued, and you will not appear to less advantage for having a couple of—or I may say, three—very silly sisters. We shall have no peace at Longbourn if Lydia does not go to Brighton. Let her go then. Colonel Forster is a sensible man and will keep her out of any real mischief; and she is luckily too poor to be an object of prey to anybody. At Brighton she will be of less importance even as a common flirt than she has been here. The officers will find women better worth their notice. Let us hope, therefore, that her being there may teach her her own insignificance. At any rate, she cannot grow many degrees worse without authorizing us to lock her up for the rest of her life."

With this answer Elizabeth was forced to be content, but her own opinion continued the same, and she left him disappointed and sorry. It was not in her nature, however, to increase her vexations by dwelling on them. She was confident of having performed her duty, and to fret over unavoidable evils, or augment them by anxiety, was no part of her disposition.

Had Lydia and her mother known the substance of her conference with her father, their indignation would hardly have found expression in their united volubility. But they were entirely ignorant of what had passed, and their raptures continued with little intermission to the very day of Lydia's leaving home.

The separation between Lydia and her family was rather more noisy than pathetic. Kitty was the only one who shed tears, but she wept from vexation and envy. Mrs. Bennet was diffuse in her good wishes for the felicity of her daughter and impressive in her injunctions that she should not miss the opportunity of enjoying herself as much as possible—advice which there was every reason to believe would be well attended to. In the clamorous happiness of Lydia herself in bidding farewell, the more gentle adieus of her sisters were uttered without being heard.

Elizabeth's tour to the Lakes was now the object of her happiest thoughts. It was her best consolation for all the uncomfortable hours which the discontentedness of her mother and Kitty made inevitable, and could she have included Jane in the scheme, every part of it would have been perfect.

"But it is fortunate that I have something to wish for," thought she. "Were the whole arrangement complete, my disappointment would be certain. But here, by carrying with me one ceaseless source of regret in my sister's absence, I may reasonably hope to have all my expectations of pleasure realized. A scheme of which every part promises delight can never be successful, and general disappointment is only warded off by the defense of some little peculiar vexation."

When Lydia went away she promised to write very often and very minutely to her mother and Kitty. But her letters were always long expected and always very short. Those to her mother contained little else than that they were just returned from the library, where such and such officers had attended them, and where she had seen such beautiful ornaments as made her quite wild; that she had a new gown, or a new parasol, which she would have described more fully but was obliged to leave off in a violent hurry, as Mrs. Forster called her and they were going off to the camp. From her correspondence with her sister, there was still less to be learned, for her letters to Kitty, though rather longer, were much too full of lines under the words to be made public.

After the first fortnight or three weeks of her absence, health, good humor, and cheerfulness began to reappear at Longbourn. Everything wore a happier aspect. The families who had been in town for the winter came back again, and summer finery and summer engagements arose. Mrs. Bennet was restored to her usual querulous serenity. And by the middle of June, Kitty was so much recovered as to be able to enter Meryton without tears, an event of such happy promise as to make Elizabeth hope that by the following Christmas she might be so tolerably reasonable as not to mention an officer above once a day, unless by some cruel and malicious arrangement at the War Office another regiment should be quartered in Meryton.

The time fixed for the beginning of their northern tour was now fast approaching, and a fortnight only was wanting of it when a letter arrived from Mrs. Gardiner, which at once delayed its commencement and curtailed its extent. Mr. Gardiner would be prevented by business from setting out till a fortnight later in July, and must be in London again within a month. As that left too short a period for them to go so far and see so much as they had proposed, or at least to see it with the leisure and comfort they had built on, they were obliged to give up the Lakes and substitute a more contracted tour, and according to the present plan were to go no farther northwards than Derbyshire. In that county there was enough to be seen to occupy the chief of their three weeks, and to Mrs. Gardiner it had a peculiarly strong attraction. The town where she had formerly passed some years of her life, and where they were now to spend a few days, was probably as great an object of her curiosity as all the celebrated beauties of Matlock, Chatsworth, Dovedale, or the Peak.

Elizabeth was excessively disappointed. She had set her heart on seeing the Lakes, and still thought there might have been time enough. But it was her business to be satisfied and certainly her temper to be happy, and all was soon right again.

With the mention of Derbyshire there were many ideas connected. It was impossible for her to see the word without thinking of Pemberley and its owner. "But surely I may enter his county without impunity and rob it of a few petrified spars without his perceiving me," thought she.

The period of expectation was now doubled. Four weeks were to pass away before her uncle and aunt's arrival. But they did pass away, and Mr. and Mrs. Gardiner, with their four children, did at length appear at Longbourn. The children, two girls of six and eight years old, and two younger boys, were to be left under the particular care of their cousin Jane, who was the general favorite, and whose steady sense and sweetness of temper exactly adapted her for attending to them in every way—teaching them, playing with them, and loving them.

The Gardiners stayed only one night at Longbourn, setting off the next morning with Elizabeth in pursuit of novelty and amusement. One enjoyment was certain—that of suitableness of companions, a suitableness which comprehended health and temper to bear inconveniences, cheerfulness to enhance every pleasure, and affection and intelligence.

Their travels through Oxford, Blenheim, Warwick, Kenilworth, Birmingham, and other locales were filled with enough sights and enjoyments to answer all that could be desired. To the little town of Lambton, the scene of Mrs. Gardiner's former residence, and where she had lately learned some acquaintance still remained, they bent their steps after having seen all the principal wonders of the country. Within five miles of Lambton, Elizabeth found from her aunt that Pemberley was situated. It was not in their direct road, nor more than a mile or two out of it. In talking over their route the evening before, Mrs. Gardiner expressed an inclination to see the place again. Mr. Gardiner declared his willingness, and Elizabeth was applied to for her approbation.

"My love, should not you like to see a place of which you have heard so much?" said her aunt. "A place, too, with which so many of your acquaintances are connected. Mr. Wickham passed all his youth there, you know."

Elizabeth was distressed. She felt that she had no business at Pemberley and was obliged to assume a disinclination for seeing it. "I must own that I am tired of seeing great houses. After going over so many, I really have no pleasure in fine carpets or satin curtains."

Mrs. Gardiner abused her stupidity. "If it were merely a fine house richly furnished, I should not care about it myself. But the grounds are delightful. They have some of the finest woods in the country."

Elizabeth said no more, but her mind could not acquiesce. The possibility of meeting Mr. Darcy while viewing the place instantly occurred. It would be dreadful! She blushed at the very idea and thought it would be better to speak openly to her aunt than to run such a risk. But against this there were objections, and she finally resolved that it could be the last resource if her private inquiries to the absence of the family were unfavorably answered.

Accordingly, when she retired at night, she asked the chambermaid whether Pemberley were not a very fine place, what was the name of its proprietor, and, with no little alarm, whether the family was down for the summer? A most welcome negative followed the last question.

Her alarms now being removed, she was at leisure to feel a great deal of curiosity to see the house herself. When the subject was revived the next morning, and she was again applied to, she could readily answer with a proper air of indifference that she had not really any dislike to the scheme. To Pemberley, therefore, they were to go.

Chapter Twenty-three

Elizabeth, as they drove along, watched for the first appearance of Pemberley Woods with some perturbation, and when at length they turned in at the lodge, her spirits were in a high flutter.

The park was very large and contained great variety of ground. They entered it in one of its lowest points and drove for some time through a beautiful wood stretching over a wide extent.

Elizabeth's mind was too full for conversation, but she saw and admired every remarkable spot and point of view. They gradually ascended for half a mile and then found themselves at the top of a considerable eminence, where the wood ceased and the eye was instantly caught by Pemberley House, situated on the opposite side of a valley into which the road with some abruptness wound. Contrary to the dark and depressing castle she had once imagined a vampire would call home, it was a large, handsome stone building, standing well on rising ground, and backed by a ridge of high woody hills. In front, a stream of some natural importance was swelled into greater, but without any artificial appearance. Its banks were neither formal nor falsely adorned. Elizabeth was delighted. She had never seen a place for which nature had done more, or where natural beauty had been so little counteracted by an awkward taste. They were all of them warm in their admiration, and at that moment she felt that to be mistress of Pemberley, in addition to the daily joys of a peaceful life spent at Mr. Darcy's side, might be something!

They descended the hill, crossed the bridge, and drove to the door. While examining the nearer aspect of the house, all her apprehension of meeting its owner returned. She dreaded lest the chambermaid had been mistaken. On applying to see the place, they were admitted into the hall, and Elizabeth, as they waited for the housekeeper, had leisure to wonder at her being where she was.

The housekeeper came, a respectable-looking elderly woman, much less fine and more civil than she had any notion of finding her. They followed her into the dining parlor. It was a large, well proportioned room, handsomely fitted up. Elizabeth, after slightly surveying it, went to a window to enjoy its prospect. The hill, crowned with wood, which they had descended, receiving increased abruptness from the distance, was a beautiful object. Every disposition of the ground was good, and she looked on the whole scene, the river, the trees scattered on its banks and the winding of the valley, as far as she could trace it, with longing. Oh, to be able to traverse such grounds at Mr. Darcy's side as they had learned to do at Rosings Park!

But these thoughts were not to be borne when such opportunity was lost to her forever through her own reprehensible behavior as well as her family's.

As they passed into other rooms, from every window there were beauties to be seen. The rooms were lofty and handsome and their furniture suitable to the fortune of its proprietor. But Elizabeth saw, with admiration of his taste, that it was neither gaudy nor uselessly fine, nor dark and depressing nor obsessively filled with items the color of blood, and with less of splendor and more of real elegance than the furniture of Rosings.

"And of this place I might have been mistress!" thought she. "With these rooms I might now have been familiarly acquainted! Instead of viewing them as a stranger, I might have rejoiced in them as my own and joined with Mr. Darcy in welcoming to them as visitors my uncle and aunt. But no, that could never be. My uncle and aunt would have been lost to me. I should not have been allowed to invite them."

She longed to inquire of the housekeeper whether her master was really absent, but had not the courage for it. At length however, the question was asked by her uncle. She turned away in alarm.

Mrs. Reynolds replied that he was, adding, "But we expect him tomorrow with a large party of friends."

How rejoiced was Elizabeth that their own journey had not by any circumstance been delayed a day!

Her aunt now called her to look at a picture. She approached and saw the likeness of Mr. Wickham, suspended amongst several other miniatures over the mantelpiece. Her aunt asked her, smilingly, how she liked it.

The housekeeper came forward and told them it was a picture of a young gentleman, the son of her late master's steward, who had been brought up by him at his own expense. "He is now gone into the army," she added. "But I am afraid he has turned out very wild and frightful."

Mrs. Gardiner looked at her niece with a smile, but Elizabeth could not return it.

"And that," said Mrs. Reynolds, pointing to another of the miniatures, "is my master—and very like him. It was drawn at the same time as the other, about eight years ago."

"I have heard much of your master's fine person," said Mrs. Gardiner, looking at the picture. "It is a handsome face. But, Lizzy, you can tell us whether it is like or not."

Mrs. Reynolds' respect for Elizabeth seemed to increase on this intimation of her knowing her master. "Does that young lady know Mr. Darcy?"

Elizabeth colored and said, "A little."

"And do not you think him a very handsome gentleman, ma'am?"

She was forced to swallow against a growing lump in her throat before she could at all reply, "Yes, very handsome."

"I am sure I know none so handsome; but in the gallery upstairs you will see a finer, larger picture of him than this. This room was my late master's favorite room, and these miniatures are just as they used to be then. He was very fond of them."

This accounted to Elizabeth for Mr. Wickham's being among them.

Mrs. Reynolds then directed their attention to one of Miss Darcy, drawn when she was only eight years old.

"And is Miss Darcy as handsome as her brother?" said Mrs. Gardiner.

"Oh! Yes, the handsomest young lady that ever was seen, and so accomplished! She plays and sings all day long. In the next room is a new instrument just come down for her—a present from my master. She comes here tomorrow with him."

Mr. Gardiner, whose manners were very easy and pleasant, encouraged her communicativeness by his questions and remarks. Mrs. Reynolds, either by pride or attachment, had evidently great pleasure in talking of her master and his sister.

"Is your master much at Pemberley in the course of the year?"

"Not so much as I could wish, sir. But I dare say he may spend half his time here, and Miss Darcy is always down for the summer months."

"Except," thought Elizabeth, "when she goes to Ramsgate."

"If your master would marry, you might see more of him."

"Yes, sir. But I do not know when *that* will be. I do not know who is good enough for him."

Mr. and Mrs. Gardiner smiled. Elizabeth could not help saying, "It is very much to his credit, I am sure, that you should think so."

"I say no more than the truth, and everybody will say that knows him," replied the other. Elizabeth thought this was going pretty far. She listened with increasing astonishment as the housekeeper added, "I have never known a cross word from him in my life, and I have known him ever since he was four years old."

This was praise, of all others most extraordinary, most opposite to her ideas. That he was not a good-tempered man had long been her firmest opinion, even after feeling herself to be attracted to him. Such feelings of approbation had grown in spite of his temper rather than because of it. Her keenest attention was awakened. She longed to hear more and was grateful to her uncle for saying:

"There are very few people of whom so much can be said. You are lucky in having such a master."

"Yes, sir, I know I am. If I were to go through the world, I could not meet with a better. But I have always observed that they who are good-natured when children are good-natured when they grow up. And he was always the sweetest-tempered, most generous-hearted boy in the world."

Elizabeth almost stared at her and thought, "Can this be Mr. Darcy?"

"His father was an excellent man," said Mrs. Gardiner.

"Yes, ma'am, that he was indeed. And his son will be just like him —just as affable to the poor."

Elizabeth listened, wondered, doubted, and was impatient for more. Mrs. Reynolds could interest her on no other point. She related the subjects of the pictures, the dimensions of the rooms, and the price of the furniture in vain. Mr. Gardiner, highly amused by the kind of family prejudice to which he attributed her excessive commendation of her master, soon led again to the subject. She dwelt with energy on his many merits as they proceeded together up the great staircase.

"He is the best landlord and the best master that ever lived," said she. "Not like the wild young men nowadays who think of nothing but themselves. There is not one of his tenants or servants but will give him a good name. Some people call him proud, but I am sure I never saw anything of it. To my fancy, it is only because he does not rattle away like other young men."

"In what an amiable light does this place him!" thought Elizabeth.

"This fine account of him," whispered her aunt as they walked, "is not quite consistent with his behavior to our poor friend."

"Perhaps we might be deceived," murmured Elizabeth, filled with more than a little guilt that she had yet to relate the truth of the situation to her aunt.

"That is not very likely. Our authority was too good."

On reaching the spacious lobby above, they were shown into a very pretty sitting room, lately fitted up with greater elegance and lightness than the apartments below, and were informed that it was but just done to give pleasure to Miss Darcy, who had taken a liking to the room when last at Pemberley.

"He is certainly a good brother," said Elizabeth as she walked towards one of the windows.

Mrs. Reynolds anticipated Miss Darcy's delight when she should enter the room. "And this is always the way with him," she added. "Whatever can give his sister any pleasure is sure to be done in a moment. There is nothing he would not do for her."

The picture gallery and two or three of the principal bedrooms were all that remained to be shown. In the gallery there were many family portraits, but they could have little to fix the attention of a stranger. Elizabeth walked in quest of the only face whose features would be known to her. At last it arrested her—and she beheld a striking resemblance to Mr. Darcy, with such a smile over the face as she remembered to have sometimes seen when he looked at her. She stood several minutes before the picture, lost in earnest contemplation and a terrible longing that made it difficult to breathe as she counted the weeks since last she had seen him, and returned to the picture again before they quitted the gallery. Mrs. Reynolds informed them that it had been taken in his father's lifetime.

There was certainly at this moment in Elizabeth's mind a more bittersweet sensation towards the original than she had ever felt at the height of their acquaintance. Many weeks had passed since having last walked with him, weeks that had given her much new knowledge to contemplate and insight into what had been previously unexplainable behavior on Mr. Darcy's part. She felt she had only recently begun to learn the truth of the man that he was, and all that she had heard and learned from his housekeeper today added still more to this new idea of him. The commendation bestowed on him by Mrs. Reynolds was of no trifling nature. What praise is more valuable than the praise of an intelligent servant? As a brother, a landlord, a master, she considered how many people's happiness were in his guardianship! How much of pleasure or pain was it in his power to bestow, and how much good he had chosen to perform! Every idea that had been brought forward by the housekeeper was favorable to his character, and as she stood before the canvas on which he was represented and fixed her eyes upon his countenance, she thought of his regard with the fully deepened sentiment of gratitude that had been steadily growing before. She remembered the warmth of his words of love and admiration for her, and softened its impropriety of expression.

When all of the house that was open to general inspection had been seen, they returned downstairs, and, taking leave of the housekeeper, were consigned over to the gardener, who met them at the hall door.

As they walked across the hall towards the river, Elizabeth turned back to look again. Her uncle and aunt stopped also, and while the former was conjecturing as to the date of the building, the owner of it himself suddenly came forward from the road, which led behind it to the stables.

They were within twenty yards of each other, and so abrupt was his appearance that it was impossible to avoid his sight. Their eyes instantly met, and the cheeks of both were overspread with the deepest blush. He absolutely started and for a moment seemed immovable from surprise, but shortly recovering himself, advanced towards the party and spoke to Elizabeth, if not in terms of perfect composure, at least of perfect civility.

She had instinctively turned away, but stopping on his approach, received his compliments with an embarrassment impossible to be overcome. Had his first appearance or his resemblance to the picture they had just been examining been insufficient to assure the other two that they now saw Mr. Darcy, the gardener's expression of surprise on beholding his master must immediately have told it. They stood a little aloof while he was talking to their niece, who, astonished and confused, scarcely dared lift her eyes to his face, and knew not what answer she returned to his civil inquiries after her family. Amazed at the alteration of his manner since they last parted, every sentence that he uttered was increasing her embarrassment, and every idea of the impropriety of her being found there recurring to her mind, the few minutes in which they continued were some of the most uncomfortable in her life. Nor did he seem much more at ease. When he spoke, his accent had none of its usual sedateness; and he repeated his inquiries as to the time of her having left Longbourn and of her having stayed in Derbyshire so often, and in so hurried a way, as plainly spoke the distraction of his thoughts.

At length every idea seemed to fail him, and after standing a few moments without saying a word, he suddenly recollected himself and took leave, his stride across the grounds so rapid and bordering on the impossible that had she told her uncle and aunt his secret, they might have believed her at that moment.

The others then joined her and expressed admiration of his figure, but Elizabeth heard not a word, and wholly engrossed by her own feelings, followed them in silence. She was overpowered by shame and vexation. Her coming there was the most unfortunate, the most ill-judged thing in the world! How strange it must appear to him! In what a disgraceful light might it not strike him! It might seem as if she had purposely thrown herself in his way again! Oh! Why did she come? Or why did he thus come a day before he was expected? Had they been only ten minutes sooner, they should have been beyond the reach of his discrimination, for it was plain that he was that moment arrived, that moment alighted from his horse or his carriage. She blushed again and again over the perverseness of the meeting. And his behavior, so strikingly altered—what could it mean? That he should even speak to her was amazing! But to speak with such civility, to inquire after her family with such a softness about the eyes and mouth! Never in her life had she seen his manners so little dignified, never had he spoken with such gentleness as on this unexpected meeting. What a contrast did it offer to his last address in Rosings Park when he put his letter into her hand! She knew not what to think or how to account for it.

They had now entered a beautiful walk by the side of the water, and every step was bringing forward a nobler fall of ground or a finer reach of the woods to which they were approaching. But it was some time before Elizabeth was sensible of any of it, and though she answered mechanically to the repeated appeals of her uncle and aunt and seemed to direct her eyes to such objects as they pointed out, she distinguished no part of the scene. Her thoughts were all fixed on that one spot of Pemberley House, whichever it might be, where Mr. Darcy then was. She longed to know what at the moment was passing in his mind—in what manner he thought of her, and whether, in defiance of everything, she was still dear to him. Perhaps he had been civil only because he felt himself at ease. Yet there had been *that* in his voice which was not like ease. Whether he had felt more of pain or of pleasure in seeing her she could not tell, but he certainly had not seen her with composure.

At length, however, the remarks of her companions on her absence of mind aroused her and she felt the necessity of appearing more like herself.

They entered the woods, and bidding adieu to the river for a while, ascended some of the higher grounds where, in spots where the opening of the trees gave the eye power to wander, were many charming views of the valley, the opposite hills, with the long range of woods overspreading many, and occasionally part of the stream. Mr. Gardiner expressed a wish of going round the whole park, but feared it might be beyond a walk. With a triumphant smile they were told that it was ten miles round. It settled the matter, and they pursued the accustomed circuit, which brought them again after some time in a descent among hanging woods to the edge of the water and one of its narrowest parts. They crossed it by a simple bridge in character with the general air of the scene. It was a spot less adorned than any they had yet visited, and the valley, here contracted into a glen, allowed room only for the stream and a narrow walk amidst the rough coppice-wood which bordered it. Elizabeth longed to explore its windings. But when they had crossed the bridge and perceived their distance from the house, Mrs. Gardiner, who was not a great walker, could go no farther and thought only of returning to the carriage as quickly as possible. Her niece was, therefore, obliged to submit, and they took their way towards the house on the opposite side of the river in the nearest direction. But their progress was slow, for Mr. Gardiner, though seldom able to indulge the taste, was very fond of fishing and was so much engaged in watching the occasional appearance of some trout in the water, and talking to the man about them, that he advanced but little.

Whilst wandering on in this slow manner, they were again surprised, and Elizabeth's astonishment was quite equal to what it had been at first, by the sight of Mr. Darcy approaching them and at no great distance. The walk being here less sheltered than on the other side allowed them to see him before they met. Elizabeth, however astonished, was at least more prepared for an interview than before, and resolved to appear and to speak with calmness if he really intended to meet them. For a few moments, indeed, she felt that he would probably strike down some other path. The idea lasted while a turning in the walk concealed him from their view; the turning past, he was immediately before them. With a glance, she saw that he had lost none of his recent civility, and to imitate his politeness as they met, she began to admire the beauty of the place. But she had not got beyond the words "delightful", and "charming", when some unlucky recollections obtruded, and she fancied that praise of Pemberley from her might be mischievously construed. Her color changed, and she said no more.

Mrs. Gardiner was standing a little behind, and on her pausing, he asked her if she would do him the honor of introducing him to her friends. This was a stroke of civility for which she was quite unprepared, and she could hardly suppress a smile at his being now seeking the acquaintance of some of those very people against whom his pride had revolted in his offer to herself. "What will be his surprise," thought she, "when he knows who they are? He takes them now for people of fashion."

The introduction, however, was immediately made; and as she named their relationship to herself, she stole a sly look at him to see how he bore it, and was not without the expectation of his decamping as fast as he could from such disgraceful companions. That he was *surprised* by the connection was evident. He sustained it, however, with fortitude, and so far from going away, turned back with them and entered into conversation with Mr. Gardiner. Elizabeth could not but be pleased, could not but triumph. It was consoling that he should know she had some relations for whom there was no need to blush. She listened most attentively to all that passed between them and gloried in every expression, every sentence of her uncle, which marked his intelligence, his taste, or his good manners.

The conversation soon turned upon fishing, and she heard Mr. Darcy invite him, with the greatest civility, to fish there as often as he chose while he continued in the neighborhood, offering at the same time to supply him with fishing tackle, and pointing out those parts of the stream where there was usually most sport. Mrs. Gardiner, who was walking arm-in-arm with Elizabeth, gave her a look expressive of wonder. Elizabeth said nothing, but it gratified her exceedingly; the compliment must be all for herself. Her astonishment, however, was extreme, and continually was she wondering, "Why is he so altered? From what can it proceed? It cannot be for *me*—it cannot be for *my* sake that his manners are thus softened. My reproofs at Hunsford could not work such a change as this. It is impossible that he should still love me."

After walking some time in this way, Mrs. Gardiner, fatigued by the exercise of the morning, found Elizabeth's arm inadequate to her support and consequently preferred her husband's. Mr. Darcy took her place by her niece, and they walked on together.

After a short silence, Elizabeth first spoke. "I wish you to know that I had been assured of your absence before I came here. Your arrival was very unexpected, for your housekeeper informed us that you would certainly not be here till tomorrow; and indeed, before we left Bakewell, we understood that you were not immediately expected in the country."

He nodded in acknowledgement of the truth of it all. "Business with my steward occasioned my coming forward a few hours before the rest of the party with whom I had been traveling. They will join me early tomorrow, and among them are some who will claim an acquaintance with you—Bingley and his sisters."

Elizabeth answered only by a slight bow. Her thoughts were instantly driven back to the time when Mr. Bingley's name had been the last mentioned between them. And if she might judge by his complexion, *his* mind was not very differently engaged.

He continued after a pause, "There is also one other person in the party who more particularly wishes to be known to you. Will you allow me, or do I ask too much, to introduce my sister to your acquaintance during your stay at Lambton?"

The surprise of such an application was great indeed; it was too great for her to know in what manner she acceded to it. She immediately felt that whatever desire Miss Darcy might have of being acquainted with her must be the work of her brother, and without looking farther, it was satisfactory. It was gratifying to know that his resentment had not made him think really ill of her.

They now walked on in silence, each of them deep in thought. Elizabeth was not comfortable, that was impossible, but she was flattered and pleased. His wish of introducing his sister to her was a compliment of the highest kind. They soon outstripped the others, and when they had reached the carriage, Mr. and Mrs. Gardiner were half a quarter of a mile behind.

He then asked her to walk into the house, but she declared herself not tired, so they stood together on the lawn. At such a time much might have been said, and silence was very awkward. She wanted to talk, but there seemed to be an embargo on every subject. At last she recollected that she had been traveling, and they talked of Matlock and Dove Dale with great perseverance. Yet time and her aunt moved slowly, and her patience and her ideas were nearly worn out before the tete-a-tete was over. On Mr. and Mrs. Gardiner's coming up they were all pressed to go into the house and take some refreshment; but this was declined, and they parted on each side with utmost politeness. Mr. Darcy handed the ladies into the carriage. The touch of his cool skin against her hand, his strong fingers so carefully holding hers in gentle assistance, was a distraction that made her heart race and her thoughts befuddled. When the carriage drove off, Elizabeth saw him walking slowly towards the house, the hand he had aided her with pressed flat against his leg. Deep in her own thoughts, she rubbed her own still tingling hand and began to replay the day's events in wonder.

The observations of her uncle and aunt now began. Each of them pronounced him to be infinitely superior to anything they had expected. "He is perfectly well behaved, polite, and unassuming," said her uncle.

"There *is* something a little stately in him, to be sure," replied her aunt. "But it is confined to his air and is not unbecoming. I can now say with the housekeeper that, though some people may call him proud, I have seen nothing of it."

"I was never more surprised than by his behavior to us," agreed her husband. It was more than civil; it was really attentive; and there was no necessity for such attention. His acquaintance with Elizabeth was very trifling."

"To be sure, Lizzy," said her aunt, "he is not so handsome as Mr. Wickham. Or rather, he has not Mr. Wickham's countenance, for his features are perfectly good. But how came you to tell me that he was so disagreeable?"

Elizabeth excused herself as well as she could. "I liked him better when we met in Kent than before. I have never seen him so pleasant as this morning."

"But perhaps he may be a little whimsical in his civilities," replied her uncle. "Your great men often are. Therefore I shall not take him at his word, as he might change his mind another day and warn me off his grounds."

Elizabeth felt that they had entirely misunderstood his character, but was unsure how best to right her previous wrongs against him without going too far or revealing too much, so she said nothing.

"From what we have seen of him," continued Mrs. Gardiner, "I really should not have thought that he could have behaved in so cruel a way by anybody as he has done by poor Mr. Wickham. He has not an ill-natured look. On the contrary, there is something pleasing about his mouth when he speaks. And there is something of dignity in his countenance that would not give one an unfavorable idea of his heart. But, to be sure, the good lady who showed us his house did give him a most flattering character! I could hardly help laughing aloud sometimes. But he is a liberal master, I suppose, and *that* in the eye of a servant comprehends every virtue."

Elizabeth here felt herself called on to say *something* in vindication of his behavior to Mr. Wickham, and therefore gave them to understand, in as guarded a manner as she could, that by what she had heard from his relations in Kent, his actions were capable of a very different construction and his character was by no means so faulty, nor Mr. Wickham's so amiable, as they had been considered in Hertfordshire. In confirmation of this, she related the particulars of all the pecuniary transactions in which they had been connected, without actually naming her authority, but stating it to be such as might be relied on.

Mrs. Gardiner was surprised and concerned. But as they were now approaching the scene of her former pleasures, every idea gave way to the charm of recollection, and she was too much engaged in pointing out to her husband all the interesting spots in its environs to think of anything else. Fatigued as she had been by the morning's walk, they had no sooner dined than she set off again in quest of her former acquaintance, and the evening was spent in the satisfactions of a intercourse renewed after many years' discontinuance.

The occurrences of the day were too full of interest to leave Elizabeth much attention for any of these new friends. She could do nothing but think, and think with wonder, of Mr. Darcy's civility, and, above all, of his wishing her to be acquainted with his sister.

Chapter Twenty-four

Elizabeth had settled it that Mr. Darcy would bring his sister to visit her tomorrow, and was consequently resolved not to be out of sight of the inn the whole of that morning. But her conclusion was false, for on the very same morning after their accidental meeting at Pemberley, these visitors came. They had been walking about the place with some of their new friends and were just returning to the inn to dress themselves for dining with the same family when the sound of a carriage drew them to a window, and they saw a gentleman and a lady in a curricle driving up the street. Elizabeth, immediately recognizing the livery, guessed what it meant and imparted no small degree of her surprise to her relations by acquainting them with the honor which she expected. Her uncle and aunt were all amazement; and the embarrassment of her manner as she spoke, joined to the circumstance itself and many of the circumstances of the preceding day, opened to them a new idea on the business. Nothing had ever suggested it before, but they felt that there was no other way of accounting for such attentions from such a quarter than by supposing a partiality for their niece. While these newly-born notions were passing in their heads, the perturbation of Elizabeth's feelings was at every moment increasing. She was quite amazed at her own discomposure. But amongst other causes of disquiet, she dreaded lest the partiality of the brother should have said too much in her favor, and more than commonly anxious to please, she naturally suspected that every power of pleasing would fail her.

She retreated from the window, fearful of being seen, and as she walked up and down the room endeavoring to compose herself, saw such looks of inquiring surprise in her uncle and aunt as made everything worse.

Miss Darcy and her brother appeared, and this formidable introduction took place. With astonishment did Elizabeth see that her new acquaintance was at least as much embarrassed as herself. Since her being at Lambton, she had heard that Miss Darcy was exceedingly proud. But the observation of a very few minutes convinced her that she was only exceedingly shy, not proud. Elizabeth searched for some visible sign of the girl's immortality but could find none. It was readily apparent that Mr. Darcy was endeavoring to use his abilities to make them both appear human and more approachable, but from habit or for the sake of Elizabeth's aunt and uncle or herself, she knew not.

Miss Darcy was tall, graceful, and as handsome as her brother, most probably attributable to her immortal charms. Still, there was sense and good humor in her face, and her manners were perfectly unassuming.

"Miss Elizabeth, it is so good to finally meet you!" cried she as she entered the room. Crossing the room so quickly she was nearly a blur, Miss Darcy took hold of Elizabeth's hands in a grip so tight it was painful, though the younger girl seemed perfectly unaware of her effect. "My brother has told me so much about you that I feel we are already the best of friends!"

Mr. Darcy stepped forward and touched his sister's elbow while giving Elizabeth an apologetic smile. Miss Darcy colored and released Elizabeth's hands. Yet Elizabeth had no need for either embarrassment or apology from either of them, for one look into his sister's eyes proved that Miss Darcy was sincerely unaware of her own strength and only overcome with a combination of shyness, excitement, and eagerness.

Elizabeth smiled at Miss Darcy. "I am afraid to ask what your brother has said about me."

Miss Darcy giggled. "Oh, but he said only the kindest of things, I can assure you. Among his many compliments regarding you were that you gave a most excellent performance on the pianoforte at Rosings."

Elizabeth colored, laughed, and looked at Mr. Darcy in astonishment. "Then he has perjured himself most terribly."

He gave a short laugh. "I said only that you played well."

"Oh, very well then. I suppose that is not quite as bad a lie," retorted Elizabeth with a smile.

Something in that smile made Mr. Darcy pause and blink as he studied her face. Only after the passage of a long moment of silence did he seem to remember the presence of his sister at his side, who was most assiduously studying them both with a knowing smile of her own.

"Perhaps we should be seated?" Mr. Darcy politely led the way to a nearby grouping of settee and chairs.

Elizabeth chose the settee, upon which Miss Darcy eagerly joined her so that they might continue talking with ease.

"Miss Elizabeth," began she as soon as they had seated. "You simply must come visit us at Pemberley before you leave so that I might hear you play."

A quick smile warmed both Mr. Darcy's face and eyes. Elizabeth understood it to mean that such a suggestion was not unwelcome.

"Oh dear, that would not do at all." Elizabeth laughed and shook her head. "I have heard nothing but that you are a most accomplished piano player, and my skills at such are quite limited by comparison. But perhaps you could perform for us."

"Oh, no, let us play a duet together instead!"

Whether from vampire glamour or natural sweetness, Elizabeth found herself to be quite charmed by Miss Darcy. She had expected to find in her as acute and unembarrassed an observer as ever Mr. Darcy had been, and was much relieved to discern such different feelings. Though the sister might suspect Elizabeth's feelings for Mr. Darcy, Elizabeth felt that she still might conceal them from Miss Darcy and her uncle and aunt at least. It was only Mr. Darcy's gaze that seemed to probe straight through into her mind and heart whenever their eyes chanced to meet, leaving her trembling with nervousness that he might see all that she hoped to keep hidden.

They had not long been together before Mr. Darcy told her that Mr. Bingley was also coming to wait on her, and she had barely time to express her satisfaction and prepare for such a visitor when Mr. Bingley's quick step was heard on the stairs, and in a moment he entered the room. All Elizabeth's anger against him had been long done away, but had she still felt any, it could hardly have stood its ground against the unaffected cordiality with which he expressed himself on seeing her again. He inquired in a friendly though general way after her family, and looked and spoke with the same good-humored ease that he had ever done—evidence that he must have at last learned to accept his immortality.

To Mr. and Mrs. Gardiner he was scarcely a less interesting personage than to herself. They had long wished to see him. The whole party before them, indeed, excited a lively attention. The suspicions of affection which had just arisen of Mr. Darcy and their niece directed their observation towards each with an earnest though guarded inquiry, and they soon drew from those inquiries the full conviction that one of them at least knew what it was to love. Of the lady's sensations they remained a little in doubt, but that the gentleman was overflowing with admiration was evident enough.

Elizabeth, on her side, had much to do. She wanted to ascertain the feelings of each of her visitors. She wanted to compose her own and to make herself agreeable to all. And in the latter object, where she feared most to fail, she was most sure of success, for those to whom she endeavored to give pleasure were prepossessed in her favor. Mr. Bingley was ready, Miss Darcy was eager, and Mr. Darcy determined, to be pleased.

In seeing Mr. Bingley, her thoughts naturally flew to her sister, and, oh, how ardently did she long to know whether any of his were directed in a like manner. Sometimes she could fancy that he talked less than on former occasions, and once or twice pleased herself with the notion that, as he looked at her, he was trying to trace a resemblance. But, though this might be imaginary, she could not be deceived as to his behavior to Miss Darcy, who had been set up as a rival to Jane. No look appeared on either side that spoke particular regard. Nothing occurred between them that could justify the hopes of his sister. On this point she was soon satisfied, and two or three little circumstances occurred ere they parted which, in her anxious interpretation, denoted a recollection of Jane not untinctured by tenderness and a wish of saying more that might lead to the mention of her, had he dared. He observed to her, at a moment when the others were talking together, and in a tone which had something of real regret, that it "was a very long time since he had had the pleasure of seeing her". And before she could reply, he added, "It is above eight months. We have not met since the 26th of November, when we were all dancing together at Netherfield."

Elizabeth was pleased to find his memory so exact. He afterwards took occasion to ask her, when unattended to by any of the rest, whether *all* her sisters were at Longbourn. There was not much in the question, nor in the preceding remark, but there was a look and a manner which gave them meaning.

It was not often that she could turn her eyes on Mr. Darcy himself. But whenever she did catch a glimpse, she saw an expression of general complaisance, and in all that he said she heard an accent so removed from *hauteur* or disdain of his companions as convinced her that the improvement of manners which she had yesterday witnessed, however temporary its existence might prove, had at least outlived one day. When she saw him thus seeking the acquaintance and courting the good opinion of people with whom any intercourse a few months ago would have been a disgrace—when she saw him thus civil, not only to herself, but to the very relations whom he had openly disdained, and recollected their last lively scene in Hunsford Parsonage—the difference, the change was so great and struck so forcibly on her mind that she could hardly restrain her astonishment from being visible. Never, even in the company of his dear friends at Netherfield or his dignified relations at Rosings, had she seen him so desirous to please, so free from self-consequence or unbending reserve, as now, when no importance could result from the success of his endeavors and even the acquaintance of those to whom his attentions were addressed would draw down the ridicule and censure of the ladies both of Netherfield and Rosings.

Their visitors stayed with them above half an hour, and when they arose to depart, Mr. Darcy called on his sister to join him in expressing their wish of seeing Mr. and Mrs. Gardiner and Miss Bennet to dinner at Pemberley before they left the country. Miss Darcy, though with a diffidence which marked her little in the habit of giving invitations, readily obeyed. Mrs. Gardiner looked at her niece, desirous of knowing how *she*, whom the invitation most concerned, felt disposed as to its acceptance, but Elizabeth had turned away her head. Presuming, however, that this studied avoidance spoke rather a momentary embarrassment than any dislike of the proposal, and seeing in her husband, who was fond of society, a perfect willingness to accept it, she ventured to engage for her attendance, and the day after the next was fixed on.

Mr. Bingley expressed great pleasure in the certainty of seeing Elizabeth again, having still a great deal to say to her and many inquiries to make after all their Hertfordshire friends. Elizabeth, construing all this into a wish of hearing her speak of her sister, was pleased. On this account as well as some others, she found herself, when their visitors left them, capable of considering the last half hour with some satisfaction, though while it was passing, the enjoyment of it had been little. Eager to be alone, and fearful of inquiries or hints from her uncle and aunt, she stayed with them only long enough to hear their favorable opinion of Mr. Bingley, and then hurried away to dress.

But she had no reason to fear Mr. and Mrs. Gardiner's curiosity. They did not wish to force her communication. It was evident that she was much better acquainted with Mr. Darcy than they had before any idea of, and it was equally evident that he was very much in love with her. They saw much to interest, but nothing to justify inquiry.

Of Mr. Darcy it was now a matter of anxiety to think well, and as far as their acquaintance reached, there was no fault to find. They could not be untouched by his politeness, and had they drawn his character from their own feelings and his servant's report without any reference to any other account, the circle in Hertfordshire to which he was known would not have recognized it for Mr. Darcy. There was now an interest, however, in believing the housekeeper, and they soon became sensible that the authority of a servant who had known him since he was four years old, and whose own manners indicated respectability, was not to be hastily rejected. Neither had anything occurred in the intelligence of their Lambton friends that could materially lessen its weight. They had nothing to accuse him of but pride. Pride he probably had, and if not, it would certainly be imputed by the inhabitants of a small market town where the family did not visit. It was acknowledged, however, that he was a liberal man who did much good among the poor.

With respect to Mr. Wickham, the travelers soon found that he was not held there in much estimation, for though the chief of his concerns with the son of his patron were imperfectly understood, it was yet a well-known fact that, on his quitting Derbyshire, he had left many debts behind him, which Mr. Darcy afterwards discharged.

As for Elizabeth, her thoughts were at Pemberley this evening more than the last. And the evening, though as it passed it seemed long, was not long enough to determine how she should feel towards *one* in that mansion. She lay awake two whole hours endeavoring to make them out.

She almost wished she could hate him as she once had, for everything had seemed easier and clearer then. But hatred had vanished long ago. The respect created by the conviction of his valuable qualities, though at first unwillingly admitted, had for some time ceased to be repugnant to her feeling. It was now heightened into somewhat of a friendlier nature by the testimony so highly in his favor, and bringing forward his disposition in so amiable a light, which yesterday had produced. But above all, above respect and esteem, there was a motive within her of goodwill which could not be overlooked. It was gratitude; gratitude not merely for having once loved her, but for loving her still well enough to forgive all the petulance and acrimony of her manner in rejecting him, and all the unjust accusations accompanying her rejection. He who, she had been persuaded, would avoid her as his greatest enemy, seemed on this accidental meeting to be most eager to preserve the acquaintance. And without any indelicate display of regard or any peculiarity of manner where their two selves only were concerned, he had solicited the good opinion of her friends and seemed bent on making her known to his sister. Such a change in a man of so much pride excited not only astonishment but gratitude—for to love, ardent love, it must be attributed. She only wanted to know how far it would be for the happiness of both that she should employ the power, which her fancy told her she still possessed, of bringing on her the renewal of his addresses. Could they truly find lasting happiness together as man and wife when so many differences still divided them? Differences of mortality, of station in life, of family?

Or should she feel, as Miss Bingley and Mrs. Hurst did, that a vampire of great wealth and high family stature could only find true and lasting happiness with one of his own kind?

Elizabeth had been a good deal disappointed in not finding a letter from Jane on their first arrival at Lambton, and this disappointment had been renewed on each of the mornings that had now been spent there. But on the third her repining was over and her sister justified by the receipt of two letters from her at once, on one of which was marked that it had been missent elsewhere. Elizabeth was not surprised at it, as Jane had written the direction remarkably ill.

They had just been preparing to walk as the letters came in. Her uncle and aunt, leaving her to enjoy them in quiet, set off by themselves. The one missent must first be attended to; it had been written five days ago. The beginning contained an account of all their little parties and engagements, with such news as the country afforded. But the latter half, which was dated a day later and written in evident agitation, gave more important intelligence. It was to this effect:

"Since writing the above, dearest Lizzy, something has occurred of a most unexpected and serious nature. But I am afraid of alarming you—be assured that we are all well. What I have to say relates to poor Lydia. An express came at twelve last night, just as we were all gone to bed, from Colonel Forster, to inform us that she was gone off to Scotland with one of his officers, to own the truth, with Mr. Wickham! Imagine our surprise. To Kitty, however, it does not seem so wholly unexpected. I am very, very sorry. So imprudent a match on both sides! But I am willing to hope the best, and that his character has been misunderstood.

Our poor mother is sadly grieved. My father bears it better. They were off Saturday night about twelve, as is conjectured, but were not missed till yesterday morning at eight. The express was sent off directly. My dear Lizzy, they must have passed within ten miles of us. Colonel Forster gives us reason to expect him here soon. Lydia left a few lines for his wife, informing her of their intention. I must conclude, for I cannot be long from my poor mother. I am afraid you will not be able to make it out, but I hardly know what I have written."

Without allowing herself time for consideration, and scarcely knowing what she felt, Elizabeth on finishing this letter instantly seized the other, and opening it with the utmost impatience, read as follows: it had been written a day later than the conclusion of the first.

"By this time, my dearest sister, you have received my hurried letter. I wish this may be more intelligible, but though not confined for time, my head is so bewildered that I cannot answer for being coherent. Dearest Lizzy, I hardly know what I would write, but I have bad news for you, and it cannot be delayed. Imprudent as the marriage between Mr. Wickham and our poor Lydia would be, we are now anxious to be assured it has taken place, for there is but too much reason to fear they are not gone to Scotland. Colonel Forster came yesterday, having left Brighton the day before, not many hours after the express. Though Lydia's short letter to Mrs. F. gave them to understand that they were going to Gretna Green, something was dropped by Denny expressing his belief that W. never intended to go there, or to marry Lydia at all, which was repeated to Colonel F., who, instantly taking the alarm, set off from B. intending to trace their route. He did trace them easily to Clapham, but no further, for on entering that place, they removed into a hackney coach and dismissed the chaise that brought them from Epsom. All that is known after this is that they were seen to continue the London road. I know not what to think. After making every possible inquiry on that side of London, Colonel F. came on into Hertfordshire, anxiously renewing them at all the turnpikes, and at the inns in Barnet and Hatfield, but without any success—no such people had been seen to pass through. With the kindest concern he came on to Longbourn and broke his apprehensions to us in a manner most creditable to his heart. I am sincerely grieved for him and Mrs. F., but no one can throw any blame on them.

"Our distress, my dear Lizzy, is very great. My father and mother believe the worst, but I cannot think so ill of him. Many circumstances might make it more eligible for them to be married privately in town than to pursue their first plan. And even if *he* could form such a design against a young woman of Lydia's connections, which is not likely, can I suppose her so lost to everything? Impossible! I grieve to find, however, that Colonel F. is not disposed to depend upon their marriage. He shook his head when I expressed my hopes, and said he feared W. was not a man to be trusted. My poor mother is really ill and keeps to her room. Could she exert herself, it would be better, but this is not to be expected. And as to my father, I never in my life saw him so affected. Poor Kitty has anger for having concealed their attachment, but as it was a matter of confidence, one cannot wonder. I am truly glad, dearest Lizzy, that you have been spared something of these distressing scenes; but now, as the first shock is over, shall I own that I long for your return? I am not so selfish, however, as to press for it if inconvenient. Adieu!

"I take up my pen again to do what I have just told you I would not. But circumstances are such that I cannot help earnestly begging you all to come here as soon as possible. I know my dear uncle and aunt so well that I am not afraid of requesting it, though I have still something more to ask of the former. My father is going to London with Colonel Forster instantly to try to discover her. What he means to do I am sure I know not. But his excessive distress will not allow him to pursue any measure in the best and safest way, and Colonel Forster is obliged to be at Brighton again tomorrow evening. In such an exigency, my uncle's advice and assistance would be everything in the world.

He will immediately comprehend what I must feel, and I rely upon his goodness."

"Oh! Where, where is my uncle?" cried Elizabeth, darting from her seat as she finished the letter, in eagerness to follow him without losing a moment of the time so precious. But before she could get halfway across the room, the door was opened by a servant, and Mr. Darcy appeared. The servant left, and Mr. Darcy entered the room, only to stop again at the sight of Elizabeth's pale, tear-streaked face and impetuous manner.

Before he could recover himself to speak, she, in whose mind every idea was superseded by Lydia's situation, hastily exclaimed, "I beg your pardon, but I must leave you. I must find Mr. Gardiner this moment, on business that cannot be delayed. I have not an instant to lose."

The next moment, he stood before her without her having seen him cross the room. Yet even this visible proof of his abilities could not add to her present distress of mind.

"Good God! What is the matter?" cried he with more feeling than politeness. Recollecting himself, he said, "I will not detain you a minute. But let me, or let the servant go after Mr. and Mrs. Gardiner. You are not well enough; you cannot go yourself."

Elizabeth hesitated, but her knees trembled under her and she felt how little would be gained by her attempting to pursue them. Calling back the servant, therefore, she commissioned him, though in so breathless an accent as made her almost unintelligible, to fetch his master and mistress home instantly.

On his quitting the room she sat down, unable to support herself, and must have looked miserable, because it seemed that it was impossible for Mr. Darcy to leave her or to refrain from saying, in a tone of gentleness and commiseration, "Let me call your maid. Is there nothing you could take to give you present relief? A glass of wine; shall I get you one? You are very ill."

"No, I thank you," replied she, endeavoring to recover herself. "There is nothing the matter with me. I am quite well. I am only distressed by some dreadful news which I have just received from Longbourn."

She burst into tears as she alluded to it, and for a few minutes could not speak another word. Mr. Darcy, in wretched suspense, could only say something indistinctly of his concern and observe her in compassionate silence.

At length she spoke again. "I have just had a letter from Jane with such dreadful news. It cannot be concealed from anyone. My younger sister has left all her friends—has eloped, has thrown herself into the power of...of Mr. Wickham. They are gone off together from Brighton. *You* know him too well to doubt the rest. She has no money, no connections, nothing but her blood that can tempt him to—she is lost forever."

Mr. Darcy was fixed in apparent astonishment.

"When I consider that I might have prevented it!" added she in a still more agitated voice. "I, who knew what he was. Had I but explained some part of it only, some part of what I had learned, to my own family! Had even a part of his true nature and character been known, this could not have happened. But it is all...all too late now."

"I am grieved indeed," cried Mr. Darcy. "Grieved—shocked. But is it certain—absolutely certain?"

"Oh, yes! They left Brighton together on Sunday night and were traced almost to London, but not beyond. They are certainly not gone to Scotland."

"And what has been done, what has been attempted, to recover her?"

"My father is gone to London, and Jane has written to beg my uncle's immediate assistance. But even if they should find him, considering who and what he is, what he is capable of doing if they should challenge him to a duel..."

Mr. Darcy grew utterly still as the shared alarm in their eyes finished that thought. In a fight between a vampire and an older, retired gentleman such as her father, there could be but one ending.

In a whisper, she continued. "We shall be off, I hope, in half an hour. But nothing can be done—I know very well that nothing can be done. How is such a monster to be worked on? How are they even to be discovered? I have not the smallest hope. It is every way horrible!"

Mr. Darcy shook his head in silent acquiescence.

"When *my* eyes were opened to his real character— Oh! Had I known what I ought, what I dared to do! But I knew not—I was afraid of doing too much. Wretched, wretched mistake!"

Mr. Darcy made no answer. He seemed scarcely to hear her and was walking up and down the room so quickly his profile was but a mere blur. Every few minutes he paused, which allowed her to see his brow contracted, his air gloomy. Elizabeth observed and instantly understood it. Her attractions for him were sinking; everything *must* sink under such a proof of family weakness, such an assurance of the deepest disgrace. She could neither wonder nor condemn, but the belief of his self-conquest brought nothing consolatory to her bosom, afforded no palliation of her distress. It was, on the contrary, exactly calculated to make her understand her own wishes, and never had she so honestly felt that she could have loved him as now, when all love must be vain.

But self, though it would intrude, could not engross her. Lydia— her very life at stake because of her utter stupidity, and the humiliation, the misery she was bringing on them all if Mr. Wickham did spare her life, soon swallowed up every private care. Covering her face with her handkerchief, Elizabeth was soon lost to everything else, and after a pause of several minutes, was only recalled to a sense of her situation by the voice of her companion.

His tone spoke likewise of compassion and restraint as he said, "I am afraid you have been long desiring my absence, nor have I anything to plead in excuse of my stay but real, though unavailing concern. Would to Heaven that anything could be either said or done on my part that might offer consolation to such distress! But I will not torment you with vain wishes, which may seem purposely to ask for your thanks. This unfortunate affair will, I fear, prevent my sister's having the pleasure of seeing you at Pemberley today."

"Oh, yes. Be so kind as to apologize for us to Miss Darcy. Say that urgent business calls us home immediately. Conceal the unhappy truth as long as it is possible, I know it cannot be long."

"I readily assure you of my secrecy. I must again express my sorrow for your distress, and wish that there might be a happy conclusion. Please give my compliments to your uncle and aunt Phillips." Then with only one serious, parting look, he went away.

As he quitted the room, Elizabeth felt how improbable it was that they should ever see each other again on such terms of cordiality as had marked their several meetings in Derbyshire. As she threw a retrospective glance over the whole of their acquaintance, so full of contradictions and varieties, she had to sigh at the perverseness of those feelings which would now have promoted its continuance, and would formerly have rejoiced in its termination.

Painfully she watched him go, and in this early example of what Lydia's infamy must produce, found additional anguish as she reflected on that wretched business. Never, since reading Jane's second letter, had she entertained a hope of Mr. Wickham's meaning to marry her sister. No one but Jane, she thought, could flatter herself with such an expectation. Surprise was the least of her feelings on *this* development. While reading the first letter's contents, Elizabeth had been all surprise, all astonishment that Mr. Wickham should marry a girl whom it was impossible he could marry for money. How Lydia could ever have attached him had then appeared incomprehensible. But now it was all too natural. For such an attachment as one outside the bonds of marriage, Lydia might have sufficient charms, as she was human and filled with the very liquid life force which many a vampire might be tempted by. A life force that would naturally and continually resupply itself only if Mr. Wickham managed enough self-discipline not to exhaust Lydia's life with his thirst. And though she did not suppose Lydia to be deliberately engaging in an elopement without the intention of marriage, she had no difficulty in believing that neither Lydia's virtue nor her understanding would preserve her from falling an easy prey.

Elizabeth had never perceived, while the regiment was in Hertfordshire, that Lydia had any partiality for him. But she was convinced that Lydia wanted only encouragement to attach herself to anybody. Sometimes one officer, sometimes another, had been her favorite, as their attentions raised them in her opinion. Her affections had continually been fluctuating but never without an object. The mischief of neglect and mistaken indulgence towards such a girl— Oh! How acutely did she now feel it!

She was wild to be at home—to hear, to see, to be upon the spot to share with Jane in the cares that must now fall wholly upon her in a family so deranged, a father absent, a mother incapable of exertion and requiring constant attendance. And though almost persuaded that nothing could be done for Lydia, her uncle's interference seemed of the utmost importance, and till he entered the room her impatience was severe. Mr. and Mrs. Gardiner had hurried back in alarm, supposing by the servant's account that their niece was taken suddenly ill. Satisfying them instantly on that head, she quickly communicated the cause of their summons, reading the two letters aloud, and dwelling on the postscript of the last with trembling energy. Though Lydia had never been a favorite with them, Mr. and Mrs. Gardiner could not but be deeply afflicted. Not Lydia only, but all were concerned in it, and after the first exclamations of surprise and horror, Mr. Gardiner promised every assistance in his power. Elizabeth, though expecting no less, thanked him with tears of gratitude, hopeful that at least he would be able to keep her father from dueling with Mr. Wickham should they discover him. And all three being actuated by one spirit, everything relating to their journey was speedily settled. They were to be off as soon as possible.

"But what is to be done about Pemberley?" cried Mrs. Gardiner. "John told us Mr. Darcy was here when you sent for us; was it so?"

"Yes, and I told him we should not be able to keep our engagement. *That* is all settled."

"What is all settled?" wondered her aunt as she ran into her room to prepare. "And are they upon such terms as for her to disclose the real truth? Oh, that I knew how it was!"

But wishes were vain, or at least could only serve to amuse her in the hurry and confusion of the following hour. Had Elizabeth been at leisure to be idle, she would have remained certain that all employment was impossible to one so wretched as herself. But she had her share of business as well as her aunt, and amongst the rest there were notes to be written to all their friends at Lambton with false excuses for their sudden departure. An hour, however, saw the whole completed, and Mr. Gardiner meanwhile having settled his account at the inn, nothing remained to be done but to go. At last, Elizabeth, after all the misery of the morning, found herself seated in the carriage and on the road to Longbourn in a shorter space of time than she could have supposed.

Chapter Twenty-five

"I have been thinking it over again, Elizabeth," said her uncle as they drove from the town. "And really, upon serious consideration, I am much more inclined than I was to judge as your eldest sister does on the matter. It appears to me so very unlikely that any young man should form such a design against a girl who is by no means unprotected or friendless, and who was actually staying in his colonel's family, that I am strongly inclined to hope the best. Could he expect that her friends would not step forward? Could he expect to be noticed again by the regiment after such an affront to Colonel Forster? His temptation is not adequate to the risk!"

"If only I could feel safe to think so," murmured Elizabeth, too filled with fear for Lydia's very life, as well as their entire family's reputation.

Her looks must have impelled her aunt to join in the attempt to comfort her.

"Upon my word," said Mrs. Gardiner, "I begin to be of your uncle's opinion. It is really too great a violation of decency, honor, and interest for him to be guilty of. I cannot think so very ill of Mr. Wickham. Can you yourself, Lizzy, so wholly give him up as to believe him capable of it?"

"Not, perhaps, of neglecting his own pecuniary interest; but of every other neglect I can believe him capable. If, indeed, it should be so! But I dare not hope it. Why should they not go on to Scotland if that had been the case?"

"In the first place," replied Mr. Gardiner, "there is no absolute proof that they are not gone to Scotland."

"Oh! But their removing from the chaise into a hackney coach is such a presumption! And besides, no traces of them were to be found on the Barnet road."

"Well, then—supposing them to be in London. They may be there, though for the purpose of concealment, for no more exceptional purpose. It is not likely that money should be very abundant on either side, and it might strike them that they could be more economically, though less expeditiously, married in London than in Scotland."

"But why all this secrecy? Why any fear of detection? Why must their marriage be private? Oh, no, no. This is not likely. His most particular friend, you see by Jane's account, was persuaded of his never intending to marry her. Mr. Wickham will never marry a woman without some money. He cannot afford it. And what claims has Lydia —what attraction has she beyond youth, health, and good humor that could make him, for her sake, forego every chance of benefiting himself by marrying well? As to what restraint the apprehensions of disgrace in the corps might throw on a dishonorable elopement with her, I am not able to judge, for I know nothing of the effects that such a step might produce. But as to your other objection, I am afraid it will hardly hold good. Lydia has no brothers to step forward, and he might imagine, from my father's behavior, from his indolence and the little attention he has ever seemed to give to what was going forward in his family, that *he* would do as little, and think as little about it, as any father could do, in such a matter."

"But can you think that Lydia is so lost to everything but love of him as to consent to live with him on any terms other than marriage?"

"It does seem, and it is most shocking indeed, that a sister's sense of decency and virtue in such a point should admit of doubt." Here Elizabeth had to stop and wipe away more tears, though these stemmed from overwhelming fury rather than sadness. "But, really, I know not what to say. Perhaps I am not doing her justice. But she is very young. She has never been taught to think on serious subjects. And for the last half year, nay, for a twelvemonth—she has been given up to nothing but amusement and vanity. She has been allowed to dispose of her time in the most idle and frivolous manner, and to adopt any opinions that came her way. Since the militia were first quartered in Meryton, nothing but love, flirtation, and officers have been in her head. She has been doing everything in her power by thinking and talking on the subject, to give greater—what shall I call it?—susceptibility to her feelings, which are naturally lively enough. And we all know that Mr. Wickham has every charm of person and address that can captivate a woman." In addition to unnatural ones that only a vampire could employ to alter a human's will to match his own. She shuddered at such privately held thoughts, but held her tongue against the urge to share secrets that must include others who were blameless in this situation. In revealing Mr. Wickham's secret, she must reveal Mr. Darcy's as well, and the lingering sensation of her feelings towards *him*, though pointless now, could not allow her to damage the reputation of one still so dear to her.

Her aunt shook her head. "But you see that Jane does not think so very ill of Mr. Wickham as to believe him capable of the attempt."

"Of whom does Jane ever think ill? And who is there, whatever might be their former conduct, that she would think capable of such an attempt, till it were proved against them? But Jane knows, as well as I do, what Mr. Wickham really is. We both know that he has been profligate in every sense of the word, that he has neither integrity nor honor, that he is as false and deceitful as he is insinuating." That he is a vampire, and worse, one without a single moral or scruple, she added to herself.

"And do you really know all this?" cried Mrs. Gardiner, whose curiosity as to the mode of her intelligence was all alive.

"I do indeed," replied Elizabeth, coloring. "I told you the other day of his infamous behavior to Mr. Darcy. And you yourself, when last at Longbourn, heard in what manner he spoke of the man who had behaved with such forbearance and liberality towards him. And there are other circumstances which I am not at liberty—which it is not worthwhile to relate. But his lies about the whole Pemberley family are endless. From what he said of Miss Darcy, I was thoroughly prepared to see a proud, reserved, disagreeable girl. Yet he knew to the contrary himself. He must know that she was as amiable and unpretending as we have found her."

"But does Lydia know nothing of this? Can she be ignorant of what you and Jane seem so well to understand?"

"Oh, yes! That, that is the worst of all. Till I was in Kent and saw so much both of Mr. Darcy and his relation Colonel Fitzwilliam, I was ignorant of the truth myself. And when I returned home, the militia was to leave Meryton in a week or fortnight's time. As that was the case, neither Jane, to whom I related the whole, nor I thought it necessary to make our knowledge public; for of what use could it apparently be to anyone that the good opinion which all the neighborhood had of him should then be overthrown? And even when it was settled that Lydia should go with Mrs. Forster, the necessity of opening her eyes to his character never occurred to me. That *she* could be in any danger from the deception never entered my head. That such a consequence as *this* could ensue, you may easily believe, was far enough from my thoughts."

"When they all removed to Brighton, therefore, you had no reason, I suppose, to believe them fond of each other?"

"Not the slightest. I can remember no symptom of affection on either side, and had anything of the kind been perceptible, you must be aware that ours is not a family on which it could be thrown away. When first he entered the corps, she was ready enough to admire him, but so we all were. Every girl in or near Meryton was out of her senses about him for the first two months. But he never distinguished *her* by any particular attention. And consequently, after a moderate period of extravagant and wild admiration, her fancy for him gave way and others of the regiment, who treated her with more distinction, again became her favorites."

It may be easily believed that however little of novelty could be added to their fears, hopes, and conjectures on this interesting subject by its repeated discussion, no other could detain them from it long during the whole of the journey. From Elizabeth's thoughts it was never absent. Fixed there by the keenest of all anguish and self-reproach, she could find no interval of ease or forgetfulness.

They traveled as expeditiously as possible, and, sleeping one night on the road, reached Longbourn by dinner time the next day. It was a comfort to Elizabeth to consider that Jane could not have been wearied by long expectations.

The little Gardiners, attracted by the sight of a chaise, were standing on the steps of the house as they entered the paddock. When the carriage drove up to the door, the joyful surprise that lit up their faces and displayed itself over their whole bodies in a variety of capers and frisks was the first pleasing earnest of their welcome.

Elizabeth jumped out and, after giving each of them a hasty kiss, hurried into the vestibule where Jane, who came running down from her mother's apartment, immediately met her.

Elizabeth, as she affectionately embraced her whilst tears filled the eyes of both, lost not a moment in asking whether anything had been heard of the fugitives.

"Not yet," replied Jane. "But now that my dear uncle is come, I hope everything will be well."

"Is my father in town?"

"Yes, he went on Tuesday, as I wrote you word."

"And have you heard from him often?"

"We have heard only twice. He wrote me a few lines on Wednesday to say that he had arrived in safety and to give me his directions, which I particularly begged him to do. He merely added that he should not write again till he had something of importance to mention."

"And my mother—how is she? How are you all?"

"My mother is tolerably well, I trust, though her spirits are greatly shaken. She is upstairs and will have great satisfaction in seeing you all. She does not yet leave her dressing room. Mary and Kitty, thank Heaven, are quite well."

"But you—how are you?" cried Elizabeth. "You look pale. How much you must have gone through!"

Her sister, however, assured her of her being perfectly well. Then their conversation, which had been passing while Mr. and Mrs. Gardiner were engaged with their children, was now put to an end to by the approach of the whole party. Jane ran to her uncle and aunt and welcomed and thanked them both with alternate smiles and tears.

When they were all in the drawing room, the questions which Elizabeth had already asked were of course repeated by the others, and they soon found that Jane had no intelligence to give. The sanguine hope of good, however, which the benevolence of her heart suggested, had not yet deserted her. She still expected that it would all end well, and that every morning would bring some letter, either from Lydia or her father, to explain their proceedings and, perhaps, announce their marriage.

Mrs. Bennet, to whose apartment they all repaired after a few minutes' conversation together, received them exactly as might be expected, with tears and lamentations of regret, invectives against the villainous conduct of Mr. Wickham, and complaints of her own sufferings and ill-usage; blaming everybody but the person to whose ill-judging indulgence the errors of her daughter must principally be owing.

She added, "If I had been able to carry my point in going to Brighton with all my family, *this* would not have happened. But poor dear Lydia had nobody to take care of her. Why did the Forsters ever let her go out of their sight? I am sure there was some great neglect or other on their side, for she is not the kind of girl to do such a thing if she had been well looked after. I always thought they were very unfit to have the charge of her. But I was overruled, as I always am. Poor dear child! And now here's Mr. Bennet gone away, and I know he will fight Mr. Wickham wherever he meets him, and then he will be killed, and what is to become of us all? The Collinses will turn us out before he is cold in his grave, and if you are not kind to us, brother, I do not know what we shall do."

Her mother's words made Elizabeth go cold all over with horror, for she spoke aloud Elizabeth's every fear, especially concerning her father's safety should he confront Mr. Wickham. She was rendered silent by her fear. The others all exclaimed against such terrific ideas. Mr. Gardiner, after general assurances of his affection for her and all her family, told her that he meant to be in London the very next day, and would assist Mr. Bennet in every endeavor for recovering Lydia. And yet this only partially allayed Elizabeth's fears, for what if her uncle were also to fight Mr. Wickham? Even if both her father and uncle stood together against Mr. Wickham at once, they would be no match. Mr. Wickham himself had told her how fast, and with what agility and strength vampires could fight. And she had seen with her own eyes how quickly they could move during the two separate instances of Mr. Darcy's great distress while in her presence. If Mr. Wickham should refuse to give up his newfound blood source...

"Do not give way to useless alarm," added Mr. Gardiner, cutting short her ever darkening thoughts. "Though it is right to be prepared for the worst, there is no occasion to look on it as certain. It is not quite a week since they left Brighton. In a few days more we may gain some news of them, and till we know that they are not married, and have no design of marrying, do not let us give the matter over as lost. As soon as I get to town I shall go to my brother and make him come home with me to Gracechurch Street. Then we may rationally consult together as to what is to be done."

Elizabeth felt some of the fear escape her in a great rush of breath. Yes, of course. Her father and uncle were rational men. They would seek the most logical course of action, not one based upon emotions as her mother was wont to do.

"Oh! My dear brother," replied Mrs. Bennet. "That is exactly what I could most wish for. And now do, when you get to town, find them out, wherever they may be. And if they are not married already, *make* them marry. And as for wedding clothes, do not let them wait for that, but tell Lydia she shall have as much money as she chooses to buy them after they are married. And above all, keep Mr. Bennet from fighting. Tell him what a dreadful state I am in, that I am frightened out of my wits—and have such tremblings, such flutterings all over me—such spasms in my side and pains in my head, and such beatings at my heart, that I can get no rest by night nor by day. And tell my dear Lydia not to give any directions about her clothes till she has seen me, for she does not know which are the best warehouses. Oh, brother, how kind you are! I know you will contrive it all."

Still, short of her father and uncle returning home alive and well, Elizabeth found that there was no other hope at all of a happy ending in this situation, for how could there be? Either Lydia would never be found at all, marking her as a victim of Mr. Wickham's dark needs for sustenance, or she would be found and made to marry the monster. Would such a union then result in Lydia's eventual death? Or would she become the most nonsensical, uncontrollable, empty headed vampire that ever existed? If she became like Wickham, would she at last learn self-discipline enough to control the dark impulses that must assuredly arise within her then? Or would she destroy their family's reputation still further with infamous acts of harm against her former fellow humans?

Whatever the result, there was no hope, no hope at all for happiness. Only darkness lie before Lydia, only darkness lie before their family, and only Elizabeth knew what truly might lie ahead for her youngest sister.

Mr. Gardiner, though he assured Mrs. Bennet again of his earnest endeavors in the cause, could not avoid recommending moderation to her, as well in her hopes as her fear. And after talking with her in this manner till dinner was on the table, they all left her to share her many long list of aches and woes to the housekeeper, who attended in the absence of her daughters.

Though her brother and sister were persuaded that there was no real occasion for such a seclusion from the family, they did not attempt to oppose it, for they knew that she had not prudence enough to hold her tongue before the servants while they waited at table, and judged it better that *one* only of the household, and the one whom they could most trust, should comprehend all her fears and solicitude on the subject.

In the dining room they were soon joined by Mary and Kitty, who had been too busily engaged in their separate apartments to make their appearance before. One came from her books, and the other from her

211

toilette. The faces of both, however, were tolerably calm, and no change was visible in either except that the loss of her favorite sister, or the anger which she had herself incurred in this business, had given more of fretfulness than usual to the accents of Kitty.

As for Mary, she was mistress enough of herself to whisper to Elizabeth, with a countenance of grave reflection, soon after they were seated at table, "This is a most unfortunate affair, and will probably be much talked of. But we must stem the tide of malice, and pour into the wounded bosoms of each other the balm of sisterly consolation."

Then, perceiving in Elizabeth no inclination of replying, she added, "Unhappy as the event must be for Lydia, we may draw from it this useful lesson: that loss of virtue in a female is irretrievable; that one false step involves her in endless ruin; that her reputation is no less brittle than it is beautiful; and that she cannot be too much guarded in her behavior towards the undeserving of the other sex."

Elizabeth lifted up her eyes in amazement, but was too much oppressed to make any reply. Mary, however, continued to console herself with such kind of moral extractions from the evil before them.

The whole party were in hopes of a letter from Mr. Bennet the next morning, but the post came in without bringing a single line from him. His family knew him to be, on all common occasions, a most negligent and dilatory correspondent; but at such a time they had hoped for exertion. They were forced to conclude that he had no pleasing intelligence to send. But even of *that* they would have been glad to be certain. Mr. Gardiner had waited only for the letters before he set off.

When he was gone, they were certain at least of receiving constant information of what was going on. On his parting, their uncle promised to prevail on Mr. Bennet to return to Longbourn as soon as he could, to the great consolation of his sister, who considered it as the only security for her husband's not being killed in a duel.

Mrs. Gardiner and the children were to remain in Hertfordshire a few days longer, as the former thought her presence might be serviceable to her nieces. She shared in their attendance on Mrs. Bennet and was a great comfort to them in their hours of freedom. Their other aunt also visited them frequently, and always, as she said, with the design of cheering and heartening them up—though, as she never came without reporting some fresh instance of Mr. Wickham's extravagance or irregularity, she seldom went away without leaving them more dispirited than she found them.

All Meryton seemed striving to blacken the man who, but three months before, had been almost an angel of light. He was declared to be in debt to every tradesman in the place, and his intrigues, all honored with the title of seduction, had been extended into every tradesman's family. Everybody declared that he was the wickedest young man in the world, and everybody began to find out that they had always distrusted the appearance of his goodness. Elizabeth, though she did not credit above half of what was said, believed enough to make her former assurance of her sister's ruin more certain. And even Jane, who believed still less of it, became almost hopeless, more especially as the time was now come when, if they had gone to Scotland, which she had never before entirely despaired of, they must in all probability have gained some news of them.

Mr. Gardiner left Longbourn on Sunday. On Tuesday his wife received a letter from him. It told them that, on his arrival, he had immediately found out his brother and persuaded him to come to Gracechurch Street; that Mr. Bennet had been to Epsom and Clapham before his arrival but without gaining any satisfactory information; and that he was now determined to inquire at all the principal hotels in town, as Mr. Bennet thought it possible they might have gone to one of them on their first coming to London before they procured lodgings. Mr. Gardiner himself did not expect any success from this measure, but as his brother was eager in it, he meant to assist him in pursuing it. He added that Mr. Bennet seemed wholly disinclined at present to leave London and promised to write again very soon. He also intended to write to Colonel Forster to seek what information they could from Mr. Wickham's fellow members in the militia.

Every day at Longbourn was now a day of anxiety, but the most anxious part of each was when the post was expected. The arrival of letters was the grand object of every morning's impatience. Through letters, whatever of good or bad was to be told would be communicated, and every succeeding day was expected to bring some news of importance.

Mr. Gardiner did not write again till he had received an answer from Colonel Forster, and then he had nothing of a pleasant nature to send. It was not known that Mr. Wickham had a single relationship with whom he kept up any connection, and it was certain that he had no near one living. His former acquaintances had been numerous. But since he had been in the militia, it did not appear that he was on terms of particular friendship with any of them. There was no one, therefore, who could be pointed out as likely to give any news of him. And in the wretched state of Mr. Wickham's finances, there was a very powerful motive for secrecy in addition to his fear of discovery by Lydia's relations, for it had just transpired that he had left gaming debts behind him to a very considerable amount. Colonel Forster believed that more than a thousand pounds would be necessary to clear his expenses at Brighton. He owed a good deal in town, but his debts of honor were still more formidable. Mr. Gardiner did not attempt to conceal these particulars from the Longbourn family.

Jane heard them with horror. "A gamester! This is wholly unexpected. I had not an idea of it."

Mr. Gardiner added in his letter that they might expect to see their father at home on the following day, which was Saturday. Rendered spiritless by the ill-success of all their endeavors, he had yielded to his brother-in-law's entreaty that he would return to his family and leave it to him to do whatever occasion might suggest to be advisable for continuing their pursuit. When Mrs. Bennet was told of this, she did not express so much satisfaction as her children expected, considering what her anxiety for his life had been before.

"What, is he coming home, and without poor Lydia?" cried she. "Surely he will not leave London before he has found them. Who is to fight Mr. Wickham and make him marry her if he comes away?"

Elizabeth gave a shocked gasp, shuddered at such words and was more happy than ever to hear that her father would soon be safe once again among them.

As Mrs. Gardiner began to wish to be at home, it was settled that she and the children should go to London at the same time that Mr. Bennet came from it. The coach, therefore, took them the first stage of their journey and brought its master back to Longbourn.

Mrs. Gardiner went away in all the perplexity about Elizabeth and her Derbyshire friend that had attended her from that part of the world. His name had never been voluntarily mentioned before them by her niece, and the kind of half-expectation which Mrs. Gardiner had formed of their being followed by a letter from him had ended in nothing. Elizabeth had received none since her return that could come from Pemberley.

The present unhappy state of the family rendered any other excuse for the lowness of her spirits unnecessary. Nothing, therefore, could be fairly conjectured from *that*, though Elizabeth, who was by this time tolerably well acquainted with her own feelings, was perfectly aware that, had she known nothing of Darcy, she could have borne the dread of Lydia's infamy somewhat better. It would have spared her, she thought, one sleepless night out of two.

When Mr. Bennet arrived, he had all the appearance of his usual philosophic composure. He said as little as he had ever been in the habit of saying, made no mention of the business that had taken him away, and it was some time before his daughters had courage to speak of it.

It was not till the afternoon, when he had joined them at tea, that Elizabeth ventured to introduce the subject.

On her briefly expressing her sorrow for what he must have endured, he replied, "Say nothing of that. Who should suffer but myself? It has been my own doing, and I ought to feel it."

"You must not be too severe upon yourself," replied Elizabeth.

"You may well warn me against such an evil. Human nature is so prone to fall into it! No, Lizzy, let me once in my life feel how much I have been to blame. I am not afraid of being overpowered by the impression. It will pass away soon enough."

"Do you suppose them to be in London?"

"Yes; where else can they be so well concealed?"

"And Lydia used to want to go to London," added Kitty.

"She is happy then," said her father drily; "and her residence there will probably be of some duration."

Then after a short silence he continued:

"Lizzy, I bear you no ill-will for being justified in your advice to me last May, which, considering the event, shows some greatness of mind."

They were interrupted by Miss Bennet, who came to fetch her mother's tea.

"This is a parade which does one good," cried he. "It gives such an elegance to misfortune! Another day I will do the same. I will sit in my library, in my nightcap and powdering gown, and give as much trouble as I can. Or perhaps I may defer it till Kitty runs away."

"I am not going to run away, Papa," said Kitty fretfully. "If I should ever go to Brighton, I would behave better than Lydia."

"*You* go to Brighton. I would not trust you so near it as Eastbourne for fifty pounds! No, Kitty, I have at last learned to be cautious, and you will feel the effects of it. No officer is ever to enter into my house again, nor even to pass through the village. Balls will be absolutely prohibited unless you stand up with one of your sisters. And you are never to stir out of doors till you can prove that you have spent ten minutes of every day in a rational manner."

Kitty, who took all these threats in a serious light, began to cry.

"Well, well," said he. "Do not make yourself unhappy. If you are a good girl for the next ten years, I will take you to a review at the end of them."

Two days after Mr. Bennet's return, as Jane and Elizabeth were walking together in the shrubbery behind the house, they saw the housekeeper coming towards them and, concluding that she came to call them to their mother, went forward to meet her.

But instead of the expected summons when they approached her, she said to Miss Bennet, "I beg your pardon, madam, for interrupting you, but I was in hopes you might have got some good news from town, so I took the liberty of coming to ask."

"What do you mean, Hill? We have heard nothing from town."

"Dear madam," cried Mrs. Hill in great astonishment. "Do not you know there is an express come for master from Mr. Gardiner? He has been here this half hour, and master has had a letter. He is walking towards the little copse."

Upon this information, they instantly ran across the lawn after their father, who was deliberately pursuing his way towards a small wood on one side of the paddock.

Jane, who was not so light nor so much in the habit of running as Elizabeth, soon lagged behind, while her sister, panting for breath, caught up with him.

Elizabeth cried out, "Oh, Papa, what news—what news? Have you heard from my uncle?"

"Yes, I have had a letter from him by express."

"Well, and what news does it bring—good or bad?"

"What is there of good to be expected?" said he, taking the letter from his pocket. "But perhaps you would like to read it."

Elizabeth impatiently caught it from his hand. Jane now came up.

"Read it aloud," said their father. "For I hardly know myself what it is about."

"Gracechurch Street, Monday, August 2.
"MY DEAR BROTHER,

"At last I am able to send you some tidings of my niece, and such as, upon the whole, I hope it will give you satisfaction. Soon

216

after you left me on Saturday, I was fortunate enough to find out in what part of London they were. The particulars I reserve till we meet. It is enough to know they are discovered. I have seen them both—"

"Then it is as I always hoped," cried Jane; "they are married!" Elizabeth read on:

"I have seen them both. They are not married, nor can I find there was any intention of being so. But if you are willing to perform the engagements which I have ventured to make on your side, I hope it will not be long before they are. All that is required of you is to assure to your daughter by settlement her equal share of the five thousand pounds secured among your children after the decease of yourself and my sister, and moreover, to enter into an engagement of allowing her, during your life, one hundred pounds per annum. These are conditions which, considering everything, I had no hesitation in complying with, as far as I thought myself privileged, for you. I shall send this by express, that no time may be lost in bringing me your answer. You will easily comprehend from these particulars that Mr. Wickham's circumstances are not so hopeless as they are generally believed to be. The world has been deceived in that respect; and I am happy to say there will be some little money, even when all his debts are discharged, to settle on my niece in addition to her own fortune. If, as I conclude will be the case, you send me full powers to act in your name throughout the whole of this business, I will immediately give directions to Haggerston for preparing a proper settlement. There will not be the smallest occasion for your coming to town again, therefore stay quiet at Longbourn and depend on my diligence and care. Send back your answer as fast as you can, and be careful to write explicitly. We have judged it best that my niece should be married from this house, of which I hope you will approve. She comes to us today. I shall write again as soon as anything more is determined on.
Yours, etc.,
"E. GARDINER."

"Is it possible?" cried Elizabeth when she had finished. "Can it be possible that he will marry her?"

"Mr. Wickham is not so undeserving, then, as we thought him," said her sister. "My dear father, I congratulate you."

"And have you answered the letter?" cried Elizabeth.

"No, but it must be done soon."

"Oh! My dear father," cried Elizabeth. "Come back and write immediately. Consider how important every moment is in such a case."

Jane eagerly nodded. "Let me write for you if you dislike the trouble yourself."

"I dislike it very much," replied he. "But it must be done."

And so saying, he turned back with them and walked towards the house.

"And may I ask—" said Elizabeth. "But the terms, I suppose, must be complied with."

"Complied with! I am only ashamed of his asking so little."

"And they *must* marry! Yet he is *such* a man!"

"Yes, yes, they must marry. There is nothing else to be done. But there are two things that I want very much to know. One is, how much money your uncle has laid down to bring it about, and the other, how am I ever to repay him."

"Money! My uncle!" cried Jane. "What do you mean, sir?"

"I mean that no man in his senses would marry Lydia on so slight a temptation as one hundred a year during my life and fifty after I am gone."

"That is very true," said Elizabeth. "Though it had not occurred to me before. His debts to be discharged, and something still to remain! Oh! It must be my uncle's doings! Generous, good man, I am afraid he has distressed himself. A small sum could not do all this."

"No," said her father. "Wickham's a fool if he takes her with a farthing less than ten thousand pounds. I should be sorry to think so ill of him in the very beginning of our relationship."

"Ten thousand pounds! Heaven forbid! How is half such a sum to be repaid?"

Mr. Bennet made no answer, and each of them, deep in thought, continued silent till they reached the house. Their father then went on to the library to write, and the girls walked into the breakfast room.

"And they are really to be married!" cried Elizabeth as soon as they were by themselves. "How strange this is! And for *this* we are to be thankful. That they should marry, small as is their chance of happiness, and wretched as is his character, we are forced to rejoice. Oh, Lydia!"

"I comfort myself with thinking that he certainly would not marry Lydia if he had not a real regard for her. Though our kind uncle has done something towards clearing him, I cannot believe that ten thousand pounds, or anything like it, has been advanced. He has children of his own, and may have more. How could he spare half ten thousand pounds?"

Elizabeth said, "If he were ever able to learn what Mr. Wickham's debts have been and how much is settled on his side on our sister, we shall exactly know what Mr. Gardiner has done for them, because Mr. Wickham has not sixpence of his own. The kindness of my uncle and aunt can never be requited. Their taking her home, and affording her their personal protection and countenance, is such a sacrifice to her advantage as years of gratitude cannot enough acknowledge. By this time she is actually with them! If such goodness does not make her miserable now, she will never deserve to be happy! What a meeting for her when she first sees my aunt!"

"We must endeavor to forget all that has passed on either side," said Jane. "I hope and trust they will yet be happy. His consenting to marry her is a proof, I will believe, that he is come to a right way of thinking. Their mutual affection will steady them. And I flatter myself they will settle so quietly, and live in so rational a manner, as may in time make their past imprudence forgotten."

"Their conduct has been such as neither you, nor I, nor anybody can ever forget. It is useless to talk of it."

It now occurred to the girls that their mother was in all likelihood perfectly ignorant of what had happened. They went to the library, therefore, and asked their father whether he would not wish them to make it known to her. He was writing and, without raising his head, coolly replied, "Just as you please."

"May we take my uncle's letter to read to her?"

"Take whatever you like and get away."

Elizabeth took the letter from his writing table, and they went upstairs together. Mary and Kitty were both with Mrs. Bennet. One communication would, therefore, do for all. After a slight preparation for good news, the letter was read aloud. Mrs. Bennet could hardly contain herself. As soon as Jane had read Mr. Gardiner's hope of Lydia's being soon married, her joy burst forth, and every following sentence added to its exuberance. She was now in an irritation as violent from delight as she had ever been fidgety from alarm and vexation. To know that her daughter would be married was enough.

She was disturbed by no fear for her felicity, nor humbled by any remembrance of her misconduct.

"My dear, dear Lydia!" cried she. "This is delightful indeed! She will be married! I shall see her again! She will be married at sixteen! My good, kind brother! I knew how it would be. I knew he would manage everything! How I long to see her! And to see dear Wickham too! But the clothes, the wedding clothes! I will write to my sister Gardiner about them directly. Lizzy, my dear, run down to your father and ask him how much he will give her. Stay, stay, I will go myself. Ring the bell, Kitty, for Hill. I will put on my things in a moment. My dear, dear Lydia! How merry we shall be together when we meet!"

Her eldest daughter endeavored to give some relief to the violence of these transports by leading her thoughts to the obligations which Mr. Gardiner's behavior laid them all under.

"For we must attribute this happy conclusion in a great measure to his kindness," added Jane. "We are persuaded that he has pledged himself to assist Mr. Wickham with money."

Mrs. Bennet waved a hand in dismissal. "Well, it is all very right. Who should do it but her own uncle? If he had not had a family of his own, I and my children must have had all his money, you know. And it is the first time we have ever had anything from him except a few presents. Well! I am so happy! In a short time I shall have a daughter married. Mrs. Wickham! How well it sounds! And she was only sixteen last June. My dear Jane, I am in such a flutter that I am sure I can't write, so I will dictate, and you write for me. We will settle with your father about the money afterwards. But the things should be ordered immediately."

She was then proceeding to all the particulars of calico, muslin, and cambric, and would shortly have dictated some very plentiful orders had not Jane, though with some difficulty, persuaded her to wait till her father was at leisure to be consulted. One day's delay, she observed, would be of small importance, and her mother was too happy to be quite so obstinate as usual. Other schemes, too, came into her head.

"I will go to Meryton as soon as I am dressed and tell the good, good news to my sister Philips," said Mrs. Bennet. "And as I come back, I can call on Lady Lucas and Mrs. Long. Kitty, run down and order the carriage. An airing would do me a great deal of good, I am sure. Girls, can I do anything for you in Meryton? Oh! Here comes Hill! My dear Hill, have you heard the good news? Miss Lydia is going to be married, and you shall all have a bowl of punch to make merry at her wedding."

Mrs. Hill began instantly to express her joy. Elizabeth received her congratulations amongst the rest, and then, sick of this folly, took refuge in her own room that she might think with freedom.

Poor Lydia's situation must, at best, be bad enough. That it was no worse, she had need to be thankful. Though in looking forward, neither rational happiness nor worldly prosperity could be justly expected for her sister, in looking back to what they had feared only two hours ago, she felt all the advantages of what they had gained. Lydia was alive and well, and that was a small miracle considering the monstrous capabilities of Mr. Wickham. As for the remainder of Lydia's future once she became Mrs. Wickham, that was still quite as dark and uncertain, and equally out of everyone's hands but the soon-to-be-married couple's.

Chapter Twenty-six

Mr. Bennet had very often wished before this period of his life that, instead of spending his whole income, he had laid by an annual sum for the better provision of his children and his wife, if she survived him. He now wished it more than ever. Had he done his duty in that respect, Lydia need not have been indebted to her uncle for whatever of honor or credit could now be purchased for her. The satisfaction of prevailing on one of the most worthless young men in Great Britain to be her husband might then have rested in its proper place.

He was seriously concerned that a cause of so little advantage to anyone should be forwarded at the sole expense of his brother-in-law, and he was determined, if possible, to find out the extent of his assistance and to discharge the obligation as soon as he could.

When first Mr. Bennet had married, economy was held to be perfectly useless, for of course they were to have a son. The son was to join in cutting off the entail as soon as he should be of age, and the widow and younger children would by that means be provided for. Five daughters successively entered the world, but yet the son was to come, and Mrs. Bennet, for many years after Lydia's birth, had been certain that he would. This event had at last been despaired of, but it was then too late to be saving. Mrs. Bennet had no turn for economy, and her husband's love of independence had alone prevented their exceeding their income.

Five thousand pounds was settled by marriage articles on Mrs. Bennet and the children. But in what proportions it should be divided amongst the latter depended on the will of the parents. This was one point, with regard to Lydia at least, which was now to be settled, and

Mr. Bennet could have no hesitation in acceding to the proposal before him. In terms of grateful acknowledgment for the kindness of his brother, though expressed most concisely, he then delivered on paper his perfect approbation of all that was done and his willingness to fulfill the engagements that had been made for him. He had never before supposed that, could Wickham be prevailed on to marry his daughter, it would be done with so little inconvenience to himself as by the present arrangement. He would scarcely be ten pounds a year the loser by the hundred that was to be paid them. For, what with her board and pocket allowance, and the continual presents in money which passed to her through her mother's hands, Lydia's expenses had been very little within that sum.

That it would be done with such trifling exertion on his side, too, was another very welcome surprise, for his wish at present was to have as little trouble in the business as possible. When the first transports of rage which had produced his activity in seeking her were over, he naturally returned to all his former indolence. His letter was soon dispatched, for, though dilatory in undertaking business, he was quick in its execution. He begged to know further particulars of what he was indebted to his brother, but was too angry with Lydia to send any message to her.

The good news spread quickly through the house, and with proportionate speed through the neighborhood. It was borne in the latter with decent philosophy. To be sure, it would have been more for the advantage of conversation had Miss Lydia Bennet come upon the town; or, as the happiest alternative, been secluded from the world in some distant farmhouse. But there was much to be talked of in marrying her, and the good-natured wishes for her well-doing which had proceeded before from all the spiteful old ladies in Meryton lost but a little of their spirit in this change of circumstances, because with such a husband her misery was considered certain.

It was a fortnight since Mrs. Bennet had been downstairs. But on this happy day she again took her seat at the head of her table, and in spirits oppressively high. No sentiment of shame gave a damp to her triumph. The marriage of a daughter, which had been the first object of her wishes since Jane was sixteen, was now on the point of accomplishment, and her thoughts and her words ran wholly on those attendants of elegant nuptials, fine muslins, new carriages, and servants. She was busily searching through the neighborhood for a proper situation for her daughter, and, without knowing or considering what their income might be, rejected many as deficient in size and importance.

"Haye Park might do if the Gouldings could quit it," said she. "Or the great house at Stoke, if the drawing room were larger, but Ashworth is too far off! I could not bear to have her ten miles from me. And as for Pulvis Lodge, the attics are dreadful."

Her husband allowed her to talk on without interruption while the servants remained. But when they had withdrawn, he said to her, "Mrs. Bennet, before you take any or all of these houses for your son and daughter, let us come to a right understanding. Into *one* house in this neighborhood they shall never have admittance. I will not encourage the impudence of either by receiving them at Longbourn."

A long dispute followed this declaration, but Mr. Bennet was firm. It soon led to another; and Mrs. Bennet found, with amazement and horror, that her husband would not advance a guinea to buy clothes for his daughter. He protested that she should receive from him no mark of affection whatever on the occasion. Mrs. Bennet could hardly comprehend it. That his anger could be carried to such a point of inconceivable resentment as to refuse his daughter a privilege without which her marriage would scarcely seem valid, exceeded all she could believe possible. She was more alive to the disgrace which her want of new clothes must reflect on her daughter's nuptials than to any sense of shame at her eloping and living with Mr. Wickham a fortnight before they took place.

Elizabeth was now most heartily sorry that she had, from the distress of the moment, been led to make Mr. Darcy acquainted with their fears for her sister. For since her marriage would so shortly give the proper termination to the elopement, they might hope to conceal its unfavorable beginning from all those who were not immediately on the spot.

She had no fear of its spreading farther through his means. There were few people on whose secrecy she would have more confidently depended. But at the same time, there was no one whose knowledge of a sister's frailty would have mortified her so much—though not from any fear of disadvantage from it individually to herself, for there seemed a gulf impassable between them. Had Lydia's marriage been concluded on the most honorable terms, it was not to be supposed that Mr. Darcy would connect himself with a family where, to every other objection, would now be added an alliance and relationship of the nearest kind with a man whom he so justly scorned.

From such a connection she could not wonder that he would shrink. The wish of procuring her regard, which she had assured herself of his feeling in Derbyshire, could not in rational expectation survive such a blow as this. She was humbled, she was grieved; she repented, though she hardly knew of what. She became jealous of his esteem when she could no longer hope to be benefited by it. She wanted to hear of him when there seemed the least chance of gaining intelligence. She was convinced that she could have been happy with him when it was no longer likely they should meet.

What a triumph for him, she often thought, if he could know that the proposals which she had proudly spurned only four months ago would now have been most gladly and gratefully received! He was as generous, she doubted not, as the most generous of his sex. But while he was mortal, there must be a triumph.

She began now to comprehend that he was exactly the man who, in disposition and talents, would most suit her. His understanding and temper, though unlike her own, would have answered all her wishes. It was a union that must have been to the advantage of both. By her ease and liveliness, his mind might have been softened, his manners improved. And from his judgement, information, and knowledge of the world, she must have received benefit of greater importance.

But no such happy marriage could now teach the admiring multitude what connubial felicity really was. A union of a different tendency, and precluding the possibility of the other, was soon to be formed in their family.

How Mr. Wickham and Lydia were to be supported in tolerable independence, she could not imagine. But how little of permanent happiness could belong to a couple who were only brought together because their passions were stronger than their virtue, she could easily conjecture.

Mr. Gardiner soon wrote again to his brother. To Mr. Bennet's acknowledgments he briefly replied with assurance of his eagerness to promote the welfare of any of his family, and concluded with entreaties that the subject might never be mentioned to him again. The principal purport of his letter was to inform them that Mr. Wickham had resolved on quitting the militia. He added:

"It was greatly my wish that he should do so as soon as his marriage was fixed on. And I think you will agree with me in

225

considering the removal from that corps as highly advisable, both on his account and my niece's. It is Mr. Wickham's intention to go into the regulars; and among his former friends there are still some who are able and willing to assist him in the army. He has the promise of an ensigncy in a regiment now quartered in the North. It is an advantage to have it so far from this part of the kingdom. He promises fairly, and I hope among different people, where they may each have a character to preserve, they will both be more prudent. I have written to Colonel Forster to inform him of our present arrangements and to request that he will satisfy the various creditors of Mr. Wickham in and near Brighton with assurances of speedy payment, for which I have pledged myself. And will you give yourself the trouble of carrying similar assurances to his creditors in Meryton, of whom I shall subjoin a list according to his information? He has given in all his debts. I hope at least he has not deceived us. Haggerston has our directions, and all will be completed in a week. They will then join his regiment, unless they are first invited to Longbourn, and I understand from Mrs. Gardiner that my niece is very desirous of seeing you all before she leaves the South. She is well and begs to be dutifully remembered to you and her mother.

Yours, etc.,

"E. GARDINER."

Mr. Bennet and his daughters saw all the advantages of Mr. Wickham's removal from the corps as clearly as Mr. Gardiner could do. But Mrs. Bennet was not so well pleased with it. Lydia's being settled in the North, just when she had expected most pleasure and pride in her company, for she had by no means given up her plan of their residing in Hertfordshire, was a severe disappointment. And besides, it was such a pity that Lydia should be taken from a regiment where she was acquainted with everybody and had so many favorites.

"She is so fond of Mrs. Forster," said she. "It will be quite shocking to send her away! And there are several of the young men, too, that she likes very much. The officers may not be so pleasant in the regiment."

His daughter's request, for such it might be considered, of being admitted into her family again before she set off for the North received at first an absolute negative. But Jane and Elizabeth agreed in wishing for the sake of their sister's feelings and consequence that she should be noticed on her marriage by her parents. They urged him so earnestly yet so rationally and so mildly to receive Lydia and her husband at Longbourn as soon as they were married, that he was prevailed on to think as his eldest daughters thought and act as they wished. And their mother had the satisfaction of knowing that she would be able to show her married daughter in the neighborhood before she was banished to the North. When Mr. Bennet wrote again to his brother, therefore, he sent his permission for them to come. It was settled that as soon as the ceremony was over, they should proceed to Longbourn. Elizabeth was surprised, however, that Mr. Wickham should consent to such a scheme, and had she consulted only her own inclination, any meeting with him would have been the last object of her wishes.

Their sister's wedding day arrived, and Jane and Elizabeth felt for her probably more than she felt for herself. Their arrival afterwards at Longbourn was dreaded by the elder Miss Bennets, and Jane more especially, who gave Lydia the feelings which would have attended herself had she been the culprit, and was wretched in the thought of what her sister must endure.

They came. The family were assembled in the breakfast room to receive them. Smiles decked the face of Mrs. Bennet as the carriage drove up to the door, her husband looked impenetrably grave, her daughters alarmed, anxious, uneasy.

Lydia's voice was heard in the vestibule; the door was thrown open, and she ran into the room. Her mother stepped forward, embraced her, and welcomed her with rapture; gave her hand with an affectionate smile to Mr. Wickham, who followed his lady; and wished them both joy with an alacrity which showed no doubt of their happiness.

Their reception from Mr. Bennet, to whom they then turned, was not quite so cordial. His countenance rather gained in austerity, and he scarcely opened his lips. The easy assurance of the young couple, indeed, was enough to provoke him. Elizabeth was disgusted, and even Miss Bennet was shocked. Lydia was Lydia still…untamed, unabashed, wild, noisy, and fearless. She turned from sister to sister, demanding their congratulations; and when at length they all sat down, looked eagerly round the room, took notice of some little alteration in it, and observed with a laugh that it was a great while since she had been there.

Mr. Wickham was not at all more distressed than herself, but his manners were always so pleasing that had his character and his marriage been exactly what they ought, his smiles and his easy address while he claimed their relationship would have delighted them all. Elizabeth had not before believed him quite equal to such assurance. But she sat down, resolving within herself to draw no limits in future to the impudence of an impudent creature such as he. She blushed, and Jane blushed. But the cheeks of the two who caused their confusion suffered no variation of color.

There was no want of discourse. The bride and her mother could neither of them talk fast enough, and Mr. Wickham, who happened to sit near Elizabeth, began inquiring after his acquaintance in that neighborhood with a good humored ease which she felt very unable to equal in her replies. They seemed each of them to have the happiest memories in the world. Nothing of the past was recollected with pain, and Lydia led voluntarily to subjects which her sisters would not have alluded to for the world.

"Only think of its being three months since I went away," cried she. "It seems but a fortnight I declare, and yet there have been things enough happened in the time. Good gracious! When I went away, I am sure I had no more idea of being married till I came back again! Though I thought it would be very good fun if I was."

Her father lifted up his eyes. Jane was distressed. Elizabeth looked expressively at Lydia.

But she, who never heard nor saw anything of which she chose to be insensible, gaily continued, "Oh! Mamma, do the people hereabouts know I am married today? I was afraid they might not, and we overtook William Goulding in his curricle, so I was determined he should know it, and so I let down the side glass next to him, and took off my glove, and let my hand just rest upon the window frame so that he might see the ring, and then I bowed and smiled like anything."

Elizabeth could bear it no longer. She got up, ran out of the room, and returned no more till she heard them passing through the hall to the dining parlor. She then joined them soon enough to see Lydia, with anxious parade, walk up to her mother's right hand and say to her eldest sister, "Ah! Jane, I take your place now, and you must go lower, because I am a married woman."

It was not to be supposed that time would give Lydia that embarrassment from which she had been so wholly free at first. Her ease and good spirits increased. She longed to see Mrs. Phillips, the

Lucases, and all their other neighbors, and to hear herself called "Mrs. Wickham" by each of them. In the meantime, she went after dinner to show her ring and boast of being married to Mrs. Hill and the two housemaids.

"Well, Mamma," said she when they were all returned to the breakfast room, "and what do you think of my husband? Is not he a charming man? I am sure my sisters must all envy me. I only hope they may have half my good luck. They must all go to Brighton. That is the place to get husbands. What a pity it is, Mamma, we did not all go."

"Very true, and if I had my will, we should. But my dear Lydia, I don't at all like your going such a way off. Must it be so?"

"Oh, lord! Yes, there is nothing in that. I shall like it of all things. You and Papa, and my sisters, must come down and see us. We shall be at Newcastle all the winter, and I dare say there will be some balls, and I will take care to get good partners for them all."

"I should like it beyond anything!" said her mother.

"And then when you go away, you may leave one or two of my sisters behind you, and I dare say I shall get husbands for them before the winter is over."

"I thank you for my share of the favor," said Elizabeth. "But I do not particularly like your way of getting husbands."

Later in the afternoon, the sisters took a short walk through the neighboring fields, with Mr. Wickham riding about them on a horse which Mr. Bennet had grudgingly loaned him. Elizabeth spent the chief of the time in observation of his actions towards his new wife.

Mr. Wickham's affection for Lydia was just what Elizabeth had expected to find it...not equal to Lydia's for him. She had scarcely needed her present observation to be satisfied that their elopement had been brought on by the strength of her love rather than by his. She would have wondered why, without violently caring for Lydia, he chose to elope with her at all, had she not felt certain that his flight was rendered necessary by distress of circumstances. And if that were the case, he was surely not the vampire to resist an opportunity of having a constant portable source for food on hand.

Lydia was exceedingly fond of him. He was her dear Wickham on every occasion; no one was to be put in competition with him. He did everything best in the world, and she was sure he would kill more birds on the first of September than anybody else in the country.

As they walked back towards home, she said to Elizabeth, "Lizzy, I never gave *you* an account of my wedding, I believe. You were not nearby when I told Mamma and the others all about it. Are not you curious to hear how it was managed?"

"No really," replied Elizabeth. "I think there cannot be too little said on the subject."

"La! You are so strange! But I must tell you how it went off. It began with such a fuss…after Mr. Darcy discovered us, he actually challenged Wickham to a duel! Wickham was so brave, and of course he accepted the challenge and met him straight away in the park, though it was dark outside and how they could possibly see to fight at such a time of night was beyond my understanding."

Utter astonishment and horror held Elizabeth in complete silence, which Lydia took for encouragement to continue.

"But after such nonsense was done with, we were married at St. Clement's because Wickham's lodgings were in that parish. And it was settled that we should all be there by eleven o'clock. My uncle and aunt and I were to go together, and the others were to meet us at the church. Well, Monday morning came, and I was in such a fuss! I was so afraid, you know, that something would happen to put it off, and then I should have gone quite distracted. And there was my aunt all the time I was dressing, preaching and talking away just as if she was reading a sermon. However, I did not hear above one word in ten, for I was thinking, you may suppose, of my dear Wickham. I longed to know whether he would be married in his blue coat.

"Well, and so we breakfasted at ten as usual. I thought it would never be over, for my uncle and aunt were horrid unpleasant all the time I was with them. If you'll believe me, I did not once put my foot out of doors, though I was there a fortnight. Not one party, or scheme, or anything. To be sure London was rather thin, but, however, the Little Theatre was open. Well, and so just as the carriage came to the door, my uncle was called away upon business with that horrid man Mr. Stone. And then, you know, when once they get together, there is no end to it. Well, I was so frightened I did not know what to do, for my uncle was to give me away, and if we were beyond the hour, we could not be married all day. But luckily he came back again in ten minutes' time, and then we all set out. However, I recollected afterwards that if he had been prevented going, the wedding need not be put off, for Mr. Darcy might have done as well."

"Mr. Darcy!" gasped Elizabeth when she could breathe again.

"Oh, yes! He was to come there with Wickham, you know. But gracious me! I quite forgot! I ought not to have said a word about it. I promised them so faithfully! What will Wickham say? It was to be such a secret!"

Jane shared a quick look of shock with Elizabeth before placing a gentle hand of restraint on their younger sister's arm. "If it was to be secret, say not another word on the subject. You may depend upon my seeking no further."

"Oh! Certainly," said Elizabeth, though burning with curiosity and worry. "We will ask you no questions."

"Thank you," said Lydia. "For if you did, I should certainly tell you all, and then Wickham would be angry."

On such encouragement to ask, Elizabeth was forced to put it out of her power by running away.

But to live in ignorance on such a point was impossible, or at least it was impossible not to try for information. Mr. Darcy had challenged Mr. Wickham to a duel, and then had been at her sister's wedding. It was exactly a scene, and exactly among people, where he had apparently least to do and least temptation to go. Conjectures as to the meaning of it, rapid and wild, hurried into her brain, but she was satisfied with none. Those that best pleased her as placing his conduct in the noblest light seemed most improbable. She could not bear such suspense, and upon the group's return to Longbourn, she hastily seized a sheet of paper and wrote a short letter to her aunt to request an explanation of what Lydia had dropped, if it were compatible with the secrecy which had been intended. She added:

> "You may readily comprehend what my curiosity must be to know how a person unconnected with any of us, and (comparatively speaking) a stranger to our family, should have been amongst you at such a time. Pray write instantly and let me understand it—unless it is, for very cogent reasons, to remain in the secrecy which Lydia seems to think necessary. Then I must endeavor to be satisfied with ignorance."

"Not that I *shall*, though," she added to herself as she finished the letter. "And my dear aunt, if you do not tell me in an honorable manner, I shall certainly be reduced to tricks and stratagems to find it out."

Jane's delicate sense of honor would not allow her to speak to Elizabeth privately of what Lydia had let fall, and Elizabeth was glad of it. Until it appeared whether her inquiries would receive any satisfaction, she had rather be without a confidante.

In the meantime, the newlyweds must be seen off, as Mr. Bennet had refused to allow them to stay overnight, and they were to proceed directly to the North to join Mr. Wickham's new regiment.

The moment of his and Lydia's departure soon came, and Mrs. Bennet was forced to submit to a separation, which, as her husband by no means entered into her scheme of their all going to Newcastle, was likely to continue at least a twelvemonth.

"Oh! My dear Lydia," cried she. "When shall we meet again?"

"Oh, lord! I don't know. Not these two or three years, perhaps."

"Write to me very often, my dear."

"As often as I can. But you know married women have never much time for writing. My sisters may write to *me*. They will have nothing else to do." She giggled as she climbed into the carriage.

Mr. Wickham's adieus were much more affectionate than his wife's. He smiled, looked handsome, and said many pretty things.

As soon as they were gone, Mr. Bennet said, "He is as fine a fellow as ever I saw. He simpers, and smirks, and makes love to us all. I am prodigiously proud of him. I defy even Sir William Lucas himself to produce a more valuable son-in-law."

The loss of her daughter was sure to make Mrs. Bennet very dull for several days. Watching their carriage being driven away, she murmured, "I often think that there is nothing so bad as parting with one's friends. One seems so forlorn without them."

Chapter Twenty-seven

Elizabeth had the satisfaction of receiving an answer to her letter to her aunt as soon as she possibly could. She was no sooner in possession of it than, hurrying into the little copse where she was least likely to be interrupted, she sat down on one of the benches and prepared to be happy, for the length of the letter convinced her that it did not contain a denial.

"Gracechurch street, Sept. 6.
"MY DEAR NIECE,

"I have just received your letter and shall devote this whole morning to answering it, as I foresee that a *little* writing will not comprise what I have to tell you. I must confess myself surprised by your application. I did not expect it from *you*. Don't think me angry, however, for I only mean to let you know that I had not imagined such inquiries to be necessary on *your* side. If you do not choose to understand me, forgive my impertinence. Your uncle is as much surprised as I am—and nothing but the belief of your being a party concerned would have allowed him to act as he has done. But if you are really innocent and ignorant, I must be more explicit.

"On the very day of my coming home from Longbourn, your uncle had a most unexpected visitor. Mr. Darcy called and was shut up with him several hours. It was all over before I arrived, so my curiosity was not so dreadfully racked as *yours* seems to have been. He came to tell Mr. Gardiner that he had found out where your sister and Mr. Wickham were, and that he had seen and talked with them both...Mr. Wickham repeatedly, Lydia once. From what I can collect, he left Derbyshire only one day after ourselves and came to town with the resolution of hunting for them. The motive professed was his conviction of its being owing to himself that Mr. Wickham's worthlessness had not been so well known as to make it impossible for any young woman of character to love or confide in him. He generously imputed the whole to his mistaken pride and confessed that he had before thought it beneath him to lay his private actions open to the world. His character was to speak for itself. He called it, therefore, his duty to step forward and endeavor to remedy an evil which had been brought on by himself. If he had another motive, I am sure it would never disgrace him. He had been some days in town before he was able to discover them. But he had something to direct his search, which was more than *we* had, and the consciousness of this was another reason for his resolving to follow us.

"There is a lady, it seems, a Mrs. Younge, who was some time ago governess to Miss Darcy, and was dismissed from her charge on some cause of disapprobation, though he did not say what. She then took a large house in Edward Street, and has since maintained herself by letting lodgings. This Mrs. Younge was, he knew, intimately acquainted with Mr. Wickham, and he went to her for intelligence of him as soon as he got to town. But it was two or three days before he could get from her what he wanted. She would not betray her trust, I suppose, without bribery and corruption, for she really did know where her friend was to be found. Mr. Wickham indeed had gone to her on their first arrival in London, and had she been able to receive them into her house, they would have taken up their abode with her. At length, however, our kind friend procured the wished-for direction. He saw Mr. Wickham and afterwards insisted on seeing Lydia.

"His first object with her, he acknowledged, had been to persuade her to quit her present disgraceful situation and return to her friends as soon as they could be prevailed on to receive her, offering his assistance as far as it would go. But he found Lydia absolutely resolved on remaining where she was. She cared for none of her friends, she wanted no help of his, and she would not hear of leaving Wickham. She was sure they should be married some time or other, and it did not much signify when. Since such were her feelings, he thought it only remained to secure and expedite a marriage, which, in his very first conversation with Mr. Wickham, he easily learned had never been *his* design. He confessed himself obliged to leave the corps on account of some debts of honor, which were very pressing, and scrupled not to lay all the ill-consequences of Lydia's flight on her own folly alone. He meant to resign his commission immediately, and as to his future situation, he could conjecture very little about it. He must go somewhere, but he did not know where, and he knew he should have nothing to live on.

"Mr. Darcy asked him why he had not married your sister at once. Though Mr. Bennet was not imagined to be very rich, he would have been able to do something for him, and his situation must have been benefited by marriage. But he found, in reply to this question, that Mr. Wickham still cherished the hope of more effectually making his fortune by marriage in some other country. Under such circumstances, however, he was not likely to be proof against the temptation of immediate relief.

"They met several times, for there was much to be discussed. Mr. Wickham of course wanted more than he could get, but at length was reduced to be reasonable. Lydia complained that they even dueled over the matter, though I did not hear mention of this directly from either of them nor could I observe any hint of a single wound on either man, so I can not ascertain this rumor's veracity.

"However the resolution was reached, once every thing was settled between *them*, Mr. Darcy's next step was to make your uncle acquainted with it, and he first called in Gracechurch Street the evening before I came home. But Mr. Gardiner could not be seen, and Mr. Darcy found on further inquiry that your father was still with him but would quit town the next morning. He did not judge your father to be a person whom he could so properly consult as your uncle, and therefore readily postponed seeing him till after the departure of the former. He did not leave his name, and till the next day it was only known that a gentleman had called on business.

"On Saturday he came again. Your father was gone, your uncle at home, and, as I said before, they had a great deal of talk together.

"They met again on Sunday, and then *I* saw him too. It was not all settled before Monday: as soon as it was, the express was sent off to Longbourn. But our visitor was very obstinate. I fancy, Lizzy, that obstinacy is the real defect of his character after all. He has been accused of many faults at different times, but *this* is the true one. Nothing was to be done that he did not do himself; though I am sure (and I do not speak it to be thanked, therefore say nothing about it), your uncle would most readily have settled the whole.

"They argued about it together for a long time, which was more than either the gentleman or lady concerned in it deserved. But at last your uncle was forced to yield, and instead of being allowed to be of use to his niece, was forced to put up with only having the probable credit of it, which went sorely against the grain. I really believe your letter this morning gave him great pleasure, because it required an explanation that would rob him of his borrowed feathers and give the praise where it was due. But Lizzy, this must go no farther than yourself, or Jane at most.

"You know pretty well, I suppose, what has been done for the young people. His debts are to be paid, amounting, I believe, to considerably more than a thousand pounds, another thousand in addition to her own settled upon *her*, and his commission purchased. The reason why all this was to be done by him alone was such as I have given above. It was owing to him, to his reserve and want of proper consideration, that Mr. Wickham's character had been so misunderstood, and consequently that he had been received and noticed as he was. Perhaps there was some truth in *this,* though I doubt whether *his* reserve, or *anybody's* reserve, can be answerable for the event. But in spite of all this fine talking, my dear Lizzy, you may rest perfectly assured that your uncle would never have yielded if we had not given him credit for *another interest* in the affair.

"When all this was resolved on, he returned again to his friends who were still staying at Pemberley. But it was agreed that he should be in London once more when the wedding took place, and all money matters were then to receive the last finish.

"I believe I have now told you everything. It is a relation which you tell me is to give you great surprise. I hope at least it will not afford you any displeasure. Lydia came to us, and Mr. Wickham had constant admission to the house. *He* was exactly what he had been when I knew him in Hertfordshire. But I would not tell you how little I was satisfied with her behavior while she stayed with us if I had not perceived, by Jane's letter last Wednesday, that her conduct on coming home was exactly of a piece with it, and therefore what I now tell you can give you no fresh pain. I talked to her repeatedly in the most serious manner, representing to her all the wickedness of what she had done and all the unhappiness she had brought on her family. If she heard me, it was by good luck, for I am sure she did not listen. I was sometimes quite provoked, but then I recollected my dear Elizabeth and Jane and for their sakes had patience with her.

"Mr. Darcy was punctual in his return, and as Lydia informed you, attended the wedding. He dined with us the next day and was to leave town again on Wednesday or Thursday. Will you be very angry with me, my dear Lizzy, if I take this opportunity of saying (what I was never bold enough to say before) how much I like him. His behavior to us has in every respect been as pleasing as when we were in Derbyshire. His understanding and opinions all please me. He wants nothing but a little more liveliness, and *that*, if he marry *prudently*, his wife may teach him. I thought him very sly—he hardly ever mentioned your name. But slyness seems the fashion.

"Pray forgive me if I have been very presuming, or at least do not punish me so far as to exclude me from P. I shall never be quite happy till I have been all round the park. A low phaeton, with a nice little pair of ponies, would be the very thing.

"But I must write no more. The children have been wanting me this half hour.
"Yours, very sincerely,
"M. GARDINER."

The contents of this letter threw Elizabeth into a flutter of spirits in which it was difficult to determine whether pleasure or pain bore the greatest share. The vague and unsettled suspicions which uncertainty had produced of what Mr. Darcy might have been doing to forward her sister's match, which she had feared to encourage as an exertion of goodness too great to be probable, and at the same time dreaded to be just from the pain of obligation, were proved beyond their greatest extent to be true! He had followed them purposely to town. He had taken on himself all the trouble and mortification attendant on such a research, in which supplication had been necessary to a woman whom he must abominate and despise, and where he was reduced to meet, frequently meet, reason with, persuade, duel, and finally bribe, the monster whom he always most wished to avoid, and whose very name it was punishment to him to pronounce. He must have won the challenge against Mr. Wickham, considering the outcome of it all. And yet how had he managed the self-restraint necessary to stay his hand from ending Mr. Wickham's cursed existence? Though Mr. Darcy was a gentleman, despite all her earlier assumptions to the contrary, he was also still capable of a man's emotions, not the least of which would be the desire for revenge against one who had done him and his family so much injustice.

Mr. Darcy could have ended the life of his family's greatest enemy. Instead, he had not only allowed such a creature to live, but he had continued on, taking so many steps to ensure that Mr. Wickham would not jilt Lydia at the alter and would indeed follow through on his promise to marry her. And he had done all this for a girl whom he could neither regard nor esteem.

Her heart whispered that he had done it for her. But it was a hope shortly checked by other considerations, and she soon felt that even her vanity was insufficient when required to depend on his affection for her —for a woman who had already refused him—as able to overcome a sentiment so natural as abhorrence against relationship with Mr. Wickham. Brother-in-law of Mr. Wickham! Every kind of pride must revolt from the connection. He had, to be sure, done much. She was ashamed to think how much. But he had given a reason for his interference, which asked no extraordinary stretch of belief. It was reasonable that he should feel he had been wrong. He had liberality, and he had the means of exercising it. Perhaps too, he had sought to force Mr. Wickham to marry Lydia as a form of delayed punishment for his actions against the Darcys.

It was painful, exceedingly painful, to know that they were under obligations to a person who could never receive a return. They owed the restoration of Lydia, her character, everything, to him. Oh! How heartily did she grieve over every ungracious sensation she had ever encouraged, every saucy speech she had ever directed towards him. For herself she was humbled, but she was proud of him. Proud that in a cause of compassion and honor, of desire for revenge and justice, he had been able to get the better of himself.

She read over her aunt's commendation of him again and again. It was hardly enough, but it pleased her. She was even sensible of some pleasure, though mixed with regret, on finding how steadfastly both she and her uncle had been persuaded that affection and confidence subsisted between Mr. Darcy and herself.

If only that were true, and furthermore, enough to surpass the many boundaries that stood between them.

The leaving of Lydia was rather hard on their mother for some time, as everyone had fully expected. But the spiritless condition which this event threw her into was shortly relieved, and her mind opened again to the agitation of hope, by an article of news which then began to be in circulation. The housekeeper at Netherfield had received orders to prepare for the arrival of her master, who was coming down in a day or two, to shoot there for several weeks. Mrs. Bennet was quite in the fidgets. She looked at Jane and smiled and shook her head by turns.

"Well, well, and so Mr. Bingley is coming down, sister," said she to Mrs. Phillips, who first brought her the news. "Well, so much the better. Not that I care about it, though. He is nothing to us, you know, and I am sure *I* never want to see him again. But, however, he is very welcome to come to Netherfield, if he likes it. And who knows what *may* happen? But that is nothing to us. You know, sister, we agreed long ago never to mention a word about it. And so, is it quite certain he is coming?"

"You may depend on it," replied the other. "For Mrs. Nicholls was in Meryton last night, I saw her passing by and went out myself on purpose to know the truth of it, and she told me that it was certain true. He comes down on Thursday at the latest, very likely on Wednesday. She was going to the butcher's, she told me, on purpose to order in some meat on Wednesday, and she has got three couple of ducks just fit to be killed."

Miss Bennet had not been able to hear of his coming without changing color. It was many months since she had mentioned his name to Elizabeth.

But now, as soon as they were alone together, she said, "I saw you look at me today, Lizzy, when my aunt told us of the present report, and I know I appeared distressed. But don't imagine it was from any silly cause. I was only confused for the moment, because I felt that I *should* be looked at. I do assure you that the news does not affect me either with pleasure or pain. I am glad of one thing, that he comes

239

alone, because we shall see the less of him. Not that I am afraid of *myself*, but I dread other people's remarks."

Elizabeth did not know what to make of it. Had she not seen him in Derbyshire, she might have supposed him capable of coming there with no other view than what was acknowledged. But she still thought him partial to Jane, and she wavered as to the greater probability of his coming there *with* his friend's permission, or being bold enough to come without it.

"Yet it is hard," she sometimes thought, "that this poor man cannot come to a house which he has legally hired, without raising all this speculation! I *will* leave him to himself."

In spite of what her sister declared and really believed to be her feelings in the expectation of his arrival, Elizabeth could easily perceive that her spirits were affected by it. They were more disturbed, more unequal, than she had often seen them.

On the third morning after his arrival in Hertfordshire, Mrs. Bennet saw him, from her dressing room window, enter the paddock and ride towards the house.

Her daughters were eagerly called to partake of her joy. Jane resolutely kept her place at the table; but Elizabeth, to satisfy her mother, went to the window—she looked—she saw Mr. Darcy with him, and sat down again in shock by her sister.

"There is a gentleman with him, mamma," said Kitty. "La! It looks just like that man that used to be with him before. Mr. what's-his-name. That tall, proud man."

"Good gracious! Mr. Darcy! And so it does, I vow. Well, any friend of Mr. Bingley's will always be welcome here, to be sure, but else I must say that I hate the very sight of him."

Both elder sisters were uncomfortable enough. But Elizabeth had sources of uneasiness which could not be suspected by Jane, to whom she had never yet had courage to show Mrs. Gardiner's letter or to relate her own change of sentiment towards him. To Jane, he could be only a man whose merit she had undervalued. But to her own more extensive information, he was the person to whom the whole family were indebted for the first of benefits, and whom she regarded herself with an interest, if not quite so tender, at least as reasonable and just as what Jane felt for Mr. Bingley. Her astonishment at his coming—at his coming to Netherfield, to Longbourn, and voluntarily seeking her again —was almost equal to what she had known on first witnessing his altered behavior in Derbyshire.

But upon further reflection, she understood. Of course he would come and see the business through to the end. As he had done with Mr. Wickham, setting to rights his perceived mistakes and staying till Lydia's marriage was completed, so too would he come with Mr. Bingley to set to rights the very wrongful separation he had caused between his friend and Jane.

She sat intently at work, striving to be composed in spite of the great pain of disappointment that arose from such a realization. She did not dare to lift up her eyes till anxious curiosity carried them to the face of her sister as the servant was approaching the door. Jane looked a little paler than usual, but more sedate than Elizabeth had expected. On the gentlemen's appearing within the room, her color increased, yet she received them with tolerable ease and with a propriety of behavior equally free from any symptom of resentment or any unnecessary complaisance.

Elizabeth said as little to either as civility would allow, and sat down again to her work with an eagerness which it did not often command. She had ventured only one glance at Mr. Darcy. He looked serious as usual, and more as he had been used to look in Hertfordshire than as she had seen him at Pemberley. That old tightness about the mouth and eyes had returned, setting his countenance into a near frown, though perhaps of determination today. And too, perhaps he could not in her mother's presence be what he was before her uncle and aunt. It was a painful, but not an improbable, conjecture.

Mr. Bingley she had likewise seen for an instant, and in that short period saw him looking both pleased and embarrassed. He was received by Mrs. Bennet with a degree of civility which made her two daughters ashamed, especially when contrasted with the cold and ceremonious politeness of her curtsey and address to his friend.

Elizabeth, particularly, who knew that her mother owed to the latter the preservation of her favorite daughter from irremediable infamy, was hurt and distressed to a most painful degree by a distinction so ill applied.

Mr. Darcy, after inquiring of her how Mr. and Mrs. Gardiner did, a question which she could not answer without confusion, said scarcely anything. He was not seated by her. Perhaps that was the reason for his silence, though it had not been so in Derbyshire. There he had talked to her friends when he could not to herself. But now several minutes elapsed without bringing the sound of his voice, and when occasionally, unable to resist the impulse of curiosity, she raised her eyes to his face, she as often found him looking at Jane as at herself, and frequently on no object but the ground. More thoughtfulness and less anxiety to please than when they last met were plainly expressed. She was disappointed and angry with herself for being so.

"Could I expect it to be otherwise!" thought she.

She was in no humor for conversation with anyone but himself, and to him she had hardly courage to speak. She inquired after his sister, but could do no more.

"It is a long time, Mr. Bingley, since you went away," said Mrs. Bennet.

He readily agreed to it.

"I began to be afraid you would never come back again," added Mrs. Bennet. "People *did* say you meant to quit the place entirely at Michaelmas, but I hope it is not true. A great many changes have happened in the neighborhood since you went away. Miss Lucas is married and settled. And one of my own daughters. I suppose you have heard of it; indeed, you must have seen it in the papers. It was in The Times and The Courier, I know, though it was not put in as it ought to be. It was only said, 'Lately, George Wickham, Esq. to Miss Lydia Bennet', without there being a syllable said of her father, or the place where she lived, or anything. It was my brother Gardiner's drawing up too, and I wonder how he came to make such an awkward business of it. Did you see it?"

Mr. Bingley replied that he did and made his congratulations. Elizabeth dared not lift up her eyes. How Mr. Darcy looked, therefore, she could not tell.

"It is a delightful thing, to be sure, to have a daughter well married," continued her mother. "But at the same time, Mr. Bingley, it is very hard to have her taken such a way from me. They are gone to Newcastle, a place quite northward, it seems, and there they are to stay I do not know how long. His regiment is there; for I suppose you have heard of his leaving the corps, and of his being gone into the regulars. Thank Heaven! He has *some* friends, though perhaps not so many as he deserves."

Elizabeth, who knew this to be leveled at Mr. Darcy, was in such misery of shame that she could hardly keep her seat. It drew from her, however, the exertion of speaking, which nothing else had so effectually done before. She asked Mr. Bingley whether he meant to make any stay in the country at present.

"A few weeks, I believe," was his reply.

"When you have killed all your own birds, Mr. Bingley," said her mother, "I beg you will come here and shoot as many as you please on Mr. Bennet's manor. I am sure he will be vastly happy to oblige you, and will save all the best of the covies for you."

Elizabeth's misery increased at such unnecessary, such officious attention! Were the same fair prospect to arise at present as had flattered them a year ago, everything, she was persuaded, would be hastening to the same vexatious conclusion. At that instant, she felt that years of happiness could not make Jane or herself amends for moments of such painful confusion.

"The first wish of my heart," said she to herself, "is never more to be in company with either of them. Their society can afford no pleasure that will atone for such wretchedness as this! Let me never see either one or the other again!"

Yet the misery, for which years of happiness were to offer no compensation, received soon afterwards material relief from observing how much the beauty of her sister re-kindled the admiration of her former lover. When first he came in, he had spoken to her but little, but every five minutes seemed to be giving her more of his attention.

When the gentlemen rose to go away, Mrs. Bennet was mindful of her intended civility, and they were invited and engaged to dine at Longbourn in a few days time.

"You are quite a visit in my debt, Mr. Bingley," added she. "For when you went to town last winter, you promised to take a family dinner with us as soon as you returned. I have not forgot, you see, and I assure you I was very much disappointed that you did not come back and keep your engagement."

Mr. Bingley looked a little silly at this reflection and said something of his concern at having been prevented by business. They then went away.

Mrs. Bennet had been strongly inclined to ask them to stay and dine there that day, as she hastened to reassure her daughters, who were merely relieved at the gentlemen's leaving and thus the end of what had been quite an awkward and long visit.

"But, though I always keep a very good table," she added. "I did not think anything less than two courses could be good enough or satisfy the appetite and pride of one who had ten thousand a year."

Chapter Twenty-eight

As soon as they were gone from view, Elizabeth sank onto the couch with a sigh of great disappointment. All hope was ended by Mr. Darcy's looks and behavior. It was obvious that he had come only to repair the damage he had caused between Mr. Bingley and Jane, and all attachments and hopes he might have once entertained for Elizabeth were sunk forever.

Jane joined her with a much quieter sigh that sounded like one of relief. "Now that this first meeting is over, I feel perfectly easy. I know my own strength, and I shall never be embarrassed again by his coming. I am glad he dines here on Tuesday. It will then be publicly seen that, on both sides, we meet only as common and indifferent acquaintance."

"Yes, very indifferent indeed," said Elizabeth with a laugh. "Oh, Jane, take care."

"My dear Lizzy, you cannot think me so weak as to be in danger now?"

"I think you are in very great danger of making him as much in love with you as ever."

Quite suddenly, they heard the front door of the house open, followed in short order by seeing the drawing room door open to admit none other than a very determined Mr. Bingley. Mr. Darcy was nowhere to be seen.

All of the ladies present jumped to their feet.

"Madam," he said by way of greeting to Mrs. Bennet, "I realize this is all very untoward. But I would like to request the honor of the presence of your daughter, Miss Bennet…alone."

"Oh!" replied Mrs. Bennet as she hurried across the room in delighted confusion. "But of course, Mr. Bingley! It is so good to see you again." She turned to her daughters, waving her hands frantically. "Come along, girls. All except you, of course, dear Jane."

Elizabeth gave her sister a quick smile of encouragement, and another to Mr. Bingley before following her family out of the room. As she pulled the door shut behind her, she just had time to clearly hear him tell her sister, "First, I must apologize for my actions when last I was here, and to heartily beg your forgiveness."

Though Kitty's giggling made it difficult to make out entirely once the door was shut, they were barely able to understand in short order that all was resolved. Mr. Bingley had announced his long restrained love for her, asked for her hand in marriage, and Jane had accepted.

Mrs. Bennet could contain herself no longer, and throwing open the door, rushed in to her eldest daughter with much cries of joy. The rest of the Bennet sisters followed, and all was much laughter for the rest of the evening, hushed in happy whispers while Mr. Bingley sought Mr. Bennet's permission, then loud again upon Mr. Bingley's return when a smile and nod to his future lady assured her that they were indeed to be married.

It was an evening of no common delight to almost all of them. The satisfaction of Miss Bennet's mind gave a glow of such sweet animation to her face as made her look handsomer than ever. Kitty simpered and smiled and hoped her turn was coming soon. Mrs. Bennet could not give her consent or speak her approbation in terms warm enough to satisfy her feelings, though she talked to Mr. Bingley of nothing else for half an hour. And when Mr. Bennet joined them at supper, his voice and manner plainly showed how really happy he was. And of course Elizabeth was happy for two reasons…joyous in her eldest sister's so long awaited engagement to the one truly perfect man for Jane, and the pride that came from the knowledge that surely today's great happiness was a direct result of strong action and encouragement upon Mr. Darcy's part. For Mr. Bingley had appeared far too nervous and lacking in confidence at his first arrival at Longbourn this afternoon, and only a stern talking to from his friend could have possibly given him the courage to return, and further, to propose.

Once their visitor took his leave for the night, Mr. Bingley turned to his eldest daughter and said, "Jane, I congratulate you. You will be a very happy woman."

Jane went to him instantly, kissed him, and thanked him for his goodness.

"You are a good girl," replied he. "And I have great pleasure in thinking you will be so happily settled. I have not a doubt of your doing very well together. Your tempers are by no means unlike. You are each of you so complying that nothing will ever be resolved on, so easy that every servant will cheat you, and so generous that you will always exceed your income."

"I hope not so," was Jane's reply. "Imprudence or thoughtlessness in money matters would be unpardonable in me."

"Exceed their income!" cried his wife. "My dear Mr. Bennet, what are you talking of? Why, he has four or five thousand a year, and very likely more." Then addressing her daughter, "Oh! My dear, dear Jane, I am so happy! I am sure I shan't get a wink of sleep all night. I knew how it would be. I always said it must be so at last. I was sure you could not be so beautiful for nothing! I remember, as soon as ever I saw him, when he first came into Hertfordshire last year, I thought how likely it was that you should come together. Oh! He is the handsomest young man that ever was seen!"

Mr. Wickham and Lydia were all forgotten by Mrs. Bennet. Jane was beyond competition her favorite child now, and at that moment, she cared for no other.

Jane's younger sisters soon began to make interest with her for objects of happiness which she might in future be able to dispense. Mary petitioned for the use of the library at Netherfield, and Kitty begged very hard for a few balls there every winter.

Mr. Bingley, from this time, was of course a daily visitor at Longbourn, coming frequently before breakfast and always remaining till after supper, unless when some barbarous neighbor, who could not be enough detested, had given him an invitation to dinner which he thought himself obliged to accept.

Elizabeth had now but little time for conversation with her sister, for while he was present, Jane had no attention to bestow on anyone else. But she found herself considerably useful to both of them in those hours of separation that must sometimes occur. In the absence of Jane, he always attached himself to Elizabeth for the pleasure of talking of her, and when Mr. Bingley was gone, Jane constantly sought the same means of relief.

"He has made me so happy," said she one evening, "by telling me that he was totally ignorant of my being in town last spring! I had not believed it possible."

"I suspected as much," replied Elizabeth. "But how did he account for it?"

"It must have been his sister's doing. They were certainly no friends to his acquaintance with me, which I cannot wonder at, since he might have chosen so much more advantageously in many respects. But when they see, as I trust they will, that their brother is happy with me, they will learn to be contented, and we shall be on good terms again, though we can never be what we once were to each other."

"That is the most unforgiving speech that I ever heard you utter. Good girl! It would vex me, indeed, to see you again the dupe of Miss Bingley's pretended regard."

"Would you believe it, Lizzy, that when he went to town last November, he really loved me, and nothing but a persuasion of *my* being indifferent or unable to love him despite his changed nature would have prevented his coming down again!"

"Ah, so you know of his immortal side then." Elizabeth nodded. "I had hoped he would tell you himself soon. Please forgive me for not doing so, but I learned of it as a secret I promised never to tell. Mr. Darcy related Mr. Bingley's history to me in a letter, but I was not given leave to share it with anyone else, and when it seemed all hope for a union between you and Bingley was lost..."

Jane hugged her sister. "It is no matter, sister. Nothing but love and utter, complete happiness can fill my heart now."

"And so you love him still? For you know Mr. Bingley is the good sort of man who would not hesitate to allow you to change your mind about marrying him if you felt otherwise about it."

Jane smiled and shook her head. "What he has become was never his choice. He has struggled so hard to learn how to control his thirst and not let it truly change the man that he still is within. Mr. and Mrs. Hurst happily supply for his needs, as well as an arrangement with the apothecary for emergencies." But here Jane blushed in modesty and could discuss such details no further.

Elizabeth smiled in understanding. "Well, then, so he made a small error in judgement with regards to your feelings, to be sure. But it is to the credit of his modesty."

This naturally introduced a panegyric from Jane on his diffidence and the little value he put on his own good qualities. Elizabeth was pleased to find that he had not betrayed the interference of his friend, for, though Jane had the most generous and forgiving heart in the world, she knew it was a circumstance which must prejudice her against him.

"I am certainly the most fortunate creature that ever existed!" cried Jane. "Oh! Lizzy, why am I thus singled from my family and blessed above them all! If I could but see *you* as happy! If there *were* but such another man for you!"

There was only one man she felt sure could ever make her as happy. But such thoughts were not safe to dwell upon ever again. She swallowed against the growing tightness in her throat and made herself smile. "If you were to give me forty such men, I never could be so happy as you. Till I have your disposition, your goodness, I never can have your happiness. No, no, let me shift for myself, and, perhaps, if I have very good luck, I may meet with another Mr. Collins in time."

The situation of affairs in the Longbourn family could not be long a secret. Mrs. Bennet was privileged to whisper it to Mrs. Phillips, and she ventured, without any permission, to do the same by all her neighbors in Meryton.

The Bennets were speedily pronounced to be the luckiest family in the world, though only a few weeks before, when Lydia had first run away, they had been generally proved to be marked out for misfortune.

One morning, about a week after Mr. Bingley's engagement with Jane had been formed, as he and the females of the family were sitting together in the dining room, their attention was suddenly drawn to the window by the sound of a carriage. They perceived a chaise and four driving up the lawn. It was too early in the morning for visitors, and besides, the equipage did not answer to that of any of their neighbors. The horses were post, and neither the carriage, nor the livery of the servant who preceded it, were familiar to them. As it was certain, however, that somebody was coming, Mr. Bingley instantly prevailed on Miss Bennet to avoid the confinement of such an intrusion and walk away with him into the shrubbery. They both set off, and the conjectures of the remaining three continued, though with little satisfaction, till the door was thrown open and their visitor entered. It was Lady Catherine de Bourgh.

They were of course all intending to be surprised, but their astonishment was beyond their expectation, and on the part of Mrs.

Bennet and Kitty, though she was perfectly unknown to them, even inferior to what Elizabeth felt.

She entered the room with an air more than usually ungracious, made no other reply to Elizabeth's salutation than a slight inclination of the head, and sat down without saying a word. Elizabeth had mentioned her name to her mother on her ladyship's entrance, though no request for an introduction had been made.

Mrs. Bennet, all amazement, though flattered by having a guest of such high importance, received her with the utmost politeness.

After sitting for a moment in silence, Lady Catherine said very stiffly, "You have a very small park here."

"It is nothing in comparison to Rosings, my lady, I dare say. But I assure you it is much larger than Sir William Lucas's," said Mrs. Bennet.

Mrs. Bennet then, with great civility, begged her ladyship to take some refreshment.

But Lady Catherine very resolutely, and not very politely, declined eating anything, and then, rising up, said to Elizabeth, "Miss Bennet, there seemed to be a prettyish kind of a little wilderness on one side of your lawn. I should be glad to take a turn in it, if you will favor me with your company."

"Go, my dear, and show her ladyship about the different walks," cried her mother. "I think she will be pleased with the hermitage."

Elizabeth obeyed and attended her noble guest downstairs. Her carriage remained at the door, and Elizabeth saw that her waiting woman was in it. They proceeded in silence along the gravel walk that led to the copse. Elizabeth was determined to make no effort for conversation with a woman who was now more than usually insolent and disagreeable.

"How could I ever think her like her nephew?" thought she as she looked at her face.

As soon as they entered the copse, Lady Catherine began in the following manner, "You can be at no loss, Miss Bennet, to understand the reason for my journey hither. Your own heart, your own conscience, must tell you why I have come."

Elizabeth looked with unaffected astonishment. "Indeed, you are mistaken, Madam. I have not been at all able to account for the honor of seeing you here."

"Miss Bennet, you ought to know that I am not to be trifled with," snapped Lady Catherine. "But however insincere *you* may choose to be, you shall not find *me* so. My character has ever been celebrated for its sincerity and frankness, and in a cause of such moment as this, I shall certainly not depart from it. A report of a most alarming nature reached me two days ago. I was told that not only your sister was on the point of being most advantageously married, but that you, Miss Elizabeth Bennet, would in all likelihood be soon afterwards united to my nephew, my own nephew, Mr. Darcy. Though I *know* it must be a scandalous falsehood, though I would not injure him so much as to suppose the truth of it possible, I instantly resolved on setting off for this place, that I might make my sentiments known to you."

"If you believed it impossible to be true," said Elizabeth, coloring with astonishment and disdain, "I wonder you took the trouble of coming so far. What could your ladyship propose by it?"

"To insist upon having such a report universally contradicted."

Elizabeth coolly said, "Your coming to Longbourn to see me and my family will be rather a confirmation of it if, indeed, such a report is in existence."

"If! Do you then pretend to be ignorant of it? Has it not been industriously circulated by yourself? Do you not know that such a report is spread abroad?"

"I never heard that it was."

"And can you likewise declare that there is no foundation for it?"

"I do not pretend to possess equal frankness with your ladyship. You may ask questions which I shall not choose to answer."

"This is not to be borne. Miss Bennet, I insist on being satisfied. Has my nephew made you an offer of marriage?"

"Your ladyship has declared it to be impossible."

"It ought to be so; it must be so while he retains the use of his reason. But your arts and allurements may, in a moment of infatuation, have made him forget what he owes to himself and to all his family. You may have drawn him in."

"If I have, I shall be the last person to confess it."

"Miss Bennet, do you know who I am? I have not been accustomed to such language as this. I am almost the nearest relation he has in the world, and am entitled to know all his dearest concerns."

"But you are not entitled to know mine. Nor will such behavior as this ever induce me to be explicit."

"Let me be rightly understood. This match, to which you have the presumption to aspire, can never take place. No, never. Mr. Darcy is engaged to my daughter. Now what have you to say?"

"Only this…that if he is so, you can have no reason to suppose he will make an offer to me."

Lady Catherine hesitated for a moment, and then replied, "The engagement between them is of a peculiar kind. From their infancy, they have been intended for each other. It was the favorite wish of *his* mother, as well as of hers. While in their cradles, we planned the union. And now, at the moment when the wishes of both sisters would be accomplished in their marriage, to be prevented by a young woman of inferior birth, of no importance in the world, and wholly unallied to the family! Do you pay no regard to the wishes of his friends? To his tacit engagement with Miss de Bourgh? Are you lost to every feeling of propriety and delicacy? Have you not heard me say that from his earliest hours he was destined for his cousin?"

"Yes, and I had heard it before. But what is that to me? If there is no other objection to my marrying your nephew, I shall certainly not be kept from it by knowing that his mother and aunt wished him to marry Miss de Bourgh. You both did as much as you could in planning the marriage. Its completion depended on others. If Mr. Darcy is neither by honor nor inclination confined to his cousin, why is not he to make another choice? And if I am that choice, why may not I accept him?"

"Because honor, decorum, prudence, nay, interest, forbid it. Yes, Miss Bennet, interest; for do not expect to be noticed by his family or friends if you willfully act against the inclinations of all. You will be censured, slighted, and despised by everyone connected with him. Your alliance will be a disgrace. Your name will never even be mentioned by any of us."

"These are heavy misfortunes," replied Elizabeth. "But the wife of Mr. Darcy must have such extraordinary sources of happiness necessarily attached to her situation that she could, upon the whole, have no cause to repine."

"Obstinate, headstrong girl! I am ashamed of you! Is this your gratitude for my attentions to you last spring? Is nothing due to me on that score? You are to understand, Miss Bennet, that I came here with the determined resolution of carrying my purpose, nor will I be dissuaded from it. I have not been used to submit to any person's whims. I have not been in the habit of brooking disappointment."

"That will make your ladyship's situation at present more pitiable, but it will have no effect on me."

"I will not be interrupted. Hear me in silence. My daughter and my nephew are formed for each other. They are descended, on the

251

maternal side, from the same noble line, and on the father's, from respectable, honorable, and ancient—though untitled—families. Their fortune on both sides is splendid. They are destined for each other by the voice of every member of their respective houses. And what is to divide them? The upstart pretensions of a young woman without family, connections, or fortune. Is this to be endured! But it must not, shall not be. If you were sensible of your own good, you would not wish to quit the sphere in which you have been brought up."

"In marrying your nephew, I should not consider myself as quitting that sphere. He is a gentleman, I am a gentleman's daughter; so far we are equal."

"True. You *are* a gentleman's daughter. But who was your mother? Who are your uncles and aunts? Do not imagine me ignorant of their condition."

"Whatever my connections may be, if your nephew does not object to them, they can be nothing to *you*."

"And what of his condition? Are you aware of his special dietary needs?" She searched Elizabeth's face, a hint of a confident smile at her mouth as if she believed the revelation of such a secret would win her point at last.

Elizabeth returned her smile. "I am aware that he is a vampire, yes. But why is that a concern for me and not your daughter?"

"My daughter will be glad to become like her cousin and join in his immortality. Can the same be said for you?"

Here Elizabeth must pause in consideration. She had not given thought to whether she would wish to become a vampire as well, only that she had grown used to the idea of Mr. Darcy's controlled need for blood. Perhaps she had, in her most private thoughts, considered whether she might eventually become a voluntary source for such needs within him, yet even this thought had never been allowed full development, for she had never truly allowed herself to think long on the possibility of being his wife.

Lady Catherine nodded. "You see, here is proof that my daughter is the perfect match for him, while one such as yourself is not. She is willing to give her all, her very mortality, for such a union. You cannot say the same."

Elizabeth lifted her chin, took a deep breath, and met Lady Catherine's stare with one of her own. "Do you not think that Mr. Darcy's wishes on this point should also be considered? For what if he should not want a vampire for a wife? If he had, he had ample opportunity to propose to Miss Bingley instead, yet he has not. Perhaps he wishes a human wife at his side, one who will help him remember the ways and emotions of the human world around him."

Lady Catherine's lips pursed with displeasure, her eyes squinting as she sought to control her feelings. After a long silence, she burst out with, "Tell me once and for all, are you engaged to him?"

Though Elizabeth would not, for the mere purpose of obliging Lady Catherine, have answered this question, she could not but say after a moment's deliberation, "I am not."

Lady Catherine seemed pleased at last. "And will you promise me never to enter into such an engagement?"

"I will make no promise of the kind."

"Miss Bennet, I am shocked and astonished. I expected to find a more reasonable young woman. But do not deceive yourself into a belief that I will ever recede. I shall not go away till you have given me the assurance I require."

"And I certainly *never* shall give it. I am not to be intimidated into anything so wholly unreasonable. Your ladyship wants Mr. Darcy to marry your daughter. But would my giving you the wished-for promise make their marriage at all more probable? Supposing him to be attached to me, would my refusing to accept his hand make him wish to bestow it on his cousin? Allow me to say, Lady Catherine, that the arguments with which you have supported this extraordinary application have been as frivolous as the application was ill-judged. You have widely mistaken my character if you think I can be worked on by such persuasions as these. How far your nephew might approve of your interference in his affairs, I cannot tell. But you have certainly no right to concern yourself in mine. I must beg, therefore, to be importuned no farther on the subject."

"Not so hasty, if you please. I have by no means done. To all the objections I have already urged, I have still another to add. I am no stranger to the particulars of your youngest sister's infamous elopement. I know it all; that the young man's marrying her was a patched-up business at the expense of your father and uncles. And is such a girl to be my nephew's sister? Is her husband, is the son of his late father's steward, to be his brother? Heaven and earth! Of what are you thinking? Are the shades of Pemberley to be thus polluted?"

"You can now have nothing further to say," snapped Elizabeth. "You have insulted me in every possible method. I must beg to return to the house."

Lady Catherine struggled to keep up as Elizabeth quickly walked back towards the house.

And still her ladyship would not cease her arguments. "You have no regard, then, for the honor and credit of my nephew! Unfeeling, selfish girl! Do you not consider that a connection with you must disgrace him in the eyes of everybody?"

"Lady Catherine, I have nothing further to say. You know my sentiments."

"You are then resolved to have him?"

"I have said no such thing. I am only resolved to act in that manner which will, in my own opinion, constitute my happiness, without reference to *you* or to any person so wholly unconnected with me."

"It is well. You refuse, then, to oblige me. You refuse to obey the claims of duty, honor, and gratitude. You are determined to ruin him in the opinion of all his friends and make him the contempt of the world."

"Neither duty, nor honor, nor gratitude have any possible claim on me in the present instance. No principle of either would be violated by my marriage with Mr. Darcy. And with regard to the resentment of his family or the indignation of the world, if the former *were* excited by his marrying me, it would not give me one moment's concern—and the world in general would have too much sense to join in the scorn."

"And this is your real opinion! This is your final resolve! Very well. I shall now know how to act. Do not imagine, Miss Bennet, that your ambition will ever be gratified. I came to try you. I hoped to find you reasonable. But depend upon it, I will carry my point." In this manner Lady Catherine talked on till they were at the door of the carriage, when, turning hastily round, she added, "I take no leave of you, Miss Bennet. I send no compliments to your mother. You deserve no such attention. I am most seriously displeased."

Elizabeth made no answer, and without attempting to persuade her ladyship to return into the house, walked quietly into it herself. She heard the carriage drive away as she proceeded upstairs. Her mother impatiently met her at the door of the dressing room to ask why Lady Catherine would not come in again and rest herself.

"She did not choose it," said her daughter. "She would go."

"She is a very fine looking woman! And her calling here was prodigiously civil! For she only came, I suppose, to tell us the Collinses were well. She is on her road somewhere, I dare say, and so, passing through Meryton, thought she might as well call on you. I suppose she had nothing particular to say to you, Lizzy?"

Elizabeth was forced to give into a little falsehood here, for to acknowledge the substance of their conversation was impossible.

Chapter Twenty-nine

The discomposure of spirits which this extraordinary visit threw Elizabeth into could not be easily overcome. Nor could she for many hours learn to think of it less than incessantly. Lady Catherine, it appeared, had actually taken the trouble of this journey from Rosings for the sole purpose of breaking off her supposed engagement with Mr. Darcy. It was a rational scheme, to be sure! But from what the report of their engagement could originate, Elizabeth was at a loss to imagine, till she recollected that *his* being the intimate friend of Mr. Bingley and *her* being the sister of Jane was enough to supply the idea at a time when the expectation of one wedding made everybody eager for another. She had not herself forgotten to feel that the marriage of her sister must bring them more frequently together. And her neighbors at Lucas Lodge, from whom Lady Catherine must have received such a report, had only set down as almost certain and immediate that which Elizabeth had looked forward to as merely possible at some future time.

In revolving Lady Catherine's expressions, however, she could not help feeling some uneasiness as to the possible consequence of her persisting in this interference. From what she had said of her resolution to prevent their marriage, it occurred to Elizabeth that she must be considering making an application to her nephew. And how *he* might take a similar representation of the evils attached to a connection with her, she dared not pronounce. She knew not the exact degree of his affection for his aunt or his dependence on her judgment, but it was natural to suppose that he thought much higher of her ladyship than *she* could do. And it was certain that, in enumerating the miseries of a marriage with *one*, whose immediate connections were so unequal to his

256

own, his aunt would address him on his weakest side. With his notions of dignity, he would probably feel that the arguments, which to Elizabeth had appeared weak and ridiculous, contained much good sense and solid reasoning.

If he had been wavering before as to what he should do, which had often seemed likely, the advice and entreaty of so near a relation might settle every doubt and determine him at once to be as happy as dignity unblemished could make him. In that case he would return no more. Lady Catherine would most probably stop by Netherfield to speak with her nephew, and his engagements to accompany his friend to Longbourn for shooting and sports must give way.

"If, therefore, an excuse for not keeping his promise should come through his friend within a few days, I shall know how to understand it," thought she. "I shall then give over every expectation, every wish for his constancy. If he is satisfied with only regretting me, when he might have obtained my affections and hand, I shall soon cease to regret him at all."

The surprise of the rest of the family, on hearing who their visitor had been, was very great. But they obligingly satisfied it with the same kind of supposition which had appeased Mrs. Bennet's curiosity, and Elizabeth was spared from much teasing on the subject. The next morning as she was going downstairs, she was met by her father, who came out of his library with a letter in his hand.

"Lizzy, I was going to look for you. Come into my room."

She followed him thither. Her curiosity to know what he had to tell her was heightened by the supposition of its being in some manner connected with the letter he held. It suddenly struck her that it might be from Lady Catherine, and she anticipated with dismay all the consequent explanations.

She followed her father to the fireplace, and they both sat down.

He then said, "I have received a letter this morning that has astonished me exceedingly. As it principally concerns yourself, you ought to know its contents. I did not know before that I had two daughters on the brink of matrimony. Let me congratulate you on a very important conquest."

The color now rushed into Elizabeth's cheeks in the instantaneous conviction of its being a letter from the nephew, instead of the aunt, and she was undetermined whether most to be pleased that he explained himself at all, or offended that his letter was not rather addressed to herself.

Her father continued. "You look conscious. Young ladies have great penetration in such matters as these. But I think I may defy even *your* sagacity to discover the name of your admirer. This letter is from Mr. Collins."

"From Mr. Collins! And what can *he* have to say?"

"Something very much to the purpose of course. He begins with congratulations on the approaching nuptials of my eldest daughter, of which, it seems, he has been told by some of the good-natured, gossiping Lucases. I shall not sport with your impatience by reading what he says on that point. What relates to yourself is as follows:

"Having thus offered you the sincere congratulations of Mrs. Collins and myself on this happy event, let me now add a short hint on the subject of another, of which we have been advertised by the same authority. Your daughter Elizabeth, it is presumed, will not long bear the name of Bennet after her elder sister has resigned it, and the chosen partner of her fate may be reasonably looked up to as one of the most illustrious personages in this land."

"Can you possibly guess, Lizzy, who is meant by this?" Mr. Bennet asked before continuing to read the letter thusly:

"This young gentleman is blessed, in a peculiar way, with everything the heart of mortal can most desire—splendid property, noble kindred, and extensive patronage. Yet in spite of all these temptations, let me warn my cousin Elizabeth, and yourself, of what evils you may incur by a precipitate closure with this gentleman's proposals, which, of course, you will be inclined to take immediate advantage of."

"Have you any idea, Lizzy, who this gentleman is? But now it comes out:

"My motive for cautioning you is as follows. We have reason to imagine that his aunt, Lady Catherine de Bourgh, does not look on the match with a friendly eye."

"*Mr. Darcy*, you see, is the man! Now, Lizzy, I think I *have* surprised you. Could he, or the Lucases, have pitched on any man within the circle of our acquaintance whose name would have given the lie more effectually to what they related? Mr. Darcy, who never looks at any woman but to see a blemish, and who probably never looked at you in his life! It is admirable!"

Elizabeth tried to join in her father's pleasantry, but could only force one most reluctant smile. Never had his wit been directed in a manner so little agreeable to her.

"Are you not diverted?"

"Oh! Yes. Pray read on." She made her lips turn up into a smile.

"After mentioning the likelihood of this marriage to her ladyship last night, she immediately, with her usual condescension, expressed what she felt on the occasion. When it became apparent that, on the score of some family objections on the part of my cousin, she would never give her consent to what she termed so disgraceful a match, I thought it my duty to give the speediest intelligence of this to my cousin so that she and her noble admirer may be aware of what they are about and not run hastily into a marriage which has not been properly sanctioned. I am truly rejoiced that my cousin Lydia's sad business has been so well hushed up, and am only concerned that their living together before the marriage took place should be so generally known. I must not, however, neglect the duties of my station or refrain from declaring my amazement at hearing that you received the young couple into your house as soon as they were married. It was an encouragement of vice, and had I been the rector of Longbourn, I should very strenuously have opposed it. You ought certainly to forgive them as a Christian, but never to admit them in your sight or allow their names to be mentioned in your hearing."

"That is his notion of Christian forgiveness! The rest of his letter is only about his dear Charlotte's situation and his expectation of a young olive-branch. But Lizzy, you look as if you did not enjoy it. You are not going to be *missish*, I hope, and pretend to be affronted at an idle report. What do we live for but to make sport for our neighbors and laugh at them in our turn?"

"Oh!" cried Elizabeth. "I am excessively diverted. But it is so strange!"

"Yes, *that* is what makes it amusing. Had they fixed on any other man it would have been nothing. But *his* perfect indifference, and *your* pointed dislike, make it so delightfully absurd! Much as I abominate writing, I would not give up Mr. Collins's correspondence for any consideration. Nay, when I read a letter of his, I cannot help giving him the preference even over Wickham, much as I value the impudence and hypocrisy of my son-in-law. And pray, Lizzy, what said Lady Catherine about this report? Did she call to refuse her consent?"

To this question his daughter replied only with a forced laugh, and as it had been asked without the least suspicion, she was not distressed by his repeating it. Elizabeth had never been more at a loss to make her feelings appear what they were not. It was necessary to laugh when she would rather have cried. Her father had most cruelly mortified her by what he said of Mr. Darcy's indifference, and she could do nothing but wonder at such a want of penetration, or fear that perhaps, instead of his seeing too little, she might have fancied too much.

Instead of receiving any such letter of excuse from his friend, as Elizabeth half expected Mr. Bingley to do, he was able to bring Mr. Darcy with him to Longbourn again before many days had passed after Lady Catherine's visit. The gentlemen arrived early. And before Mrs. Bennet had time to tell him of their having seen his aunt, of which her daughter sat in momentary dread, Mr. Bingley, who wanted to be alone with Jane, proposed their all walking out. It was agreed to. Mrs. Bennet was not in the habit of walking and Mary could never spare time, but the remaining five set off together. Mr. Bingley and Jane, however, soon allowed the others to outstrip them. They lagged behind, while Elizabeth, Kitty, and Darcy were to entertain each other. Very little was said by either. Kitty was too much afraid of him to talk. Elizabeth was secretly forming a desperate resolution. And perhaps he might be doing the same.

They walked towards the Lucas's, because Kitty wished to call upon Maria, and as Elizabeth saw no occasion for making it a general concern, when Kitty left them she went boldly on with him alone. Now was the moment for her resolution to be executed, and while her courage was high, she immediately said, "Mr. Darcy, I am a very selfish creature, and for the sake of giving relief to my own feelings, care not how much I may be wounding yours. I can no longer help thanking you for your unexampled kindness to my poor sister. Ever since I have known it, I have been most anxious to acknowledge to you how gratefully I feel it. Were it known to the rest of my family, I should not have merely my own gratitude to express."

"I am sorry, exceedingly sorry," replied Mr. Darcy in a tone of surprise and emotion, "that you have ever been informed of what may, in a mistaken light, have given you uneasiness. I did not think Mrs. Gardiner was so little to be trusted."

"You must not blame my aunt. Lydia's thoughtlessness first betrayed to me that you had been concerned in the matter, and of course I could not rest till I knew the particulars. Let me thank you again and again, in the name of all my family, for that generous compassion which induced you to take so much trouble and bear so many mortifications and such personal danger for the sake of discovering them."

"If you *will* thank me, let it be for yourself alone. That the wish of giving happiness to you might add force to the other inducements which led me on, I shall not attempt to deny. But your *family* owe me nothing. Much as I respect them, I believe I thought only of *you*."

Elizabeth was too much embarrassed to say a word, her heart both racing and attempting to fly up into her throat at once. But no, she should not dare to hope...

After a short pause, Mr. Darcy stopped and she followed suit, turning to face him though she could hardly bear to look at him for fear of all that he might see in her expression.

In a voice so quiet as to almost be lost to her ears, her companion murmured, "You are too generous to trifle with me. If your feelings are still what they were last April, tell me so at once. *My* affections and wishes are unchanged, but one word from you will silence me on this subject forever."

A glow of warmth and hope and love burned within her, rising to her cheeks and forming a smile upon her face. She dared to look at him, letting her silence and her eyes be her answer of encouragement as wild emotions choked all words within her.

His eyes widened; she saw her own hope reflected in them as he continued. "Then, if your feelings have changed, I must tell you that you have utterly and completely bewitched me. All that I am, all that I can ever hope to be in this changed existence of mine, I gladly and wholly offer to you. I love you, Elizabeth Bennet. Please do me the honor of becoming my wife."

Smiling harder than she ever had reason to before, Elizabeth managed to choke out, "Yes."

An expression of heartfelt delight spread over his face, making him appear rather more like an angel than a vampire. Even if she had not already loved him, in that moment with so much love shining upon his countenance, he would have surely earned her heart.

They walked on without knowing in what direction. There was too much to be thought and felt and said for attention to any other objects. She soon learned that they were indebted for their present good understanding to the efforts of his aunt, who had called on him at Netherfield and related her journey to Longbourn, its motive, and the substance of her conversation with Elizabeth. Lady Catherine had emphatically dwelled upon every expression of Elizabeth's, with the belief that doing so must assist her endeavors to obtain that promise from her nephew which Elizabeth had refused to give. But unluckily for her ladyship, its effect had been exactly the opposite.

He smiled, and she found herself hoping she might see him do so again every day for the rest of her life, as he said, "It taught me to hope as I had scarcely ever allowed myself to hope before. I knew enough of your disposition to be certain that, had you been absolutely, irrevocably decided against me, you would have acknowledged it to Lady Catherine frankly and openly."

Elizabeth colored and laughed as she replied, "Yes, you know enough of my frankness to believe me capable of *that*. After abusing you so abominably to your face, I could have no scruple in abusing you to all your relations."

"What did you say of me that I did not deserve? For, though your accusations were ill-founded and formed on mistaken premises, my behavior to you at the time had merited the severest reproof. It was unpardonable. I cannot think of it without abhorrence."

"We will not quarrel for the greater share of blame annexed to that evening," said Elizabeth. "The conduct of neither, if strictly examined, will be irreproachable. But since then, we have both, I hope, improved in civility."

"I cannot be so easily reconciled to myself. The recollection of what I then said, of my conduct, my manners, my expressions during the whole of it, is now, and has been many months, inexpressibly painful to me. Your reproof, so well applied, I shall never forget: 'had you behaved in a more gentlemanlike manner.' Those were your words. You know not, you can scarcely conceive, how they have tortured me

—though it was some time, I confess, before I was reasonable enough to allow their justice."

"I was certainly very far from expecting them to make so strong an impression. I had not the smallest idea of their being ever felt in such a way."

"I can easily believe it. You thought me then devoid of every proper feeling, I am sure you did. The turn of your countenance I shall never forget, as you said that I could not have addressed you in any possible way that would induce you to accept me."

"Oh! Do not repeat what I then said. These recollections will not do at all. I assure you that I have long been most heartily ashamed of it."

Mr. Darcy mentioned his letter. "Did it soon make you think better of me? Did you, on reading it, give any credit to its contents?"

She explained what its effect on her had been, and how gradually all her former prejudices had been removed so that she might acknowledge what had been hidden all along...her true feelings towards him.

"I knew that what I wrote must give you pain, but it was necessary. I hope you have destroyed the letter. There was one part especially, the opening of it, which I should dread your having the power of reading again. I can remember some expressions which might justly make you hate me."

"The letter shall certainly be burned if you believe it essential to the preservation of my regard. But, though we both have reason to think my opinions not entirely unalterable, they are not, I hope, quite so easily changed as that implies."

Mr. Darcy shook his head. "When I wrote that letter, I believed myself perfectly calm and cool. But I am since convinced that it was written in a dreadful bitterness of spirit."

"Perhaps the letter began in bitterness, but it did not end so. The adieu is charity itself. But think no more of the letter. The feelings of the person who wrote, and the person who received it, are now so widely different from what they were then that every unpleasant circumstance attending it ought to be forgotten. You must learn some of my philosophy. Think only of the past as its remembrance gives you pleasure."

He laughed. "I cannot give you credit for any philosophy of the kind. Your retrospections must be so totally void of reproach that the contentment arising from them is not of philosophy, but, what is much better, of innocence." With a sigh, he shook his head. "But with me, it is not so. Painful recollections will intrude which cannot, which ought not, to be repelled. I have been a selfish being all my life, in practice, though not in principle. As a child I was taught what was right, but I was not taught to correct my temper. I was given good principles, but left to follow them in pride and conceit. Unfortunately an only son—for many years an only child—I was spoiled by my parents, who, though good themselves, allowed, encouraged, almost taught me to be selfish and overbearing; to care for none beyond my own family circle; to think meanly of all the rest of the world; to wish at least to think meanly of their sense and worth compared with my own. Such I was, from eight to eight and twenty, and such I might still have been but for you, dearest, loveliest Elizabeth! What do I not owe you! You taught me a lesson, hard indeed at first, but most advantageous. By you, I was properly humbled. I came to you without a doubt of my reception. You showed me how insufficient were all my pretensions to please a woman worthy of being pleased."

"Had you then persuaded yourself that I should?"

"Indeed I had. What will you think of my vanity? I believed you to be wishing, expecting my addresses."

"My manners must have been in fault, but not intentionally, I assure you. I never meant to deceive you, but my spirits might often lead me wrong. How you must have hated me after *that* evening."

"Hate you! I was angry perhaps at first, but my anger soon began to take a proper direction."

"I am almost afraid of asking what you thought of me when we met at Pemberley. You blamed me for coming?"

"No indeed. I felt nothing but surprise."

"Your surprise could not be greater than *mine* in being noticed by you. My conscience told me that I deserved no extraordinary politeness, and I confess that I did not expect to receive *more* than my due."

"My object then was to show you, by every civility in my power, that I was not so mean as to resent the past. And I hoped to obtain your forgiveness, to lessen your ill opinion, by letting you see that your reproofs had been attended to. How soon any other wishes introduced themselves I can hardly tell, but I believe in about half an hour after I had seen you."

He then told her of Georgiana's delight in her acquaintance, and of her disappointment at its sudden interruption. This naturally leading to the cause of that interruption, she soon learned that his resolution of following her from Derbyshire in quest of her sister had been formed before he quitted the inn, and that his gravity and thoughtfulness there had arisen from no other struggles than what steps and actions such a purpose must comprehend.

Here she must hesitate again before asking, "Lydia made mention of a duel."

Mr. Darcy bowed his head, studying the grass passing beneath their feet as they continued their walk together. After a long moment, he sighed. "It is true. I did give way to my vengeful feelings and challenge him. At the time, I believed I was doing so solely to force him to do the honorable thing and marry your sister. However, upon further reflection, I see now that it was also for my own personal revenge. I have for many years harbored strong feelings towards Wickham, which only grew in his attempts to further divide you from me."

At her look of confusion, he explained, "I believe that, knowing me as long as he had and as well as he had, Wickham saw even before I myself understood my growing feelings for you. Upon this discovery, he began to pay you special attention. The timing was too much of a coincidence. He was using the vampire glamour to enamor you to him so that he might turn you against me with his lies."

She thought back to that day upon first meeting Mr. Wickham, of how he had paid her little special attention until after encountering Mr. Darcy and Mr. Bingley. Only then had Mr. Wickham sought her confidence, only to then tell her things about Mr. Darcy that were aimed to make her fear and loathe Mr. Darcy's very existence.

She sighed and nodded. "I believe you are correct."

"I am sorry if this pains you further." His voice was a low murmur, soft with regret and apology, drawing a smile from her.

"It only pains my opinion of myself and what very few attractions I believed I might have held for him. But I still do not understand why he would be attracted to Lydia. Surely there were any number of girls in Brighton equally as bereft of intelligence who would submit to his charms? Choosing one such as Lydia seems to have been a most unwise choice on his part. What a life of misery he will lead with her at his side!"

"If he had sought her affection solely for her blood, then this would be true. But as we fought in the park in London, he confessed that he had additional motives in seducing her, namely to tarnish hers, and by extension your entire family's, reputation. It was his endeavor to make you an ineligible match for me."

Her throat closed up. It took all her effort to whisper, "And if you had not succeeded in forcing him to marry her?"

He stopped, turned to face her, and held her hands tenderly within his own. "My dearest Elizabeth, all the scandalous relatives in the world could not destroy my love for you. Though I will confess that I am unsure how I would have earned *your* love if I had been unable to assist your family in this way and thereby prove myself a changed man."

She smiled and shook her head through sudden tears. "I began to understand my true feelings for you after you wrote that letter. And then when we met again in Derbyshire, I knew for certain that I loved you, that you could be the only man possibly suited for me. While I certainly appreciate your timely and courageous assistance that you have provided my family, it only strengthened my already growing respect for you."

A tear of happiness slid down her cheek. Smiling, he wiped it away with a finger, tucked her hand under his arm, and began walking again, giving them both a moment to compose themselves.

Once she was able to speak more easily, she asked, "But how did you ever manage not to end Mr. Wickham's life? For I can well imagine the strength of such a desire after all he has done to yourself and your family and friends."

Mr. Darcy's smile faded, replaced by his more usual expression of contemplation. "You will laugh at me in disbelief. But I believe it was you who stayed my hand. Or rather, the idea of what you thought of me, and how you might consider me if I gave in to such a base desire for revenge. Now confess it…would you not think less of me if I had ended Wickham's life?"

She hesitated, considered then sighed. "My esteem that I then felt for you would not have been lessened. But perhaps the level of respect that I have for you now would not be *quite* so high."

He smiled at the return of his beloved, teasing Elizabeth and patted her hand at his arm.

She expressed her gratitude again for all that he had done. But it was too painful a subject to each to be dwelt on any farther.

After walking several miles in a leisurely manner, and too busy to know anything about it, they found at last, on examining their watches, that it was time to be at home.

"What could have become of Mr. Bingley and Jane!" was a wonder which introduced the discussion of their affairs. Mr. Darcy was delighted with their engagement; his friend had given him the earliest information of it.

"I must ask whether you were surprised?" said Elizabeth.

"Not at all. When I went away, I felt that it would soon happen."

"That is to say, you had given your permission." She laughed. "I guessed as much."

"Not my permission but rather my encouragement, support, and guidance as to how best to make apologies and broach the subject," admitted Mr. Darcy. "On the evening before my going to London, I made a confession to him which I believe I ought to have made long ago. I told him of all that had occurred to make my former interference in his affairs incorrect. His surprise was great. He had never had the slightest suspicion. I told him, moreover, that I believed myself mistaken in supposing, as I had done, that your sister was indifferent to him, and as I could easily perceive that his attachment to her was unabated, I felt no doubt of their happiness together."

Elizabeth could not help smiling at his easy manner of directing his friend. "Did you speak from your own observation when you told him that my sister loved him, or merely from my information last spring?"

"From the former. I had narrowly observed her during the visit which I had lately made with him here, and I was convinced of her affection."

"And your assurance of it, I suppose, carried immediate conviction to him."

"It did. Bingley is most unaffectedly modest. His diffidence had prevented his depending on his own judgment in so anxious a case, but his reliance on mine made everything easy. I was obliged to confess one thing, which for a time, and not unjustly, offended him. I could not allow myself to conceal that your sister had been in town three months last winter, and that I had known it and purposely kept it from him. He was angry. But his anger, I am persuaded, lasted no longer than he remained in any doubt of your sister's sentiments. He has heartily forgiven me now."

Elizabeth longed to observe that Mr. Bingley had been a most delightful friend, so easily guided that his worth was invaluable. But she checked herself. She remembered that Mr. Darcy had yet to learn to be laughed at, and it was rather too early to begin.

In anticipating the happiness of Mr. Bingley, which of course was to be inferior only to his own, he continued the conversation till they reached the house. In the hall they reluctantly parted.

Chapter Thirty

"My dear Lizzy, where can you have been walking to?" was a question which Elizabeth received from Jane as soon as she entered their dining room, and from all the others when they sat down to table. She had only to say in reply that they had wandered about till she was beyond her own knowledge. She colored as she spoke, but neither that, nor anything else, awakened a suspicion of the truth.

The evening passed quietly, unmarked by anything extraordinary. The acknowledged lovers talked and laughed, the unacknowledged were silent. Mr. Darcy was not of a disposition in which happiness overflows in mirth. And Elizabeth, agitated and confused, *knew* that she was happy rather than *felt* herself to be so, for, besides the immediate embarrassment, there were other evils before her. She anticipated what would be felt in the family when her situation became known. She was aware that no one liked him but Jane, and even feared that with the others it was a dislike which not all his fortune and consequence might do away.

At night she opened her heart to Jane. Though suspicion was very far from Miss Bennet's general habits, she was absolutely incredulous here.

"You are joking, Lizzy. This cannot be! Engaged to Mr. Darcy! No, no, you shall not deceive me. I know it to be impossible."

"This is a wretched beginning indeed! My sole dependence was on you, and I am sure nobody else will believe me if you do not. Yet, indeed, I am in earnest. I speak nothing but the truth. He still loves me, and we are engaged."

Jane looked at her doubtingly. "Oh, Lizzy! It cannot be. I know how much you dislike him."

"You know nothing of the matter. *That* is all to be forgotten. Perhaps I did not always love him so well as I do now. But in such cases as these, a good memory is unpardonable. This is the last time I shall ever remember it myself."

Miss Bennet still looked all amazement. Elizabeth again and more seriously assured her of its truth.

"Good Heaven! Can it be really so! Yet now I must believe you," cried Jane. "My dear, dear Lizzy, I would—I do congratulate you—but are you certain? Forgive the question—are you quite certain that you can be happy with him?"

"There can be no doubt of that. It is settled between us already that we are to be the happiest couple in the world. But are you pleased, Jane? Shall you like to have such a brother?"

"Very, very much. Nothing could give either Mr. Bingley or myself more delight. But we considered it, we talked of it as impossible. And do you really love him quite well enough? Oh, Lizzy! Do anything rather than marry without affection. Are you quite sure that you feel what you ought to do?"

"Oh, yes! You will only think I feel *more* than I ought to when I tell you all."

"What do you mean?"

"Why, I must confess that I love him better than I do Mr. Bingley. I am afraid you will be angry."

"My dearest sister, now *be* serious. I want to talk very seriously. Let me know everything that I am to know without delay. Will you tell me how long you have loved him?"

"It has been coming on so gradually that I hardly know when it began. But I believe I must date it from a letter of explanation that he wrote in Kent after his first asking for my hand in marriage."

In shock, Jane insisted that she properly explain it all from the beginning, and giving into her earnest entreaties, Elizabeth related all that had occurred in Kent, then Pemberley, and finally the full details of Mr. Darcy's aid in Lydia and Mr. Wickham's marriage. Once all had been told, she satisfied Jane by her solemn assurances of attachment.

When convinced on that article, Miss Bennet had nothing further to wish. "Now I am quite happy, for you will be as happy as myself. I always had a value for him. Were it for nothing but his love of you, I must always have esteemed him. But now, as Mr. Bingley's friend and your husband, there can be only Mr. Bingley and yourself more dear to me. But Lizzy, you have been very sly, very reserved with me. How little did you tell me of what passed at Kent and Pemberley and Lambton! I owe all that I know of it to another, not to you."

Elizabeth told her the motives of her secrecy. She had been unwilling to mention Mr. Bingley's circumstances for fear of causing Jane more undue pain, and the unsettled state of her own feelings had made her equally avoid the name of his friend. But now she would no longer conceal anything from her. All was acknowledged, and half the night spent in conversation.

"Good gracious!" cried Mrs. Bennet as she stood at a window the next morning. "That disagreeable Mr. Darcy is coming here again with our dear Bingley! What can he mean by being so tiresome as to be always coming here? I had no notion but he would go a-shooting, or something or other, and not disturb us with his company. What shall we do with him? Lizzy, you must walk out with him again, that he may not be in Bingley's way."

Elizabeth could hardly help laughing at so convenient a proposal, yet was really vexed that her mother should be always giving him such an epithet.

As soon as they entered, Mr. Bingley looked at her so expressively and shook hands with such warmth as left no doubt of his good information. He soon afterwards said aloud, "Mrs. Bennet, have you no more lanes hereabouts in which Lizzy may lose her way again today?"

Mrs. Bennet's lips pursed with displeasure. "I advise Mr. Darcy and Lizzy and Kitty to walk to Oakham Mount this morning. It is a nice long walk, and Mr. Darcy has never seen the view."

"It may do very well for the others," replied Mr. Bingley; "but I am sure it will be too much for Kitty. Won't it, Kitty?"

Kitty owned that she had rather stay at home. Mr. Darcy professed a great curiosity to see the view from the Mount, and Elizabeth silently consented.

As she went upstairs to get ready, Mrs. Bennet followed her, saying, "I am quite sorry, Lizzy, that you should be forced to have that disagreeable man all to yourself. But I hope you will not mind it. It is all for Jane's sake, you know, and there is no occasion for talking to him, except just now and then. So, do not put yourself to inconvenience."

During their walk, it was resolved that Mr. Bennet's consent should be asked in the course of the evening. Elizabeth reserved to herself the application for her mother's. She could not determine how her mother would take it, sometimes doubting whether all his wealth and grandeur would be enough to overcome her abhorrence of the man. But whether she were violently set against the match, or violently delighted with it, it was certain that her manner would be equally ill adapted to do credit to her sense. And she could no more bear that Mr. Darcy should hear the first raptures of her joy than the first vehemence of her disapprobation.

In the evening, soon after Mr. Bennet withdrew to the library, she saw Mr. Darcy rise also and follow him, and her agitation on seeing it was extreme. She did not fear her father's opposition, but he was going to be made unhappy; and that it should be through her means—that *she*, his favorite child, should be distressing him by her choice, should be filling him with fears and regrets in disposing of her—was a wretched reflection. She sat in misery till Mr. Darcy appeared again, when, looking at him, she was a little relieved by his gentle, hopeful smile.

In a few minutes he approached the table where she was sitting with Kitty, and while pretending to admire her work, said in a whisper, "Go to your father, he wants you in the library."

She was gone directly.

Her father was walking about the room, looking grave and anxious. "Lizzy, what are you doing? Are you out of your senses, to be accepting this man? Have not you always hated him?"

How earnestly did she then wish that her former opinions had been more reasonable, her expressions more moderate! It would have spared her from explanations and professions which it was exceedingly awkward to give. But they were now necessary, and she assured him, with some confusion, of her attachment to Mr. Darcy.

"Or, in other words, you are determined to have him. He is rich, to be sure, and you may have more fine clothes and fine carriages than Jane. But will they make you happy?"

"Have you any other objection than your belief of my indifference?"

"None at all. We all know him to be a proud, unpleasant sort of man. But this would be nothing if you really liked him."

"I do, I do like him," replied she with tears in her eyes. "I love him, Papa. Indeed he has no improper pride. He is perfectly amiable. You do not know what he really is. Pray do not pain me by speaking of him in such terms."

"Lizzy, I have given him my consent. He is the kind of man, indeed, to whom I should never dare refuse anything which he condescended to ask. I now give it to *you*, if you are resolved on having him. But let me advise you to think better of it. I know your disposition, Lizzy. I know that you could be neither happy nor respectable unless you truly esteemed your husband; unless you looked up to him as a superior. Your lively talents would place you in the greatest danger in an unequal marriage. You could scarcely escape discredit and misery. My child, let me not have the grief of seeing *you* unable to respect your partner in life. You know not what you are about."

Elizabeth, still more affected, was earnest and solemn in her reply. At length, by repeated assurances that Mr. Darcy was really the object of her choice, by explaining the gradual change which her estimation of him had undergone, relating her absolute certainty that his affection was not the work of a day but had stood the test of many months' suspense, and enumerating with energy all his good qualities, she did conquer her father's incredulity and reconcile him to the match.

"Well, my dear," said he when she ceased speaking, "I have no more to say. If this be the case, he deserves you. I could not have parted with you, my Lizzy, to anyone less worthy."

To complete the favorable impression, she then told him what Mr. Darcy had voluntarily done for Lydia. He heard her with astonishment.

"This is an evening of wonders, indeed! And so Darcy did everything; made up the match, gave the money, paid the fellow's debts, and got him his commission! So much the better. It will save me a world of trouble and economy. Had it been your uncle's doing, I must and *would* have paid him. But these violent young lovers carry everything their own way. I shall offer to pay him tomorrow, he will rant and storm about his love for you, and there will be an end to the matter."

He then recollected her embarrassment a few days before on his reading Mr. Collins's letter, and after laughing at her some time, allowed her at last to go, saying as she quitted the room, "If any young men come for Mary or Kitty, send them in, for I am quite at leisure."

Elizabeth's mind was now relieved from a very heavy weight, and after half an hour's quiet reflection in her own room, she was able to join the others with tolerable composure. Everything was too recent for gaiety, but the evening passed tranquilly away. There was no longer anything material to be dreaded, and the comfort of ease and familiarity would come in time.

When her mother went up to her dressing room later that night, she followed her and made the important communication. Its effect was most extraordinary, for on first hearing it, Mrs. Bennet sat quite still and unable to utter a syllable. Nor was it under many, many minutes that she could comprehend what she heard, though not in general backward to credit what was for the advantage of her family, or that came in the shape of a lover to any of them. She began at length to recover, to fidget about in her chair, get up, sit down again, wonder, and bless herself.

"Good gracious! Lord bless me! Only think! Dear me! Mr. Darcy! Who would have thought it! And is it really true? Oh! My sweetest Lizzy! How rich and how great you will be! What pin-money, what jewels, what carriages you will have! Jane's is nothing to it—nothing at all. I am so pleased—so happy. Such a charming man! So handsome! So tall! Oh, my dear Lizzy! Pray apologize for my having disliked him so much before. I hope he will overlook it. Dear, dear Lizzy. A house in town! Everything that is charming! Three daughters married! Ten thousand a year! Oh, Lord! What will become of me. I shall go distracted."

This was enough to prove that her approbation need not be doubted, and Elizabeth, rejoicing that such an effusion was heard only by herself, soon went away. But before she had been three minutes in her own room, her mother followed her.

"My dearest child, I can think of nothing else! Ten thousand a year, and very likely more! 'Tis as good as a lord! And a special license. You must and shall be married by a special license. But my dearest love, tell me what dish Mr. Darcy is particularly fond of, that I may have it tomorrow."

This was a sad omen of what her mother's behavior to the gentleman himself might be, and Elizabeth found that, though in the certain possession of his warmest affection and secure of her relations' consent, there was still something to be wished for in life. But the morrow passed off much better than she expected, for Mrs. Bennet luckily stood in such awe of her intended son-in-law that she ventured not to speak to him unless it was in her power to offer him any attention or mark her deference for his opinion.

Elizabeth had the satisfaction of seeing her father taking pains to get acquainted with him, and Mr. Bennet soon assured her that he was rising every hour in his esteem.

"I admire all my three sons-in-law highly," said he. "Wickham, perhaps, is my favorite. But I think I shall like *your* husband quite as well as Jane's."

Elizabeth's spirits soon rising to playfulness again, she wanted Mr. Darcy to account for his having ever fallen in love with her. "How could you begin? I can comprehend your going on charmingly when you had once made a beginning. But what could set you off in the first place?"

"I cannot fix on the hour, or the spot, or the look, or the words, which laid the foundation. It is too long ago. I was in the middle before I knew that I *had* begun."

"My beauty you had early withstood, and as for my manners—my behavior to *you* was at least always bordering on the uncivil, and I never spoke to you without rather wishing to give you pain than not. Now be sincere…did you admire me for my impertinence?"

"For the liveliness of your mind, I did."

"You may as well call it impertinence at once. It was very little less. The fact is that you were sick of civility, of deference, of officious attention. You were disgusted with the women who were always speaking, and looking, and thinking for *your* approbation alone. I roused an interested you because I was so unlike *them*. Had you not been really amiable, you would have hated me for it. But in spite of the pains you took to disguise yourself, your feelings were always noble and just, and in your heart, you thoroughly despised the persons who so assiduously courted you. There—I have saved you the trouble of accounting for it, and really, all things considered, I begin to think it perfectly reasonable. To be sure, you knew no actual good of me—but nobody thinks of *that* when they fall in love."

"Was there no good in your affectionate behavior to Jane while she was ill at Netherfield?"

"Dearest Jane! Who could have done less for her? But make a virtue of it by all means. My good qualities are under your protection, and you are to exaggerate them as much as possible. And in return it belongs to me to find occasions for teasing and quarrelling with you as often as may be, and I shall begin directly by asking you what made you so unwilling to come to the point at last. What made you so shy of me when you first called and afterwards dined here? Why, especially when you called, did you look as if you did not care about me?"

He smiled. "Because you were grave and silent and gave me no encouragement."

"But I was embarrassed."

"And so was I."

"You might have talked to me more when you came to dinner."

"A man who had felt less might," was his quick reply.

"How unlucky that you should have a reasonable answer to give, and that I should be so reasonable as to admit it! But I wonder how long you *would* have gone on if you had been left to yourself. I wonder when you *would* have spoken if I had not asked you! My resolution of thanking you for your kindness to Lydia had certainly great effect. *Too much*, I am afraid, for what becomes of the moral if our comfort springs from a breach of promise? For I ought not to have mentioned the subject. This will never do."

He could not help but chuckle. "You need not distress yourself. The moral will be perfectly fair. Lady Catherine's unjustifiable endeavors to separate us were the means of removing all my doubts. I am not indebted for my present happiness to your eager desire of expressing your gratitude. I was not in a humor to wait for any opening of yours. My aunt's intelligence had given me hope, and I was determined at once to know everything."

"Lady Catherine has been of infinite use, which ought to make her happy, for she loves to be of use." She gave him a saucy grin. "But tell me, what did you come down to Netherfield for? Was it merely to ride to Longbourn and be embarrassed? Or had you intended any more serious consequence?"

"My real purpose was to see *you*, and to judge, if I could, whether I might ever hope to make you love me. My avowed one, or what I avowed to myself, was to see whether your sister were still partial to Bingley, and if she were, to make the confession to him which I have since made."

She could not help but tease him with, "Shall you ever have courage to announce to Lady Catherine what is to befall her?"

He laughed. "I am more likely to want more time than courage, Elizabeth. But it ought to be done, and if you will give me a sheet of paper, it shall be done directly." Rising to her challenge impressively, he held out a hand for the requested materials.

Shaking her head in disbelief, she searched a nearby writing table for paper and quills. "And if I had not a letter to write myself, I might sit by you and admire the evenness of your writing, as another young lady once did. But I have an aunt, too, who must not be longer neglected."

From an unwillingness to confess how much her intimacy with Mr. Darcy had been overrated, Elizabeth had never yet answered Mrs. Gardiner's long letter. But now, having *that* to communicate which she knew would be most welcome, she was almost ashamed to find that her uncle and aunt had already lost three days of happiness, and immediately wrote as follows:

> "I would have thanked you before, my dear aunt, as I ought to have done, for your long, kind, satisfactory, detail of particulars; but to say the truth, I was too cross to write. You supposed more than really existed. But *now* suppose as much as you choose; give a loose rein to your fancy, indulge your imagination in every possible flight which the subject will afford, and unless you believe me actually married, you cannot greatly err. You must write again very soon, and praise him a great deal more than you did in your last. I thank you, again and again, for not going to the Lakes. How could I be so silly as to wish it! Your idea of the ponies is delightful. We will go round the Park every day. I am the happiest creature in the world. Perhaps other people have said so before, but not one with such justice. I am happier even than Jane; she only smiles, I laugh. Mr. Darcy sends you all the love in the world that he can spare from me. You are all to come to Pemberley at Christmas.
> Yours, etc."

Mr. Darcy's letter to Lady Catherine was in quite a different style. And still different from either was what Mr. Bennet sent to Mr. Collins in reply to his last.

> "DEAR SIR,
> "I must trouble you once more for congratulations. Elizabeth will soon be the wife of Mr. Darcy. Console Lady Catherine as well as you can. But if I were you, I would stand by the nephew. He has more to give.
> Yours sincerely, etc."

Miss Bingley's congratulations to her brother on his approaching marriage were all that was affectionate and insincere. She wrote even to Jane on the occasion to express her delight and repeat all her former professions of regard. Jane was not deceived, but she was affected, and though feeling no reliance on her, could not help writing her a much kinder answer than she knew was deserved.

The joy which Miss Darcy expressed on receiving similar information was as sincere as her brother's in sending it. Four sides of paper were insufficient to contain all her delight and all her earnest desire of being loved by her sister.

Before any answer could arrive from Mr. Collins, or any congratulations to Elizabeth from his wife, the Longbourn family heard that the Collinses were come themselves to Lucas Lodge. The reason for this sudden removal was soon evident. Lady Catherine had been rendered so exceedingly angry by the contents of her nephew's letter that Charlotte, really rejoicing in the match, was anxious to get away till the storm was blown over. At such a moment, the arrival of her friend was a sincere pleasure to Elizabeth, though in the course of their meetings she must sometimes think the pleasure dearly bought when she saw Mr. Darcy exposed to all the parading and obsequious civility of her husband. He bore it, however, with admirable calmness. He could even listen to Sir William Lucas when he complimented him on carrying away the brightest jewel of the country, and expressed his hopes of their all meeting frequently at St. James's with very decent composure. If he did shrug his shoulders and shake his head with disbelief, it was not till Sir William was out of sight.

Mrs. Phillips's vulgarity was another, and perhaps a greater, tax on his forbearance. Though Mrs. Phillips, as well as her sister, stood in too much awe of him to speak with the familiarity which Mr. Bingley's good humor encouraged, yet whenever she *did* speak, she must be vulgar. Nor was her respect for him, though it made her more quiet, at all likely to make her more elegant. Elizabeth did all she could to shield him from the frequent notice of either, and was ever anxious to keep him to herself and to those of her family with whom he might converse without mortification. And though the uncomfortable feelings arising from all this took from the season of courtship much of its pleasure, it added to the hope of the future. She looked forward with delight to the time when they should be removed from society so little pleasing to either, to all the comfort and elegance of their family party at Pemberley.

Chapter Thirty-one

Happy for all her maternal feelings was the day on which Mrs. Bennet got rid of her two most deserving daughters. With what delighted pride she afterwards visited Mrs. Bingley and talked of Mrs. Darcy may be guessed. For the sake of her family, Elizabeth wished she could say that the accomplishment of her mother's earnest desire in the establishment of so many of her children produced such happy effect as to make Mrs. Bennet a sensible, amiable, well-informed woman for the rest of her life. But such was not to be. Though perhaps it was lucky for her husband, who might not have relished domestic felicity in so unusual a form, that she still was occasionally nervous and invariably silly.

Mr. Bennet missed his second daughter exceedingly; his affection for her drew him oftener from home than anything else could do. He delighted in going to Pemberley, especially when he was least expected.

Mr. Bingley and Jane remained at Netherfield only a twelvemonth. So near a vicinity to her mother and Meryton relations was not desirable even to *his* easy temper or *her* affectionate heart. The darling wish of his sisters was then gratified...he bought an estate in a neighboring county to Derbyshire, and Jane and Elizabeth, in addition to every other source of happiness, were within thirty miles of each other.

Kitty, to her very material advantage, spent the chief of her time with her two elder sisters. In society so superior to what she had generally known, her improvement was great. She was not of so ungovernable a temper as Lydia, and removed from the influence of Lydia's example, she became, by proper attention and management, less irritable, less ignorant, and less insipid. From the further disadvantage of Lydia's society she was of course carefully kept, and though Mrs. Wickham frequently invited her to come and stay with her, with the promise of balls and young men, her father would never consent to her going.

Mary was the only daughter who remained at home, though at least she was necessarily drawn from the pursuit of accomplishments by Mrs. Bennet's being quite unable to sit alone. Mary was obliged to mix more with the world, but she could still moralize over every morning visit. And as she was no longer mortified by comparisons between her sisters' beauty and her own, it was suspected by her father that she submitted to the change without much reluctance.

As for Mr. Wickham and Lydia, their characters suffered no revolution from the marriage of her sisters. He bore with philosophy the conviction that Elizabeth must now become acquainted with whatever of his ingratitude and falsehood had before been unknown to her, and in spite of everything, was not wholly without hope that Mr. Darcy might yet be prevailed on to make his fortune. The congratulatory letter which Elizabeth received from Lydia on her marriage explained to her that, by his wife at least, if not by himself, such a hope was cherished. The letter was to this effect:

"MY DEAR LIZZY,

"I wish you joy. If you love Mr. Darcy half as well as I do my dear Wickham, you must be very happy. It is a great comfort to have you so rich, and when you have nothing else to do, I hope you will think of us. I am sure Wickham would like a place at court very much, and I do not think we shall have quite money enough to live upon without some help. Any place would do of about three or four hundred a year. But however, do not speak to Mr. Darcy about it, if you had rather not.
"Yours, etc."

As it happened that Elizabeth had *much* rather not, she endeavored in her answer to put an end to every entreaty and expectation of the kind. However, such relief as it was in her power to afford, by the practice of what might be called economy in her own private expenses, she frequently sent them. It had always been evident to her that such an income as the Wickhams', under the direction of two persons so extravagant in their wants and heedless of the future, must be very insufficient to their support. And whenever they changed their quarters, either Jane or herself were sure of being applied to for some little assistance towards discharging their bills. Their manner of living, even when the restoration of peace dismissed them to a home, was unsettled in the extreme. They were always moving from place to place in quest of a cheap situation, and always spending more than they ought. His affection for her soon sunk into indifference, hers lasted a little longer, and in spite of her youth and her manners, she retained all the claims to reputation which her marriage had given her.

Lydia also retained her mortality, for Mr. Wickham soon had to agree with Mr. Darcy's wisdom upon this point. Lydia, for that total want of self-discipline or care for anyone but herself, was difficult enough to control. As a powerful immortal who would be tempted to prey upon every human who crossed her path, Lydia would have been insupportable and a danger to the secrecy of all vampires in existence. And though she could not be taught to keep her husband's different nature a secret, those who heard her outlandish stories about vampires learned to discount all her claims as nothing more than a very great jest.

Though Mr. Darcy could never receive Mr. Wickham at Pemberley, for Elizabeth's sake he assisted him further in his profession. Lydia was occasionally a visitor there when her husband was gone to enjoy himself in London or Bath, and with the Bingleys they both of them frequently stayed so long that even Mr. Bingley's good humor was overcome and he proceeded so far as to talk of giving them a hint to be gone.

Miss Bingley was very deeply mortified by Mr. Darcy's marriage. But as she thought it advisable to retain the right of visiting at Pemberley, she dropped all her resentment, was fonder than ever of Georgiana, almost as attentive to Mr. Darcy as heretofore, and paid off every arrear of civility to Elizabeth.

Pemberley was now Georgiana's home, and the attachment of the sisters was exactly what Darcy had hoped to see. They were able to love each other even as well as they intended. Georgiana had the highest opinion in the world of Elizabeth, though at first she often listened with an astonishment bordering on alarm at her lively, sportive manner of talking to her brother. He, who had always inspired in herself a respect which almost overcame her affection, she now saw the object of open pleasantry. Her mind received knowledge which had never before fallen in her way. By Elizabeth's instructions, she began to comprehend that a woman may take liberties with her husband which a brother will not always allow in a sister more than ten years younger than himself. By Elizabeth's behavior in general, she learned how to act as a human woman ought, and through constant practice and instruction from her brother, she soon learned to both control and utilize her own vampire abilities when in other humans' company. In this way, Darcy's responsibilities in protecting his sister's secret were gradually relinquished to Miss Darcy herself, offering them all the hope that one day she would be fully capable of an existence independent of her brother's protection should she choose it.

Lady Catherine was extremely indignant on the marriage of her nephew. She gave way to all the genuine frankness of her character in her reply to the letter which announced their marriage's arrangement, sending him language so very abusive, especially of Elizabeth, that for some time all intercourse was at an end. But at length, by Elizabeth's persuasion, he was prevailed on to overlook the offence and seek a reconciliation. And after a little further resistance on the part of his aunt, her resentment gave way, either to her affection for him or her curiosity to see how his wife conducted herself, and she condescended to wait on them at Pemberley in spite of that pollution which its woods had received, not merely from the presence of such a mistress, but the visits of her uncle and aunt from the city.

With the Gardiners, they were always on the most intimate terms. Mr. Darcy, as well as Elizabeth, really loved them, and they were both ever sensible of the warmest gratitude towards the persons who, by bringing her into Derbyshire, had been the means of uniting them.

As for her own mortality, Elizabeth and Mr. Darcy decided that she should remain mortal for now, for this allowed her to retain all those dear human traits that softened her husband's immortal ways and allowed him to feel connected in some small part to the human existence he had lost. And of course they would have many youthful years together still before she might grow weary of aging and reconsider.

Until that day's arrival, her vulnerability as a human was both a joy and a treasure that Darcy was honored to have the protection of for as long as she chose to retain it.

The End

www.ingramcontent.com/pod-product-compliance
Lightning Source LLC
Chambersburg PA
CBHW070811180626
46818CB00001B/212